TIMEHUNTERS

BLADE OF SHADOW

BOOK FOUR

SARA SAMUELS

BLADE OF SHADOWS
BOOK 4

TIMEHUNTERS

SARA SAMUELS

Published by Sara Samuels

Denver, CO 80237

First Edition

Copyright ©2025 Sara Samuels

All Rights Reserved.

Cover design by Krafigs Designs

Editing by Rainy Kaye

Formatting by Storytelling Press

"In the deepest shadows, where trust turns to ash and secrets bleed like open wounds, whispers haunt the air, and poison seeps through silence. Come closer, dear reader, fear not. For every betrayal is a riddle, a cipher hiding a powerful truth, and every dark revelation is a key that will drag you deeper into the enigma at the heart of this tale."

"To those who carry dreams in their hearts, for the ones who dare to believe in themselves, even when the path is steep and the nights are long. May you always find light in the darkest moments, strength in every struggle, and the courage to keep reaching for the stars, no matter how far they seem. Your dreams are the wings that will carry you forward—never let them go."

FAMILY TREE

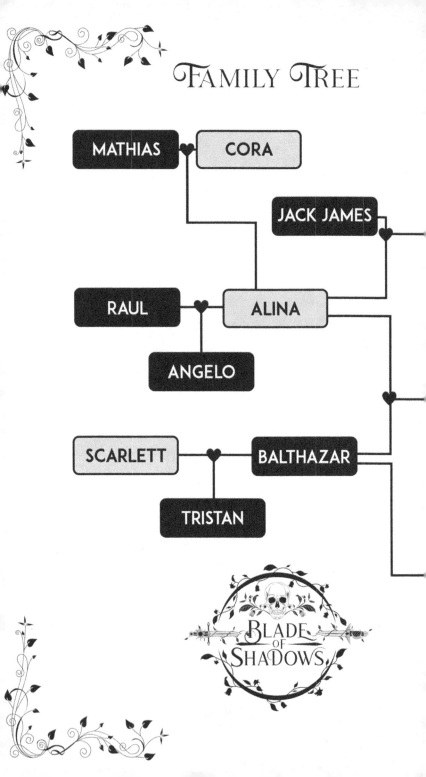

MATHIAS ♥ CORA

JACK JAMES ♥

RAUL ♥ ALINA

ANGELO

SCARLETT ♥ BALTHAZAR

TRISTAN

BLADE OF SHADOWS

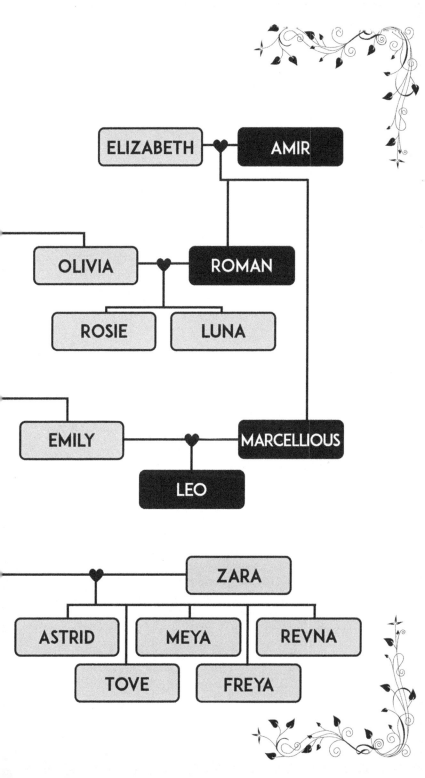

AUTHOR'S NOTE

Dear Reader,

Thank you for embarking on this journey with me. As you prepare to dive into the series' fourth book, I cannot stress enough how important it is to have read the first three books, along with the villains' book. Every installment is a crucial piece of the larger puzzle, and trust me—you don't want to miss a single moment.

So far, we've traveled through time alongside our beloved characters: from the ancient wonders of Rome in Timeborne to the perilous hunt for the Blade of Shadows in 1800s America in Book Two, and then to Roman's journey into the modern world, and where our characters uncovered the chilling truth about the Timehunter Society in Book Three. This journey ended with the shocking revelation that Olivia's mother is still alive. Now, in Timehunters, the stakes are higher than ever as our heroes continue their pursuit of the Moon Dagger in Wales 1597, where destiny awaits.

I hope you're ready because this book will change everything. The biggest secret I've been keeping is about to be revealed—and once you know the truth, there's no going back.

I've poured my heart into this series, and I hope it sweeps you into an unforgettable adventure. Buckle up—this is going to be a ride like no other.

With all my love,
Sara

PROLOGUE

ALINA

The sharp scent of fear mingled with the coppery stench of blood as I leaned in closer to the writhing figure chained to the wall. His whimpers were muffled by the gag wedged in his mouth, but his eyes—wide and wet—screamed the terror that his bound lips could not.

The meager light from a small window above cast sinister shadows over the grimy, rotting dungeon floor. The air was oppressive, with the sickening scent of decay and desperation. I paid little attention to my surroundings, consumed by my single-minded pursuit—to retrieve the cursed moon dagger at any cost.

"Where is it?" I whispered, my voice a serpent's hiss as the blade of my dagger traced the outline of an old scar on his cheek—a souvenir from our last encounter. He shook his head frantically, his skin quivering under the cold steel.

"Think carefully," I said. "The moon dagger and the ancient scrolls of time are not trinkets you can forget about."

∞ 1 ∞

The dagger tip pricked his skin, a bead of crimson swelling up like a promise.

Fourteen years… It had been fourteen years since I first made death my ally. Fourteen years of screams and silence, and bloodshed and betrayal…

Each cry I extracted, every drop of blood I spilled, was a note in the symphony of my existence, a testament to the ruthless efficiency I'd honed. My hands, once hesitant and unsure, now moved with the precision of a master craftsman, carving agony into flesh with the finesse only a seasoned killer could possess.

A putrid stench permeated the air, suffocating and overpowering my senses. The smell of rotting flesh permeated the room, a reminder of my failure and a warning of the horrors that awaited if I couldn't retrieve the weapon. But I pushed on, determined to uncover the dagger's whereabouts despite the overwhelming stench of death surrounding me.

My victim's muffled cries echoed off the stone walls as I slid the cold, sharp dagger beneath the gag. With a yank of my hand, I sliced through it with ease, catching his flesh in the process. Blood spewed from the gaping wound, staining my hands in thick crimson. The man's body convulsed in agony, but I reveled in the power coursing through me with each passing second.

"Please," he finally choked out, the word garbled and desperate.

I knew better than to trust the pleas of those who harbored secrets. Secrets that could unlock the power I sought, the power we all coveted.

I leaned in, letting my breath dance across his ear.

"Your pain will end when you speak the truth," I assured him, though we both understood the lie for what it was.

His mouth twisted into a grimace as he clenched his teeth

and shook his head, refusing to speak. Steeling myself, I leaned in close, my resolve unwavering, and whispered, "You made your choice."

With velvety finesse, I traced the cold blade across his neck, drawing a thin line of crimson blood that trickled down his chest. The air was tense as we both knew the weight of this moment and its irreversible consequences.

His eyes, wide with the realization of his impending doom, met mine for a fraction of a second before I ended his life. I unfastened his shackles, and his body crumpled to the ground, joining the others who had fallen by my hand. I stood above their lifeless forms, the finality of my actions settling in like a thick fog. My heart thudded dully against my ribs, the only sound in a world gone mute. No moon dagger. No scrolls. Only the stillness of death as my constant companion.

"Any luck?" The voice pricked at the bubble of solitude that had surrounded me. I turned, finding Mathias leaning against the dungeon doorway, his arms crossed over his chest, his features cast in shadows that hid his thoughts.

"Father, it's you!" I cried. As if propelled by the strings of our shared bloodline, I leaped over my fallen prey and closed the distance between us, each step shedding the weight of my recent kill. Father's eyes followed my approach, gleaming with pride. He received me with open arms, the familiar scent of leather and steel wrapping around me like a cloak of affirmation.

I buried my face in his chest as he embraced me tightly. Tears streamed down my face as I whispered, "I've missed you so much."

"I have missed you too, my daughter," my father replied, his voice thick with emotion. He placed a tender kiss on my forehead before leaning back.

"Alina," he said, scanning the decomposing bodies scattered around the room. "Look at you—my daughter, my protégé. You've exceeded my every expectation."

I allowed myself the briefest of smiles, basking in his rare praise, feeling the darkness inside me purr with contentment.

"Your precision and ruthlessness," he said, his grin wolfish and wide. "You've become a lethal assassin, and I love it!"

The echoes of our footsteps mingled with the whispers of the past as we navigated the dimly lit corridors out of the dungeon and upstairs to Salvatore's study. The door creaked open, revealing walls lined with books that held secrets darker than their leather-bound covers. I turned to my father, impatience for news scratching at my throat.

"Father, give me news! What do you know?"

Father paced before the hearth, where embers fought a losing battle against the cold.

"Olivia and Roman have infested Wales. Those fools, Roman and Malik, are scurrying about for supplies like rats." He slammed a fist onto the desk, causing the candlelight to shiver. "And Olivia... She's pregnant. Breeding yet another weakling into this world."

His disdainful tone painted an ugly picture of derision for life itself.

"They're searching for the moon dagger, thinking it will save them. And Emily—may the abyss swallow her soul—is on the brink of spewing out her spawn any moment now." His laughter was cruel, a symphony to my ears.

I leaned against the cool wood of the bookshelf, letting the shadows envelop me.

"Children," I muttered, the word leaving a sour taste. "It disgusts me how Olivia and Emily are such enthusiastic breeders as if the world needs more of their kind."

The concept of nurturing life was foreign, anathema to the essence of who I had become.

"Indeed," Father said, the firelight casting sinister shapes upon his face. "Breeding weakness when we strive for power —foolishness."

A smirk teased the edges of my lips as my father's voice dripped with scorn.

"Oh, Marcellious has been captured and soon will be poisoned to death," he said, his eyes alight with malice. "He will reveal my location to Balthazar, and that's when I will capture him."

Father leaned in closer, lowering his voice to a venomous whisper. "I hate that motherfucker."

"Delicious," I cooed, reveling in the thought of our enemies unraveling before us.

The door creaked open, and the sudden intrusion sliced through our conspiratorial bubble. Salvatore's imposing figure filled the doorway, his presence an unexpected storm cloud darkening the room.

"My Lord, I have come to tell my daughter the news!" Father's words tumbled out in a hasty greeting, but his voice betrayed a tremor of fear.

Salvatore raised an eyebrow. "I see. You come when you don't think I'm here."

"Forgive me," Father stammered, his composure fraying at the edges like worn fabric. "It's not what it looks like."

He bowed low.

Salvatore said nothing, quietly studying my father. I shook where I stood, fearing Salvatore's wrath.

"Mathias, you know how much I loathe it when you dare to communicate with your daughter without my presence," Salvatore said through clenched teeth. "Tell me, have you finally brought me some news I want? Or are you foolishly scheming behind my back once again? Remember my power over you and how easily I could obliterate everything you hold dear."

His voice was laced with a dangerous edge, his eyes burning fiery.

I caught the undercurrent of danger, realizing my father's blunder. Salvatore's power was absolute, his displeasure a sentence we could ill afford. Stepping forward, I sought to weave a mend into the fabric of our rapport.

"My Lord, forgive me," I said, my tone smooth as silk yet edged with urgency. "My father came, and we wanted to catch up."

A calculated risk, to interject—but necessary. We could not allow Salvatore's displeasure to find root when we were so close to our dark victory.

Salvatore's gaze, sharp as the edge of a scythe, swept over us, measuring our worth—or lack thereof. A silence swelled in the room, filled with the weight of his deliberation. Then, as if the heavens had parted to spare us from divine retribution, the corner of Salvatore's lip twitched upward in a semblance of a smile.

"Very well," he said, his voice low and steady like serenity after chaos. "I appreciate loyalty and obedience. You may continue."

I swallowed hard, my throat tight with apprehension, while a wave of relief washed through me at his words. Father straightened up, though the sweat on his brow betrayed his lingering unease.

"Our ragged group finally reached the shores of Wales," Father said, his muscles tensed. "Malik, Roman, and Marcellious ventured out to gather supplies for our imminent search in the cave. I received intel that Raul Costa captured Marcellious; his days are numbered. With his death, I will continue my mission to dismantle the clan individually."

A troubled look flickered across Father's face. "My men also reported that Balthazar has allied with Raul Costa to extract information from Marcellious about Emily's whereabouts. Once Marcellious reveals my location, I know Balthazar will arrive at my estate. I will then capture him and kill his son Tristan and bring him immense pain, just like I did when I killed his daughters those long years ago. His love for his children sickens me, and I want to continue to make him miserable and suffer."

"Does Balthazar remember his past connections to Olivia and Roman?" Salvatore asked.

"Balthazar doesn't remember a damn thing," Father said. "He isn't strong enough to kill Olivia. I believe deep down he still cares for her."

"And do Olivia and Roman remember their previous lives as Isabelle and Armand?" Salvatore pressed.

"No, nothing at all. Olivia is pregnant again, and neither she nor Roman has any memory of their pasts," Father said with a satisfied grin, reveling in his successful manipulation of their memories.

"And Malik?" Salvatore settled on the settee, his arms stretched across the back.

Father sat on the opposite side of the settee.

Salvatore removed his arms from the back of the sofa and edged away from Mathias.

"I have Malik wrapped around my finger," Father said. "He is absolutely clueless in everything. Soon, Balthazar will be imprisoned, and everything will be in our hands. Malik is completely oblivious to my true nature. He thinks I saved him. I followed the plan perfectly."

Salvatore and I shared a knowing look.

"Are you sure he doesn't suspect anything about your allegiance to me?" Salvatore prodded.

A dark smirk crept across Father's face.

"No," he drawled, relishing the thrill of it all. "I love playing the part of the kindly, beloved count. Once the truth is revealed, Malik and Marcellious will be utterly *crushed*. They'll realize this seemingly sweet old man has betrayed them." He gestured toward himself. "And, by then, Marcellious will be dead."

The following words dripped from Father's lips like molten honey. "Olivia is pregnant and utterly helpless. She's at my estate in Wales. Roman is too busy nursing his fragile wife to see the danger under his nose."

His grin widened into a grotesque mask of triumph. "I carefully orchestrated this game of power, placing each piece on the chessboard with precision. Victory is within our grasp."

Joy bubbled within me, dark and exhilarating. I reveled in the thought of the chaos we would wreak.

"Everything is falling into place," I whispered, my heart pounding with anticipation and power. The vision of a world cloaked in shadows, bending to my will, filled my mind. A world where I stood above all, the ultimate purveyor of darkness.

Victory will be mine.

My lips curled into a sinister smile.

Father brushed his fingers against the polished, acorn pommel of a familiar dagger strapped to his side. His lips twisted into a sardonic smile.

My heart raced as I saw the gleaming knife. It seemed to beckon me, whispering seductively in my mind. I felt a sudden urge to grip it tightly, to feel its weight and power in my hand.

"I brought it," he said, the words laced with triumph as he stood and extended the weapon toward me.

"My dagger!" I held the dagger like a mother might embrace her beloved newborn. It gleamed ominously in the dim light of the study, its edge promising deceit and disruption.

"Now that you've brought Alina's dagger back to her," Salvatore said, "it's time to bring our plan to motion. And, so, Mathias, you have my permission to travel back to your estate with Alina. You shall depart at the full moon."

"How will I explain my long absence?" I asked, my voice trembling with uncertainty. "Olivia saw Balthazar stab me outside our shop in Seattle."

My father held up a slender finger. "We have already set a story in motion. Timehunters captured you. Since Olivia was unaware of their existence and her own abilities, her mind would have deceived her into believing she had witnessed your murder. All we must do is sow seeds of doubt in her memory. I have also convinced Lee of the story's truth. He will support it without question. Don't worry, my dear. We have thought of everything. Go to Olivia. She will be uncertain, disoriented by your sudden presence."

He leaned closer, the scent of his ambition as heady as the darkest incense. "Keep her off balance. That's where we need her."

I nodded, understanding the gravity of the task at hand. With her unwavering determination, Olivia now carried the vulnerability of her condition—a weakness to be exploited.

"We want her to focus on you, not her quest to find the moon dagger," he said, his gaze sharp and calculating. "*You* will be the key to finding the next blade—not Olivia and her insipid companions."

The mission was clear. I would infiltrate their ranks, a

serpent in Eden, weaving distrust and discord until they were too entangled in their suspicions to see the real threat. It was more than subterfuge; it was artistry, and I would paint their downfall with strokes of calculated chaos.

"What if our plan falls apart? What if everything goes wrong?" I blurted out, fear taking a sudden and powerful hold of my heart.

Salvatore's dark eyes snapped to mine. He drew back his hand as if ready to strike me for daring to question our carefully crafted plan. I flinched and closed my eyes, bracing for impact.

Instead, he let out a terrifying roar that echoed through the room. "What are you so afraid of?"

"What if Zara or Lazarus come back?" I asked, trembling. "What then?"

My gaze darted to my father. His expression conveyed a warning directed at me—*Watch what you say*. I nodded and turned my attention back to Salvatore.

Salvatore shook his head. "Forget about them. They've been gone too long to be a threat."

His words didn't reassure me. My mind raced with all the possibilities and dangers that could arise if my enemies returned. "But what if they come back stronger than before?"

Salvatore's expression hardened as he leaned forward, his voice low and powerful. "Don't underestimate me or what I've given you. Remember who made you a Timeborne and how easily I can crush and kill you."

His words lingered in my mind, and my head ached with confusion and fear. He claimed to have created me as a Timeborne, but that went against everything my ex-husband had taught me with his wild theories about solar eclipses. Despite my doubts, I couldn't contradict Salvatore; his power was beyond anything I had ever witnessed, and I didn't want to risk facing his terrifying wrath. But deep down, the question burned within me—Did this enigmatic and manipulative being create me? Or was there something darker and more sinister at play?

I shook my head, my attention captured by the thoughts of Zara and Lazarus. I remembered the horrifying sensation of icy scales slithering up my legs, making me freeze in terror. Dozens of snakes had coiled around me, summoned by Lazarus, trapping me in a suffocating embrace. I had wanted to scream, but my lips were sealed shut as the serpents pressed against my face, their heads seeking entry into my mouth.

And Zara… I shuddered as I recalled our first meeting. I had stepped into a stream, and something caught my foot and held me tight. Twigs and debris tangled around my ankle. I couldn't untie the knot in my shoelaces, and my shoe was stuck between two rocks and branches. It was her doing… the demoness Zara. I thought I would die in that icy stream. And then she proceeded to taunt and torment me, letting me know she had me in her sights from that day forward.

A sheen of icy sweat covered my body at the recollections. I loathed and feared Zara and Lazarus.

"You know I have eyes and ears everywhere," Salvatore said, a sly grin creeping across his face. "I would know if Zara or Lazarus were lurking nearby."

I straightened up. "Why are you telling me this now?"

Salvatore chuckled and placed a hand on my shoulder.

"Because I don't want you to be afraid, my beautiful serpent," he said softly. "Zara and Lazarus may think they have the upper hand, but they are weaker than me. I still hold all the strings in this game."

His words sent shivers down my spine as I gazed into his intense, piercing eyes.

He rose from his seat and extended a hand toward me.

"We're so close to victory, my love," he whispered with conviction, pulling me to stand before him. "I can feel it in my bones."

With that, he drew me in for a passionate kiss that was powerful and full of emotion. He cupped my face with his hands, his fingers entwining in my hair as he deepened the kiss.

My whole being felt electrified, as if every cell in my body was awakening for the first time. We lingered in the kiss, my body heated and wet with desire. I couldn't remember the last time I had been kissed so passionately. It was as if the world around us had ceased to exist, leaving only the two of us entwined in our own little bubble of sadistic bliss.

Eventually, we broke apart, and he rested his forehead against mine, his breaths coming out in uneven puffs. "It's been too long since we've satisfied our passion, my love."

I couldn't help the smile that spread across my face.

"I agree," I replied, feeling bold and uninhibited.

When Salvatore had taken me under his wing, I'd been drawn into a world of darkness and seduction. His every touch ignited a fire within me, and we'd become passionate lovers, consumed by each other's desires. But as the years had passed, he'd pulled away from me, drawn to another woman who bore him three sons. They were being groomed to become the next Lords of Shadows while I remained on the outskirts of his life. Yet, in those rare moments when he would return to my bed, I couldn't resist him. My body craved his touch, even as my heart longed for something more.

A warm sense of approval washed over me, like a comforting embrace, as I sensed my father's gaze fixed on

Salvatore and me. A subtle thrill tingled through my being, lifting the hairs on my arms in a silent dance of contentment. As I stealthily glanced at him, his eyes held a proud glint, like jewels glistening in the sun. We both knew that keeping Salvatore happy was our ultimate goal, our duty. Every move we made, every word we spoke, was carefully calculated to please him and maintain his favor. It was a delicate dance we were all too familiar with now. Our lives revolved around pleasing Salvatore.

Yet, as Salvatore's lips captured mine again, I knew I was caught in a dangerous game with no way out but surrendering to his will.

"Olivia and Roman have the sun dagger," Father said, interrupting the moment. "They are actively searching for the moon blade. Now that you are back, Alina, you will be the one who finds the moon dagger. Once you have both knives in your possession, you will kill Roman and Olivia and the rest of the people she loves."

A surge of power coursed through me, igniting a fiery determination. After all this time, our plans were finally coming to fruition.

I looked at Salvatore with a fierce expression. "My love, I will make you proud. We have waited so long for this moment."

I tightened my hold on the hilt of my dagger.

Salvatore's piercing gaze turned dark and predatory as he lunged forward, his hand snaking out to grab my throat. His fingers were like steel, digging into my skin with a force that made me gasp for air.

"You will succeed, my beautiful serpent," he hissed. "You will be unstoppable...but follow the plan precisely and keep your emotions in check. One wrong move could ruin everything."

He leaned closer, his hot breath tickling my ear. "Make Olivia believe your story. Play the role of the devoted mother who has finally been reunited with her daughter. Be patient with her, and above all, do not reveal your true nature to her."

His grip tightened on my throat. "Once you possess both blades, then you may unleash your wrath. But not a moment sooner than that."

When he released me, I gasped for breath. A chill ran down my spine at the thought of wielding such power. Salvatore's eyes gleamed with excitement and anticipation as he watched me.

Wet desire pooled between my legs. His rough treatment of me always turned me on.

He glared at me with a twisted smile before addressing my father. "And *you*, my dear ally, have the full force of my army of Timehunters at your disposal. Use them wisely, for our time is finally at hand. We will become the all-powerful rulers of the universe, and none shall stand in our way!"

A savage hunger for power consumed me, driving me to contemplate unspeakable acts in pursuit of our grand vision. My heart raced with sadistic anticipation, imagining the delicious moment when I would strut into Olivia's presence, relishing the look of abject horror that would inevitably spread across her face as she realized her mother was alive.

CHAPTER ONE

ROMAN

"Where are we going?" Malik asked as we left the lavish Noir room in Mathias' estate.

"Rosie," I said, the name like a talisman against the darkness that threatened to engulf us. "We must check on her."

We needed to ensure she was safe, untouched by the turmoil that had seized our lives.

Silence hung heavily between us as Malik and I strode toward the front room, our footsteps echoing against the marble floors of Mathias' opulent estate.

Malik glanced at me, his intense eyes searching mine for a strength I wasn't sure I possessed.

"Let's hurry this up," he barked, urgency lacing his voice. "We can't leave your wife vulnerable with those two monsters lurking around." My heart raced at the thought; my love for her was eclipsed only by the frustration she ignited within me. Her stubbornness often led her into perilous situations, and now it had driven her to seek out Balthazar, ensnared in Belladonna's shadow, with Mathias looming ominously beside her. What possessed her to descend into that abyss, determined to confront her greatest adversary alone, while I remained powerless above?

The air was thick with tension, a palpable cloud that followed in our wake as if it also sensed the unease coursing through our veins. I could feel Malik's restlessness mirroring my own; he had always been the one to seek balance in the chaos, striving to mend what was broken. Now, with Marcellious snatched from us by those relentless Timehunters, there was a void no amount of determination could fill.

"Damn it," Malik muttered. "If only Marcellious were here."

Lines of frustration etched deeper into his face.

We glanced into the room where Osman and Rosie sprawled on the carpeted floor, playing with wooden blocks. Osman looked so silly pretending to be a child. Satisfied, I eased back, not wanting to disturb them.

"I can't stand the thought of my wife with those two demons, Balthazar and Mathias." I clenched my fists, the leather of my gloves creaking with the motion. "I'm going to go downstairs to the dungeon. I'm going to see that everything is alright."

Without another word, we strode forward, each step carrying the weight of our resolve. We were warriors, bound by a purpose that went beyond ourselves, beyond even the confines of time. And though the shadows whispered of dread and despair, we would not falter.

Malik and I departed into the depths of uncertainty, leaving behind the deceptive splendor of the estate for the grim reality that awaited us below.

The stairwell spiraled downward, a stone artery leading to

the dungeon's heart. The air grew damp, carrying a musty scent that clung to my nostrils. My thoughts were a tangled web—the image of my wife, who had already endured more than her fair share, of Rosie, innocent and vulnerable, a vivid splash of color against the drab uncertainty of Marcellious' absence.

"Almost there," Malik murmured, his voice a low growl of frustration. He was like an animal on edge, desperate for action, for a wrong to right. I shared his sentiment, the gnawing helplessness clawing at my insides.

We reached the bottom of the stairs, the coolness of the dungeon level seeping into my bones. It was a chill that no fire could chase away, a reminder of the dangers lurking within these walls.

We turned the final corner and halted abruptly. My gaze landed on Lee, and I did a double take. Then, my attention was drawn further down the hallway. There, amidst the shadows, stood a woman—her presence incongruous in this dim underworld. Her eyes, pools of history and sorrow, fixed on another figure before her—my wife.

"Mom? You're alive?" Olivia's voice broke through the stillness, a mixture of disbelief and awe as she stared at the woman.

"Yes, honey. I've been alive this whole time," the woman said with a knowing smile.

Olivia's knees buckled. I lunged forward, catching her limp form just as it grazed the cold floor. Her skin was pale, starkly contrasting the vibrancy she always emanated.

"She's fine. She's just shocked to see me." The strange woman's declaration did little to ease the vice around my heart.

I cradled Olivia in my arms, her unconscious state rendering her a sleeping beauty lost in a nightmare.

"Malik!" My voice echoed off the walls, a plea laced with urgency. "I need your help!"

Malik strode over, his face set with determination. We had faced countless perils together, but none so personal, so wrenchingly intimate as this moment with Olivia's vulnerability laid bare between us.

Malik's eyes smoldered embers at the woman.

"Malik, you look more handsome than ever," she said, her voice dripping with insincerity.

"Enough!" I said, an edge of ferocity cutting through my tone. "We have to get Olivia out of here."

Lee barreled toward us, his muscles rippling with determination as we hoisted Olivia's lifeless body between us. Urgently, we scaled the stairs, sweat beading on our brows as we raced against time to reach safety with our precious burden.

"We must care for her," I said, more to myself than to anyone else, as we navigated the labyrinthine hallways of the estate. Malik paced beside me, each step a thunderous beat in tune with the wild tempest brewing within him.

Upon reaching Olivia's bedroom, we gently laid her on the plush bed. Her serene face belied the moment's chaos, and my hands shook as I brushed a lock of hair from her forehead. The weight of guilt crushed my chest as I stared at my wife's pale, unconscious body. I shouldn't have allowed her to be alone with those madmen, leaving her vulnerable and defenseless. I hoped she would wake up soon and forgive me for my mistake.

"Who was that woman?" I asked, turning to Malik with a gaze that sought answers.

"Olivia's mother," he spat out, the words laden with bitterness.

Shock coursed through me, rooting me to the spot. How

could this be? Olivia had told me she'd witnessed her mother be killed by Balthazar.

"Can I help?" A maid had appeared at the doorframe, wringing her hands.

"Water," I commanded, my voice hoarse. She scurried away and then returned with a basin and cloth.

As I wrung the cloth, water droplets fell like tears onto the wooden floor. I traced the contours of Olivia's cheek with a tenderness borne of desperation.

"Come back to us, my love," I whispered, a silent prayer for her swift return to consciousness.

Olivia's eyelids fluttered, and I felt relieved as she returned to the waking world. I cradled her in my arms, feeling the rise and fall of her chest against mine—a rhythm that sang a counterpoint to the erratic drumming of my pulse.

"Oh, god, Roman. I'm so happy to see you. You will not believe it," she murmured, her voice weak but filled with wonder. "I just had the strangest dream. I saw my mother live in the flesh, and Lee was with her. I think my pregnant brain is making things up. Mathias beheaded Tristan. Balthazar was captured."

The room seemed to constrict around us, the air growing heavy with the weight of her words. Malik, pacing like a caged beast, spun toward us, his eyes ablaze with an intensity that pinned me to the spot.

"It wasn't a fucking dream, Olivia." His voice tore through the silence, each syllable sharp and incendiary. "She's fucking alive."

The profanity jolted through me—Malik, always the peacemaker, his decorum now shattered by the magnitude of our reality.

Olivia's brow furrowed as she tried to piece together the fragments of her consciousness.

"My mom is alive?" Her incredulous whisper was a knife to my gut. "I thought she was dead. How is this possible? I saw it happen with my eyes. Balthazar stabbed her in the chest, and there was a funeral. Everything in my head is jumbled. I don't know what's going on. I need to speak to my mother."

The urgency in her voice clawed at me, but the strategist within knew better than to act on impulse. My grip tightened around her, protective and resolute.

"No," I said, anchoring her gaze with mine. "You should rest. Today has been hard on you. Malik and I have to come up with a plan. We must figure out what the next step is. This throws everything off with Lee's and your mother's arrival. We should focus on finding the dagger, but instead, we must deal with Alina's sudden appearance."

Conflicting emotions warred across Olivia's face, her need for answers wrestling with the understanding that reck-lessness could cost us dearly. My mind raced, already sifting through possibilities, contingencies, and allies. In this twisted game where the board had been overturned and the pieces scattered, I knew one thing for certain—we were far from checkmate.

Olivia whipped around to face Malik, her eyes wide and pleading. Her shaky voice barely managed to whisper, "Did you know?"

The tension in the room crackled like a live wire.

"No! Mathias did not tell me anything," Malik said. "I feel so used in this whole twisted plan!"

He could barely contain his rage, a raw, palpable force that seemed to vibrate through the air.

"Malik, please—" Olivia extended a hand and stroked his arm, her eyes brimming with concern.

"Don't touch me!" His shout echoed off the walls, and

Olivia recoiled. There was a wildness in his eyes that I hadn't seen before.

"Malik, you need to calm down," Olivia said, though her voice quivered slightly. "I'm tired of the secrets. We need to speak with my mother to hear her truth."

A sharp rapping at the door cut through the turmoil. Malik flung open the door to reveal Alina and Lee standing there, their presence an unwelcome intrusion into our chaos.

"Olivia?" Alina's voice was soft, almost hesitant.

With a sudden burst of energy, Olivia pushed herself up and lunged into Lee's open arms. I could sense the love and longing in their hug.

"I missed you so much, Lee. So, so much," Olivia whimpered.

"My dear Little Moon," Lee said. "Not a single day has passed since you left that I haven't thought of you. I'm sorry, Little Moon. I'm sorry I didn't tell you the truth."

Olivia clung to him before facing her mother, her eyes alight with a thousand unanswered questions. "Mom, how are you standing here, alive in the flesh? Where have you been all these years?"

The demand hung heavily in the air.

Alina met her daughter's gaze, the weight of years etched onto her face. Silence fell upon the room.

I stood to the side, my arms crossed over my chest as Alina stepped forward with open arms toward Olivia.

"I will tell you everything, my darling," she said, her voice a blend of joy and sorrow. "I'm so happy to see you! I know you have many questions, and I will answer them all. But first, I need to check on Emily. I was told she had her baby today."

Olivia's expression hardened, her eyes flickering with the pain of recent revelations.

"She just learned her father is Balthazar and is devastated," she stated flatly. "She witnessed the brutal death of Balthazar's son. She has never met you. After everything she has endured today, I don't think she is ready to see you."

"The last time I saw Emily, she was just a tiny newborn," Alina said, her voice quivering.

"Please," Oliva said, "be gentle with her."

Olivia and I proceeded down the candle-lit corridor toward Emily's room with Alina close at our heels. My footsteps echoed heavily against the stone floor, each a dull reminder of the uncertainty gripping our lives.

The sight of Emily cradling the baby to her chest while tears streamed down her face twisted something deep within me. Her soft sobs filled the room, each one punctuated by a whispered plea for Marcellious.

"Disgusting," Alina muttered, but I caught it. Disgust? At her flesh and blood in distress?

Before I could question or chastise, Olivia was at Emily's side, whispering words of comfort and smoothing back her hair. Alina cleared her throat to assert her presence, but it was a clumsy intrusion against the backdrop of Emily's grief.

"Emily," I began, my voice steady despite the turmoil, "it's alright. We're going to find Marcellious, I promise."

"Everyone, leave! I don't want to see anyone right now. I want to be alone." Emily's forceful and raw voice broke through her tears. She didn't look at Alina.

Olivia rested her hand on Emily's trembling shoulder. "Emily, I know you're going through a lot today, and I feel every ounce of your pain, but there is someone special you probably want to meet."

Emily's heart clenched with betrayal as she met Olivia's gaze, her pain mirrored in the woman's conflicted expression.

"This is your mother," Olivia said softly, her words laced with regret and guilt.

The room fell silent, all eyes fixed on Emily, waiting for her reaction to this revelation. Would it bring healing or only deepen the wounds that were still raw and bleeding?

But instead of finding solace in the truth, Emily's agony erupted into a deafening scream, her voice rising to an unearthly pitch like a banshee's cry. "Get out!" She spat at her mother, tears streaming down her face. "I want no one in this room." Her words hung heavy in the air, thick with anger and pain.

Alina took a hesitant step forward, reaching out as if to smooth over the chasm that had opened between them.

"Emily, honey, let me explain," she pleaded, her words trembling with desperation. "Balthazar meant nothing to me. It was a past connection."

"Past connection?" Emily's shriek cut through Alina's defense like a knife. "I don't want to hear anything from your mouth, especially after discovering that Balthazar is my father! I'm disgusted. Do you know how many times he tried to kill me? You bore me but abandoned me. I wish I'd never been born!"

I remained an observer, a statue rooted in place as emotions raged around me. Alina's face contorted in pain, her composure slipping away under the weight of Emily's condemnation.

"No, Emily," Alina said, her voice straining against the tide of rejection. "I tried to protect you. He never wanted anything to do with you or be a part of your life. I wanted you to have the best life, so I left you with Philip."

Emily clutched the baby closer, her body shaking with inconsolable sobs. "But you cared for your other daughter, Olivia! Yet you abandoned me!"

The accusation hung heavy, a testament to a lifetime of perceived inequality.

Alina's composure snapped, her scream piercing the already fraught atmosphere. "I love you both! My life was brutal and harsh!"

The room felt smaller, the air thicker with each word spoken, each secret unraveled. I watched, still powerless, as the fabric of trust continued to tear, the threads of their bond fraying beyond recognition.

My fingers found Olivia's amidst the tension that crackled through the air, her palm cool and clammy within my grasp. She turned to me, a flicker of disbelief in her eyes.

"I'm shocked to see Emily so riled," she whispered, her voice barely more than a breath.

She stepped toward Emily, her hand slipping from mine to reach out with words meant to soothe. "Emily, we will find Marcellious and return him to you."

Lee's silhouette filled the doorway, commanding the attention of everyone in the room.

"I will find my son and bring him back to you," he said with unwavering conviction. "I raised him and will do whatever it takes to have him by your side again."

His gaze locked on Alina. "I think you should go. Emily and the baby need their rest."

Without a word, Alina receded into the shadows of the hallway, leaving behind a trail of stifled emotions and unanswered questions.

A hush descended as Emily's tear-streaked face turned toward Lee. His steady gaze seemed to smooth out the raw edges of her anger.

"I believe you, Lee," she said, her voice steadying. "Marcellious has told me so many things about you. Your presence here eases my pain."

With trembling arms, she presented the bundle cradled against her chest. "Meet Leo."

Lee approached with solemnity reserved for sacred moments, extending his arms to receive the infant. As he gazed down at the baby, his expression softened, reverence shining in his eyes like a lighthouse beacon amidst stormy seas. "You have given Marcellious a beautiful son, Emily. I give you my word. I will bring Marcellious back."

As I stood there, watching the exchange, a silent vow settled in my heart alongside Lee's promise—a gladiator's oath to protect and fight for this family, torn and mended by the threads of fate and blood.

Olivia stormed out of the room, her fury a living thing that seemed to burn the air around us. I trailed closely behind, my mind racing, but my demeanor as steady and resolute as a centurion on watch.

"How could she just stand there, Roman?" Her words were sharp, each one slicing through the tension. "After all these years?"

"Easy," I murmured, placing a hand on her shoulder in a silent bid to steady her tempest and protect her as if I could shield her from the storm of emotions battling within her.

Alina was waiting just outside, her face etched with concern and something else—perhaps regret or fear. As Olivia's eyes met hers, I felt a shift inside me. Every muscle tensed, every sense heightened. The gladiator in me took over, ready for any threat, real or perceived.

"Olivia, honey, please let me tell you the story," Alina said, her voice threaded with a weariness that spoke of long-held burdens. "I'm tired of all these secrets and lies."

Before Olivia could retort, heavy footsteps echoed down the hallway. Mathias appeared, his presence dominating the space as he approached.

"You will get the whole truth, my dear," he told Olivia, his gaze fixed on Alina with an intensity that left no room for doubt. "Alina will tell you everything."

Even if they were to tell us their side of the story, could we trust it? Would it be enough to satisfy our burning questions and doubts? Or would we always wonder if there was more to the truth, hidden just out of our reach?

CHAPTER TWO

OLIVIA

We headed downstairs, a somber procession led by Malik's silent determination, Roman's steady presence at my side, Lee's watchful eyes scanning for unseen threats, and Mathias' enigmatic composure. Behind us, Alina's footsteps were a hushed whisper of deception. In contrast, my footfalls echoed loudly with my cumbersome and awkward gait, evidence of the life growing inside me. The weight of my pregnant belly slowed my steps, but I trudged on determinedly despite the ache in my back and the heaviness in my limbs.

"My whole life was upended in an instant," I murmured, the words tumbling like shards of broken glass. "All these years, I thought she was dead. Where was she?"

Roman squeezed my hand, anchoring me to the present amidst the chaos. "Patience, Olivia."

"Roman, I need answers! I need someone to tell me the truth. Where's she been all along?" The desperation in my voice clawed its way up from my gut, demanding to be heard.

Alina's calm voice floated behind us. "My dear, I can hear you perfectly well."

I spun hastily to face her, the sudden movement causing me to wobble slightly on my unsteady feet. My pregnant belly protruded outward, throwing off my balance and adding another layer of vulnerability to my stance. The group stopped behind me, their footsteps echoing faintly in the room's stillness. Despite my physical discomfort, I stood tall and determined, ready to face challenges.

"I've been on a goose chase," I spat, the bitterness stinging my tongue. "About you, the daggers, the journals, everything. While all this time, you were alive!"

Alina's expression remained serene in the dim light filtering through the windows, as if our world hadn't just tilted on its axis. She approached with measured steps, her hands reaching to bridge the chasm between us.

"Olivia, please—"

"No!" I recoiled from her touch, anger flaring hot and fierce. "Before we start unraveling your web of secrets and stories, we need to find Marcellious. You must understand that."

"And Marcellious is Emily's husband?" Alina asked.

"Yes, and my twin brother, who Timehunters have taken," Roman interrupted. "The longer he's with Timehunters, the madder, the more insane, and the more poisoned he will be. He will spill secrets—*our* secrets—if he survives."

Her eyes held sorrow, but it was too late for regret or explanations. There was no room for anything else until we secured Marcellious' safety. And so, amid the dust motes dancing in the shafts of light and the heavy silence of our entourage, we stood at an impasse, the weight of a mother's absence and her daughter's fury hanging thick in the air.

Mathias exhaled, rubbing a hand over his face before saying, "We should all go talk in my dining room." His tone left little room for argument.

The oak door to the dining room groaned open, a fore-boding echo to our heavy hearts as we filed in. The table, once a place of communion, now felt like an arena where secrets bared their fangs. We took our seats silently, the wood and velvet chairs providing cold comfort. I settled into my spot, unable to shake the sensation of my world unraveling.

Mathias clenched his fists as he spoke, his voice trembling with determination. "I won't rest until we find Marcel-lious. My network of connections will be looking for him at once."

Malik leaned toward Mathias.

"Maybe you know where he is," he said, his voice barely above a whisper but laden with a venom I'd never heard from him before. "Why did you keep the truth from me that Alina was alive? You used me! You made me do all your dirty work. But you lied to me whenever I asked you about Alina's dagger. You could have told me she was alive. I thought we were allies, Mathias!"

Mathias let a honeyed smile play on his lips as if Malik had merely commented on the weather. "You have no right to question my intentions. I had to keep Alina a secret for her protection and safety."

Malik stood abruptly, fists clenched, his voice thunderous in the otherwise still room. "I have done everything you asked. I brought you the daggers. You could have told me why!"

All eyes snapped to Malik. Even Alina's stoic facade cracked slightly at the edges. I flinched with each syllable.

"Now poor Marcellious is captured by those bloody ruth-less Timehunters. He will become a lunatic under their influence!"

Mathias remained unflappable, his voice a calm counter

to Malik's storm. "Do not raise your voice to me. We will find him."

Malik was panting now, chest heaving as though each breath battled the rage within. "You know everything. Like you said, you have connections. You should *know* where he is."

In that charged moment, the air thick with accusations and desperation, the world seemed to pivot on the axis of Mathias' response. Would he reveal the threads that bound us all, or would he sever them, one by one, with continued secrecy?

"You forget who you're talking to," Mathias said, his voice low and laced with a threat that sent shivers down my spine.

Malik's face contorted with fury.

"I could throw you in my dungeon and force you to inhale poison with Balthazar," Mathias said.

"Is that a threat, old man?" Malik's shout bounced off the high ceilings, his challenge hanging between them like a gauntlet thrown. The room, filled with the weight of unsaid truths and accusations, felt smaller, suffocating.

"Malik, please," Roman intervened. "You need to breathe."

Malik was a force of nature. With blazing eyes, every word he spoke was like a burst of lightning.

"You swore you were the most powerful darkness of all time. How could Marcellious be taken under your watch? You should have protected him." He jabbed a finger toward Mathias, accusation sharp as a dagger's edge.

The shouting escalated, voices overlapping into a cacophony of betrayal and confusion. Roman's pleas, Malik's accusations, Mathias' denials; it was a mad family reunion where every member threw their grievances like punches.

Alina sat back, a slight smile creasing her lips, observing it all as if she had watched a chess match unfold. I stood there, helpless, watching the fracturing of our little trust.

It was as if the long-buried secrets were clawing their way to the surface, leaving us all gasping for air amidst the debris of our shattered illusions.

The darkness spilled from Mathias like ink in water, its tendrils reaching out. His now-shadowy form rose, wrapping his hands around Malik's neck and hauling him to his feet. Malik's face began to turn an alarming shade of purple as the shadows coiled around his throat, squeezing tighter. I felt a surge of panic and bolted forward, Roman at my heels.

"Mathias," I screamed, my voice raw and desperate. The chaotic scene around us was a blur. All my focus was on Mathias and the life he held in his hands.

Malik's eyes bulged, and his face turned red as Mathias' fingers tightened around his throat.

"Stop this!" I pleaded, tears streaming down my face. "He's just upset. Please don't hurt him. I'm your granddaughter. If you care for me at all, let him go."

Mathias was beyond reason, his eyes ablaze with a wrath that darkened the air around us.

"I reunited you with Roman and Olivia. I gave you Rosie. I let you live. I healed you," he said, his voice a thunderous rumble that shook the room. "And now you question me? Do you know what I do to those who do not accept my kindness? I bring them down to their knees!"

My hands shook as I reached for the shadowy strands, trying to pull them away from Malik's neck. They were cold and slippery, resisting my touch like living things. Beside me, Roman grappled with Mathias, trying to break his concentration to disrupt the flow of his dark power.

"Please, Mathias, if you love me!" I said, my voice

breaking with fear. My mind raced, trying to piece together the puzzle of secrecy and lies that had ensnared us all. "Let Malik go!"

Roman's face was etched with confusion, mirroring my own bewilderment. What game was he playing, where we were but pawns oblivious to the rules? The questions circled in my head, a whirlwind of doubt and suspicion, but no answers came.

"Please," I whispered again, a last-ditch effort to reach whatever humanity was left within Mathias. "I know you love me. Don't do this."

The tension in the room felt like a bowstring drawn taut, ready to snap at any moment. In that unbearable silence, I waited, hoping against hope that my plea had found its mark.

Mathias' hand dropped to his side, and the darkness choking the air recoiled back into the shadows. Malik staggered backward, gasping for breath, his face flushed with rage and humiliation. He straightened, his chest heaving as he locked eyes with me, his expression raw and unforgiving.

"I don't need your pleading or begging for him to stop," he said, his voice hoarse but laced with defiance. His dark gaze shifted to Mathias, who stood silent, a storm still swirling in his ancient eyes. "I thought I was dark, but there's a bigger monster at play."

Pushing past the tension that hung between us like a heavy curtain, Malik turned on his heel. "I'm done here. I'm going to the caves to dig for the moon dagger. That is still our best lead."

"I'll go too," Roman said from beside me, determination lining his words.

Malik faced Roman. "No, you need to protect your wife," he countered, his eyes briefly softened as they met mine.

I stifled the urge to protest; I didn't need protecting. Roman's posture told me he was torn, so I touched his arm.

"Go with Malik and calm him down," I said. "I'll be here with Lee. He'll protect me."

Roman's gaze bore into mine, filled with warmth and adoration. He leaned in, his lips brushing against mine as if they were made of feathers. Then he kissed me, a soft and gentle embrace that spoke volumes without a single word. I could feel the love and tenderness pouring from him, warming every inch of my body. The world stood still as we shared a sweet, tender kiss that filled my heart with joy.

As we slowly pulled apart, my hand instinctively reached up and pressed against my racing heart. Roman smiled softly. He stooped down to press a tender kiss on my swollen belly, his voice filled with anticipation as he whispered, "I can't wait to meet you, little one." As he rose to stand back up, our eyes met and locked in a powerful gaze that seemed to ignite the air around us with fiery passion. In that searing instant, it was as if time stood still and nothing in the world existed except for the two of us and our unborn child.

Without another word, Roman followed Malik out of the room, their footsteps a fading echo against the stone floors. The departure left a vacuum, and into it settled an awkward silence. Mathias, Lee, and Alina arranged themselves around the dining table, an uneasy truce settling among us.

"Please, forgive my outburst," Mathias said, his voice uncharacteristically soft. As our gazes locked, his eyes scoured mine for recognition, revealing the kind man my grandfather used to be before he showed me the evil that lurked inside.

I sighed, the anger and fear ebbing away. It wasn't easy, but family ties had a way of binding even the most frayed hearts.

"Our one weakness is family," Mathias said quietly. "I want to be a happy family and be whole."

The words felt heavier than I expected, laden with the hope that we could somehow move past the secrets and the darkness that seemed to shadow our every step.

Mathias settled back into his ornate chair, the ancient wood creaking. Shadows flickered across his face as the candles on the table danced and swayed.

His deep voice cut through the tense air, its low rumble resonating with authority. "You must understand, Olivia, everything I told you this morning about my life was true. But yes, Malik is right about me orchestrating this plan against Balthazar. I am the mastermind behind it all. For too long, he has been a dangerous and ruthless monster, constantly trying to kill you and those you love. I created a plan to eradicate him once and for all.

"I had Malik play his part in it. He summoned Marcellious to get close to Balthazar and retrieve his dagger and your mother's. I couldn't do it myself because Balthazar and I have a long and bitter history."

Mathias' words hung heavily in the air, punctuated by the crackling of the candles and my heart thumping as I processed everything he had just revealed.

A shiver ran down my spine as I hugged myself tightly, searching for warmth in the cozy room. My mind raced, trying to piece together the fragments of truth that were slowly coming to light.

"Also, I didn't want Balthazar to know I was alive," Mathias said, his gaze steady and solemn. "I love you and Emily so much and would do anything to protect you. I would never hurt either of you. I want to have my family close. Please don't be afraid of me."

Afraid? The word echoed in my head. How could I not fear the unknown, the shrouded past unraveling before me?

"Balthazar is locked up and will never escape. I promise you," Mathias said as if reading my thoughts. "And I need to share my ugly past with Balthazar with you."

He paused, his words hanging between us like a specter.

"I once had a wife and a training school, teaching my students to correct their innate darkness. I taught them they may have been born this way, but it didn't mean they had to live that way. Balthazar was my greatest student, closest ally, and friend, once upon a time, until one day he destroyed my school, wanting power."

My breath caught in my throat.

"He blamed me for every bad thing that happened to him." Mathias clenched his hands into fists. "He killed my beautiful wife Cora in vengeance. He went after my daughter, Alina, but he fell in love with her. Still, he tried to kill her. Balthazar is the most dangerous darkness, and I will protect you and Emily at all costs."

His declaration was fierce, an oath carved from years of hidden battles.

"The truth is, Olivia," he added, softer now, "I had no idea Alina was alive until Lee told me."

"Lee?" The name tumbled out of me, disbelief shading my tone. My gaze snapped to him, searching for confirmation. Lee met my eyes, his expression unreadable, then he gave a slow, measured nod.

"You and Lee know each other?"

Mathias nodded, a haunted look passing over his features. "Yes, I've known Lee for a long time. For years, I thought Alina was dead."

Something shifted inside me, some barrier crumbling at

the realization that the webs of our lives were more inter-twined than I'd ever imagined.

"I had a purpose," Mathias murmured, almost to himself. "I want joy in my life. I want to be one big, happy family."

He turned toward Alina, who lurked silently in the corner.

"I think it's time your daughter knows the truth," he said. "She only knows bits and pieces. Tell her the truth, Alina. She needs her mother back."

Tears pricked the corners of my eyes, the weight of years of longing and confusion pressing down on me. The truth. It was what I'd sought all along, and now it seemed closer than ever.

But with it came the realization that the path ahead was paved with revelations that would change everything. And those revelations might reveal more lies than I could stomach.

CHAPTER THREE

OLIVIA

The grandeur of Mathias' estate felt like a cruel contradiction to the turmoil that churned within me. Gilded edges and velvet drapery mocked my confusion as I sat at the head of the long dining table, its surface gleaming under the flickering glow of countless candles nestled within crystal chandeliers. The chair beside me remained conspicuously occupied, the ghost of my mother's absence over the years replaced by her tangible, but no less haunting, presence.

"Mom," I started, my voice steadier than I felt, "I want answers. I went through fourteen years with you gone, presumed dead. What happened?"

Alina's gaze met mine across the table. Lines of hardship etched into her face that I remembered smooth and laughing, but the same steel-blue eyes bore into me with an intensity I couldn't escape.

"Olivia," she began, her voice laced with a weariness that seemed to reach beyond the confines of this room, "everything I will tell you is dark and vicious. I just wanted to protect you."

A chill crawled up my spine. Malik's earlier outburst replayed in my mind, his anger ricocheting off these opulent walls and shattering the illusion of safety and family that Mathias' estate had promised. Now, hearing my mother confirm the darkness that swirled around our lives, it felt as if the final pillar of my childhood had been kicked out from under me.

"Protect me from what?" The question was barely a whisper, fear knotting my stomach.

"From Balthazar," she said with a bitter edge. "He killed me when you were a child. You and I were going to get ice cream. He stabbed me."

Her fingers trembled slightly as she traced the edge of the fine china before her.

The memory surged forward unbidden. The scream that had torn from my throat on that day echoed in my ears; the sight of blood blossoming on her shirt seared into my vision forever.

"I saw it," I gasped, the horror of that moment still vivid in my mind. "How did you recover?"

The silence between us held a weight of years, of buried secrets and truths too dangerous to speak aloud. My heart hammered against my ribcage, demanding the closure I had been denied for over a decade. Alina's eyes never left mine, reflecting the pain we both carried.

"Recover," she said softly, almost to herself, "is perhaps not the right word. There was, in fact, no killing. But I can understand why you thought that. Instead, I was whisked away by *Timehunters*."

She reached across the table, stopping short of touching my hand. Her fingers hovered there, trembling with the dread of her own story—a tale I knew would unravel the last threads of the life I thought I understood.

My heart pounded against my chest, and each beat resounded like the toll of a funeral bell as I waited for her to speak.

"Olivia," she said, her voice barely above a whisper, "I thought I was dead and wished I was because the pain, torture, and suffering I went through was unbearable. I woke up in a dark room, chained to the wall, beaten, and starved nearly to death. I was in the unforgiving grasp of Salvatore."

I flinched at her words, feeling the cold, feeling the cold bite of the metal around her wrists, the sting of starvation that had gnawed at her once vibrant spirit.

"Salvatore?" I echoed, the unfamiliar name bitter on my tongue. "I've never heard of him."

"Few have," she replied, her eyes distant as if peering into that shadowy abyss again. "He was watching me when we went to get ice cream. He's very powerful, more powerful than anyone I have ever met. After Balthazar... after that monster stabbed me, Salvatore took me. He made me his prisoner."

I struggled to draw a breath, to understand how this specter named Salvatore fit into the puzzle of our shattered lives.

"Prisoner?" I managed to ask, the word tasting of fear and confusion.

"Ruthless," she confirmed with a nod, haunted. "He had been watching us, waiting for an opportunity. I pleaded with everything I had. I lied to him, told him I had no children— that you were the child of a friend, and I looked after you."

The child of a friend... The phrase seemed so cold, devoid of the illusion of warmth I'd clutched to my chest as a child.

The air seemed to thin, and I gasped, trying to fill my lungs with something other than the dread that seeped from every word she spoke. How many nights had I cried myself to sleep, thinking my mother was dead? And all along, she had been enduring tortures unimaginable.

"Mom..." My voice trailed off, leaving a silence filled with the echoes of chains and the ghostly touch of unseen watchers.

"He's been the Timehunter leader all this time," she said, her gaze piercing mine with the ferocity of one who had stared down evil itself. "And the creator of Timebornes."

"A Timehunter leader and a creator of Timebornes?" Confusion swirled within me like a vortex. "But Dad said that if a baby was born during a solar eclipse during that exact moment of darkness, it creates Timebornes. You're telling me some man named Salvatore created us instead?"

Mom shook her head. "Salvatore claims he orchestrated the Eclipsarum Obscura, which means he created the power during the solar eclipse to create Timebornes and bring darkness within the dagger."

"Created us?" I repeated, feeling the ground of reality shift beneath my feet. Every truth I had held onto was being peeled away, layer by layer, revealing a core of uncertainty and fear.

"Olivia," she said, reaching across the void between us, her hand trembling like a leaf poised to fall. "There is so much you do not know hidden from you."

And at that moment, amidst the glinting cutlery and the brooding portraits of ancestors long gone, I understood that the path to truth would be as treacherous as any darkened labyrinth, with a Minotaur called Salvatore lurking at its heart.

The chandelier above cast a somber glow over the dining table, its candlelight shifting with the tension in the air.

I leaned forward, my hands clasped together to still their shaking.

"How did you live? How did you survive? More importantly, how did you get away?" The questions escaped me, raw and desperate.

My mother's eyes held a distant fire that had been kindled in the darkest places.

"Calm down, honey," she said, though her voice quivered with suppressed anguish. "I survived. I... I served him as his whore all these years. It was survival, nothing more. Salvatore is a formidable figure, known in certain circles as a Shadow Lord. His mastery of dark magic is unparalleled, and he can manipulate darkness, travel through time with ease, and hunt down his enemies ruthlessly. He is considered by many to be the most fearsome and elusive monster they have ever encountered. After so many years of planning... I finally escaped him."

A cold shiver ran through me. "How did you escape someone so powerful, so dark? That's impossible!"

I couldn't mask the disbelief in my voice.

"You don't understand," she replied, her gaze now steady, revealing a hint of the strategic mind that had outwitted a dark sorcerer. "Salvatore's power has grown weak through time. His minions, who once executed his every whim, now took orders from afar, giving me a sliver of opportunity. So, I bided my time. And when the moment came, I ran to Lee for help."

"To Lee?" The name felt strange on my lips, an echo from a childhood spent in play, not plots and schemes.

Lee stepped forward, his face a mixture of sorrow and resolve. He briefly took Mom's hand. "Your mother turning up after all these years... It shocked me as much as it has you. I was aware of the Timehunters, always cautious, always hiding our abilities to ensure they would never find us. I never for a moment thought they would have captured her."

He glanced at my mother, a silent understanding passing between them. "When I found her, broken yet defiant, the only way I could protect her was through Mathias."

I sat back, the pieces of this twisted puzzle refusing to fit together—my mother, a prisoner turned fugitive, Lee, a child-hood ally turned protector, and Mathias, an enigmatic figure whose role in this web of secrets was still unclear. The room spun around me, a carousel of truths and lies, and at its center stood Salvatore—the Shadow Lord who claimed dominion over time itself.

Golden light cascaded from above, scattering luminous patterns that danced across the dining room table. The tension was nearly tangible in the lavish space, wrapping around me like the cool Welsh mist outside the estate.

"How did you know Mathias?" I asked, my voice barely rising above a whisper, an anxious tremor betraying the semblance of calm I fought to maintain.

Lee's face was shadowed, and his eyes flitted to the gilded cornices as if seeking guidance from the ornate decor.

"He came to me when you were young," he said, his tone laced with a reluctance that seemed to age him further. "When Alina... When we thought she had died, Mathias showed up out of nowhere. He claimed he was Alina's father and wanted to be part of your life. He watched you from afar, never intruding too close. We kept in touch, but nothing serious."

"Did my papa know Mathias?" I pressed, my pulse quick-ening at the thought of my father being ensnared in this web of deceit.

"No, he didn't." Lee shook his head, his jaw tightening.

"We had to protect your father from the truth. The risk was too great, and the less he knew, the safer he would be."

He took a slow breath. "When Alina returned, we needed a solid plan to defeat Balthazar. First, we deal with that asshole. The rest shall follow."

The revelations settled upon my shoulders like the heavy velvet drapes adorned the tall windows. I was enveloped by the lore of my lineage, a narrative I could never have imagined to be so intricately woven into the fabric of darkness we all now sought to unravel.

The tension in the room wound tighter as Mathias, his eyes reflecting the soft glow of the chandelier above, leaned forward to address the growing list of questions that hung heavy in the air. Though laced with a certain weariness, his voice carried an undeniable authority that commanded attention.

"I contacted Malik," he said, the name dropping like a stone into still water, "and together we secured Balthazar's dagger. It was imperative to weaken him—to ensure your mother's safety."

A shiver ran down my spine at the mention of the weapon tied so closely to our family's turmoil. Resolve etched into Mathias' features, a manifestation of years spent plotting.

"Your mother is an expert in excavation," he said. "She's essential in helping us locate the moon dagger and ultimately defeating Balthazar."

He tapped lightly on the walnut table, betraying a hint of impatience or perhaps anxiety. It wasn't easy to discern.

"All I ever wanted," he said, the words escaping him like a sigh, "was to be reunited with my family. To be reunited with you, Olivia, and Emily."

His sentiment echoed through the lavish dining room, bouncing off the gilded frames of portraits that watched over us—silent guardians of a legacy fraught with secrets. The notion of family, once a simple concept, now seemed like a puzzle where pieces kept appearing and disappearing at will.

"My father doesn't know that Alina is alive?" I asked, the words tasting bitter on my tongue. The thought of him being kept in the dark twisted something deep inside me.

Mathias regarded me with a look that seemed to carry the weight of untold stories. The shadows in his eyes betrayed the turmoil that must have been boiling beneath his composed exterior.

"Your father…" His voice caught in his throat, and he gazed at the floor momentarily before regaining his composure. With a deep breath, he shifted the topic to our current predicament, skillfully avoiding my question about my father's involvement.

I clutched my hands together, striving to quiet the turmoil inside.

"Honey, but you must know Salvatore is hunting you," Mom said with certainty.

"Now that Balthazar is locked up, I have someone else after me," I murmured, trying to piece together the fragments of this twisted narrative. "Salvatore," I repeated, the name tasting like poison on my tongue. The Shadow Lord. The one who claims to have created the Timebornes, who commands the Timehunters with an iron grip. A man who bends time to his will, shrouded in secrecy and fear. My pulse hammered. And now he was after me.

The question hung between us, tinged with disbelief and a creeping dread that had begun to take root.

Lee's face softened, empathy etching lines into his weathered features. The silence stretched taut, a fragile thing ready to snap under the weight of unspoken truths and revelations yet to come.

Mathias' eyes were like dark stones as he leaned back in his chair, a false veneer of ignorance playing across his face. "He's after the sun and moon daggers mostly. But you have become his target since you possess one of the blades and are looking for the next blade."

"What I want to know is why are all these people after these blades? Balthazar, Raul, his men, and now this Salvatore person?" My voice was steady, but my heart raced with fear and curiosity. "I heard these blades can make the world dark and vicious. I've heard they can destroy all darkness and cure it from killing daily."

I narrowed my eyes at him, trying to discern the truth. "But a part of me thinks that there is something more powerful about these blades that no one is telling us."

Mathias met my gaze, his expression unreadable. "I don't know much about these blades."

I studied him. He said the words so smoothly, like a master of deceit, and I felt a coldness settle in my stomach.

A golden glow spilled across the room, offering no comfort against the chill seeping into my bones. My mother, Alina, fidgeted with the edge of the tablecloth, her face etched with lines of hardship and secrets.

"Every time I had a lead on a blade, I found nothing," she said, her voice barely above a whisper, "and I was tortured and beaten by Salvatore. Master manipulator. Liar. When I escaped, I was excited to see you all grown up. I watched you from afar."

"Cut the bullshit," I snapped, unable to contain the roiling emotions inside me. "You tried to kill me many times, according to the journal."

The words felt heavy, accusatory, and raw.

Alina's posture stiffened. "I was trying to protect you. I

know how crazy it sounds. I want to defeat Balthazar and these Timehunters once and for all."

Confusion clouded my mind as I tried to digest her words. Could she be telling the truth? My gut twisted with uncertainty, the journal's accusations echoing in my skull.

"Mom…" I hesitated, my throat tight. I circled to the beginning of this conversation. So many things weren't adding up. "I saw you get killed. I attended the funeral."

Lee rose to his feet, placing a gentle hand on my shoulder. "She had a closed casket. Your father didn't want you to be scarred for life. We wanted you to have a better memory."

His voice trembled as he spoke, his eyes never leaving mine. "The Timehunters and Salvatore… they're ruthless. They'll stop at nothing to get their hands on the sun dagger, which you possess, and soon the moon dagger. They'll hunt you down relentlessly." He took a deep breath before continuing, "They'll do anything to possess such powerful artifacts."

I swallowed hard, feeling the weight of his words, the burden of a destiny I hadn't chosen. The opulent dining room suddenly felt like a cage, trapping me with revelations I couldn't escape, truths I wasn't sure I could face. None of this made sense. My mother had died. Lee had witnessed it, too. She'd had a funeral. Did they put pillows in the casket? Was it all some ginormous plot? Oh, my head hurt with all the missing pieces of the story.

The tension in the room was so thick I could hardly breathe.

Mathias pushed himself up from his chair and moved toward the grand fireplace, his eyes reflecting flames that seemed to be devouring more than just the aged logs within.

"I just want to protect my family," he said again, vulnerability seeping through his stoic demeanor. "Balthazar is locked up. You don't need to worry about him. Our next simple step is to find the moon dagger and destroy the evil."

"Roman, Malik, and their team of workers will start digging in the caves to find it," I replied, my voice barely above a whisper. "We will eventually find the dagger, but right now, we must find Marcellious and get him home safely."

Marcellious was key, yet he was out of reach.

"Like I said, we will find Marcellious, I promise you. But now it's late, and you should get some rest. You've had a long day, and we're all tired," Mathias said, but there was an unmistakable command underneath the gentleness. His authority had always been absolute, but now, everything felt different.

Before I could respond, Alina moved toward me with arms open wide, her eyes shimmering with unshed tears. But I couldn't do it—I couldn't step into the warmth she offered. Not yet.

"So much has happened," I whispered, my voice trembling with emotion. "Emily gave birth. I found out that Mathias is my grandfather. And you...after all these years of believing you were dead, here you stand in front of me."

A wave of conflicting emotions washed over me—relief, confusion, anger. Above all, I felt a deep need for time to process everything.

"And now this Shadow Lord named Salvatore is after me. Marcellious is missing, and I don't know where to start looking." My words came out in a rush. "Please give me some space to figure things out."

She froze, arms still suspended midair. Her eyes dimmed, and she slowly lowered her arms, nodding in silenced pain.

"I'm in a room full of monsters," I muttered.

Turning away from my mother's and Mathias' gazes, I

ascended the staircase, which creaked under the burden of my heavy steps. With each rise, echoes of the earlier revelations rang louder in my ears.

A part of me didn't believe Mom's story. How could one survive someone so powerful and ruthless as Salvatore? Points in the story don't make sense, or I was too tired.

"Salvatore created the Timebornes?" The words slipped from my lips, a question meant for the shadows that danced along the halls. My mind couldn't wrap around that Salvatore created Timebornes—it didn't make sense.

I longed for a simpler life where Roman and I could hide away deep in the woods, safe from anyone who might come after us.

But my dreams of peace were shattered when I first traveled through time. A calm existence was no longer an option. Who was this Salvatore man? And when would I have to confront him face-to-face? The thought made my stomach turn, yet I couldn't shake the feeling that our paths would inevitably cross one day.

CHAPTER FOUR

ROMAN

Malik, Osman, and I trudged down the hill toward the yawning mouth of the cave, our way lit only by the meager glow of a crescent moon. The darkness surrounded us, thick with the night's secrets and untold threats lurking just beyond our sight. Malik breathed heavily beside me, each exhale a gust of silent fury. Osman walked ahead, his figure a shadow against the lesser dark.

"Malik," I said, my voice low, "we need to keep level heads."

He looked at me, his eyes glinting with the same ferocity that had ignited at Mathias' estate.

"Easy for you to say," he spat, not breaking stride.

I clenched my jaw, feeling the weight of my frustration. Alina's presence at Mathias' place was a thorn in my side, sharp and unwelcome. Raul's words from the tavern echoed in my head, painting her in hues darker than the night around us. It didn't sit right with me how she lingered like a specter over everything we did—everything Malik had suffered.

"Mathias be damned," I muttered. "He thinks he made you powerful? Gave you Rosie?"

The thought was laughable, a pitiful attempt by a man bloated on self-importance. I knew Malik's strength; it was his own, hard-earned and honed through trials that would have broken lesser men.

"Rosie was never his to give," I said, louder this time, my words slicing through the tension. "And power isn't handed to you by the likes of him. It's taken, fought for."

I hoped my conviction would seep into Malik and bring him peace.

Malik grunted, a noncommittal noise, but the set of his shoulders eased ever so slightly. We continued our descent in silence, the only sounds those of our footsteps and the distant calls of nocturnal creatures hidden in the wilderness.

As much as I wanted to believe Malik and I were united, Alina's lurking shadow divided us, a constant reminder of past deceptions and the pain they wrought. I couldn't shake the discomfort of having her near, of knowing what Raul had insinuated about her true nature. Her presence filled me with unease, a nagging feeling I couldn't shake.

Then, there was the revelation of their shared child. Despite Raul's claim that the child had died due to his experiments, a part of me couldn't help but question the truth. Was he lying? Or perhaps the child truly was gone. Alina seemed to hold so many secrets close to her chest, leaving me to wonder how much more there was to uncover. Her connection to Olivia, the woman I'd come to love deeply, only twisted the knife further.

Each step closer to the cave was further from the mess of lies and manipulations we left behind. But even in the sanctuary of darkness, there was no escaping the web that entangled us all.

I gripped Malik's shoulder, trying to ground him. "We can figure this all out."

He jerked away from my touch, his eyes wild in the moonlight. "Why is it that people I trusted let me down?" His voice was barely a whisper but carried the weight of deep hurt and anguish.

I understood all too well—the world felt like a chessboard, and we were pawns amidst the kings and queens of deceit.

"Trust is a luxury we can't afford right now," I replied.

With my brother gone, the path ahead was murky, our plans adrift in a sea of chaos.

"Let's focus on what we can control," I said, more to convince myself than to reassure Malik.

Our steps grew heavier as we approached the cave, its gaping maw looming like an abyss, ready to swallow us whole. Its immensity struck me silent; this was no mere hole in the earth—it was a cathedral of shadows and secrets.

"We're going to dig until we find the moon dagger," I said, my resolve hardening with each syllable. The dagger was the key to understanding, power, and securing a future I could no longer envisage clearly.

Osman nodded, his silhouette etched against the darkness. "It's our goal."

"Then let's find it," I said, steeling myself. Whatever lay within the cavernous depths, it couldn't be worse than the dread that had taken root in my soul.

We paused to retrieve supplies covered with a tarp outside the caverns. Once we stepped through the stone opening, I held my lantern high. The interior was vast, stretching to infinity. We began our search, staying close yet breaking off to explore different threads.

The air inside the cave was cool and brackish, like the breath of a slumbering beast.

I wiped the sweat from my brow, my hands coated in the

fine dust that carpeted the cavern floor. We'd been searching for hours, our fingertips brushing against the indifferent stone, hoping for a sign of the elusive dagger.

"Roman," Osman's voice cut through the silence. "There is something you must be aware of. Once you locate the Moon dagger, it will not work immediately. The two blades have been separated for far too long."

The gravity of his words hung heavy in the air, sending shivers down my spine as I contemplated the consequences of reuniting the ancient daggers.

My fingers stilled on the cold rock as I turned to face him. The flickering light of our torches cast dancing shadows on his earnest face.

"A very specific scripture is used to awaken it, different than Timeborne blades," he continued. "The scripture to make them work is a dead language. Only the true owner can activate it. Ancient scriptures of time reveal specific instructions."

"What do you mean?" I asked, my mind reeling. "How do you know so much? How do you know they won't activate?"

My lantern cast long shadows across his face.

Osman's uneasy movements stirred the dirt beneath his feet. His eyes evaded mine as he gazed at the scattered debris on the ground.

"There are these ancient scrolls," he said, his voice low and wary. "They hold the key to activating the blades properly. My father and a group of men dedicated their lives to studying them, even before I was born. But many of them have since passed. If they were to fall into the wrong hands, it could spell disaster for us all."

His statement hung between us, reinforcing what we already knew—We needed to find the dagger before anyone else did.

"Then we must ensure they end up in the right hands," I said with newfound resolve. The search wasn't just for power but to ensure the daggers didn't get into the wrong hands. And I would see it through, for Malik, for myself, and for the ghosts that lingered in the shadows of our purpose.

"How did something so powerful come to be?" My question echoed off the jagged walls.

"These blades hold an extraordinary tale," Osman said, "one that I learned when I was just a boy."

He took a deep breath, his eyes distant as if lost in memories.

"It is believed that these blades were created during the first solar eclipse in the Ancient Uragit," he said. "Legends speak of how the eclipse itself brought forth their existence but also brought about the destruction of Uragit. A new city or realm was formed in its place—Solaris."

A faint glimmer of awe slid through his voice at the mention of this mythical city.

"But there are darker tales surrounding these blades as well," he said. "Some believe that a thirst for power consumed those who wielded them and that their lust for control led to the downfall of Uragit. And yet, despite all the stories and legends, one thing remains certain—something significant happened during that solar eclipse."

His expression darkened. "When my father and other scholars from Anatolia began to delve into the mysteries of Solaris, they were met with fierce resistance from the Timehunters. The Timehunters eradicated every last one of them, not allowing them to explore or understand why Solaris came to be. It was as if the Timehunters were guarding a powerful secret."

A note of bitterness crept into his voice.

"My father, however, discovered something ground-breaking about Solaris," Osman said. "But before he could share it with anyone, he was killed by the very people who claimed to protect our world—again, the Timehunters."

His fists tightened, the pain of his loss raw in his expression.

"After my father's death, I was left an orphan, forced to fend for myself on the streets. But then Reyna and her father showed me kindness, taking me in and caring for me. As we grew up together, I couldn't help but fall deeply in love with her. Her father blessed us to marry, and Reyna became my everything—a strong and fierce woman who completed me. But now she has been taken from me, and if I don't find her soon and bring her back to Anatolia, her father will surely seek my life."

His voice trembled with emotion as he spoke of his beloved Reyna, his eyes clouded with pain and determination.

The blades were not just relics; they bore the scars of history, of lives destroyed by greed and the unquenchable thirst for power.

"I can only imagine," I said, clapping a hand on Osman's shoulder. The rough fabric of his tunic was damp with the night's dew. "I promise we will look for her. Don't lose hope. Hope is the last thing to die."

Exhaustion gnawed at my muscles, an unwelcome companion whispering defeat. I turned back to face Osman and Malik. Their faces bore the same weariness that burdened my soul.

"We should regroup," I said, my voice barely carrying over the hush that enveloped us, "and return with a larger crew. We need more hands, more eyes... This is bigger than we anticipated. With more men here, the faster we can find the blade."

The agreement was wordless. Together, we retraced our

path up the hill, the cave's mouth disappearing from sight but never from our minds. Home beckoned with the promise of respite, however fleeting, from the daunting task ahead.

Our ascent toward the estate was quiet. Each of us was lost in thought as we navigated the uneven terrain. The night held a chill that seeped into my bones, and overhead, the stars were obscured by a blanket of clouds, ominous and foreboding.

Malik's silhouette was drawn tight against the dark, like a bowstring pulled to its limit. "Balthazar is in the dungeon, yet I'm more worried by those not imprisoned."

I glanced over my shoulder at the gaping mouth of the caverns, their deep recesses shrouded in darkness like the maw of some colossal beast. There was no disagreeing with him. We were out of our depth, and remembering Balthazar's imprisonment only added weight to our failure.

I placed a hand on Malik's shoulder, trying to exude a calm I didn't quite possess. "We'll figure this out," I reassured him. He clenched his fists and glared at me, his eyes blazing with anger like sparks from flint. "You don't know what it's like to be used, Roman," he spat out through gritted teeth. "I was kept in the dark. Mathias told me he saved me and gave me Rosie. It's not right. It's all lies."

His pain was a raw wound exposed to the biting air.

"Don't worry, I'm here with you. Don't panic," I said, though the hollowness of my promises rang in my ears. We were all adrift, clutching at straws in hopes of finding solid ground.

We trudged back in silence, the estate coming into view through the mist. Its windows were dark, save for a few that spilled warm light onto the dewy grass. Once we crossed the threshold, Alina awaited us there, her presence an unwanted stain on the night.

"Did you find the blade?" she asked as we trudged into the drawing room, our bodies heavy with fatigue.

Malik's face contorted with barely restrained ire. "I think it's best if you stay out of our fucking way."

The shadows played across Alina's features as she stepped closer, oblivious or indifferent to his turmoil. "What's wrong, Malik? We used to be friends. We did so many fun things together."

Osman's eyebrows furrowed, and his eyes darted back and forth between Alina and Malik. His lips were pursed, and his body was tense.

"Don't come near me," Malik growled, his voice a low rumble of thunder. "I am not the same man I used to be."

He stormed past her, leaving the room in his wake, while Alina stood there, a statue of feigned innocence.

Alina's voice quivered with a blend of confusion and hurt. Her gaze lingered on Malik's back, disappearing into the shadows.

"I don't know why he's so angry with me," she said. "He's treating me like *I'm* the monster."

I sighed, the weight of the day's trials pressing down my shoulders.

"It's been a long day for all of us," I said, keeping my tone even. "We are all going through a lot."

The words felt empty, but civility was a cloak I had learned to drape over my true feelings when necessary.

"Your tenderness is a balm, Roman," Alina cooed, reaching out to caress my cheek, her touch light but unwelcome. "My daughter's so lucky to have such a strong man."

She pressed her body to mine, and I recoiled.

"Take your hand off of me," I said firmly.

Her eyes widened in shock, but I couldn't find it within myself to care. Raul Costa's words reverberated through my mind, leaving a bitter taste in my mouth as I recalled the tragic fate of her child, Angelo. The innocent boy, betrayed by the very man meant to protect him, his life stolen by poison—administered by his own father, Raul, who did not even deny the crime.

"I'm sure Costa would love to hear you're back."

"Raul?" Her voice cracked, a mix of yearning and surprise painting her features. "It's been ages."

"Yes, I saw him not too long ago." I narrowed my eyes. "He had much to say about you."

Before she could come up with a retort, I added, "Good night, Alina. And keep your *fucking* hands off me."

I picked up the hand that had caressed my cheek and flung it away.

With that dismissal hanging between us, I turned on my heel and strode away, leaving her in the dimly lit corridor. Her shock became unreadable as the distance grew between us.

The door to Olivia's and my room creaked open, its hinges protesting the late hour as much as my weary bones. Before I could step fully inside, Olivia burst from the shadows, throwing her arms around me with a force that nearly drove the remaining breath from my lungs. As our lips met in a fervent kiss, the sensation felt like an explosion of emotions, a symphony of relief and unspoken fears. The softness of her lips against mine, the way they moved in perfect harmony, ignited a fire within me. Our bodies pressed together as much as possible, given her growing belly. I could feel her warmth radiating through her clothes, adding to our embrace's intensity. We sought comfort and reassurance in each other's warmth, our hearts beating.

Our passionate exchange was a language without words, but the intensity of our embrace spoke volumes. At that moment, nothing else existed but us, lost in a sea of emotions and passion.

"My flaming fire," I murmured against her hair, the intoxicating aroma of lavender wrapped around me, a soothing spell I never wanted to break. I longed to stay cocooned in her embrace, enveloped by her warmth and the lingering essence of vanilla.

But as much as I craved her touch, the pressing matter demanded my attention.

"How did your conversation with your mother go?" I asked, my stomach twisting with unease at the thought of Alina's overbearing presence.

She trembled in my embrace; the quiver of uncertainty didn't need words to express itself. Her eyes, wide and glimmering in the dim light, held stories of turmoil she had yet to say.

"Roman." Her voice quavered as she spoke. "I don't know what to do. I want to believe my mother's story, but parts of it don't add up. The words of Mathias and Lee echo in my mind, conflicting with her version of events. I'm struggling to trust and understand."

She leaned into my touch, a silent plea for reassurance that I ached to provide.

"I don't know who to trust. With Mathias telling me who he is, and Balthazar captured, I don't know." Her words tumbled out like stones in an avalanche. "Then my mother tells me that she was imprisoned by a powerful man named Salvatore, that he is some Shadow Lord, and that he is after me. Everything is jumbled and confusing, and I feel so scared and unsafe."

I pulled her close, enveloping her in my arms. "If you feel unsafe, I will take you somewhere else where you feel protected," I said, a vow etched in the very marrow of my bones. "Anywhere you need to be, we'll go together."

Her eyes searched mine, seeking the truth behind my promise. In them, I saw the reflection of our shared resolve, fragile but unbroken.

Olivia's fingers clung to mine with a fervor that spoke volumes, her grasp seeking the anchor of my presence. The room, awash in the pale moonlight filtering through the window, felt too vast, as if it could swallow us whole with its shadows and secrets. She sat on the edge of the bed, the tension in her shoulders betraying her unease.

"When you were gone," she said, her voice barely above a whisper, "you were away for over a month. What took so long?"

The weight of untold stories pressed against my chest.

"Everything went well at first," I said. "We met Osman, who we brought back with us. Raul took away his betrothed. But then... Balthazar and Raul showed up." I hesitated. My next words would shake the already fragile ground beneath us. "Raul... he told us his life story—about how he met and loved your mother. And that they had a child together."

Her hand flew to her mouth, eyes widening in disbelief as if she had just seen a ghost.

"What? That's impossible," she stammered, her voice trembling with shock and confusion. "In her journal, she never mentioned having a child with Raul. Instead, she wrote of being chained and tortured by him."

Olivia's voice cracked, the image she held of her mother splintering before us.

"Raul painted a different picture," I said, trying to ease the blow. "He spoke of how he lost his son, and Alina... she gave him another son. Then he condemned his own son to an agonizing death, using him as a test subject for his cruel experiment.

Olivia shook her head, her breaths ragged and quick as she tried to process the information.

"That's insane," she said, her voice trembling. "In my mother's journal, she never mentioned anything like this. She only wrote about the horrors of being held captive by Raul, his cruel experiments on her, and her daring escape after a year. Someone must be lying. Is it Raul? My mother?"

I touched her arm, feeling the tremble beneath her skin. Truth seemed as elusive as the shifting shadows of the flickering candle on the nightstand.

The weight of the revelations pressed heavily upon us, and the room felt far too small for the enormity of our troubles.

"There is much to unravel," I said, "but I want to get Marcellious back and find the dagger."

She grasped my hand, her grip both delicate and desperate.

I smiled. "And I will always keep you safe and protect you. I love you so much, Olivia, and together we will conquer this."

Together, we extinguished the candle's flame, its light flickering and dancing before finally surrendering to the darkness of the night. I pulled Olivia close, wrapping my arms around her in a protective embrace. The cool air of the room enveloped us, but warmth radiated from our entwined bodies as we held each other tightly. The silence of the estate mocked us, a stark contrast to the storm of emotions raging within.

With Olivia's steady breathing beside me, I closed my eyes, willing sleep to take me. But rest proved elusive; my mind was a battlefield, replaying every word, every lie, every half-truth that had been uncovered. The house, once a sanctuary, now felt like a lair where monsters roamed with human faces, their intentions as obscured as the shadows that danced across the walls.

As I finally drifted into a restless slumber, the thought haunted me—the notion that what lurked beneath the surface of those around us could be more terrifying than any creature of the night.

CHAPTER FIVE
OLIVIA

It had been a week since my mother returned, and the atmosphere in the house was thick with a tension that clung to my skin. I stayed close to Emily, helping her with baby Leo and his innocent coos, which starkly contrasted with the chaos unfurling around us. Avoiding my mother became a silent routine; we orbited each other, careful not to collide.

Lee and Mathias were relentless in their search for Marcellious, their determination as doggedly persistent as the fear that kept me awake at night. Their quest for the dagger consumed Osman, Malik, and Roman.

Roman would return home each night, his eyes heavy with burdens he tried to shield me from. Silently, he would slip into bed with me, his warm body pressing against mine as we intertwined in the language of touch. Our lovemaking was slow and deliberate, each movement filled with a raw passion that could only be conveyed through our bodies. Roman fought to stay awake despite his fatigue as we explored each other's desires. As we finally reached the peak of our pleasure, he would collapse beside me, his chest rising and falling rapidly in pure exhaustion and satisfaction. Every moment spent in this intimate embrace reminded us of our undying love for one another.

Amidst the turmoil, thoughts of Balthazar haunted me. The dungeon where he languished felt like a gaping mouth beckoning with forbidden knowledge. Questions gnawed at me, like who my mother and Mathias were and the nature of Malik and Mathias' relationship. Would Balthazar tell me the truth about my mother in his Belladonna delirium? I found my resolve hardening like forged steel. Tonight, I decided I would have answers.

Mathias kept the keys hidden inside a book of ancient lore on the third shelf of the study. Their weight was reassuring in my palm as I slid them into the pocket of my cloak. Taking them felt like plunging into icy waters—a shock to my system but strangely invigorating.

With quiet steps, I slipped through shadow-draped hallways, the keys a silent promise against my thigh. My heart thrummed a nervous rhythm, yet the pull toward the dungeon was undeniable, a magnetic force that drew me toward the truth I sought from the man who could upend everything I believed.

That night, the manor was steeped in silence as if holding its breath, bracing for the secrets buried within its stone walls. The luxurious chambers where Alina had ensconced herself were far removed from the rest of us. Her laughter and the clinking of fine glassware barely permeated the thick tapestries as she indulged in her newfound opulence.

Emily's gentle lullabies to baby Leo drifted through the corridors, accompanied by Rosie's soft giggles starkly contrasting the turmoil within me.

Clutching the cold metal of the keys, my fingers trembled slightly—not from the chill of the night, but from the weight of what I was about to do. Each step toward the dungeon felt like descending into the depths of an evil abyss. The air grew colder, damper.

My mind was consumed by the memories of Roman's and my passion, spent in the cloak of night, hidden from prying eyes. The echo of our lovemaking lingered as a bittersweet reminder that kept me going through my long, lonely days. I yearned for his warmth, his strength, but tonight, I walked alone in the darkness. My heart ached with longing, and his absence made my steps heavy.

As I edged closer to the dungeon door, my pulse quickened. Was it fear or determination that fueled my resolve? With a deep breath to steady myself, I slid the key into the lock, its click echoing ominously in the hollow space. The door creaked open, protesting the disturbance.

Inside, shadows clung to the walls, and the usual stench of belladonna poison was notably absent. My eyes adjusted to the dimness, drawn to a corner where Balthazar sat crumpled against the stone. His figure was hunched over something— or someone. It was Tristan, or rather what remained of him. His head rested on his father's lap, a tragic tableau that reeked of grief and regret.

"I'm sorry for failing you, my son," Balthazar murmured, his voice cracked and thick with sorrow. He stroked Tristan's hair, oblivious to my presence. "I should have been a better father. I should have given you a better life. I should have put the past away and moved on. I wanted to bring your sisters back."

Sisters? My breath caught in my throat, my heart aching at the raw pain in his words.

He continued, lost in his lamentations. "And now my greatest enemy has trapped me. Long ago, I had a wife. A Loving family. A wonderful life. Until they were taken away from me, I tried to look for my Freya but couldn't find her. I only have my daughter Emily now, but she doesn't want me. Oh, Tristan. I should have been a better father and left my past behind."

His words trailed into the darkness, leaving a heavy silence in their wake. There he was, the feared Balthazar, broken and weeping, a monster mourning his child. I clenched the keys tighter, knuckles whitening. This man, this...father—Was he the beast I believed him to be, or something more complicated?

The chill of the dungeon seeped into my bones as I stood there, transfixed by Balthazar's despair. In his grief, I saw not just the villain of my tales but a fragment of the man he might once have been—a man shattered by loss, twisted by vengeance.

The truth I sought seemed more elusive than ever.

The keys jangled in my hand. Balthazar's head snapped up, his bloodshot eyes locking onto mine with a ferocity that made me recoil.

"Why have you come, Olivia?" he said, his voice dripping with disdain and something else—pain, perhaps? "To gloat? Are you filled with glee to find me here, locked up and tortured?"

The dim light glinted off the thick glass that separated us, casting eerie shadows across his haggard face.

"*You,* my dear, should be scared," he said. "Mathias and Alina are the biggest monsters out there."

I gasped, my heart pounding against my ribcage. His words were like a physical blow, jarring and unexpected.

"Mathias has only shown me kindness and respect," I said, but my voice trembled with the uncertainty that had taken root deep within.

Balthazar's laugh was hollow and mocking as it bounced

off the stone walls. He turned away from me, his fingers lingering on Tristan's lifeless form as if drawing strength—or maybe seeking forgiveness—from the son he'd outlived. Then, he crawled toward me, chains clanking, with a fluid motion that belied his earlier despair.

"Mathias is the biggest monster. The greatest actor," he hissed through the barrier between us, his voice laced with a venom meant for someone not present. He pressed his callused palms against the glass. "That despicable monster killed my daughters. He took my wife from me. His daughter, your fucking mother, killed my Scarlett. He is using you, pretending to be the greatest host, protecting you, being the nice grandfather. But once he possesses those blades, he will kill you and show you no mercy."

He withdrew, finding and cradling his son's lifeless head.

My breath caught in my throat. I searched his face for signs of deceit, for the manipulation I'd been warned about. Yet, looking into his eyes, I saw not just the simmering anger but also the flicker of genuine fear, a father's torment over lost children. Could a man so broken still weave such intricate lies?

The cold of the underground chamber seeped into my skin, but it was nothing compared to the icy dread that began to crystallize in my stomach. What if Balthazar spoke the truth?

My fingers tightened around the cold metal keys, my heart pounding in my chest. The heavy silence of the dungeon was punctuated only by Balthazar's low sobs as he cradled his son's head. A shiver ran down my spine.

"Who is Scarlett? Who are Balthazar's daughters?" I whispered, the questions echoing off the stone walls. "You are nothing but a monstrous fiend, Balthazar. You have caused me immeasurable suffering. With one cruel act, you snuffed out the life of my innocent child and tore away a piece of my soul. You left me shattered and battered, bleeding from wounds that may never heal."

The words fell into the darkness like stones into a well, their truth reverberating back at me. He lifted his head, and tears streaked the grime on his cheeks.

"I had no idea you were carrying a child," he choked out. "A child is a blessing. I loved my children. They were my greatest joy. They were all taken away from me ruthlessly. If I destroyed the life inside you, I am deeply sorry. The loss of a child…"

His voice trailed off, held by a spider's web of grief.

Confusion laced with an unwelcome surge of sympathy made my stomach churn. I had never seen Balthazar so vulnerable, in so much pain. The torment in his voice and his small confessions made me feel a bit sad for him.

"I'm sorry about Tristan," I said, my voice softer than intended. "Mathias shouldn't have killed him so brutally. He could have struck him with a sword and merely wounded him. But beheading him was awful."

Balthazar snapped his gaze to mine. "Leave this place. Mathias and Alina are vicious monsters. Leave!"

"Flabbergasted" was too mild a word for what I felt.

"All you do is lie," I spat, pressing my hands against the cool glass, needing the barrier between us.

Balthazar's face contorted with anger, his eyes blazing with all-consuming fire.

"You think I have always been like this, an evil monster who takes pleasure in causing pain and suffering? You are wrong. There was a time when I was not consumed by such darkness." His voice trembled with emotion as he spoke. "I was a father of five with a wife. The Timehunters killed them and destroyed my home. It was Mathias who sent them. He was jealous of my life and the happiness I enjoyed. But Darknesses shouldn't be happy—that seems to be an unwritten law. Your mother, the fucking whore, turned me against Malik. She made me imprison him. She killed Layla. The monsters are up *there*." He stabbed his forefinger overhead. "You're too blind to see it. You and your gladiator."

His ferocity hit me like a physical force, and I stumbled backward, my breath coming in short gasps. How could a man who spoke of love and loss also speak such vile words? The contradictions of Balthazar—the grieving father, the scorned lover, the ruthless killer—swirled before me, obscuring the line between truth and lies.

The last echo of Balthazar's claims pulsed in my ears. Alina—my *mother*—and Mathias were vicious monsters? The words tangled with my thoughts, a knot I couldn't untie. Despite the dread that twisted my stomach, something about his accusations felt uncomfortably plausible.

"Prove you're not lying," I said, though the distance between us was less for safety and more for preserving my crumbling resolve. "If there's one thing you can tell me, where is Marcellious?"

A devious grin stretched across Balthazar's face, splitting it like a crack in a stone statue. My skin crawled with unease.

"Why bother asking me where he is when Mathias knows? He's just toying with you, painting himself as the hero while he and Raul are thick as thieves." Balthazar's voice dripped with malice, his eyes glinting with a cunning light that revealed his true intentions. I could practically taste the deceit on his breath.

Bile rose in my throat at the implications, but I shoved it down with a fierceness born of fear.

"Balthazar, stop turning me against Mathias," I said, my voice carrying an authority I didn't feel. "I know you're trying to poison my mind again, just like you did with me before with Roman.

His eyes, dark pools reflecting years of torment, softened as he looked past me, somewhere distant and unreachable.

"You should worry less about Marcellious and worry about your unborn child," he murmured, his voice laced with a regret that seeped through the thick glass. "Leave and live with your gladiator and protect your unborn child. One minute, they are here. The next, they are gone."

He splayed his bony fingers.

I swallowed hard against the lump forming in my throat. His words carried the weight of genuine loss—a feeling I knew all too keenly.

"I fucked up a lot," he said, a shadow passing over his features. "My wife always said to leave the past behind, and I should have listened to her."

A haunted look claimed his gaze. "You remind me of my beautiful Viking wife. Don't believe Mathias or Alina. They are the greatest monsters, your *majesty*."

I looked at Balthazar in disbelief. Why was he calling me "your majesty?"

"Your *majesty*," he echoed mockingly, yet with a hint of reverence that unsettled me further.

Is he making fun of me? I stood frozen, the damp air of the dungeon clinging to my skin. Could the heart of a monster still recognize truth? Or was this another layer of deception as intricate and convoluted as the labyrinth that held him captive?

A chill crept down my spine, whispering doubts and fears I had long suppressed. And in the gloom of the dungeon, under the scrutiny of a broken man, the foundations of everything I believed began to tremble.

The heavy thud of boots on stone shattered the charged silence.

"That's enough, Balthazar!" The thunderous and commanding voice radiated authority as it cascaded down the stairwell.

My heart lurched against my ribcage, jolting me from the hypnotic web of Balthazar's revelations. I jerked back, the keys in my hand clinking faintly, a chime of trepidation. My gaze snapped toward the source of the outburst, where the shadows morphed into the imposing figure of Mathias.

His presence was like a storm cloud bursting forth, his eyes fierce with an intensity that could rival the sun's blaze— terror seared through my veins, ice-cold and paralyzing. The air turned thick, suffused with the acrid scent of danger, and every instinct screamed at me to flee.

I stood petrified, my breaths coming in shallow gasps. Once a mere prison for the condemned, the dungeon now felt like an arena where hidden truths clashed with the facade of trust I had clung to. Suddenly, a chilling realization gripped me—Mathias' sinister intentions were far from over, and Balthazar's fate was the key to unraveling the darkness lurking beneath our feet.

Just as I grasped what lay ahead, Mathias beelined toward a handle in the wall, and I knew he was about to make his next deadly move.

CHAPTER SIX
OLIVIA

The air in the dungeon was tense; the musky scent of old metal mingled with fear.

Without a word, Mathias reached for a rusty metal handle protruding from the wall. He turned it with a twist of his wrist, and a hissing sound filled the chamber.

"Mathias, no!" I screamed.

From the corner of the dank cell, a guttural howl erupted as Balthazar writhed in agony, the poison seeping through invisible vents and enveloping him in its deathly embrace. Malik and Roman, their faces etched with horror and disbelief, rushed toward us, but they were too late to stop the vile act.

"Shut off the poison!" My voice broke, the words barely escaping through the lump in my throat. When no one moved, I looked for the source. A dull, iron handle protruded from the wall to Balthazar's cell. I lunged toward it and cranked it off.

Mathias turned to me, his eyes unnervingly calm amidst the chaos.

"He's telling his ridiculous tales, and they need to stop," he said, his voice steady, soothing in its madness. The sickening click of the handle still echoed in my ears. "All this crazy talk. Calling you 'your majesty.' He's telling you lies. He wants you to feel sorry for him."

My gaze flicked back to Balthazar, who now clutched the severed head—Tristan's—his tears mixing with bloodstains.

"Why did you behead Tristan?" I asked, trying to keep my voice level, not to let it tremble with fury and fear.

"You and Emily were in danger," Mathias replied, speaking as if explaining something trivial, like why the sky was blue. "He wouldn't listen. He put you through hell. I wanted to protect you and your unborn child."

His words were meant to be comforting, but they felt like daggers, each stabbing deeper than the last.

I rolled my eyes, unable to hold back my contempt. *Can this moment get any weirder?* A carousel of doubts and truths spun wildly inside my mind, each more grotesque and nightmarish than the last.

The metallic tang of blood and poison sat heavy on my tongue. Alina's entrance was like a match struck in a room doused in gasoline. She sauntered in, her eyes alight with the fire of triumph, her stride confident and mocking.

Still reeling from the venom that pulsed through his veins, Balthazar fixed her with a glare that could have melted steel.

"Well, well, well, if it isn't the serpent herself," he said, his voice laced with contempt and pain.

"In the end, you lost; I won," Alina said with a sneer as she took in Balthazar's haggard form, trapped behind bars. "You're caged like an animal."

His bitter and hoarse laughter filled the space between us. The sound was jarring, a symphony of agony as the belladonna seeped into every crevice of his cell, into his very pores.

"Everyone in this room, especially your daughter and

Malik, should know who you are," he spat the words, disgust curling through his voice.

"Let's start with the fake journal you created, painting a picture of our toxic relationship. Claiming I killed your family. But everyone should know it was you. You threw yourself at me."

He leaned in closer, his eyes blazing with anger. "And then there's the night of the incident. You started to play with yourself in front of your dead sister, fingering yourself and begging me to fuck you like an animal."

Alina's face contorted with rage.

"You never wrote about how you poisoned my mind against Malik, weaving lies until I was convinced he was plotting against me. You craved all the power and sought to eliminate anyone who stood in your way." His voice shook with anger and sorrow. "And what of Layla? You disfigured her and crushed her soul without a second thought. Then you ran to Raul with your whoring—"

"It was you who fucking killed Layla?" The words erupted from Malik like a volcano, raw and destructive. He was upon Alina in two strides, hands closing around her delicate neck with the strength of unleashed fury.

"Malik, stop!" I cried out, frozen in horror.

Roman threw himself at Malik, desperately trying to unfurl his fingers from Alina's throat.

"Get your filthy fucking hands off my daughter!" Mathias bellowed, shoving Roman aside. He slammed Malik against the glass wall with enough force to shudder through the room. My mother staggered to the side, clutching her neck, while Malik's chest heaved with suppressed violence.

"Enough!" Mathias' command cut through the chaos, but Malik was already storming away, and the echo of his footfalls was a thunderous reminder of the dangerous undercurrents swirling among us.

Mathias turned his cold gaze back to Balthazar, his voice icy with finality. "Enough with your lies, Balthazar, about Alina. Game over. You lost. You'll be gone once Olivia and Roman find the moon dagger."

He swiveled toward me, his expression softening into a fatherly concern that didn't reach his eyes. "Come, Olivia. Roman and Alina, let's go. There's nothing to see here."

I squared my shoulders, defiance blooming within me. "I'm not a child, Mathias. If I want to stay, I will."

This was my stand, my moment to assert my right to seek the truth amidst the web of deceit.

My mother stepped forward, her face a mask of maternal worry, yet it did little to hide the steel in her voice.

"Stay if you want, but he will tell you lies. But as you wish," she sighed as though each word pained her. "I just want to protect you from this sickening monster."

Her plea clashed with the memories of her written words, the pages that spoke of love once fierce and consuming.

"But, Mom, your journals say you loved him despite everything and wanted to help or fix him to be a better person. Now, you despise him. I'm confused." My voice wavered, betraying my turmoil.

"Monsters can't change. They grow hungrier for power," she replied, her tone resolute, her eyes dark pools of conviction.

Balthazar's scornful laugh cut through the air.

"You wanted those blades to rule the world with darkness. That's all you cared for," he said, his accusation a sharp jab at her polished armor of righteousness.

The chamber seemed to contract, the walls pressing in as the weight of their shared past bore down on us. Lies, love, and the lust for power tangled before my eyes, leaving me to sift through the wreckage for shards of truth.

Mom's silhouette spun with a viper's quickness, her eyes narrowing into slits as she faced Balthazar. "You dare speak to me this way?"

"I never loved you," Balthazar spat, the poison in his cell nothing compared to the vitriol in his tone. "You spread your legs to every fucking man. You killed my Scarlett because you were jealous that I moved on with my life."

His accusation hung heavy in the air, an invisible fog that seemed to weave through the iron bars to wrap around us all.

"You know the secrets of Olivia's destiny," he said, and the ground beneath my feet turned cold. "You're afraid she will learn of it and destroy you all. But she will learn, and there will be no turning back."

A look of shock passed between Roman and me, a silent understanding that the scene unraveling before us was more than just a clash of past lovers—it was the collapse of history itself. My hand flew to my stomach as it tightened, a sharp contraction seizing me. My knees buckled, and I crumpled onto the cold stone floor, gasping, the world tilting dangerously.

"Take care of her." Balthazar's voice carried through the air, raw and jagged with pain, each word drenched in anguish. "Before her mother tries to kill her again."

Roman's arms wrapped around me with unwavering strength as he lifted me from the cold, unyielding stone that had broken my fall. His gaze locked onto mine, a storm of worry swirling in his eyes before he turned and began navigating the labyrinthine corridors of the estate. Every step he took carried us farther from the chaos behind us in Balthazar's cell.

"Everything… it's all unraveling," I whispered, my trembling fingers clutching the fabric of Roman's shirt as if it were my last anchor. My voice wavered, struggling to rise above the suffocating fog of pain and confusion. "Balthazar… he was crying for his son. They say poison forces the truth to spill from even the most guarded tongues."

Roman's jaw tightened, a flash of steel in his expression as we ascended the echoing staircase, each step a whisper against the cold marble.

Each step echoed beneath our weight, a grim reminder of the fragile ground we were treading—literally and metaphorically. "You shouldn't have gone down there, Olivia. You need rest," he murmured.

"He told me that Raul and Mathias are working together," I continued, my mind racing as much as my heart. Each breath fanned the flames of doubt that Balthazar's words had sparked.

"Rest now," Roman said, brushing a strand of hair from my forehead as he laid me down on the softness of my bed, a striking difference from the challenging reality we had departed from. "We'll sort through these things later."

As he turned to leave, I reached out, my fingers wrapping tightly around his hand. "Do you believe any of it, Roman?"

A storm of emotions flickered across his face—doubt, fear, something else I couldn't name—but instead of hiding behind his usual mask, he exhaled softly and sat back down. He didn't let go of my hand.

"I don't know, Olivia," he admitted, his voice quieter, rougher. "But whatever it is, I'm not letting you face it alone."

The weight of uncertainty pressed against my chest like a stone, heavy and suffocating. "Stay," I whispered. "Just for a little while."

He didn't hesitate. Shifting beside me, he stretched out on

the bed, his warmth chasing away the icy dread curling inside me. His arm slid around my waist, pulling me closer and grounding me in something real. I pressed my face against his chest, feeling the steady, unshaken rhythm of his heartbeat—a stark contrast to the storm raging inside me.

In the hush that followed, one truth burned through the chaos: I believed Balthazar's words deep down beneath every doubt and desperate hope. Every single one.

And that belief terrified me more than any blade, battle, or poison.

As sleep crept in, the chilling realization settled like a shadow over my soul—whatever came next would shatter everything I thought I knew about my family and myself. And there would be no turning back.

CHAPTER SEVEN

MALIK

I stormed toward the exit of Mathias' estate, my wrath a living thing clawing at my insides.

"Watch Rosie," I told the maid, my voice sharp enough to cut glass.

She nodded with wide eyes as she scooped the child into her arms. I didn't wait to see if Rosie's face crumpled into tears or clung to hope; there was no space in my head for anything but the blistering anger.

As I made my way out, my boots clattered against the wooden floor, slamming the door behind me with a resounding thud that seemed to echo my fury. The house—the cage of my own making—fell away behind me as I strode toward the stables. My fingers itched for action, anything, to unleash this torrent within.

Upon reaching the stables, I swung the door open, and it banged against the wall. The horses startled at the intrusion, their eyes rolling with nerves. I approached the nearest stall, the one housing a chestnut mare with a blaze running down her nose, Swiftwind. She snorted, sensing my mood, but I had no patience for gentleness. I grabbed her halter and led her out, saddling her with swift, jerky movements.

Once mounted, I dug my heels into Swiftwind's flanks, and we shot forward like an arrow from a bow. The rhythm of her hooves pounding the earth became the soundtrack to the chaos in my mind. Trees blurred past as we tore through the familiar paths, the wind lashing against my face, doing nothing to cool the heat of my anger.

Then came the haunting thoughts, the dangerous game I'd played with fate not once but twice. Olivia and Roman, unwitting pawns in a match where I had lost control of the pieces long ago. Memories flickered, cruel and taunting—fire licking at ancient timber, screams filling the night air—an earlier life's tragedy that I had hoped would remain buried. Yet, here I was again, threading the needle between salvation and damnation, and the eye was ever-narrowing.

I leaned into Swiftwind's gallop, urging her faster as if I could outrun the regret that clung to me like a shroud. The forest became a green blur, shrouded with shadows, and I welcomed the numbness that riding always brought. It was a temporary escape, a momentary lapse in the relentless tide of self-recrimination that threatened to drown me. But even as Swiftwind's powerful strides carried me further away from the house, there was no escaping the truth—I had screwed up. And this time, the cost might be more than I could bear.

Swiftwind's hooves pounded the earth with a rhythmic fury that matched the turmoil in my chest. I could no longer tell where her heartbeat ended, and mine began, our syncopated pulsing a testament to the chaos ensnaring my thoughts. The secrets I harbored were a poison coursing through my veins, and I was its sole antidote—a cure I couldn't administer.

"Marcellious," I hissed into the rush of wind. He had been

right beside me, within arm's reach, and then, just like that, snatched away by malevolent forces I could neither predict nor understand. How could I have allowed it? How could I be so careless? Anger at myself bubbled and seethed—a cauldron of self-loathing ready to erupt.

The canter slowed to a trot, and Swiftwind's breath came out in labored puffs. Every snapped twig or rustle in the underbrush felt like an accusation, a reminder of my failure. We were in this together—Roman, Marcellious, and me—and the weight of their fates bore down on me with the gravity of a thousand moons.

"Mathias won't find him," I muttered to Swiftwind, though she offered no solace. "He's telling them lies when I know he's not even looking."

My grip on the reins tightened. Trusting Mathias, a man whose motives were as murky as the ocean's depths, was a fool's errand. But what choice did I have?

My chest constricted, a vice around my heart. I should've kept them close and seen the danger simmering beneath the surface. Instead, I led them straight into the mouth of the beast, blinded by my hubris and deafened by my arrogance. If only I hadn't taken them for supplies, hadn't left the safety of our sanctuary. Regret gnawed at me, a relentless hound with a taste for my spirit.

"Forgive me," I whispered to the wind, the trees, and the gods who had turned their backs on us long ago. "I'll find you, Marcellious. I swear it."

The words were a vow etched in the marrow of my bones. But promises, I knew all too well, were fragile things—easily made and more easily broken.

Then there was that other disturbing fact—Alina was alive.

That sentence snaked through the chaos like poison, tightening around my heart with every repetition. She was a specter from the past, resurrected to haunt the present, and her survival threatened to unravel everything we had worked for. How she managed to cheat death was beyond me, and I shuddered at the implications of her return.

Swiftwind's breaths came in heated gusts, fogging the cool air in a cloud that dissipated as quickly as it formed. We raced through the forest, the looming trees standing sentinel over our desperate flight. But it wasn't just an escape; it was a pursuit of answers, guidance, and any semblance of control in a world that seemed determined to slip through my fingers like grains of sand.

The house appeared as we rounded a bend, its wooden frame modest and unassuming amidst the wild. Zara's abode was the only place left where wisdom might be found, where I could sift through the wreckage of my decisions and salvage some hope. I needed her insight, her foresight, something to cling to in this maelstrom.

"Easy, girl," I murmured, pulling back on the reins to slow Swiftwind. The horse snorted, her sides heaving, and together, we approached the house nestled in the embrace of the forest.

I dismounted, my boots sinking into the loamy soil, ground tied Swiftwind, and strode toward the door with determination etched into every line of my body. I had come for counsel but also for absolution, for some sign that the path I trod wasn't leading us all to ruin.

"Zara," I called out, urgency lacing my voice. "We must talk immediately. The plan is getting out of control."

I hammered my fists against the weathered wood of Zara's door, the sound echoing like a drumbeat of my fraying nerves. The door creaked open as if she had been waiting just beyond it, her piercing eyes meeting mine with an unsettling calm.

"Malik," she said, stepping aside to allow me entry into the humble space crowded with books and jars of mysterious contents used for healing.

I burst past the threshold, my voice raw with panic and frustration. "Everything is a fucking mess. We put Olivia and Roman in danger."

"Malik, calm down," Zara said, her voice steady as a rock amidst my storm. But I couldn't stop; the floodgates had opened.

"And Marcellious... he's gone," I continued, stalking through the small main room, my boots scuffing against the wooden floor. "He's been taken by Raul and his Timehunters. You were right about everything!"

Zara shoved me hard against the back of the worn-out couch. I stumbled before tumbling onto the cushions.

"Why are you here?" Her voice cracked like a whip, each word a pointed barb aimed at my already raw conscience. "You're only supposed to be here if Roman and Olivia are dead, imprisoned, or worse."

I struggled to regain my composure, my mind spinning from the abruptness of her anger.

"Fuck, Zara, I—" My words were cut off as I caught a glimpse of her face, contorted not just with fury but with disappointment.

"Stop it!" She advanced on me, jabbing her finger toward my chest. "Compose yourself. I can't even understand you."

Her admonishment felt like a splash of cold water. I shook my head, trying to clear the fog of my emotions and piece together the fragments of our conversation that now seemed scattered across the floor like the pages of one of her tomes.

Regaining my breath, I pushed myself into a sitting position. As I looked up at Zara, a smile cracked through the turmoil on my face. Despite her sternness, a familiar warmth coursed through me. She had been more than a mentor; she was the closest thing to family I had left, like my mother. Through centuries of upheaval and lifetimes of loss, she had remained a constant, guiding me with a firm hand after Balthazar betrayed me.

"Slow down and tell me what's going on," she said, her voice softening. "What happened? You came here in such a rush."

"I can't believe you were right about everything," I said, each word laced with the gravity of our shared history. "Everything you warned me about Mathias, Alina, and their monstrous ways is true."

Zara's eyes held mine, searching for sincerity, for the trust woven into the fabric of our relationship.

"Even after I showed you the past," she said, her voice low but laced with an unmistakable ache, "even after I cared for you like my own son, you still doubt me." She paused, her expression hardening though the pain lingered in her tone. "We're fighting for the same side, Malik. I've suffered just as much, if not more, at the hands of the same enemies you despise. Don't forget, you *saw* it. You saw how Mathias orchestrated the slaughter of my family by those Timehunters. You *know* what they've done.

"I know, Zara," I said. "I saw it all unfold. But now Balthazar... he's been captured. And Alina... She's alive. Every single truth that you have said and shown me is believable. I feel disgusted with myself for not trusting you one hundred percent."

Anguish twisted my features as I confronted the gravest truth. "I was used by Mathias and put Olivia and Roman in danger!"

The confession whipped me, the sting of guilt sharp against my failures.

"Zara," I whispered, the words barely escaping my lips, "I'm lost without your guidance."

Silence enveloped us, and in her eyes, I saw the reflection of our unspoken understanding—the promise that we would see this through together, no matter the cost. I pushed to stand.

A torrent of regret swept through me as I paced across the timeworn planks of Zara's secluded refuge. The air was thick with my self-loathing, a suffocating cloud that refused to dissipate.

Zara gripped my shoulders, anchoring me back to the present.

"Malik, stop." Her voice was a force to be reckoned with, pulling me from the quicksand of my thoughts. "Don't be angry. Don't drown yourself in guilt over Balthazar's capture. He deserves this. He needs time to reckon with the pain and devastation he's inflicted on Olivia and so many others. Let him stay captive. Let him confront his sins."

Her reminder was a spear through my heart, for I knew the pain and the vengeance that fueled her every move. It was a pain we shared, a bond forged in the fires of loss and injustice. How could I doubt her? How could I not see that every step she took was pursuing retribution for those timeless wounds? In the steadying grasp of her hands, the chaotic pulse of my heart slowed. The anger that had threatened to consume me ebbed away, leaving behind the embers of resolve.

She had cared for me through the ages, her guidance the compass by which I navigated the perilous waters of our shared destiny. In the quiet strength of her hold, I found the courage to let go of my rage, to trust in the path she had laid before us.

"What about Alina?" I asked. "She's alive, which means Olivia is in danger."

The thought of Alina, with all her cunning and malice, set loose upon the world once more sent shivers down my spine.

Zara's words rang out in the quiet room, her voice firm and commanding. There was no room for argument.

"Alina should be the one worrying about Olivia, not the other way around," she said, her steel eyes fixed on me. "You must protect Olivia and Roman so they can fulfill their destiny. But you also know that Alina and Mathias will stop at nothing to prevent that from happening. As members of the darkness, our sworn duty is to protect and care for the Timebornes. We were never meant to hunt them down and destroy them."

Her gaze pierced through me, reminding me of my oath to protect Timebornes. The sacred duty that was now mine.

I swallowed hard, feeling the weight of destiny upon my shoulders. Protecting the Timebornes wasn't just a mission— it was a calling. One I couldn't fail. Not now, not ever.

"Zara," I said, "you were always right about Mathias. I wanted to believe there was some part of him that wasn't as you said."

Regret tinged my voice, the taste of it bitter on my tongue.

She regarded me with an unwavering gaze, disappointment etched deeply into her features. "After everything we've endured together, all the sacrifices I've made for you, you still doubt me. I've protected you, Malik. I helped raise Rosie as if she were my own, yet you still question me.

Her words settled on my shoulders, heavier than any physical burden.

"I'm sorry," I said, my voice breaking. "I'm so sorry to have doubted you. I'm just shocked by recent events. I want to take Roman and Olivia out of there immediately. It doesn't feel safe. Especially since she's about to have her baby."

"Not yet," Zara interjected sharply, halting my cascade of worries. "Not till the moon dagger is found. Olivia needs to possess both blades."

My heart clenched. "Everything feels so fragile right now. Olivia is about to have a baby. Emily just birthed baby Leo, and Mathias killed Tristan. If I hadn't ordered Roman to bring him, he wouldn't be dead." A pang of guilt cut through me. "I can't bring myself to feel sorry for Balthazar, but it's still heartbreaking. He's lost another child."

"Malik, you can't shoulder the blame for this," she said, stepping closer, her presence steady and reassuring. "We need Mathias to believe he's in control, that we're nothing more than pawns in his game. You must play the part—act clueless, the loyal and obedient student. Mathias and Alina aren't acting on their own. Salvatore's will dictates every move they make."

Her eyes flickered to the side as if she couldn't bear to look at me. "And Salvatore...he is weak. Weakened for some time now." She took a deep breath before continuing, "He is desperate for the blades you and I are tasked with protecting. You must stay strong, follow Lazarus' orders, and protect Olivia and Roman."

I couldn't help but ask, "How is Lazarus?"

A slight tremor passed through Zara's body. "Lazarus is also weakening with each passing day. But I have hope that once the blades are reunited, they will restore some of his strength. But they will strengthen Salvatore, too."

A grimace formed on my face. "Let's hope Olivia is willing to embrace her fate and everything can be restored to its former glory. Have Roman and Olivia begun to recall their past yet?"

"Roman has some fragments of memories, but Olivia's recollection is still minimal. It seems like there needs to be a catalyst for her to remember," Zara said. "Malik, you know that everything will change once she remembers who she is and her destiny with Roman. Even Balthazar doesn't recall their connection together."

"You only remembered your destiny when Lazarus allowed it," I said. "Maybe if Olivia sees him, she will remember too."

"Lazarus is constantly monitoring and protecting Olivia from a distance along with us," she said. "You must pretend to be an obedient and loyal student under Mathias' command. Let him believe he has control while Lazarus watches him and Salvatore."

Her words were filled with longing and determination. Her eyes held mine, imploring me to understand. "Let him think he's in charge. We are watching him."

I nodded, feeling the mantle of my duty settle back upon me. The game was far from over, and I had a part to play. For now, I would wear the mask of ignorance, biding my time until the moment to strike presented itself. For Olivia, for Roman, for all Timebornes, I would not falter.

"It's upsetting that Tristan is dead," Zara said, a hint of sorrow lacing her usually unwavering tone. "But now I know why Mathias did that. Balthazar did love Tristan."

She turned away slightly, her gaze falling on an old photograph on the mantel. "Mathias wanted to bring Balthazar to his knees by destroying the only thing Balthazar truly cares about—his children."

Her silence was heavy, filled with unsaid truths and

secrets too dangerous to voice. I could only imagine the weight of her knowledge.

"Zara," I said, "I'm losing control. This past week has been... challenging."

The words felt like an understatement. Every action and every decision seemed to be teetering on the brink of disaster.

"I want to put Olivia and Roman in safety, not danger. I keep putting them in harm's way." My throat tightened, the conflict between duty and emotion threatening to overwhelm me. "I don't know if I can keep putting on this facade. I want to rip Mathias apart, piece by piece."

She faced me again, her eyes steady and reassuring. "Patience, Malik. Keeping the facade is hard, especially given the past you shared with Olivia and Roman. But we are closer than you think…so close."

The room seemed to close around us, the shadows whispering of battles yet to come and the fragile lives that hung in the balance. I found a flicker of strength in Zara's unwavering gaze to continue the fight.

"If any harm comes to them," I said, my voice low and laced with a threat I couldn't quite contain, "I won't be able to live with myself."

"Malik." Zara's tone was as firm as granite. "Stay focused on your duty. Don't let your emotions cloud your judgment. Find the dagger. Once you have it, get everyone out of that house—no delays, no mistakes."

Her eyes held mine, unblinking, a silent command that brooked no argument.

A heart-wrenching moan shattered the silence. My body tensed as I turned to Zara with confusion and concern.

"There's something you should know—I have Marcellious," she said, her tone softening but still edged with steel.

The revelation brought a tumultuous mix of relief and

confusion. How had she found Marcellious? I had to see for myself.

I stood in the sparse light of Zara's living room, the scent of dried herbs and something metallic lingering in the air. My heart was a heavy drumbeat in my chest, echoing the shock that gripped me as her words settled into my consciousness.

"He's here," she said, her voice steady with a gravity that pulled at my soul. "I had someone get him away from the Timehunters."

"Marcellious is here?" My voice was a mere whisper, disbelief painting each syllable. How? The walls of this modest house felt too close, the reality of his presence pressing down on me.

Zara nodded. "He was in an abandoned home not far from here. He's here, healing slowly."

Images of Marcellious, broken and battered, flashed before my eyes.

"I have to go tend him," Zara said, her expression turning grave as she moved toward the noise with a purposeful stride.

The sight that greeted us in the adjacent room struck me with cold dread. Marcellious lay on a makeshift bed. His body was wracked with convulsions. He was a shadow of his former self—beaten, bruised, and emaciated—his skin pallid and slick with sweat.

Zara approached the bed. She whispered words meant to soothe him, but his body continued to thrash wildly, revealing the depth of his agony.

I tried to steady his flailing arms and legs, the muscles beneath his battered skin twitching uncontrollably. It was like trying to restrain the sea itself—unpredictable and over-powering.

"Get a bottle of Calabar healing potion," Zara said over the chaos, her eyes never leaving Marcellious' tormented face. "It's an antidote for belladonna. It's in the next room in a cupboard across the bed."

Driven by the urgency in her voice, I bolted for the door, my heart pounding against my chest. I burst into the next room, my mind racing.

The sight before me slammed into my senses like a rogue wave, halting my step. There, upon the unadorned bed, lay a woman, naked, her skin a moonlit tapestry against the linen.

She was not merely beautiful but the incarnation of every unspoken dream that had ever danced at the edges of my consciousness. Her form was a delicate interplay of shadow and light, curves and lines composing artistry so natural that it seemed to mock the notion of flaw.

I sucked in a breath as a strange captivation took hold of me, a magnetism I had never known. It was as if her very presence reached into the deepest vaults of my being, touching a part of me that was hidden even from me.

Time slowed, and I faltered, ensnared by something beyond visual allure. She was the embodiment of vulnerability and strength entwined, a silent siren call that spoke directly to the dormant protector within me.

Duty roared back into focus, a clarion call that could not be ignored. With a wrenching effort, I tore my gaze away from the enigmatic figure on the bed, chastising myself for the lapse.

"Do what you came to do, Malik," I muttered, scouring the room for the potion that promised salvation. As lonely as I was, I could not yield to temptation. And yet, as I knew all too well, when did I ever listen to reason when it came to a woman—especially one as captivating as the one who lay before me?

CHAPTER EIGHT

MALIK

I stood before the bed of this bewitching, unknown woman, utterly captivated. The sheet slipped from the woman's fingers, fluttering like a surrendering flag before it settled over the edge of the bed. It was an inadvertent revelation, a moment too swift to undo. Her body, a silhouette of curves and grace, was bared to my unintended gaze. The shock that etched her features mirrored the paralysis seizing my own. Words, typically my allies, deserted me in the face of such unexpected beauty.

Her hair, a cascade of ebony waves, framed a face that seemed sculpted from the finest marble, with high cheekbones and a delicately pointed chin. Her eyes, a startling azure, gleamed like fragments of the Mediterranean Sea, their depths hinting at stories untold and wisdom far beyond her years.

Her appearance exuded an ethereal beauty, yet there was a subtle frailty in her frame, a slenderness that suggested a strong gust of wind could easily topple her.

However, this impression was deceptive. Beneath her seemingly delicate exterior lay a resilience that might have been forged from years of silent perseverance and intellectual rigor. Her olive-skinned heritage lent her an exotic allure, a blend of cultural richness and history that painted her as Scheherazade, with tales waiting to be whispered into the ears of an enraptured audience—namely, me.

Her duality—her delicate appearance and formidable strength—made her fascinating. She was a living contradiction, a beautiful enigma with a core of unyielding strength and intellect that shone brighter than the jewels in the Ottoman treasury.

"What a beautiful woman," I whispered, my voice so faint it barely rippled the heavy tension between us.

Her skin was flawless, the warmth of olive skin, except for the cruel patches of violet bruises staining her flesh—a silent testament to the suffering she had endured.

"She has the face of an angel," I murmured again as if the words could soften the harsh reality of her wounds, as if naming her beauty could create a fragile shield against the truth.

Compunction twisted inside me, and I struggled to stitch my scattered thoughts into coherence.

"I'm so sorry," I managed, feeling the unfamiliar stumble of my tongue as I spoke. "I had no idea someone was in this room."

My voice sounded alien, halting, and insecure—unlike the composed man I was known to be.

With each stutter, my desire to retreat grew, to give her the sanctuary of solitude.

"I'll come back," I said to her, though I couldn't quite discern whether it was a promise or a plea.

"It's all right," she said with a softness that seemed at odds with the bruises that flowered on her skin. There was a grace to her movements as she pulled the sheet up, trying to cover what was already seen, wincing slightly as it grazed her tender wounds.

I could not move, my feet rooted in place despite my best intentions.

"I'll leave now," I said, fumbling over the words that felt like stones in my mouth. It was strange, this sensation that washed over me—a mixture of desire and concern, something I hadn't felt stirring within me for years.

The intrusive, primal thought crept into my mind without warning—*I want to possess her.*

The flood of longing and craving for this woman was overwhelming, filling me with a fierce ache that pulsed through every fiber of my being. The intensity of my desire was palpable, a burning fire that threatened to consume me whole. I could feel the pull toward her, like a magnet drawing me closer and closer until I was lost in the depths of yearning.

Her eyes held mine, clear and questioning.

"Why are you here?" she asked gently, shifting beneath the thin barrier of linen. "What do you need?"

The urgency of my mission resurfaced, pulling me back from the edge of distraction.

"The antidote," I replied, my voice steadier as I clung to the purpose that brought me here. "I'm here to get the antidote for belladonna poisoning. For Marcellious," I stammered.

"Please continue—get the Calabar," she said, her surprising and telling knowledge of the remedy.

As I moved to the cupboard facing the bed, where the dark-green vials were kept, my glance swept over her again. The sight of her—so broken yet enveloped in quiet dignity—ignited a protective flame within me. How did she come to be in such a state? The urge to shield her from any further harm rose fiercely in my chest.

Securing the vial of Calabar extract for Marcellious, I felt its weight in my hand and heart.

This gorgeous woman needed more than a mere herbal antidote; she needed someone to ensure no more pain would come to her. As odd as it felt, I wanted to be the man to protect and care for her.

I sat on the bed beside her, the wooden frame creaking under my weight.

"What happened? Did the Timehunters hurt you? Were you and Marcellious kept in the same place?" My voice was a whisper, rough with concern.

"Yes," she replied, her voice trembling. "Raul Costa captured us. It was awful." The pain in her eyes mirrored the bruises marring her skin, each one a silent testament to the horrors she had endured.

Gently, I peeled the sheet from her arms, revealing the map of her suffering. She flinched, but she didn't pull away. My fingers hovered over each bruise, the urge to soothe her wounds overwhelming.

"Did they violate you?" I asked, the words scraping from my throat, raw with the need to understand the full extent of their cruelty.

"No," she whispered, her voice a fragile mix of relief and lingering sorrow. "It was heading in that direction, but I would have fought them with everything I had." She hesitated, her gaze dropping. "When Marcellious was brought into captivity, their attention was focused on him."

Her courage astounded me, and my hand, as if with a will of its own, continued to gently trace the shadows of violence upon her skin. The connection felt sacred and necessary. I needed to know more and understand everything that had happened.

"Take your hand off her. She's betrothed. I don't think her

betrothed would like this." Zara's voice sliced through the charged air, startling me.

I retracted my hand as if burned, my heart sinking. This beautiful, exotic woman was already taken.

Zara's stern gaze bore into me, and with a sharp tilt of her head, she signaled me to follow her into the hall.

"You cannot touch her like that," she hissed, her words laced with warning and anger. "Not after everything she has endured. And certainly not when she has already been promised to another man."

"Who is her betrothed?" I asked, my voice taut with an edge I couldn't suppress.

"His name is Osman," Zara replied calmly.

The name struck me like a physical blow.

"Osman?" I repeated. "The Osman, I know?"

Confusion clashed with a sharp pang of betrayal, a storm brewing in my chest.

"Yes, the same man Roman and Marcellious met at the tavern, the one helping you excavate the cave. I placed him there."

Every piece of the puzzle clicked into—a place with agonizing clarity. The setup, Osman's story, it was all Zara's doing. And there I stood, unwittingly caught in the center of a game I hadn't even realized was being played.

The realization struck me, a heavy stone sinking in my gut. Osman's betrothed, Reyna, was the woman I couldn't tear my thoughts from. She was *his*. A bitter taste of irony filled my mouth as I mused over the cruel jest fate played on me. Was it not enough that I'd crossed paths with Timehunters and lived to tell the tale? Now, I found myself entangled in feelings for a woman promised to another, shackled by emotions I couldn't escape.

"Malik." Zara's voice snapped me back to reality. "You

should leave here and head back. You've been here long enough, and they'll start wondering."

"Right," I said, my mind racing. "Do you think it best to take Reyna and Marcellious with me now? It would look better if I said I found them in the forest. And I can't have Mathias asking questions about my whereabouts."

My story must be convincing; my reputation as a solitary wanderer would lend credence to the tale.

Zara scanned out the window for any signs of danger.

"Yes, I think you should take them with you," she finally said, her voice laced with concern. "Marcellious' healing is slow, and Reyna is badly bruised. I don't want them in any more danger."

"I will protect them both with my life, Zara," I said. "No one, and nothing will harm them while they are under my care. You have my word."

A small smile tugged at the corners of Zara's lips. "I know, Malik. I've always known how fiercely protective you are. And when Mathias asks how you found them, you'll tell him that while trying to restore your energy, you stumbled upon them in the forest, abandoned and left for dead."

We returned to Reyna's room. She studied me, her eyes wide with uncertainty.

"Reyna, my dear, you're going to go with Malik," Zara said gently but firmly, her voice carrying an edge of finality.

Reyna nodded.

As we made our way to Marcellious' bed, I couldn't help but notice how Reyna's presence seemed to fill the space around us. The antidote was cold in my hand as I administered it to Marcellious, who writhed under its influence until, mercifully, he calmed.

"Is there a cart we can use to transport him?" I asked, considering the logistics of moving an incapacitated man.

Zara shook her head. "Showing up at Mathias' estate with a cart would raise too many questions, anyway."

"Then we make do," I replied. "I'll fashion a stretcher out of sticks and secure it to my horse's back."

"Can you manage?" she asked, doubt lining her brow.

"I have to," I said. "Reyna will ride with me."

The thought of Reyna riding behind me, her arms wrapped around my waist, her body pressed against mine, sent an unexpected surge of heat through my veins. Forcing the distraction aside, I returned to the task at hand. Marcellious needed us, and I had no room for anything else—not desire, not doubt, only duty.

The forest floor was littered with the debris of nature's own making, and from this disarray, I selected the sturdiest branches.

"Help me with these branches," I said, setting about creating a makeshift stretcher with practiced hands.

As Zara handed me strips of cloth to bind the wood together, my resolve hardened. I would transport Marcellious and Reyna safely, no matter the personal cost.

Zara's hands moved in unison with mine, silent but efficient, as we constructed a makeshift stretcher. It wasn't elegant, but it would serve its purpose. We secured it to Swiftwind's back, ensuring the knots were tight so they wouldn't give way under Marcellious' weight.

Inside, Reyna stood unsteadily, dressed in a traveling dress and overcoat. My gaze lingered on her longer than it should have—her angelic face and graceful figure captivating me in ways I couldn't ignore. A fierce longing stirred within me, an ache to pull her into my arms and kiss her, to let every ounce of unspoken affection spill forth. At the same time, an equally powerful instinct surged—a need to shield her from the world, to ensure no harm ever touched her.

I caught Zara's glare of reproach and hurried toward Marcellious' room.

"Careful," I murmured as we lifted him, swaddled in blankets like a newborn. His body was limp, the sedative holding him in a merciful grip of unconsciousness. We settled him onto the stretcher, and I couldn't shake the feeling that we were preparing for a journey far more precarious than any I had undertaken before.

Reyna leaned heavily against a tree, her legs trembling as she attempted a step. Without thinking, I reached out, slipping an arm around her waist to steady her. She leaned into me, her breaths shallow and labored, her vulnerability tugging at something deep inside me.

Zara's sharp gaze fixed on us, her expression darkening with warning. "Watch yourself, Malik," she said, her voice low but firm. "She's betrothed. We don't need to repeat what happened with Isabelle. Reyna belongs to another, and you *will* respect that."

I nodded, swallowing the lump in my throat.

"Of course," I said, chastened, though the warmth of Reyna's body against mine sent conflicting messages racing through my mind.

With care, we hoisted Reyna onto Swiftwind, and then I mounted, positioning her behind me. The moment her hands settled on my shoulders, light as a whisper yet heavy with meaning, a sense of elation mixed with forbidden longing washed over me. I focused on the rhythm of the horse's breath, anything to distract from the sensation of her touch.

Zara disappeared into the cabin, returning with a satchel filled with supplies—vials of Calabar, bandages, and other necessities. Her eyes met mine, a solemnity in their depths. "You need to care for her. She's hurting, she's weak, and she's going through more than you know."

"I understand," I said, taking the satchel from Zara's hands. "And I won't forget her situation."

The words *she's betrothed* echoed relentlessly in my mind, a mantra I clung to in a futile attempt to temper the emotions stirring within me.

"Be discreet with these." Zara gestured toward the supplies. "Lee can vouch that he had them."

Her implicit trust in me did nothing to alleviate the weight of responsibility now resting on my shoulders.

"Reyna will be cared for," I said, securing the satchel in a hidden compartment of my saddle. Reyna needed protection, and whether fate or poor luck had led me to her, I wouldn't let her down. Nor would I abandon Marcellious. Both had suffered greatly.

Zara climbed onto a flat-topped boulder, her stature above our makeshift litter. She leaned close to Reyna, her fragile form shrouded in a cloak that did little to disguise the tremors that occasionally coursed through her. I could not hear Zara's tenderly spoken words, but I saw their impact; Reyna's eyes glistened with a sheen of tears, the kind born from whispered encouragements or shared secrets.

"Even the strongest warriors face setbacks. Everything will be alright, my dear," was all that drifted on the wind to my ears.

A solitary tear tracked down Reyna's cheek, carving a clean path through the dust of her trials. She nodded subtly—whether in agreement or determination, I couldn't be sure.

Zara turned her keen gaze upon me, her eyes flashing an unspoken warning mingled with an ironclad resolve.

"Remember your duty and stick to the plan," Zara continued as she stepped forward, her movements fluid as she closed the distance between us.

"Don't come back here. Stay the course. It will get harder, Malik, but don't let it break you. Don't lose control."

Her commands were etched into my mind, each a beacon to guide me through the coming storm. I touched her shoulder, a gesture of parting between warriors faced with separate battles. And, in a moment brimming with the unspoken fears and hopes that clung to our mission, I leaned forward and brushed my lips against her cheek—a silent vow to fight, to protect, to survive.

"Now," I murmured, letting my breath ghost over the loose strands of her hair, "it's time to fight the ultimate battle."

"Be well, my friend." She nodded before leaping off the stone on which she had been standing.

With those words lingering between us like a sacred oath, I straightened and looked over my shoulder at Reyna, offering a reassuring smile.

Gripping the reins with a white-knuckled grip, I dug my spurs into Swiftwind's flanks, urging the powerful steed onward. The path ahead was uncertain, and responsibility weighed heavily on me. How many lives would be lost in the treacherous months ahead?

CHAPTER NINE

MALIK

The rhythmic cadence of our horse's hooves against the hard-packed earth provided a steady undertone to my racing thoughts as we made our way toward the caves. A sliver of the moon provided the barest illumination.

Reyna's touch scorched me from the inside out. Her fingers grazed my shoulders with an inadvertent intimacy as she adjusted her position, and my gut clenched with a desire that was becoming painfully hard to ignore.

"Are you alright?" Reyna asked, her voice soft and laced with concern, stoking the fire within me.

"Fine," I managed to grunt.

As much as I tried to focus on the path ahead, my mind couldn't help but wade through the murky waters of self-reflection. It seemed to be my curse, falling for women whose hearts were promised to others, eternally reaching for what was beyond my grasp.

Reyna shifted closer, perhaps seeking solace from the jarring motion of our journey, or maybe it was something else, a need that mirrored my own. She nestled her head against my shoulder, a gesture so innocent yet fraught with meaning. She wrapped her arms around me, holding on as if I were the anchor in this vast, unpredictable world. My body responded to her nearness with a ferocity that left little room for denial.

Osman doesn't deserve her, I thought with a bitter edge. *She needs passion, someone who can match her fire and make her feel alive. Someone like me.*

I'd always prided myself on being the kind of man who could sweep a woman off her feet—bringing danger, excitement, and seduction together in an irresistible whirlwind. Yet here was Reyna, fierce and breathtaking, tethered to Osman —the embodiment of predictability and safety.

Osman, the scholar, the bookworm, I scoffed inwardly, my grip tightening on the reins to keep my hands from straying to where they longed to be—entwined in the silky strands of Reyna's hair, tracing the curves of her body pressed so intimately against mine. *She deserves a man who lives on the edge and embraces the thrill of the unknown. Not him.*

My jealousy flared, hot and sharp, as we continued our trek. I had to remind myself to breathe and maintain the facade of stoic calm, even as every fiber of my being screamed to claim what I so desperately wanted. But duty called, and with a heavy heart, I focused on the path before us, leading us back to the realities of Roman, Osman, and the fate that awaited us at Mathias' wretched estate.

"So... how long have you been betrothed to Osman?" My voice seemed too loud in the stillness of our journey, grating against the quiet.

She shifted slightly, her head still resting on my shoulder, but she remained ensconced in her world, her arms loosely around me, a touch that was both torture and ecstasy. The silence stretched, and I was left with only the sound of our horse hooves and Marcellious' pained groans punctuating the air.

"Marcellious," I murmured, glancing back at him with concern and impatience, "hang in there."

The sooner we reached the caves, the sooner he could get the desperately needed help. And the sooner I could rid myself of this tormenting proximity to Reyna.

Her secrets tantalized me, just out of reach. She knew things—about Osman, Roman, and this tangled web we found ourselves in. What power did her silence hold? Why did she withhold her words as if they were precious gems locked away in a fortress?

"Reyna, how did you meet Osman?" I tried again, probing for any sliver of connection, any hint of her thoughts. But she was like a statue behind me, her presence both comforting and maddening. Her lips parted, a breath as if she might speak, but then sealed shut again, trapping whatever secrets lay within.

I sighed, resigning myself to the void between us.

"It's alright. You don't have to say anything. Osman will be so happy to see you. He's missed you terribly," I said, though the words tasted bitter on my tongue.

That bastard.

Osman, the unworthy recipient of her affections. How could she choose him when someone like *me*—someone who truly understood the allure of danger and passion—was beside her?

All I could do was ride on, the silence an unyielding barrier, and my desires a silent storm raging within.

The cave loomed before us, its gaping maw swallowing the last rays of twilight. As we drew near, figures emerged from the shadows, their faces alight with hope and relief. Roman sprinted toward us.

"By God's grace! You found them both," he said, rushing to his brother's side. "Thank the heavens."

Properly in his composure, Osman approached with a restraint that belied his excitement. His eyes found Reyna, and with a grace that mocked me, he reached up to help her down from the horse. But when she winced at his touch, my heart clenched an echo of pain for her discomfort—and a surge of jealousy for the intimacy I craved but could not claim.

That should be my woman, not yours. The thought snarled within me, wild and untamed, a beast caged by duty and circumstance. In moments like this, the hollowness in my chest felt infinite. Love, I realized bitterly, was an illusion—a cruel mirage. My job and my duty were tangible and grounded in reality. But this ridiculous, tormenting thing called love? It would never find a home within me.

Roman crouched beside Marcellious, concern furrowing his brow.

"What have they done to you?" He looked at me. "He looks awful. We need to get him to the estate, and everyone will be relieved to see him alive."

"Let's move," I said, voice edged with urgency, pushing aside the distraction of my longing.

"Reyna should ride with me," Osman interjected, calm but firm. He glanced in my direction—an expression that might have been apologetic if I cared enough to dissect it.

Reyna climbed onto his horse without a word, and they settled together. The sight of her so close to him sent another surge of jealousy coursing through me, but I swallowed it down.

We set off into the dark, the rhythmic pounding of hooves

on the earth the only sound to punctuate the silence, each of us racing toward an uncertain fate.

As stars pierced the veil of night, we arrived at Mathias' doorstep. Roman didn't bother with formalities; he threw open the front door and bellowed, "We need a doctor!"

Oliva, Alina, Emily, and Mathias poured from the house and gathered around Marcellious, their faces a tableau of shock and fear. But beneath the alarm on Alina and Mathias' faces, something else lurked—something I recognized all too well. The faintest flicker, a glint in the eye, spoke of deceit. They played their parts admirably, the concerned family, yet I knew the truth of their hearts. They had cast Marcellious into danger with purposeful intent and carried resentment that he was alive.

My jaw tightened as I watched them, the weight of unsaid accusations heavy on my tongue. The night wrapped around us, a cloak of secrets and lies, as I watched a scene rife with betrayal.

Mathias' voice was a barrage of urgency as he bore down on me with question after question. "What happened? How did you find him? Where was he?"

His eyes, dark and probing, sought the truth in mine.

I ignored him. Emily's eyes shimmered with relief, her hands clasped over her mouth as if holding back sobs. Stoic and silent, Lee lifted Marcellious from the stretcher with Roman's help. Osman left Reyna's side to assist while Emily fluttered behind like a concerned bird. They moved grimly up the staircase.

Amid the swirling chaos of concern for Marcellious, Reyna—pale and wincing—seemed to fade into the background, forgotten even by her betrothed. Osman's focus had become an echo of the household's collective obsession with

Marcellious' condition. Only Olivia seemed to notice Reyna's quiet suffering.

"Immediately draw her a bath," she told a maid.

In stark contrast to the flurry of movement and voices, Mathias and Alina remained unnervingly composed. Their calmness was sharp, deliberate, and too perfect. It was a thin veneer of tranquility that only emphasized the treachery simmering beneath their polished exteriors.

"Malik, how did you find them?" Mathias pressed, his voice cutting through the din of the hallway.

"The night called for blood," I said, my voice low and even. "I went to kill. I needed sustenance. But fate led me to them, broken and bruised on the forest floor, teetering at death's edge."

My hand instinctively moved toward Reyna, a silent gesture of protection, a shield against the scrutiny she didn't deserve.

"Who saved you and Marcellious? What happened?" Mathias pressed, his relentless questions cutting through the air like the edge of a blade.

Reyna, standing tall despite her injuries, met his gaze unflinchingly. "Someone attacked Raul and his men. A woman unleashed a powerful smoke and saved us. We were put on horses, and I saw... Raul's face—half of it was burned." She paused, the memory flickering in her eyes. "I believe Raul and his men didn't make it."

A flicker of some unknown emotion danced across Alina's face, swallowed by her shadows.

The air felt heavy with the weight of unspoken truths, with everything hidden behind each set of eyes in the room. As I stood there, the guardian of secrets and protector of hearts, I knew our fates were as entwined as vines in the darkest parts of the forest.

"We're grateful to be alive," Reyna said.

"Grateful doesn't begin to cover it," I murmured, my gaze lingering on her.

"We traveled through the woods, desperate and terrified, until we collapsed. We were lucky Malik found us when he did," she continued, her voice edged with raw truth. "If not, we'd be dead." Her words sent an involuntary shiver down my spine.

Mathias leaned in, his brow furrowed with concern—or was it suspicion?

"Are you sure it was a woman?" he asked.

"Mathias, stop interrogating," Olivia cut in, her voice halting Mathias in his tracks. "She needs food, rest, and a bath. She needs care. She survived—that's all that matters."

I nodded in silent appreciation toward Olivia. Stepping aside, I let the weight of my protective stance ease off.

"She needs to be with a woman, not a man," I said, feeling the heat of the moment dissipate as the household shuffled into motion, turning their attention to more immediate needs.

Lee, Roman, Osman, Emily, and Marcellious had already vanished upstairs, a trailing echo of footsteps marking their passage. I pivoted, intent on checking on Rosie, when Mathias' voice stopped me.

"Forgive me, Malik, for my earlier insults," he said, his tone uncharacteristically soft, laced with a rare vulnerability. "I should have told you about Alina. I'm so sorry for throwing you against the glass. I should have been honest from the start."

"There's no need to beg for forgiveness," I replied evenly, masking the turmoil beneath the surface. "If anyone needs forgiveness, it's me. I overstepped." As I turned away, my thoughts were already racing ahead, threading through the shadows of what lay before us.

I hope we find that damn blade so I can leave and protect my loved ones, I thought, the urgency of our quest burning like a fire in my chest. But I knew my desire was nothing more than folly—our enemies were the darkest of the dark. Something horrible could happen at any time. I hoped I would be ready when that time came.

CHAPTER TEN

OLIVIA

The majestic halls of Mathias' estate were quieter than usual, the air thick with anticipation and a tinge of worry. I lingered at the threshold of Marcellious' room, where the heavy scent of medicinal herbs and incense swirled in a stifling dance, masking the underlying stench of sickness. His body was a battleground, writhing one moment in the throes of Belladonna's cruel withdrawal, then collapsing into fitful sleep the next.

Lee moved his hands with a healer's grace over Marcellious, whispering words of an ancient tongue that seemed to coax the pain from his limbs.

Emily, her face etched with concern, never left Marcellious' side, offering sips of water or mopping his brow with a cloth dipped in cool water, all while splitting her focus between him and baby Leo.

"Is he getting any better?" I asked, my voice barely above a whisper as if afraid to disturb the precarious peace.

"Slowly," Lee replied without looking up, his focus unbreakable. "The poison has deep roots, but we're untangling them individually."

I found Reyna in the sun-drenched conservatory, a sanctuary of greenery that hummed with life. She sat on a wrought-iron bench, gazing out at the manicured gardens with a distant look in her eyes. A book lay open on her lap, forgotten. Her recovery was ongoing, the color slowly returning to her cheeks, yet there was a fragility about her, a sense that she was holding herself apart from the world around her.

"Reyna," I said, approaching her with hesitant steps, "how are you feeling today?"

"Better, thank you," she said, her voice soft like the rustle of leaves. "And how are *you?*" she asked, her attention flitting toward my belly and back to her lap. Her gaze did not meet mine, and she offered no more words to bridge the gap between us.

"Well enough," I said, touching my tummy. But I didn't think she registered a word I said.

Osman passed by outside, his silhouette intersecting our line of sight. A flicker of recognition crossed her expression, and she seemed as though she might call out to him. Instead, she watched silently as he continued, her lips pressed into a thin line.

"Would you like to walk in the garden?" I asked, hoping to coax her into the world again.

"Maybe later." Her attention drifted back to the gardens beyond the glass. "Thank you, Olivia."

I left her there, wrapped in the solace of solitude, the gentle hum of bees, and the whisper of leaves in her chosen company. I felt a kinship with her, a shared understanding of being lost in the shadows of grand events. Yet I knew better than to intrude further; some paths to healing needed to be walked alone.

All I knew about her was what Roman had told me—she

was a Timebound on the run to find answers about the sun and moon dagger, and she was far from home. The weight of her captivity under Raul hung heavy in my thoughts. I could only begin to imagine the horrors she had endured.

Back in my chamber, I paced restlessly, the plush carpet beneath my feet doing little to dull the tension coiling within me.

Emily had started by never leaving Marcellious' side, tending to him with quiet devotion. But exhaustion eventually pulled her away, and now she sat huddled in the corner of the room, her mind undoubtedly overwhelmed with worry and distress. She had just given birth to Leo, and now her husband had returned home battered and broken, leaving her caught between the needs of the two people she loved most.

Each member of our small community carried their battles within them. Still, for Emily, it seemed especially burdensome as she navigated the challenges of new mother-hood while supporting her wounded spouse.

Beyond the panes of my window, the green expanse of the grounds spread far, bathed in the golden hues of the afternoon sun—a stark contrast to the shadowy depths of the caves where Roman and his team were toiling away.

They had been gone since dawn, a caravan of determined souls seeking the elusive moon dagger. With Malik at his side, Roman had more helpers now, more hands to dig through the earth, and eyes to scan for the shimmer of ancient metal. Each day without them pulled at me, a relentless tide tugging at the shore of my patience. I longed to be among them, to feel the cool touch of the cavern walls and the thrill of discovery in the air.

"Olivia, honey." The soft call drifted through my chamber door, my mother's voice as gentle as ever, reaching out to bridge the chasm between us.

I did not move to answer, nor did Emily, who sat quietly in the corner, lost in the labyrinth of her thoughts.

"Olivia," my mother said again, this time with a hint of persistence. "I've brought some lavender tea. It's quite soothing."

"Thank you, Mother, but I'm fine," I replied, my gaze fixed on the distant tree line where the world disappeared into shadow and mystery.

"Your father would have wanted—"

"Please, Mother," Emily cut in, her voice firm as she rose to stand beside me, "Leave it be."

Silence followed, stretching taut before the soft sound of retreating footsteps. My mother, ever the hovering phantom of concern, lingered long enough to remind us of her presence before fading into the hallway. She had learned to weather our rebuffs, yet she persisted, as steady and unyielding as the ivy climbing the stone walls outside.

Neither Emily nor I trusted her. Her story about what happened after Balthazar stabbed her was riddled with holes and inconsistencies. The revelation from Roman about her secret son with Raul only deepened the shadows of doubt. She had selectively written in her journal, omitting critical details and twisting the narrative to suit her design. And when Balthazar unveiled disturbing truths—claiming that my mother and Mathias were monsters to be feared—whatever fragile trust I had in her crumbled further.

Yet I had neither the time nor energy to untangle her web of lies.

"Roman should be here," I muttered to Emily, my voice tight with frustration. "Not buried in those caves day after day."

"Perhaps," Emily said softly, "but he's doing what he believes is necessary. Just as we must endure this waiting."

"Endure." The word tasted bitter on my tongue, a reminder of the helplessness that seemed to cling to my skirts like morning dew. I was no fragile woman to be kept aside while the world churned and changed beyond my reach. And yet, here I was, staring out at the horizon, wishing for the sight of Roman returning victorious, the moon dagger in hand.

"Come," Emily said, taking my arm gently. "You must be excited about your upcoming birth. Let's talk about it."

"Thank you, sister, but no," I replied, allowing a faint smile to tug at my lips. "I'd like to walk outside to clear my head."

"As you wish," Emily said with a nod. "I'll return to Marcellious' chamber."

The sun was climbing toward noon when Reyna found me in the gardens. Her steps were cautious, and she faltered slightly on the dew-covered grass. I turned to face her, noting the pallor of her skin, which even the warm morning light failed to soften.

"Olivia," she began, her voice trembling just enough to betray her unease, "I would like to go and see Osman at the cave. I want to check on their progress."

She wrapped her arms tightly around herself as if warding off a chill only she could feel. Her eyes burned with determination, but fear lingered beneath the surface, shadowing her expression.

"I have been away from home for so long," she continued, her voice quieter now. "The longer Osman and I remain here searching for the blade, the more worried my father will become. He'll start looking for me soon."

Her words struck a deep chord within me, igniting a spark of purpose that had been smothered under layers of idleness. The image of Roman toiling in the caves day after day surged into my mind, stoking a sense of urgency I could no longer ignore.

"I deeply apologize, Reyna," I said, my tone heavy with regret. "We've been selfish in our actions. Instead of sending you and Osman back home, we've pulled him into our search for the blade."

"There's no need to apologize, Olivia," Reyna replied gently, though concern flickered in her voice. "Our journey to Wales was meant to uncover answers, and I am grateful that Osman can aid you in your quest. I hope that progress is being made."

"Then we'll go together," I said, the decision breaking through like a beam of clarity. "We can't sit here, waiting for news to trickle in while we're shrouded in safety."

A glimmer of relief softened her expression. "Truly? You'd do that?"

"Of course," I said, my restlessness finally finding an outlet.

Reyna smiled. "And we'll bring them food. They must be starving, working all hours without a proper break."

"Oh, my god," I breathed, realization dawning on me. "Why didn't I think of that before? To bring them food..." Shame flickered through me as I realized how consumed I'd been by my concerns, oblivious to their relentless efforts.

"Let's not waste any time then," Reyna said, her voice gaining strength. "I'll prepare the food. We'll make it a feast to bolster their spirits."

"Perfect," I said, the thrill of action quickening my pulse. "And maybe we can help in other ways too. It's about time we did more than wait."

Our plans were nearly set when the faint rustle of silk on marble heralded Alina's arrival. She swept into the room with an air of forced grace, her eyes bright with a spark of unbidden enthusiasm.

"I couldn't help but overhear," she said, clasping her hands together in a gesture that seemed part plea, part performance. "You're going to the caves, aren't you? Take me with you."

I stiffened, exchanging a brief, strained glance with Reyna.

"Mother," I said gently, though my patience frayed at the edges, "this isn't an excursion. It's dangerous, and we'll be fine on our own."

For a fleeting moment, disappointment flickered across her face, unguarded and raw. But before she could respond, Mathias strode into the room, his presence heavy and commanding, like a storm cloud darkening the horizon.

"Listen to your mother," he said. "You're heavy with child, Olivia. Your safety must come first."

His words, though cloaked in concern, wrapped around me like chains. The warmth that once defined his gaze now seemed a veil for something colder, something darker.

"Mathias," I replied, my voice steady despite the turmoil roiling beneath the surface, "I'm aware of my condition, but I don't need a bodyguard or protection."

The memory of Balthazar's son flashed in my mind, and the brutal moment of his death was seared into my consciousness. Mathias had called it justice, but the savagery of the act lingered like a shadow in my dreams, painting him in ominous shades of malice.

"Olivia, dear," Mathias said, stepping closer, his hand raised as if to offer a benediction or perhaps to seize control. "Consider what you risk."

Was his concern genuine, or did he savor the power he

held over us all? The doubt gnawed at me, sharp and relentless, a weight I couldn't cast off.

"I have considered it," I said, summoning what was left of my resolve. "And I must go. Not just for myself, but for all of us."

Mathias narrowed his eyes ever so slightly, and I wondered if I'd glimpsed the man's true face behind the guise of benevolence. "You must take care."

"Fine," I relented, the word tasting like acid on my tongue. "My mother can come, but only for protection."

A flicker of softness passed through my mother's gaze as though I had granted her the world. But beneath my concession, resentment churned, simmering like a storm held barely in check.

The carriage rattled along the uneven path, its wheels clattering against stones as we left Mathias' estate behind. Our bountiful food offering sat in a hand-woven wicker basket between Reyna and me, overflowing with colorful fruits, freshly baked bread, and savory dishes. My mother sat opposite me, her eyes sharp and vigilant as if scanning for unseen threats. I stared out the window, tracing the elaborate woodwork of the carriage door with my fingers, trying to ignore the growing tightness in my belly.

"Are you alright, Olivia?" Reyna asked, her voice tinged with concern.

"Fine," I said through gritted teeth, pressing one hand against my abdomen. "It's just... discomfort."

The lie fell flat even to my ears.

A sharp contraction tore through me, and I gasped, my free hand gripping the seat for support.

"Olivia," my mother said, reaching out to steady me, her touch feather-light yet unwelcome. "You need to stay calm. Take deep breaths. Take a couple with me…"

She inhaled deeply, but I ignored her.

"Mom, I don't." My words were cut short as another contraction, fiercer than the last, wrenched through me. I clutched at the seat, panic rising alongside the pain.

"Olivia, this journey might not have been wise," Reyna said, caution threading her usually serene tone. She exchanged a look with my mother, who bit her lip but remained silent.

"Stop," I snapped, my frustration bleeding into my tone. I hadn't meant for it to sound so sharp, but I refused to appear fragile. "I'm not a porcelain doll. We continue."

Reyna nodded in reluctant agreement. My mother, however, glowered, her disapproval radiating in silence.

The carriage wheels crunched over gravel, the noise colliding with the muffled discomfort filling the interior. As we neared the caves, my mother's voice rose.

"Olivia, your birth was much like this—rushed, unexpected, amidst the shadows of an ancient cave in Peru. Your father and I—"

"Stop talking about the past. Stop talking about me!" I snapped, cutting through her reverie with impatience.

My discomfort mounted, each contraction a stark reminder of the present, of the imminent life I carried, not the one long since lived.

A heavy silence fell, the air thick with unspoken words and the moment's weight. The carriage halted at the mouth of the caves. As we disembarked, Reyna offered me a steadying arm, which I reluctantly accepted. My feet found the uneven ground outside, and I noted how the air smelled of earth and sweat, the tang of men at work.

Ahead, the entrance yawned wide, a portal into darkness lined by the silhouettes of laborers chiseling away at history. Malik emerged from the shadows, his expression darkening when he saw us. His gaze landed on my mother first, and his jaw tightened.

"Why is she here?" he spat, jabbing a finger in her direction. Then his eyes shifted, flickering between Reyna and me. The incredulity on his face hardened into a scowl. "Why are Reyna and you here? You're pregnant!"

I met his glare unflinching. "Malik, I—"

A spasm of pain clenched at my midsection, more insistent than the last. My breath hitched as I doubled over, bracing my hands against the cool stone wall of the cave entrance.

"Olivia!" Reyna's voice was sharp with concern, her urgency breaking through the haze of pain. She rushed to my side, her hands steadying me. "We're going home!"

I shook my head, gasping as another contraction rippled through me.

"No," I managed through gritted teeth. The thought of retreat, of abandoning this mission when we were so close, was unbearable.

Malik appeared beside us, looming like a dark storm cloud. His brow furrowed deeply, his frustration palpable.

"Get Roman!" he barked to one of the hired men nearby, who nodded before disappearing into the cave's depths. "He can talk some sense into her! Olivia is so damn stubborn!"

As Malik turned back to me, his expression softened—a rare and unsettling vulnerability slipping through his gruff exterior. But his gaze didn't linger on me. Instead, his eyes darted toward Reyna, holding something raw and unspoken. This flash of emotion on his face was disconcerting, as though he couldn't contain it any longer. Why would Malik be drawn to Reyna? She was engaged, for heaven's sake. Such feelings had no place here; they should be locked away, not displayed so openly, like a wound for all to see.

I tried to focus on steadying my breathing.

Roman's voice echoed through the dim expanse of the cave, tinged with panic as he burst into view.

"Why did you come here?" His words tumbled out in a rush, each syllable etched with worry. "You and Reyna should be resting. Reyna has only begun to recover, and you, my love…"

His words trailed off as he hurried to my side.

I lifted my chin, meeting his concern with a determined stare, even as another contraction threatened to bend me double.

"We came to feed you," I said, the simplicity of our gesture juxtaposed against the complexity of our current dilemma.

Beside me, Reyna stood resolute, her pale cheeks flushed with the effort to remain upright despite her healing wounds.

Protective instincts radiated off Roman like heat from a fire. "No! Go home!"

"Please," I said, clutching his arm, feeling the tense coil of strength beneath his sleeve. "Just five minutes. I want to see the caves, see the progress."

"Olivia…" He began, yet something in my gaze must have reached him because he faltered. "Fine, but only five minutes."

It was a small victory, but it was enough to ease the tightness in my chest. Roman's attention shifted to one of the workers, and I followed his gaze to see Osman and Reyna standing off to the side. They were carefully unpacking the baskets we'd brought, laying out our humble offering—lunch for the weary searchers—with quiet efficiency.

The sight warmed me, and despite everything, I felt a thread of connection to these people, this place, and the shared purpose that bound us together and drove us forward.

The air inside the cave was cool and damp, a vivid contrast to the oppressive heat outside. Roman led the way, his lantern casting jagged, ominous shadows on the uneven walls. Alina's voice danced around us like the flutter of a curious bird, each question more eager than the last.

"Is this the same path you take every day?" she asked, her eyes wide with fascination and lingering frailty.

"Every day," Roman said, the corners of his mouth lifting in a rare smile as he indulged her curiosity. "We have marked the safe routes with these symbols here."

He gestured toward faint etchings carved into the cave wall.

I trailed behind them, watching their exchange. At first, I was content to listen, feeling a vicarious thrill through Alina's wonder. But soon, the sameness of the conversation—the endless cycle of questions and answers—began to dull my senses. My mind wandered, restless for something beyond the reach of their chatter.

As I squinted through the darkness, a faint flicker caught my eye. It danced along the edge of my vision, a stray beam of light that seemed out of place in the pitch-black cave. Driven by an impulse I couldn't quite explain, I veered off the marked path, letting the allure of the strange illumination guide me. The voices of Roman and Alina became a distant murmur, dissolving into the stillness that enveloped me as I ventured deeper.

The passage narrowed, then opened into a hidden chamber. The source of the light revealed itself—not a torch or lantern, but a crack in the cave ceiling where daylight seeped through. The golden light filtered down, cutting through the darkness with an ethereal glow that transformed the room. The space felt otherworldly, the soft illumination lending it an almost sacred intimacy.

"Interesting," I murmured, my breath misting in the chilled air of the secluded chamber. An entrance yawned open from the opposite wall, beckoning me further into the earth's shadowy embrace. Compelled by a strange mix of discovery—and perhaps a touch of rebellion—I crossed the threshold.

The passage led to another chamber, bathed in an impossible brilliance. Natural light poured in from some unseen source, filling the space with a serene, almost scared glow. I stood motionless, transfixed by the silence that seemed to ring louder than any sound, pressing against my eardrums with its weight.

"How odd," I whispered, my words dissipating into the stillness like smoke. "It's so quiet."

As I stepped deeper into the chamber, my breath caught in my throat. Before me lay a pit, its depths alive with serpents; their scales shimmered in the ethereal light, shifting and writhing in a mesmerizing yet menacing dance. My heart pounded against my ribs, each beat a primal echo of fear. My hand instinctively shot out to the wall, fingers grasping the handle of a lit torch carelessly propped against the cold stone.

The pit hissed and undulated with life, and every movement sent a wave of terror clawing up my spine. The air was heavy with the musk of reptiles and damp earth, the scent clinging to my nostrils and threatening to suffocate me.

"Child..." said a voice, ancient and sibilant, slithered through the chamber, weaving through the symphony of hisses and coils. It called to me, yet my body remained rooted in place, paralyzed by fear and awe.

Slowly, I lifted my gaze to find the source of the voice. An old man stood on the far side of the pit, leaning heavily on a twisted cane. His eyes held the weight of eons, and they locked onto mine with unsettling intensity. His short, wild hair jutted out in untamed spikes streaked with silver, hinting at a lifetime of unrestrained chaos. Round glasses, slightly askew, framed his piercing gray eyes, which glinted with a cold, calculating intelligence. His appearance was striking, like a raptor transformed by years into something more enigmatic and foreboding. And the way he moved...

A torrent of images surged through my mind, vivid and unrelenting, as though my memories were clawing their way back to me. The dank stone walls of a dungeon materialized. First, the clang of metal reverberated as a shadowed figure pounded on the bars of his prison, desperate for freedom.

Next, I ran—lungs burning with exertion, a blade gleaming in my hands. The Blade of Shadows, its edge dripping with power, pulsing with its thirst for conflict. I tore through an unrecognizable landscape, pursued by unseen assailants whose malicious shouts echoed like war cries.

Finally, a crown appeared, resplendent yet oppressive in its weight. It simmered before me, a tantalizing mirage always just beyond my grasp. I reached for it, but it dissolved into nothingness, leaving only its burden etched into my soul.

"Do you remember?" the old man asked, his voice a thread connecting me to these fragmented glimpses of another life—my past life.

Shaking, I clutched the torch like a lifeline, the heat of its flame grounding me back in the present, away from the phantoms of who I once was.

Ahead, the pit of snakes writhed with sinister purpose, their scales glinting like shards of malice under the eerie glow. My heart raced, a staccato rhythm of panic and defiance. I couldn't tear my eyes away from them as they slithered closer, their movements hypnotic and horrifying. A part of me burned with curiosity, drawn to their serpentine intent, but fear and dread coiled tightly within me. Should I stay and face them or run for my life?

CHAPTER ELEVEN
OLIVIA

The snakes writhed, their scaled bodies weaving an eerie, living tapestry before my eyes. My pulse quickened as the mass of serpentine forms coiled and twisted, their movements almost sentient, as though they were more than mere guardians—they were protectors of secrets buried deep within this hidden chamber.

"Child, don't be afraid of my pets. They won't harm you," the old man rasped, his voice dry and brittle, like the rustle of ancient parchment. It mirrored the sound of his slithering companions, adding an unsettling harmony to the air.

I stood frozen, fear grabbing me icily in my chest. His voice stirred something deep within me, a distant thread of familiarity tugging at the edges of my memory. I knew him, but how? From where? The room seemed to shrink, its walls pressing in with the weight of history I couldn't name but feel in my bones.

"I need to get help from my husband," I stammered, the words tumbling out as I took an instinctive step back. "You stay there."

The hissing rose like a whispered warning, a chorus of serpentine voices that sent a chill skittering down my spine.

Then, the mass of snakes shifted, parting like a dark sea to reveal what lay beneath their undulating forms. The moon dagger. Its hilt glinted faintly in the dim, otherworldly light, its blade nestled within the heart of the writhing nest.

My breath hitched. I couldn't believe my eyes. The moon dagger was right there.

"The old man and the snakes are protecting it," I whispered, the realization landing heavily within me. Fear and something far deeper—a strange, electric pull—shivered through my veins. Destiny. That was what it felt like, pulsing through me as though the dagger itself called to me.

"Olivia?" The voice echoed through the cavernous space, faint yet familiar.

My heart leaped as I scanned the shadows but saw no one.

I turned back to the old man, who was watching me with an intensity that made the air around us seem to vibrate.

"I've been protecting the moon dagger for you, my dear," he said, his tone soft yet weighted with purpose. "Only you have the power to possess it."

His words were cryptic, yet they resonated deep within me, stirring a dormant knowledge that felt both foreign and intimately familiar. How could this be meant for me? And why? My fingers twitched at my side, an unconscious yearning to reach out and grasp the hilt guarded by serpents. But I remained still, caught between wonder and fear, as the weight of his revelation pressed down on me like an unseen force.

"Who are you?" The question fell from my lips tentatively, like a leaf quivering on the verge of its final descent.

The withered man's eyes seemed to hold centuries within their milky depths.

"My child, you have known me for a long time, though you don't remember. That is the curse," he said, his voice both a balm and a blade. "There are fragments you will start to remember. I had to make a sacrifice. Be patient. Accept." His gaze pierced through the veil of time, burdened with a sorrow that clawed at my chest. His words carried an aged authority, a blend of wisdom and mystery that quickened my pulse.

"I met your husband back in Rome in another century. You both have a destiny far greater than you realize, but the key lies in your past life. That life is the thread that weaves it all together."

A shudder rippled through me, rattling the fragile lock on memories buried just out of reach. His words were a riddle, each syllable a puzzle piece that didn't quite fit, yet impossible to ignore. He had known Roman in Rome?

"Olivia!" The voice sliced through the fog enveloping me, its urgency snapping the world back into focus. I turned sharply, my heart racing toward the sound.

"Roman!"

Relief poured through me as he emerged from the shadows, his form solid and real. A woman's silhouette flanked him, her movements swift with shared urgency.

The torch slipped from my fingers, clattering to the cave floor and rolling away until it came to rest against the jagged stone wall. The air seemed to shift, reality stretching taut like a thread about to snap.

"Olivia, don't run off like that!" Roman's voice reverberated through the air and anchored me back to the present moment.

He wrapped my trembling form in his arms. His warmth seeped into my bones, chasing away the chill from our cryptic chamber. The scent of leather and musk clung to him, a comforting familiarity that eased my anxious heart. I was safe with him by my side at that moment.

I glanced back to where the ancient-looking man and his slithering guardians should have been, but the space was barren, an empty cavity in the earth where secrets once lay. Only shadows clung to the corners as if they, too, wondered at the sudden emptiness.

"Where did they go?" The words tumbled out, barely audible, a breath caught in the stillness. The old man, the serpents, the moon dagger—everything had been swallowed by the cave's insatiable darkness, leaving behind a silence that buzzed in my ears like the echo of a scream.

Roman held me tighter, his embrace firm yet tender, an anchor against the tumult swirling in my mind. His breath was warm against my hair, and his voice trembled with a raw emotion that made my heart ache.

"I was so afraid I'd lost you," he whispered, the words laced with relief and worry. "I would die if anything happened to you."

He pressed his lips to mine with an unbridled hunger and desperation. His touch was gentle and fierce, as if he had been holding back for ages and could finally let go. There was a primal need in his kisses, as if he wanted to claim and possess me wholly. And I felt it, too, the fear that lay beneath his every touch, the terror of losing me forever and never finding solace again in this world or the next.

My lips responded instinctively, melting into his kiss' warm, urgent pressure. My heart fluttered wildly as if trying to match the intensity of his emotion. In that moment, time unraveled, stretching out into eternity as our bodies pressed together, fitting seamlessly like two halves of a whole. But even as the warmth of his embrace consumed me, the shadow of what I had seen lingered, tugging at the edges of my mind.

As we reluctantly ended our embrace, the tension in my heart turned into a jumble of words. "Roman," I said, trembling, "I saw something... terrifying. There was a man beyond a pit of snakes and beneath them, the moon dagger. He was in that dark cavern over there." My hand shook as I pointed to the ominous void, torn between the urge to run toward it or flee as far as possible.

His eyes sparkled with excitement and concern as he peered into the shadows from where I had emerged. His gaze scanned the dark interior, but his expression quickly fell. He stepped cautiously inside, his silhouette melting into the murkiness before reappearing empty-handed and bewildered. The cavern was void of the old man, the serpents, and the moon dagger.

"Olivia, my love, there's nothing here," he said, his voice tinged with confusion.

My mother stepped past Roman, her curiosity tugging her toward the cave. She peered into its depths, her brows knitting together. "Honey, there's nothing here. Sweetheart, I think your pregnancy is affecting you."

Her tone was soft, but it only underscored the disbelief in her eyes.

I clenched my fists, the weight of what I had seen pounding through me like a relentless drumbeat. The gleam of the moon dagger, the serpents' menacing hiss, and the frail man's cryptic words—they had been real, as tangible as the ache now tightening my chest. Yet, how could I convince them when the evidence had vanished like smoke in the wind?

Heat surged to my cheeks, a stubborn fire igniting beneath the cold mantle of their doubt.

"It was there!" I screamed. My heart was a thunderous

drum in my chest, each beat resonating with the conviction of what I'd witnessed.

A sharp, searing pain gripped my abdomen, stealing the air from my lungs. I staggered, clutching at my belly, as the ground pitched beneath me. The cool earth rushed up to meet my knees, grounding me even as my mind whirled with the indelible images etched into my memory. Every scale, every hiss, every glint of moonlit metal—they were real, a truth I couldn't deny.

"Olivia!" Roman's voice broke through the haze, sharp and frantic. He was at my side instantly, his strong arms lifting me effortlessly. The warmth of his body enveloped me, a stark contrast to the cool cavern air and the chill of their disbelief. "Alina! Grab the torch Olivia dropped. We need light!"

His pace quickened, each step carrying us further from the cave and deeper into the safety of the sunlit expanse beyond, yet, as we crossed the threshold between shadow and light, an ethereal and intimate voice brushed against my ears, soft as a whisper and heavy with purpose.

"You need to return to the cave. You must return. I will be waiting for you." The chamber's familiarity tugged at the fringes of my memory, a haunting melody I couldn't quite place.

"Who are you?" I murmured, my voice barely audible, more to myself than anyone else. My eyes remained shut as if shielding me from the confusion and pain swirling within. The question hung unanswered, lost in the stillness, as Roman pressed forward, his grip steady and unyielding, carrying me farther from the enigmatic depths.

"Roman!" I clutched at his sleeve, desperation sharpening my tone.

"The man! We must go back! He wants us to go back. I don't know who he is, but he wants us to return."

My heart thundered in my chest, each beat amplifying the urgency of the phantom's plea.

Roman paused, the crease between his brows deepening. Concern flickered in his eyes. "Olivia, love, there was no one there."

His words were gentle, yet they stung, laced with the undertone of disbelief.

My mother's voice cut through from the periphery, sharp and clear. "She doesn't know what she's talking about."

She eyed me with worry and skepticism, wringing the fabric of her skirt.

"Delirium," Roman muttered.

"Stay with me, my love," he said, tightening his hold on me. His embrace was warm and grounding, yet it couldn't tether the certainty that swirled within me, a tide that refused to recede. "I will get you safely home."

Home. The word lingered in the air like an unwelcome guest. It should have brought relief, a sanctuary from the chaos. But instead, it felt like a shroud, smothering the undeniable truth clawing at the edges of my consciousness. The man's plea echoed in my mind, relentless and haunting, "You need to return to the cave. You must return. I will be waiting for you."

The overwhelming weight of responsibility consumed my entire being as I desperately searched my mind for the cave's location. The fate of humanity hung in the balance, and our survival depended on finding it. But what if my memory failed me? What if we were doomed to face extinction because of my shortcomings? Panic clawed at my insides, threatening to consume me whole. Failure was not an option, yet it loomed over us like a dark cloud waiting to unleash its fury. The pressure was suffocating, crushing my spirit with each passing moment. We had to find that cave, or all would be lost.

CHAPTER TWELVE
ROMAN

Cradling Olivia in my arms, I turned on Alina, fury burning in my eyes, the weight of my frustration as heavy as the limp body I carried.

"You should never have brought her here," I growled, my voice a low, dangerous rumble that reverberated against the cold stone walls of the cave's mouth. "What kind of mother endangers her child like this?"

Alina squared her shoulders. "Olivia insisted on going to the caves. You know she wouldn't have stayed behind."

"Damn it, Alina! This isn't some game where—"

"Enough, Roman!" she snapped, her voice slicing through my anger like a whip. Her hands balled into fists at her sides, trembling with restrained emotion. "Arguing now won't change what's happened."

I knew she was right, but admitting it would have been like swallowing broken glass. Instead, I shifted Olivia in my arms, feeling her labored breaths against my chest, and sprinted toward the waiting carriage. She felt fragile in my arms, her body limp and unresponsive, as if the life had been drained from her. Every step I took was measured, driven by sheer willpower to keep her safe.

"Malik! Osman!" I bellowed, my voice carrying over clattering tools and murmured conversations among our hired hands. "Work's done. We're leaving now! Pack up immediately! Now is not the time for questions. Move!"

Their eyes darted back and forth; their hands shook as they fumbled to comply with my command. The air was thick with tension, and I could sense their fear mixing with mine. But there was no space for it, not when Olivia's well-being hung precariously in the balance.

I didn't wait for their responses or see if they followed. All that mattered was getting Olivia to safety. My boots pounded against the ground, kicking up dust clouds as I closed the distance to the carriage, each stride was steady, my grip unyielding despite the strain in my arms.

"Osman, help me with her," I pleaded as I neared the carriage, my voice tight with urgency. Nothing could happen to her. I wouldn't let it.

He rushed forward, his usually placid face creased with concern as he opened the carriage door and assisted me in laying Olivia down onto the cushioned bench inside.

"We'll have you home soon," I murmured, brushing a stray lock of hair from Olivia's fevered brow.

Osman's gaze was fixed on the sky, his eyes narrowed in a mix of fascination and dread. I followed his line of sight, squinting against the sun's glare, my mind still reeling from the urgency of Olivia's condition.

"The solar eclipse is coming," Osman said flatly.

We all stopped in our tracks, turning to him in disbelief. Even Olivia, weak as she was, managed a feeble, "What?"

"Look at the sun." Osman pointed upward. "It will be here within a week or a few days."

The news settled upon us with unexpected weight. An eclipse was a bad omen at the best of times, but now—with everything so precariously balanced—it felt like a harbinger of disaster. The air seemed to grow colder, and the shadows around us stretched out like dark fingers.

Malik's violent wash of anger surged, threatening to drown us all in its destructive waves. His voice shook with a feral growl as he screamed, "The solar eclipse approaches! Its cursed presence weakens all darkness, leaving me vulnerable. I won't be able to protect you and Olivia!"

"Don't worry," I said with a false sense of calm, trying to reassure him while my heart pounded frantically. "We'll find a way to protect you and get through this together."

Deep down, I knew the danger ahead, and fear clawed at my insides.

Malik tugged me aside, his face etched with lines of genuine fear. "If only you knew how a solar eclipse affects the darkness. I have no power during it."

"Malik," I said, touching his shoulder, trying to infuse confidence into my voice, "Don't worry. We've faced worse than celestial shadows. We'll face this together."

Reyna touched Malik's back, and the surge of power that emanated from her was palpable.

Malik jerked away from her touch.

"Thank you," he said, nodding to her before turning away.

I frowned, stupefied by their interaction.

Olivia's form was limp, her face pale and drawn. I tried to make out the words she mumbled, but they slipped away, unintelligible whispers carried off by the wind. Her head lolled to one side, and I adjusted it so she might rest easier.

"Get moving! We need a doctor," I bellowed to the coachman, who snapped the reins with a sense of purpose. The horses leaped into action, their hooves thundering against the ground, pulling us toward the refuge of Mathias' house. Behind us, the others mounted their horses in a symphony of leather creaks and animal snorts, ready to escort us back.

The carriage rocked and heaved over the uneven terrain, each jolt sending a silent prayer from my lips that Olivia would hold on just a little longer. The weight of leadership pressed down upon me like the coming eclipse threatened to darken the sky—inescapable, all-consuming. But now was not the time for doubt; whatever lay ahead, we would deal with it.

The gates to Mathias' estate swung open as if anticipating our frantic return. Dust billowed in our wake, a cloud of unease that choked the air we breathed. As I leaped from the carriage before it even halted, Osman was at my side, his expression grim.

"There was truth in Malik's words," he said, voice low but carrying weight. "He will lose his power. All darknesses are vulnerable. We have to get home."

His words were like a cold hand squeezing my heart. What did that mean for all of us if Malik's strength weakened during the eclipse? And what if Olivia went into birth during the eclipse?

I raced into the house holding Oliva, the door banging against the wall, echoing through the hallways.

"Lee!" I bellowed, my voice reverberating off the marble. The feel of Olivia in my arms—her warmth, the unsteady rise and fall of her shallow breaths—was all I could focus on.

Lee emerged from the parlor, his face creased with concern. "What happened?" he asked, his eyes darting between Olivia and me.

"Maybe she's in labor?" Emily's voice quivered with tension. She hovered by Lee's side, wringing her hands. "It's normal to have a baby at eight months. Marcellious' doctor is here. Let him check her."

"Please," I said, my voice raw with worry. Olivia's breaths came shallow and uneven in my arms.

The doctor stepped into the foyer, his medical bag already open. His gentle hands worked with precision as he examined her. I held my breath, watching every flicker of his expression, searching for reassurance.

"She's not in labor," he said, and relief surged through me. "But she needs bed rest. Complete bed rest."

The order lingered in the air, sounding like a reprieve and a sentence. Olivia needed more than rest; she needed protection, especially now with the eclipse looming and the threats it posed. But for now, bed rest was the immediate prescription, and I would ensure it was enforced—for her sake and the sake of the life she carried.

"Thank you, doctor," I said, my gaze drifting back to Olivia, whose stillness belied the storm I knew was raging within her. We would weather this storm together, as we had all the others. I would be the light to hold it at bay.

I navigated the narrow hallway to our bedchamber, Olivia's warmth pressed against me, her fragile form unmoving in my arms. Gently, I laid her down on the bed, the soft mattress molding around her. Her chest rose and fell with shallow breaths, yet her eyes bore into mine, defiant and fiery.

"Roman, I can't just lie here," she said, trying to push herself up despite her body's apparent exhaustion. "I'll go crazy confined to these four walls."

"Olivia," I said, pressing a firm hand to her shoulder and coaxing her back onto the pillows. "You need to rest. It's not just about you anymore. Think of the child."

She let out an exasperated sigh, her gaze drifting away

from me. "Resting is a silent madness, Roman. I need to be part of what's happening. I can't be left out."

I crouched beside the bed, cupping her hand in mine. "Your strength is in your resilience right now, not your actions," I said.

Leaving her to contemplate my words, I stepped into the dim corridor, each step pulling me deeper into the weight of everything unraveling around us. As I approached the adjacent room where Marcellious lay, the air grew heavier, thick with the pungent scent of herbs and despair.

Marcellious was worse than I had imagined—his face was ashen, his chest rising and falling in labored gasps. His body was wracked by an invisible torment that refused to release its hold. Lee stood over him on the opposite side of the bed, a mixture of determination and despair etched into his features.

"I need to take him to the future," Lee stated without preamble, his voice carrying the weight of a father's love battling against the tide of inevitability.

Mathias entered behind me, filling the room with an aura of authority and concern. "What is this talk? You want to go to the future?"

"Mathias, look at him," Lee said, motioning toward Marcellious' frail, trembling form. "He needs medical care— the kind they have in the 21st century. You might have magic and old knowledge, but there are things only the future can provide."

"Nonsense," Mathias countered, his voice a low rumble of certainty. "I helped Malik survive Belladonna's bite. Surely, you, Lee, can do the same."

"Marcellious is not Malik," Lee snapped. His voice wavered, a thin thread of anguish laced through the anger. "He's a Timeborne, not a darkness."

Mathias stepped closer, his expression unreadable. "He will be alright. He will come through. We need time."

"Promises don't heal the sick, Mathias!" Lee's voice cracked, and his desperation laid bare. "You assured Marcellious of safety under your care, yet look at my boy—sick, dying."

"Malik survived Belladonna because of what I did for him," Mathias said with quiet intensity as if the words themselves could ward off the grim reality before us.

"This is no poison to be purged," Lee said. "He needs more than herbs and incantations. He needs to return with me to my time, where medicine can do what magic here cannot."

Before Mathias could respond, a violent cough tore through Marcellious' frame. Blood flecked his lips, his convulsions throwing him into a desperate fight for every breath. Lee and I pressed down on his limbs, trying to steady him, to keep him anchored in this world.

Marcellious' eyes snapped open, wild with fever and fear. His lips trembled as a single word escaped, hoarse and haunting.

"Lazarus," he gasped. His voice cracked, but the name cut through the air like a blade. "He's coming... going to destroy Salvatore."

I leaned in closer, my heart hammering in my chest. The name Lazarus chilled me to the bone.

"Stay with us, Marcellious," I said, my voice barely above a whisper, as much a plea to the heavens as to my brother. "We're going to save you. You have to fight."

Mathias' grip on my shoulder felt like the weight of an impending storm, his fingers digging in with a desperation that mirrored the panic in his eyes. The air thickened with tension as he peered down at Marcellious, whose chest heaved with shallow, ragged breaths.

"Mathias, let me go," I snapped through gritted teeth, my body twisting in an attempt to free myself.

He hesitated, the sinews of his hand standing out against his pale skin, before finally releasing me. My arm ached from the pressure.

Mathias stepped toward Marcellious, his face etched with lines of worry that seemed to deepen with every second. "Marcellious, tell me again what you said…. Who are Lazarus and Salvatore?"

I wedged myself between Mathias and Marcellious, my heart pounding in my chest. Mathias' expression was tight with annoyance.

"Roman," he said, his voice low and controlled but crackling with impatience, "Marcellious just mentioned some names. Don't you think we need to know who they are? They could hold the key to our survival.

I felt a growl rise in my throat, my protective instincts roaring to life. "Leave my brother alone," I snarled, my voice like steel. "Can't you see that he's sick and dying? That should be our priority, not some names he happened to mention. If those names are crucial to you, why don't you ask Reyna? Maybe she knows who they are."

The words spat out of me like venom, fueled by my fear for Marcellious and my frustration with Mathias' focus on the mysterious names.

"Mathias, you saw enough," Lee interjected, his voice sharp and unwavering. "My boy is sick and needs help. I'm taking him to the future. He's delusional, and he's dying."

Mathias' lips pressed into a thin line, the weight of his pride and reluctance visible in the rigid set of his shoulders. But after a tense moment, he relented with a curt nod. "Very well. We will do what we must for Marcellious."

Relief coursed through me, mingling with the urgency

pounding in my chest. There was no time to waste—not with the eclipse looming and its ominous weight pressing down on us.

Mathias turned sharply on his heel, flickering his gaze between Lee and Marcellious before leaving the room. His footsteps echoed down the hall with an air of finality.

I stood there, staring at Lee with desperation and frustration. The heavy silence in the room was punctuated only by Marcellious' labored breathing.

"Will he make it?" I asked.

"I don't know," Lee admitted, the exhaustion in his voice like a physical weight pressing down on him. His shoulders sagged, and his face was etched with lines of worry. "This whole plan... it's spiraling out of control."

"Out of control?" I echoed, incredulous. "What an understatement. I'm tired of all these secrets you're keeping from me. What aren't you telling me, Lee?"

Lee took a deep breath, his expression heavy with unspoken truths.

"Roman," he said, "there is so much I want to share with you, but it's too dangerous. All I can tell you is that Mathias and I have known each other for many years. We first crossed paths after I thought Alina had died. He approached me one day, claiming to be her father and wanting to watch over her daughter, Olivia, in her absence. I allowed it, not knowing what else to do.

"Then, one day, Alina returned, telling me the Timehunters had taken her hostage. That's when Mathias revealed the truth about Balthazar and how he targeted Olivia. He declared we had to put an end to these dangerous people once and for all. That's also when I learned that Marcellious had been captured by the Timehunters, despite Mathias' assurances that everything would be okay."

Lee's voice wavered as he continued, "Marcellious and I have been separated for far too long, and now that I'm back, he's sick and delusional from the poison they gave him. I must take him away from here and find someone to heal him properly before it's too late."

Tension coiled tighter within me. "And what about Olivia's father? Does Jack know Alina is alive?"

Lee's face hardened. "No. He can't know. The trials Olivia endured with Tristan were immense. I can't—won't—risk Jack discovering any of this. He and Alina had a rocky relationship. It was hard on him after she left."

The secrets we kept seemed to multiply, each one a thread in a web that threatened to entangle us all.

Malik stepped into the room, his expression grim. "I think Lee is right. He should take Marcellious to the future. After everything we've encountered, I don't trust anyone. We're in a pit of vipers here."

Before I could respond, Emily appeared in the doorway, her presence a silent storm of worry. Her eyes searched mine, seeking reassurance—perhaps an escape from the darkness looming over us.

"I will go too," Emily said, unable to mask the urgency in her voice. "Marcellious is my husband; I must be there for him."

Malik grunted, folding his arms. "Emily and her son will go with you."

"Then it's settled," I said. "You will all time travel at the next full moon."

Leaving the room as the echo of our decision lingered, I made my way to check on Olivia. The house seemed to hold its breath, anticipation and fear mingling in the stale air. I found her sitting up, defiance etched into her posture despite the pallor of her skin.

I brushed my fingertips against her cheek, my heart aching for her.

"Olivia," I said, my tone gentle yet filled with concern, "how are you feeling, my flaming fire?"

Leaning in, I kissed her forehead tenderly, hoping to offer comfort. The warmth of her skin against mine reminded me of the passion that burned between us. I only wanted her to feel at peace and free from pain.

"Okay," she said, but her voice lacked conviction.

"You need rest," I said.

She shook her head, stubbornness lighting her eyes. "No, Roman. I know you don't believe me, but I know what I saw in the cave. The old man said that he knows you and that you have met each other in Rome."

A chuckle escaped me, unbidden. "Olivia, I met a lot of people in Rome."

Her expression sharpened, growing intense, almost feverish. "He had this presence... like the shadows bent toward him, drawn to him." She shivered, her voice trembling with the weight of her recollection. "He moved with deliberate, almost predatory grace. Each step he took echoed softly in the cave as if the ground recognized him." Her gaze grew distant, caught in the vivid memory. "And the snakes guarded the moon dagger, coiled and slithering like living sentinels, protecting something so precious. I saw it, Roman. I saw it all."

"Olivia, my love, there was no one in there," I replied, maintaining a gentle firmness.

The battle lines were drawn between us, invisible yet palpable. She clung to her vision with a tenacity that frustrated and impressed me. As much as I wanted to dismiss her claims, a small part of me couldn't shake the nagging thought that the truth might be buried in her words. But now wasn't the time to dwell on impossibilities. Immediate dangers loomed, and every moment spent debating felt like a betrayal of those relying on me.

The weight of her sadness hung heavy in the air, almost suffocating. The shimmer of unshed tears glistened in her eyes, threatening to fall. Her pain and vulnerability crashed over me like a cold, unrelenting tide, washing away my resolve and leaving me raw.

"Maybe you're right," I said at last, my voice softening in her despair. "But the baby is coming soon, Olivia. You must watch over yourself and protect the life growing inside you."

I placed my hand gently over hers, resting protectively on her belly. "Let the men handle this. You stay here and rest. We'll find the blade."

She nodded, but her eyes remained distant, clouded with worries and visions only she could see. I felt an unfamiliar helplessness. In protecting her, I asked her to deny every instinct she had to fight alongside us.

My mind churned with unease as I turned away to give her space. Who was this man she spoke of? And why did his alleged words linger in the corners of my thoughts like a shadow refusing to fade?

I rubbed my arms where Mathias' grip had left its mark— too firm, too fraught with urgent strength. What was he not saying? I could sense the cogs turning in his mind at Lazarus' and Salvatore's names.

My memory flashed back to Olivia's warning that Salvatore, the man who had once held her mother captive, was now targeting us. He wanted to claim the legendary blades for himself. The air seemed charged with unspoken truths, thick with secrets no one dared to reveal.

I stayed by Olivia's side, holding her close until her breath evened out and sleep finally claimed her. Even then, I couldn't bring myself to leave. Her haunting expression lingered in my mind—a stark reminder that we were all pawns in a far more dangerous game. The urgency to retrieve the moon dagger gnawed at me like a relentless ache, but doubt and fear whispered insidiously at the edges of my thoughts. Were we truly capable of finding it before our enemies did? Or were we blindly walking into the trap that would seal our downfall?

CHAPTER THIRTEEN

OLIVIA

The sheets twisted and tangled around me as I tossed in bed, suffocating under the oppressive silence of Mathias' grand estate. My mind churned, unable to shake the echoes of that encounter in the cave today, the hiss of serpents, the cryptic gaze of the old man, and the fleeting glimpse of the moon dagger.

Moonlight crept through the curtains, casting pale streaks across the room. My eyelids grew heavy, surrendering to the pull of sleep. But it came with a familiar companion—the dream, relentless and haunting—I gripped the Blade of Shadows tightly, running across a battlefield littered with the fallen. The ground was a grotesque mosaic of twisted bodies, broken soldiers strewn like discarded marionettes. Lifeless horses lay sprawled, their glassy eyes frozen in eternal terror, while the earth drank the dark, viscous blood pooling beneath them.

Panic clawed at my chest as I spun, searching for pursuers. The air was thick with the whistle of arrows slicing through the night.

Amid the chaos, he appeared—a man cloaked in darkness, his presence commanding and unrelenting. His voice broke the stillness like the crack of a whip, each word dripping with malice. "You can't keep running from me or my dark soldiers. You have lost this battle."

I froze, the blade becoming an extension of my fierce resolve. I planted my feet on the blood-soaked ground. The man was Salvatore. He was my predator, and I was his prey.

"I might have lost today, but I will never allow you to take the Blade of Shadows," I said, my voice reverberating with an authority that felt ancient and powerful.

His laughter was a cold wind that sought to wither my defiance.

"Oh, such big words," he sneered, each step forward exuding a predator's confidence. "But you forget, I am the Shadow Lord and hold all the power. Speaking of Shadow Lords, where is Lazarus, the all-powerful? Where are your devoted protectors, Balthazar and Zara? I don't see your fearless husband either."

He glanced around the battlefield, his words landing like blows, chipping away at my defenses. "At this moment, you need them the most, but here we are—just you and me."

His eyes glinted with malicious glee as he reveled in my vulnerability. A cruel smile twisted his lips, sharp and mocking.

"I'll make this easy for you. Don't bother answering my questions. Just hand over the blades, and I won't kill you. You will be my prisoner, but I will allow you to live."

"Never," I spat. "Never will I allow you to possess the blades."

The dream pulsated with the tension of our standoff, the forces of light and darkness clashing in an eternal struggle. Salvatore's shadow loomed larger, his malice saturating the air, but I stood firm, unyielding.

With a defiant cry, I thrust the sun and moon blades skyward, their edges catching the ghostly light of an unseen celestial body. My lips moved of their own accord, uttering the sacred script of the Blade of Shadows. The words felt familiar, a long-forgotten chant etched deep within my soul, resonating with the pulsating power of the daggers.

"*'Iinani 'adeu qiwaa alsama' aleazimati, wa'atlub mink 'an tutliq aleinan linurka*," I said, the air around me crackling with ancient magic. The meaning hummed through my mind —*I call upon the great forces of the sky. I ask of you to unleash your light.*

A blinding radiance enveloped the blades, igniting them with a power that seemed to tear the fabric of my dream. Salvatore's face contorted in agony as he clawed at the air, his scream piercing the cacophony of battle that faded into the background. The blades, now alive with furious energy, pushed him back.

"You will never possess them, Salvatore," I said, my voice laced with a command that defied time. "I am breaking them apart, and you will never find or possess them."

The world around me spun violently, the ground beneath my feet giving way to a maelstrom of wind and raw energy. My heart thundered as the sun and moon blades trembled in my hands, radiating an unholy intensity. Then, with a deafening crack like thunder splitting the heavens, the blades wrenched apart, severing their bond. Shockwaves rippled through the battlefield, scattering shadows and silencing the chaos.

Sweat dripped from my brow as the tempest roared around me, yet I remained untouched—a solitary force standing firm in the eye of the storm as the world unraveled.

And then, silence.

My eyes snapped open to the stillness of Mathias' estate

bedroom. The chaos of my dream receded, leaving me gasping for breath, my heart racing against the soft, steady rhythm of Roman's slumber beside me. The room was cloaked in shadows, yet the vivid imagery of the dream clung to my mind with an unsettling clarity.

"I saw everything," I whispered to the darkness, my voice trembling under the weight of revelation. "So clearly... so real."

Salvatore's name echoed in my mind, a shadowy specter of menace, intertwining the past with the present. A fragment of memory from my life as Isabelle flitted through my thoughts—a fleeting wisp just out of reach. Was there a connection? How did I know him? What secrets lay buried in the depths of history, taunting me with their elusive nature?

Despite the room's warmth, I shivered, an urgent need rising within me to collect myself and steady the tremors as reality and dreams collided. The name Salvatore lingered, a puzzle from a long-forgotten era, demanding to be placed. My resolve solidified—I would not rest until the mysteries of my lineage and destiny were unraveled.

The chill of the night air brushed against my skin as I slipped from beneath the silken sheets, careful not to disturb Roman's peaceful slumber. My pulse thrummed in my ears, a relentless reminder of the chaos unfurled in my dreams.

"Who is this Shadow Lord, Lazarus? And Balthazar and Zara... protectors of my past," I murmured to myself, the words feeling foreign yet familiar on my tongue. "How very odd. Balthazar, my protector? More like my biggest enemy. And who is Zara?"

None of it made sense—the visions, the voices, the veiled threats. They wove a tapestry of confusion and unease that clung to me like a second skin.

Thirst clawed at my throat, grounding me with its raw,

tangible need amidst the intangible swirl of my thoughts. Rising quietly, I padded across the room, careful to keep my steps light on the cool marble, avoiding any sound that might disturb the silence—an old habit from childhood nights spent slipping through the shadows. The estate was silent, draped in the heavy velvet of night. I descended the grand staircase with deliberate, soundless steps, the weight of unspoken secrets pressing down my shoulders.

Halfway down the staircase, a murmur of voices halted my descent. Pressing myself into the shadows, I leaned around the edge of the wall. The faint glow of a single candle illuminated two familiar figures—my mother and Mathias, locked in a hushed conversation.

"What happened in the caves today?" Mathias asked, his voice low but probing.

"Olivia saw a pit of snakes, an old man... and the moon dagger," my mother replied, her tone laced with concern and conviction.

"Did you see this as well?" Mathias' inquiry held a note of skepticism.

"Of course not," Mom answered sharply. "But I know it was Lazarus. He's protecting the moon dagger. Everything disappeared when I walked up."

"Have patience," Mathias said, his tone measured, almost dismissive. "It wasn't Lazarus. He has never approached Olivia or Roman. It couldn't have been him. She was likely imagining things."

Shock rippled through me, sharp and piercing. How could they dismiss what I had experienced so easily? Was my mind truly playing tricks on me?

"How can you say everything is handled?" Mom asked, her voice rising with barely contained frustration. "You claim to have everyone wrapped around your finger, and now

Marcellious and Reyna have returned from Raul. Lazarus appeared with his pit of snakes. Everything feels like it's slipping out of control. Even Malik could be manipulating you, Father."

Mathias didn't respond.

"And Balthazar," Mom continued, her voice trembling with anger, "he's out of control. He just revealed all my secrets to Olivia. And worst of all, every word he said was the truth."

Their exchange hung in the air like a toxic mist, thick and suffocating, unraveling everything I thought I knew. Secrets, lies, and betrayals were the threads binding my family together.

I pressed my back against the cool stone wall, my breaths shallow and uneven as I wrestled with the weight of their revelations. What else had been hidden from me? What other truths lay buried in the hearts of those I loved and trusted?

I had come for water, but the thirst that drove me now was far more consuming—a hunger for answers, for the truth buried beneath their layers of deceit.

My pulse hammered in my ears, a frantic drumbeat against the night's stillness. I was a shadow within shadows, my breath a silent witness to the treachery unfolding before me. The revelation that Balthazar had spoken only truth cut through me, a betrayal sharper than any blade.

"Everything is under control," Mathias' voice murmured, smooth and assured yet tinged with an edge of menace. "Olivia's mind is clouded with pregnancy. She sees threats where there are none."

The rage bubbling within me burned cold. Clouded with pregnancy? The words echoed in my mind, igniting a silent fury that clenched my fists at my sides. How dare he?

"I have the loyalty of all the players," Mathias continued,

his confidence unnerving. "Balthazar's recent... indiscretions will be addressed. A little more poison should keep him subdued."

"Poison?" my mother repeated, her voice steady but tinged with something darker. "And what of Salvatore? You said his eyes see all."

Salvatore. His name felt like a curse, coiling through my thoughts like a serpent. Another figure in this labyrinth of deceit, his presence loomed even in absence.

"He watches, yes," Mathias replied, his voice low and malicious. "He knows our every move."

"Does Balthazar remember, Father?" Mom asked, her words hanging heavy in the air. "His past with Olivia?"

"Impossible," Mathias scoffed, dismissing her concern with his hand. "If he did, he'd recall everything. And we can't allow that, can we?"

A surge of icy dread coursed through me, freezing me in place. Who was I in this intricate web of lies and manipulation? Was I merely another pawn in their insidious game?

Mathias' body shuddered a brief tremor that seemed out of character for his otherwise composed demeanor. It was subtle, but it struck me as a crack in his armor, a fleeting glimpse of the strain beneath his facade.

"Are you alright?" Mom asked, her voice tinged with alarm.

"Something's wrong," Mathias said, his usual veneer cracking as he gripped the back of a chair for support. "The solar eclipse is coming, and I am losing my power. It's fading away, and the pain is immense."

His confession struck me as a stark reminder of the forces at play that threatened to engulf us all. The eclipse was a harbinger of change, a time when the balance of power could shift, not in our favor.

I clutched the wall, my mind racing. This was far beyond familial discord. It was a war rooted in ancient grudges, and somehow, I stood at its very center—a pawn in a game that spanned lifetimes. How could I navigate this labyrinth of deceit and danger when every step seemed to lead to ruin?

Slipping away from my hiding place, I vowed to uncover the truth, no matter the cost. But first, I needed to steady the storm within and confront whatever lay ahead with clear, resolute eyes. My family's fate—and my unborn child's future—depended on it.

Fury burned through me like wildfire. It was a trap—everything. My mother, Mathias—puppets in a grand scheme that had tangled me at its core. They had underestimated me, but no longer.

I stormed toward the study with every fiber screaming for action, where muffled voices rose and fell behind the closed door.

"No, Osman! We can't risk it," Reyna's voice came through, tinged with frustration.

"But we must!" Osman countered, his tone calm yet unwavering.

I pushed the door open without hesitation, barging into their heated conversation. Their heads snapped toward me, shock etched across their faces.

"Osman, you must take me to the cave. *Now.*" My voice left no room for argument.

"Olivia, no. You're with a child. The danger—" Reyna began, her words laced with the overprotection I could no longer bear.

"Osman," I interrupted, fixing him with a glare that dared him to refuse, "I am going, with or without you."

The tension hung between us like a blade poised to fall.

Finally, Osman sighed and nodded, his resignation evident. "Very well. But we proceed carefully."

Under the shroud of night, we set out for the caves. Reyna and I sat on the wagon's box seat while Osman rode horseback. The silence of the journey was broken only by the rhythmic clomping of hooves on the dirt road.

Strapped to my thigh, the sun dagger pulsed with a warmth that seemed to echo my heartbeat. When we reached the caves, we dismounted and secured the horses. Osman moved ahead, promising to return with light.

"Osman, wait," Reyna called, her voice tinged with worry, but he had already vanished into the cavern's depths.

"Olivia, please, stay here," Reyna said.

"Of course," I lied, eyes drawn toward one of the darkened corridors.

She hesitated, studying me with skepticism before hurrying after Osman.

The moment she disappeared into the shadows, I moved. Determination drowned out the whispers of fear that clawed at the edges of my mind.

"I don't think I went this deep before," I murmured, my fingertips grazing the rough stone walls as I ventured further. The cavern loomed around me, its oppressive darkness closing in like a living thing.

Each step carried me deeper into the unknown, the air growing colder and heavier with each breath. The silence was absolute, broken only by my heartbeat pounding in my ears. Despite the chill, my movements were steady, driven by an instinct that felt older than myself, as though I had walked these paths in another life.

"Stay focused," I whispered. "You can do this, Olivia."

I paused, pulling the sun dagger from its holster and clutching it tightly. The familiar weight of the blade grounded me, a fragile anchor in the sea of chaos swirling around me. The life growing inside me was my strength and vulnerability —a promise of hope amidst the shadows of loss that haunted my past. I had already lost so many, including an unborn child. Fear gnawed at the edges of my resolve, but there was no turning back now. The answers I sought were here, waiting to be unearthed.

Ahead, a faint light flickered in the darkness, pale and otherworldly, beckoning me deeper into the cave's depths. Each step I took felt like crossing a threshold between the living and the dead, the echoes of my boots swallowed by the oppressive stillness.

Finally, I stumbled into the clearing. It was the same room from yesterday, illuminated by a light that had no discernible source. The old man stood beside the pit of writhing snakes, his presence as unyielding and enigmatic as before. The serpents twisted and coiled like a living tapestry of menace, their movements hypnotic and disquieting. Relief surged through me, momentarily displacing my fear. He was real. The vision had been real.

"Olivia," the old man said, his voice resonating with a calm that belied the dread-laden air. His eyes, ancient and all-knowing, locked onto mine, their gaze heavy with unspoken truths.

I halted, panting, the remnants of anger toward my mother still burning. What other lies had she tangled into the threads of my life? How much had she kept hidden, and why?

"You came back," he said, his tone almost gentle. "Don't be afraid."

"I am," I admitted, my voice trembling. "I'm scared of you, the snakes, what tomorrow will bring."

The sun dagger felt warm in my hand, its presence a

small, fierce comfort against the swell of uncertainties pressing down on me.

The faintest hint of a smile touched his lips, one that spoke of empathy and understanding. "You should never be afraid. If I were not on your side, I would not have woven protectors into the fabric of your destiny. Walk toward me. My snakes will not harm you."

His words, spoken with quiet assurance, spurred my feet into motion. Each step was an act of courage, a declaration that the unknown would not cow me. The air grew heavier as I approached, his gaze pressing down on me, yet I refused to falter.

The serpents, a writhing carpet of scales and hisses, parted like the sea before me, granting passage. Their retreat felt like an unspoken acknowledgment—a recognition of my purpose, my right to be here.

Nestled in a crevice, bathed in an ethereal glow that pierced the shadows of the cave, lay the moon dagger. Its silver blade shimmered like the surface of a tranquil pond, catching the moonlight that filtered through a narrow crack in the cave's ceiling. My heart hammered against my ribs, a frantic rhythm heralding triumph as my hand closed around the hilt. The metal was cold, biting even, yet it felt like home —a piece of my soul I hadn't known was missing.

I lifted the moon dagger, its weight both physical and symbolic, turning it over in my hands. Majestic as it was, it lacked the radiant brilliance of the sun dagger that had always been by my side. Devoid of its rightful power, it felt incomplete—just as I had once been, before fate had forged me into something more.

"This is it," I whispered, the words almost a prayer. "I have them both now."

But their dormancy pressed heavily against my palms, a

reminder that possession alone was not enough. Memories of my dream surfaced, vivid and haunting—the blades ablaze with power, defying the darkness. I remembered the words I had spoken in that otherworldly battlefield—words of separation, of breaking a bond that had endured through time.

"It was me," I murmured, a realization dawning. "I separated them, didn't I?"

"Yes, Olivia," the old man's voice echoed, calm and certain. "You did. But it was necessary, then, to protect the world from their combined force. Now, the time has come to reunite them, to awaken their true potential."

Anxiety coiled in my stomach, tightening with each beat of silence. "What do I have to do? What are the words to bring them back to life?" My voice was edged with urgency.

Before he could answer, the old man staggered, his body folding like a marionette whose strings had been cut. He collapsed with a muted thud, the sound reverberating through the cavern and echoing the sudden drop of my heart.

"No!" I cried out, rushing to his side.

His eyes were closed, his face a map of pain—or perhaps something deeper, an unseen battle etched into the lines of his features. I dropped to my knees beside him, the cold stone biting through the fabric of my skirt.

"What happened?" My voice trembled as I reached out tentatively, unsure if my touch could bring comfort or solace.

The old man's breaths were ragged, each one a struggle that seemed to siphon the last remnants of life from his frail body. His hand, unexpectedly strong, grasped mine with a force that sent a jolt through my frayed nerves.

"The solar eclipse is coming," he said, his words punctuated by the labor of his chest rising and falling. His hand, surprisingly strong, gripped mine with an urgency that sent a jolt through my already frayed nerves. "You must remember the past."

Confusion swirled within me, mingling with the fear and adrenaline that had been my constant companions since setting foot in this forsaken place. "Remember what? How can I—"

"Salvatore is your greatest enemy," he interrupted, his gaze locking onto mine with a piercing intensity that made the air around us feel heavy. "Mathias and your mother... they are your enemies too."

The floor beneath me felt unsteady, as though it might give way at any moment, plunging me into an abyss of betrayal.

Before I could process the magnitude of his words, his grip loosened, and his frail body began to fade—dissolving into the encroaching shadows that crept along the cave walls. A cry of disbelief escaped my lips, raw and broken, only to be swallowed by the oppressive silence.

I sat there, alone, the truth of his warning heavy on my heart.

A sharp pain seared through my abdomen, startling in its intensity. I doubled over with a gasp, clutching at the cold, unyielding rock for support.

Not now. Panic flared inside me, white-hot and blinding. This couldn't be happening—not here, not in the depths of a cave, cloaked in darkness and far from any help. Another contraction tore through me, stronger and more relentless, leaving me gasping for breath.

"Please, not yet," I whispered, my plea a desperate prayer to the child within me, to the fates that seemed intent on testing my limits. The cave around me blurred, shadows pressing closer as I braced myself against the unyielding stone. Alone and terrified, I fought against the waves of pain, with nothing but the silent echoes of the serpents as my witnesses.

CHAPTER FOURTEEN

OLIVIA

The damp air clung to my skin as I huddled in the caves near Mathias' estate. My breaths came in ragged gasps, and a scream ripped from my throat as another contraction tore through me, stronger and more unforgiving than the last. The pain felt alive, an unrelenting force clawing its way through every fiber of my being.

"Olivia!" Reyna's voice echoed through the cavern, fragmented and distorted as it bounced off the jagged stone walls. The disorienting sound deepened the void around me, amplifying my isolation. "I can't find you! Roman is coming, too."

"Reyna!" I cried out, my voice hoarse and strained between the crushing waves of pain. The sound ricocheted back at me, an eerie reminder of our loss. I pressed my palms against the rough, cool surface of the cave wall, leaning heavily into it as if it could bear the weight of my agony.

My gaze fell to the daggers on the damp cave floor, their metallic sheen muted in the dim light. No one could see them —not Reyna, not Osman, and certainly not my mother or Mathias. I couldn't let them fall into the wrong hands. With trembling fingers, I scooped them up, fumbling to secure them in the holster strapped to my thigh.

The pain consumed me, each contraction melding into the next until time itself seemed to unravel. I was adrift in a void of suffering, the boundaries of reality blurred and shifting.

Through the haze, Reyna's hand suddenly found mine. Her touch was firm yet gentle, a lifeline anchoring me back to reality.

"Everything is going to be alright," she said, her voice steadier now that she had found me. Her calm tone clashed with the chaos I felt within. "Let's get you out of here."

With her arm wrapped around my waist, Reyna tried to guide me through the labyrinthine tunnels, but the cave seemed to conspire against us. Each path led us in frustrating circles, the oppressive darkness closing in like a living thing. My legs shook, barely able to carry me as another contraction bent me double, the force of it robbing me of breath.

"Focus on your breathing," Reyna urged, her words a tether pulling me from the edge of despair. Her presence was my only solace amidst my body's rebellion.

The cave refused to release us, and despair gnawed at the edges of my resolve with each dead end.

"Almost there," she whispered repeatedly, though we both knew we were no closer to escape than when we started.

The contractions intensified, a relentless tide, and Reyna's words became a distant echo, drowned out by the sound of my screams.

Panic clawed at my throat, each breath shallower than the last. "I can't do this," I gasped, my voice barely a whisper against the echoing void. "I'm going to give birth here, in this cave. We'll never make it out in time."

My voice broke as reality crashed down on me. The cave walls closed in.

"Olivia, listen to me." Reyna's voice cut through the despair. Her hands were firm on my shoulders, grounding me. "You're strong—stronger than anyone I know. You can do this."

Strength felt like a distant memory, a tale from another life. I sank to the cold ground, the unforgiving stone a harsh reminder of our plight. Overhead, another crack sliced the stone, revealing the waning night sky. My mind raced to the child within me, their life hanging in the balance of these shadowed corridors.

"Pray, Olivia," Reyna said. "Someone will find us."

She sounded sure, but her eyes betrayed a flicker of doubt.

I closed my eyes, lips moving in silent supplication to any deity that might be listening. Then Reyna was there again, her voice a soft command. "Take off your gown. I've seen births before. Our healer taught me a few things through observation."

With trembling hands, I obeyed, the fabric slipping away from my loose chemise. I clutched the discarded dress to my chest, a feeble barrier against the wave of vulnerability that engulfed me. The stone beneath me felt impossibly cold, yet it was nothing compared to the fear coursing through my veins.

Then, a familiar roar pierced the labyrinth, a primal sound reverberating off the walls. *Roman.* His voice carried the same raw fury that had electrified the air the first time we met in Rome. He must have been furious—furious that I had left and had ventured into this treacherous underground maze without him.

"Roman!" I tried to shout back, but my voice was weak, a frail echo of his intensity swallowed by the vast expanse of the cavern. He would find us; I clung to that hope. Yet fear gnawed at me. His anger—was it for my reckless departure or for what awaited us both? For the unknown fate of our child, conceived in love but now overshadowed by darkness?

"Focus, Olivia." Reyna pressed her hands to my back. "He's coming for you, for both of you."

Her words were a lifeline, tethering me to hope amid fear and uncertainty. Another wave of pain surged through me, threatening to drag me under. But Roman was near—I could feel it deep in my bones. He would find us, and we would face whatever came next together.

"Roman!" The name escaped my lips in a hoarse gasp, echoing through the cavern only to return as a haunting, distorted whisper. My plea felt as futile as trying to grasp the fleeting shadows that danced with each fresh stab of pain. Overhead, the first delicate rays of dawn filtered through a narrow fissure, teasing the oppressive darkness with the faintest promise of light.

Time stretched, each moment an eternity marked by the unrelenting rhythm of my contractions. The faint trickle of sunlight grew bolder, its golden streaks illuminating the rough stone walls. Yet even as daylight inched forward, a cold premonition settled in my chest—the solar eclipse was near. Its arrival would cast the world into an unnatural twilight, a veil of foreboding that seemed to mirror the chaos within me.

When despair threatened to consume me, a silhouette emerged from the gloom. Roman. His presence cut through my haze of agony like a beacon, his eyes locking onto mine with unyielding determination. Behind him, Malik staggered, his face pale and etched with suffering. The eclipse was already clawing at his strength, stripping him of the power that made him who he was.

"I'm in so much pain," I whispered, my voice crumbling under the weight of distress as tears blurred my vision.

Malik's knees buckled, his form crumpling to the cold, unforgiving ground.

"Malik!" Roman's voice was edged with panic as he knelt beside his friend, but his gaze never strayed far from me.

"Roman," I gasped through gritted teeth. "I can barely take it."

Pain lanced through me with renewed ferocity, commanding every fiber of my being. Each breath felt like a battle; every moment stretched into an eternity.

The air hung heavy, saturated with the mingling scents of damp earth and fear. Reyna crouched beside Malik, her arms steadying his trembling form. The once formidable figure now quaked like a shadow of himself slumped against her.

"Stay with me," she said, her voice a steady drumbeat against the chaos.

"Take him away, Reyna," Roman commanded, his tone sharp but laced with urgency.

"No," Malik rasped, his voice weak yet defiant, a flicker of fire burning behind his words. "You're not taking me out of here."

Reyna slipped her arm beneath Malik's shoulders, hoisting him with a grunt. Malik swayed as he fought to catch his balance. Finally, with his arm around her shoulder, he staggered beside her. Their shadows merged into one as they disappeared into the labyrinthine paths of the cave, leaving Roman and me alone with the encroaching darkness and the storm of my labor.

Roman's hands shook as he fumbled with a torch, striking flint until sparks caught and flame bloomed, casting a warm glow against the cold stone.

As another contraction ripped through my body, I

couldn't help but scream in agony. The sound was primal and wild, reverberating off the cave walls. Roman was by my side, massaging my back and offering words of comfort. His presence eased some of the pain, but I could still feel every sharp throb in my abdomen as I rode out the wave of contractions.

"I found the moon dagger," I managed between labored breaths, my voice quivering but resolute. "I have them both now."

Roman's face, illuminated by the flickering torchlight, registered shock. "How?"

"The old man. He's real," I said, my words cut short as another contraction gripped me, stealing my breath and silencing any further explanation.

Confusion etched itself deeply across his features, his mind racing to make sense of my revelation.

When the spasm subsided, and I could draw a shaky breath, I said, "The old man was waiting for me. Roman, we're in danger. I overheard Mathias and Mom talking. They want to kill us. The old man warned me—they're my biggest enemies."

The weight of my words hung heavy in the air, the gravity of the revelation pressing down on both of us. I braced for disbelief, for denial, but instead, Roman nodded. His gaze locked onto mine, steady and resolute. "I believe you, my love. But right now, I need you to focus on the baby and your breathing. We'll face this together."

The stakes were higher than ever. All we had was each other and a fragile life fighting to emerge into a world shadowed by danger.

Pain crashed over me in relentless waves, each one building higher than the last. Roman's hands were gentle yet unyielding as he helped me shift against the rough cave floor.

"Pull up your chemise," he said.

I obeyed, the coolness of the subterranean air brushing against my fevered skin. Through the narrow slit in the cave's ceiling, the celestial dance of moon and sun drew nearer to an embrace. The light that trickled through wavered with the rhythm of the impending eclipse.

"You're giving birth, Olivia. The baby's coming. I see a head…" Roman's face was a picture of awe and fear. "I don't know what to do."

"Roman!" I cried out, not in pain this time but in desperate need. "You have to help me deliver the baby."

My plea echoed off the cavern walls, amplifying the direness of our situation. His throat bobbed as he swallowed hard, his eyes meeting mine with a mixture of terror and determination.

"We need a midwife," he muttered, almost to himself.

"Stop wishing for solutions we don't have!" The command burst from me with the force of another contraction. "I only need you, Roman! You're the only one I can trust."

He squeezed my hand with a promise that he wouldn't let go.

His gaze shifted upward, his expression torn.

"I wish Amara were here," he whispered, the name heavy with memories of comfort and guidance, her absence a palpable ache.

"Roman!" My voice rang out sharper than I intended, but urgency demanded it. The sliver of sky visible through the cave's fissure darkened rapidly as the eclipse drew closer to totality. "The solar eclipse is coming fast."

His eyes locked on mine again, steadying me. "Don't worry. Just think about birthing the baby. Give me a push."

Drawing every ounce of strength I had left, I bore down,

focusing on the life within me. Silent prayers echoed in my mind—prayers for survival, hope, and the fragile future we desperately fought to protect. The darkness crept closer, an unwelcome specter at the threshold of our moment.

The pain swelled, consuming, threatening to splinter my resolve. Then, amidst the cacophony of anguish, a featherlight touch brushed against my sweat-drenched forehead.

A soft and sure whisper cut through the din of my cries. "You can do this, Olivia. You've got this."

The familiar and reassuring words were a melody against the discord of my suffering. My tear-blurred eyes fluttered open, and the sight before me pierced through the fog of pain.

Amara. She stood before me, ethereal, her presence an impossibility.

"Amara?" The name slipped from my lips, laden with disbelief. "How are you real? It can't be!"

Yet there she was, as real as the stark stone walls that encircled Roman and me.

Amara stepped forward without hesitation, an aura of quiet authority bending the air around her. She placed her hands on Roman's chest, firm but gentle, and nudged him back.

"I will deliver the baby," Amara said, her voice carrying the weight of timeless wisdom. She stepped forward, pressing the sun and moon daggers into Roman's hands. "Keep these safe. Their power must not be left unguarded." Her gaze softened as she met his. "Now, go. Be by your wife's side, Roman. Comfort her."

Stunned into silence, Roman and I exchanged glances, the impossible unfolding before us as we clung to hope amidst the shadows.

His mouth fell open, his eyes wide with astonishment.

"Do you see what I see?" he asked, his voice barely above a whisper.

I struggled to comprehend the scene unfolding before us, utterly awestruck by the sight of Amara—our once-dear friend—returning from beyond the veil at the precise moment we needed her most.

"Give me one big push," Amara instructed, her voice steady and clear, a lifeline in the tumult of my agony.

Summoning every ounce of strength left within me, I gathered it like a warrior preparing for battle. With a raw, primal roar, I pushed against the relentless tide of pain, willing our child into the world.

And then—silence. A profound stillness blanketed us as if the universe itself held its breath.

The quiet shattered with a sound more powerful than any thunder—a sharp, piercing cry, fragile yet fierce in its defiance of the void. My breath caught as my eyes sought Amara through the haze, her form glowing with an otherworldly light that seemed to radiate from within her. Tears streamed down my face, no longer from pain but from overwhelming relief and awe. I never thought I'd see this moment. I never thought I'd see Amara again.

"You have a daughter," Amara said, her voice soft and reverent.

Joy burst into my chest, filling every corner of my being. Beside me, Roman let out a shaky sob, his tears mingling with mine as they traced paths of gratitude down our faces. Amara moved with a grace that defied reality, cradling our newborn daughter before gently placing her on my chest. The warmth of her tiny body against mine was a miracle; each breath she took was a testament to the trials we had overcome.

"Oh my god, she's here," I whispered, the words choked by overwhelming emotion.

Amara smiled down at us, her expression tender, her eyes shining with pride.

"You did so good, my love," Roman said, stroking my hair. "You were incredible."

Amara's gaze shifted to the tiny life nestled between us. Her smile deepened as she said. "Looks like your daughter is a Timeborne."

A chill rippled through me, starkly contrasting the warmth of my baby cradled against my chest. Beside me, Roman drew a shaky breath, his wide eyes reflecting the gravity of the moment. Amara's gaze shifted to the glint of metal catching the dim light—the Timeborne dagger lying innocuously at my side.

Amara picked up the blade with hands trembling from both exhaustion and reverence. It was more than a weapon; it was an artifact of destiny, a symbol of our trials and triumphs, now destined to pass into the hands of a new generation. She turned to Roman and extended it toward him.

Roman accepted the dagger, his fingers curling around its hilt. The weight of the blade was a sharp contrast to the fragile life he had just helped bring into the world. For a moment, he stood still, the gravity of its significance sinking into his soul.

Darkness enveloped us, but a light stronger than any eclipse bound us together—a family forged through time and trials. Our tears fell silently, an unspoken ode to the love and wonder that held us in this sacred moment, deep in the heart of the earth.

As I held our newborn daughter close, her tiny breaths a miraculous rhythm against the stillness of the cavern, I nuzzled her soft, delicate nose. "Welcome to the world, little one," I whispered, my voice filled with awe. "Your day of birth is February 25, 1598, and you shall be a woman who is not bound by time's constraints."

"All that matters is that you're safe and the baby is here," Roman said, his steady voice grounding me amidst the whirl-wind of emotions. He leaned forward, pressing his lips to my forehead and my cheek. His eyes, warm and unwavering, radiated a love so profound it felt like a force of nature—unbreakable, eternal. It consumed us both, growing stronger with each passing heartbeat. We were rooted together at that moment, intertwined like ancient trees, reaching deeper into the earth.

"What shall her name be?" I asked softly, the question rising instinctively. A name held power, especially for someone destined to transcend the boundaries of time.

Roman's gaze fell to her tiny face, his thumb brushing gently against her cheek. His features softened as he considered.

"Luna," I proposed, struck by the poetic balance of light and darkness, the celestial dance that had heralded her arrival.

He nodded, the faintest smile playing on his lips. Then, after a moment of thought, he added, "She graced her way into the world amidst chaos. We should name her Grace."

"Luna Grace," I whispered, feeling the name resonate deeply, as though it was always meant to be hers.

"Luna Grace it is," he said with a tender smile, blending the serenity and tumult surrounding her birth.

As we basked in the glow of new life, Roman turned to Amara, his brow knit in confusion. "How is it you're here, Amara?"

Before she could reply, a resonant voice filled the cavern, reverberating off the ancient rock walls. "Amara, my love, it's time for us to go."

My heart stuttered as I recognized the voice before even seeing him—the old man.

Amara moved toward him. "Lazarus, can you believe it? They have a daughter, a Timeborne, just like you said."

"Exactly as it was meant to be," he replied, his tone steeped in an ageless wisdom that transcended comprehension.

Roman and I exchanged a startled glance, the weight of their words crashing over us like a tidal wave. Their connection and intimacy spoke of a bond that defied the boundaries of life and death, of time itself.

"Lazarus?" Roman's voice faltered, his brow furrowed in disbelief. "I knew you as Gaius in Ancient Rome."

The old man—Lazarus, Gaius—turned to Roman, his gaze piercing and timeless. "Roman," he said, his voice carrying a resonance that bridged centuries.

"Both of you... you're here—Gaius and Amara." Roman's voice cracked as he held Luna Grace closer to his chest, protective instincts flaring as though their presence might whisk her away into the realms of time they navigated so effortlessly.

The excruciating pain of childbirth gradually faded into a state of profound astonishment.

Lazarus—once known as Gaius—stepped forward, his face etched with the shadows of sunlight no longer obscured by the moon. The faint glow highlighted the scars and lines of a life wrought with danger and hardship.

"In Rome, I was Gaius to you, Roman," he said, his voice steady yet burdened with truths too vast to grasp. "But that name was a mask, a deception crafted to shield me from my enemies. My true name is Lazarus." His words carried the weight of centuries, layered with secrets and untold stories. "There's much I wish I could tell you, but my time here is short. I must take Amara back to where she belongs before it's too late. Protect your wife, your daughter, and yourself. Great danger surrounds you, and the final battle is closer than you think."

His voice wavered briefly as if bearing the sorrow of what lay ahead. The gravity of his warning settled deep in my chest, igniting a fierce resolve to protect my family from the shadows creeping ever closer.

Lazarus and Amara began to fade as his words lingered in the air, their forms dissolving into shimmering translucence. Their departure was quiet, like a sigh carried on the wind, but it left behind the unmistakable weight of an impending storm.

"Wait!" Roman's voice cracked with desperation, echoing through the cavern.

But they were gone, leaving only the flickering shadows on the stone walls and Luna Grace's soft, insistent cries.

My strength ebbed, the events of the day—both physical and emotional—demanding their toll. Exhaustion gripped me, and my body trembled under its weight.

"Olivia?" Roman's voice reached me, distant and tinged with alarm.

The edges of my vision blurred, the cave narrowing to a dark tunnel as I struggled to stay conscious. Roman's figure became a smear of light and shadow, the torch's glow dimming to a faint glimmer before plunging into darkness.

"Olivia!"

The deafening sound of Roman's terrified scream echoed in my ears as the suffocating darkness swallowed me. My body convulsed, every muscle screaming in agony as I was dragged into the abyss. My heart pounded frantically, love and fear intertwining until it finally shattered like glass. At that moment, I was certain that I was dying, falling into a slow, agonizing descent into nothingness.

CHAPTER FIFTEEN

ROMAN

The damp air clung to my skin as I stood in the dim, oppressive cave. My heart thundered in my chest like a war drum, each beat a deafening reminder of the stakes. Olivia lay pale and lifeless on the cold stone floor, a crimson stain spreading beneath her. The sight of her so still, so fragile, seized my breath, choking me with despair. Clutched against my chest, our newborn wailed, her feeble cries ricocheting off the cavern walls, a haunting reminder of the life we had just brought into this world.

Olivia is dying. The thought sliced through me with brutal clarity, leaving no room for doubt. I couldn't let that happen —not Olivia. She was my life, my soul, my everything.

With trembling resolve, I dropped to my knees beside her, sliding one arm beneath her knees and the other around her back. I pressed the baby close, her fragile form a small weight against my chest, anchoring me in the chaos. Rising to my feet was an agonizing struggle, a careful balancing act to ensure Luna Grace didn't slip from my hold. But there was no time for hesitation. Every second mattered.

As I navigated the treacherous path toward the cave's

mouth, I focused on the faint slivers of light ahead. Luna's cries pierced the shadows, their urgency propelling me forward. I couldn't afford to falter. Not when their lives hung by such a delicate thread.

A hunched figure emerged from the darkness, leaning heavily against the cave wall.

"Malik!"

The solar eclipse had drained him, leaving him a hollow version of the warrior I once knew. Beside him stood Reyna, her face etched with lines of worry, her posture taut with unspoken fear.

"We have to go!" I said the command was a more desperate plea than an authoritative order.

Reyna met my gaze, her eyes holding a storm of hidden troubles.

"We have a problem," she said, and something in her tone told me that our plight had just deepened into a chasm from which we might not all emerge.

With Olivia cradled securely in my arms, my focus remained on Luna. I lurched toward Reyna, every step driven by the urgency to ensure she was safe.

"Take the child," I said, my voice raw with panic and exertion.

The baby's wails pierced the thick air as Reyna carefully wrapped her arms around the newborn, cradling its tiny form against her chest.

"Raul and his men have surrounded the cave," Reyna said, her voice steady despite the dire weight of her words.

I froze, my blood thundering in my ears. "Fuck, can this get any worse… I thought Raul was burned to death!"

"Raul has half a face and one eye now," she replied, her tone calm but the imagery horrifying. The darkness mercifully veiled the gruesome picture her words conjured, but the thought alone was enough to churn my stomach.

Gritting my teeth, I adjusted my grip on Olivia, determination searing me. With one last glance at Malik, who nodded weakly, I pressed forward toward the cave's mouth, ducking beneath jagged rocks and skirting piles of debris. Behind me, Reyna and Malik followed, their steps, careful yet swift, shadowed phantoms in the gloom.

Emerging from the cave was like stepping into a nightmare. The scene outside was straight from hell's darkest depths. Raul stood at the forefront, his charred face a grotesque mask of hatred. One side was a ruin of melted flesh, his single eye gleaming with malice amidst the carnage of his visage.

"You little bitch!" he snarled, his voice a guttural growl that made my blood run cold. "Look what you did to my face!" His hatred was directed at Reyna, who stood firm despite the venom in his words, clutching my child with unwavering resolve.

The stench of scorched flesh wafted on the wind, a nauseating reminder of the violence that had twisted him into this monstrous figure. But I couldn't dwell on vengeance or fear. Olivia's life hung in the balance, and time was slipping through my fingers like grains of sand. Without proper care, I would lose her—and the thought of a world without Olivia made the air around me feel unbreathable.

Everything felt like a blur of motion—rock, sky, the looming shadows of Raul's men—yet I forced myself forward, Olivia's fragile weight pressing against me. Each step was a battle against the fear clawing at my throat.

She's going to die. The thought echoed relentlessly in my mind, a chilling refrain I refused to accept. I couldn't—wouldn't—let it become reality.

Reyna's voice cut through the haze of my dread.

"Oh, Raul, I did such a bad job. I have to finish what I started. I have to make sure everyone lives happily." The resolve in her tone was a stark contrast to the gentle way she then turned to Malik, offering him the bundle in her arms. "Hold the baby."

Malik extended trembling arms, cradling the newborn with all the strength his weakened body could muster. Despite his exhaustion, he held her as though she were the most precious thing in the world.

Reyna lifted the hem of her dress, revealing twin blades strapped to her thighs. In one fluid motion, she unsheathed them, their polished steel catching the dim light.

Reyna was upon Raul's men before they could react, a deadly whirlwind of precision and fury. The guards, weakened by the fire, were no match for her. Her movements were a dance of lethal grace, her blades singing as they struck.

Who is this woman? And what the hell happened to Osman. The thought slammed into me as I watched her, mesmerized and horrified. My mind raced, trying to piece together what had happened.

The clash of steel against steel rang out, interspersed with the guttural cries of the fallen. And then... silence.

Reyna stood amidst the carnage, her chest rising and falling with controlled breaths, her blades dripping crimson. Only Raul remained, stumbling backward, his one good eye wide with terror.

"Roman," Reyna said, her voice steady yet charged with purpose, as she pointed one bloodied blade at our disfigured adversary. "I must end this."

My heart pounded against my ribs, an erratic drumbeat. "No. Don't. We take him with us."

Surprise flickered across her face, but she nodded.

Without hesitation, she bound Raul's hands with practiced skill, the ropes biting into his scorched skin. He struggled feebly, his strength no match for hers.

With an almost effortless motion, Reyna heaved him into the wagon like a grain sack. Her calm efficiency belied the chaos that had unfolded, but there was a sense of unyielding determination in her actions—a resolve that matched my own.

I watched, bewildered by the woman who had just single-handedly turned the tide of our desperate situation.

Who was Reyna? What other secrets did she carry?

"Reyna..." I began, but the words lodged in my throat, inadequate and feeble.

"I'll explain later, Roman," she interrupted. "We have to move now."

I shifted Olivia in my arms, her pale face contrasting the deepening shadows around us. Osman approached, mouth set in a grim line. Gently, I handed her over to him, my hands lingering on her cool skin, feeling the slow pulse at her throat. She was alive, but barely.

"Be careful with her," I murmured.

Osman nodded, cradling Olivia with tenderness. I mounted the horse and reached down as Osman lifted Olivia up to me. Her body was limp, her chest rising and falling with faint breaths that tugged at my heartstrings. I held her close.

"Stay with me, Olivia," I said.

Behind me, Malik's grip on the baby tightened, his hands trembling as the lingering effects of the eclipse left him sapped of strength. He passed the newborn to Reyna with great effort, the small bundle seeming impossibly fragile in the transition.

"You're still not recovered from the eclipse," Reyna said,

her voice firm but tinged with concern as she cradled the baby.

"Let me at least drive the horses!" Malik said, his pride battling his physical frailty.

"Fine," Reyna said, though her eyes spoke volumes of her doubts. She watched him climb onto the buckboard and take the reins with determination.

I adjusted Olivia in front of me, one arm wrapped around her back while the other gripped the reins. For a moment, my gaze met Reyna's as she climbed into the wagon beside Malik, the baby secure in her embrace. Her expression was unreadable, a mask that concealed whatever thoughts churned behind those sharp eyes.

"Let's move out," I called, my voice steady despite the chaos.

The horse beneath me responded to the subtle pressure of my heels, and we surged forward, Osman falling in line behind us, his mount stepping carefully over the uneven terrain. The clatter of wagon wheels joined the rhythmic hoofbeats as we left the chaos of the cave behind, the grim silence of our group broken only by the occasional creak of the wagon and the soft, distressed murmurs of the baby.

The shadows of the trees blurred past as we pressed on, each of us lost in our grim contemplations. Olivia's limp form was a weight against my chest—both physical and emotional —her shallow breaths barely perceptible. My heart raced with dread, urgency driving me onward as fear threatened to consume me.

"I don't know who you are, Reyna, but thank you," I said, my voice cutting through the wind that whipped against my face.

Reyna nodded, her focus on the infant cradled in her arms. The baby's tiny fists flailed weakly, a soft wail escaping her lips before Reyna murmured soothing words too low for me to catch. Her practiced motions only deepened the mystery of who this woman was—and how much more she might be hiding.

As the estate's towering silhouette emerged through the thinning woods, hope fought against the fear clutching my chest. The familiar grounds loomed ahead, promising aid and safety, though the weight of uncertainty hung heavy in the air.

"Osman!" I called, barely slowing my horse as we approached the gates, now swung wide in welcome.

Osman urged his horse closer, reaching for Olivia with gentle hands. Her pallor was haunting, her once vibrant complexion now ghostly under the cloudy skies.

"We need a doctor!" My shout echoed across the court-yard, carrying the weight of desperation.

After I dismounted, I snatched Olivia back into my embrace and bounded toward the grand entryway, the doors thrown wide in anticipation of our arrival.

"Clear a path!" I bellowed, and servants scrambled aside as I carried Olivia upstairs; their faces blanched with shock at the sight of her bloodied gown and unresponsive state.

Reyna followed close behind, the baby now quiet in her arms. Her heels clicked a steady rhythm against the marble steps, a dramatic difference from the erratic pounding of my boots as I ascended.

"Please," I whispered to no one in particular, "let her be saved."

Once I laid Olivia on the bed, the infant began to wail, her cries cutting through the tense silence of the room.

"The baby is hungry," Reyna said.

Without hesitation, I took Luna from Reyna, cradling her awkwardly against my chest as I rushed down the hall.

Bursting into Emily's chambers, I found her sitting in bed, her face softening as she saw the bundle in my arms.

"Oh, my goodness, Roman," Emily said, her voice tinged with relief and wonder. "Olivia had the baby. Give her here."

Her outstretched arms were a lifeline, and I gently transferred the newborn into her embrace. "Please, feed her," I said, my voice barely audible over my heart pounding. I didn't wait for a response, already turning on my heel and sprinting back to Olivia's room, the echo of my boots chasing me down the corridor.

The doctor had arrived and was bent over Olivia, his face etched with concentration as he examined her still form. My chest tightened as I took in the pale pallor of her skin, her lifeless appearance, a knife twisting in my gut.

"Sir," the doctor said, "you must leave the room."

"That's my wife," I growled, my voice laced with desperation and anger.

"Exactly why you can't be here," he countered, his gaze unwavering. "You'll do more harm than good. Let me work."

I clenched my fists, my body vibrating with the urge to fight him, to stay. But his words were an immovable wall, and with a reluctant step, I exited the room. The door closed behind me with a quiet click that sounded far too final.

Pacing the hallway, my mind reeled, clawing for a shred of control that continued to slip through my grasp. My eyes landed on the window, where I saw Reyna and Osman standing by the wagon, Raul still bound and immobilized in its bed.

The cold air hit me like a slap as I stormed onto the estate grounds, my breath visible in the brisk night. Reyna turned toward me, her expression unreadable, while Osman kept a watchful eye on Raul.

"Raul," I snarled a low growl as I approached him. "How did you find us? What do you want?"

He squinted at me, his one good eye glinting with defiance and resignation. Despite his battered and bound state, a smugness lingered in his expression.

"Roman," he said, his voice rasping but steady, "I believe I still have something you need—something you might have forgotten about."

"Spit it out," I snapped, my patience fraying under worry and weariness. My voice cut through the cold air like a blade.

Raul's breath was labored, his face pale and drawn, beads of sweat glistening on his charred skin. "I have come to inform you of something," he said, his tone urgent despite his obvious pain.

I fought to steady my trembling hands, my body shaking with equal parts rage and exhaustion. "And what is it you came here to tell me?"

Reyna stepped forward, her presence commanding as she extended her hand. In her palm rested a dagger, its polished blade catching the faint light.

"Raul had this," she said evenly. "I took it from him while he writhed in pain from the burns. I believe it belongs to Olivia—or perhaps to you?"

Relief washed over me as I realized that Olivia's beloved dagger had been returned.

"Thank you, Reyna," I said, my voice softening as I met her unwavering gaze. Her bravery had once again proven invaluable.

She gave a curt nod and stepped back, allowing me to refocus on Raul.

"Reyna saved my child," I said, my voice cold with contempt. "She fought off your men and risked her life. What did you hope to gain by attacking us?"

Raul's lips curled into a bitter smirk, his good eye narrowing as he stared at me. "Power, Roman," he spat. "It's always power. But now… it's slipping away. Just like everything else."

His words hung heavy in the air, their bitterness a stark reflection of his defeat. Disgust coiled in my gut, twisting tighter with every passing moment.

"You're beaten, Raul," I said, my tone laced with contempt. "Yet here you are, tied like an animal. Tell me—was it worth it?"

A hollow laugh escaped him, devoid of joy or hope. "Nothing is ever worth it in the end," he muttered, his voice little more than a whisper.

His words lingered in the cold night air, heavy with a truth I wasn't ready to accept. I needed answers, but they wouldn't come from a broken man whose schemes had crumbled to dust.

Mathias emerged from the estate, his steps purposeful as his gaze fell on Raul.

"What have we here?" he said, his voice tinged with disdain. He stopped before the wagon, glaring at Raul's bound, battered form. "Costa, you're an evil man. It seems fate has seen to your punishment."

He turned to me, his expression unreadable. "Let's take him to the dungeon where he belongs."

The cold, damp air of the dungeon enveloped us as I followed Mathias down the narrow stone corridor, our footsteps echoing off the walls. Raul's disheveled form dragged between us, his head bowed, the fight drained from him. Shadows clung to the edges of the hall like silent spectators as we reached an iron-barred door.

Mathias didn't hesitate, securing Raul inside with practiced efficiency. The soft click of the lock echoed through the chamber, a quiet yet absolute finality to his fate. Together, we sealed him within the same glass enclosure that held Balthazar, his own reflection staring back at him—a ghost of his own making.

"Pathetic," Mathias muttered, his gaze lingering on Raul with contempt. Without another word, he turned on his heel and disappeared into the shadows.

Laughter, cruel and mocking, broke the silence that followed. Balthazar crawled from the shadows like a wraith, his eyes gleaming with mirth as they found Raul's disfigured visage.

"Oh, look at you!" he sneered, his voice dripping scornfully. "You're hideous. Your face burned to a crisp. A fitting look for someone who's spent his life playing with fire."

"Shut up!" Raul growled, his voice hoarse but brimming with fury. His one good eye glared at Balthazar, blazing with rage and humiliation.

"Who did this to you?" Balthazar prodded further.

"Reyna," Raul spat, the name leaving his lips like venom. "She's insane. Dangerous. Fucking crazy. I had captured her before I acquired Marcellious. She may have the face of an angel, but she's capable of unspeakable things.

"Once I had my fun with Marcellious—broken him completely—I threw him into a cell with Reyna. That's when she escaped," Raul growled, his voice laced with bitterness. "She doused me and my men with some kind of liquid—a poisonous substance that ignited into searing flames on contact. I wouldn't be surprised if she and Marcellious were lovers."

"Reyna and Marcellious? Lovers?" I said, disbelief dripping from every word. "Preposterous."

Raul's smirk deepened, the scars marring his face twisting with malice. "Oh, but I found her hugging him, whispering everything would be alright. Go on, tell Marcellious' wife that he betrayed her. Let's see how loyal they remain."

A surge of fury bubbled within me, but I swallowed it down, focusing instead on the battles I faced beyond the confines of this wretched dungeon. My newborn child. Olivia. This man's petty insinuations were nothing compared to the storms raging within the estate's walls.

I stepped closer to the barriers that separated us.

"You're lying!" I spat out, unable to contain the disbelief and contempt in my voice.

Raul's response was a slow, wicked grin that deepened the shadows etched into his ravaged face. His one good eye gleamed with satisfaction, a predator relishing his prey's unease.

"Lying? You see what she did to my face and my men," he hissed. "She's deadly, but who is she? And why isn't she chained down here with the rest of us?"

His voice dripped with suspicion and malice, the words laced with venom. The stench of sweat and blood thickened the air, mingling with the metallic tang of fear.

I let out a low, humorless laugh, bouncing off the damp stone walls and mingling with Balthazar's mocking chuckle.

"Are you telling me a woman bested you?" I sneered, my tone cutting like a blade. "How pathetic."

Regaining my composure, I stared Raul down. "Tell me, Raul. Why did you take Marcellious? Why did you take Reyna hostage? Whose orders were you following?"

Raul seemed to shrink back, his shoulders sagging under defeat. His eyes darted around the dungeon as if searching for an escape, but there was none. The walls closed in, the air thick with tension.

"I don't know who he is," he muttered, almost as if

speaking to himself. "I just follow his orders. He is a powerful man."

I narrowed my eyes, stepping closer. "A powerful man? Is he a Timehunter like you—only stronger, more connected? Does he belong to a greater society that wields even more control over time and space?"

Raul's silence was answer enough, but Balthazar's sharp voice cut through the oppressive quiet before he could respond. "Why don't you tell Roman how you are now the only Timehunter left in Italy, thanks to me? I destroyed your pathetic band of vermin on the night of your masquerade."

His words left a cold silence in their wake. I looked at Raul, his form now less formidable, a lone figure in the grand scheme of our conflict—a pawn discarded after the play.

"Was your society in Italy destroyed by Balthazar?" I asked, my voice low, disbelief threading through each word.

The flickering light of the torches danced across Raul's hollowed features, casting shadows that stretched like skeletal fingers along the stone walls.

"Yes," he replied, his tone devoid of the venom it once carried, now hollow and resigned. "But let us set aside the fate of my society for a moment."

I stiffened, sensing a darker truth about to unravel.

"I came to your cave for a different purpose," Raul continued, his voice sharpening like the edge of a blade. "To warn you."

"Warn me?" I echoed, the disbelief twisting into something colder.

Raul's gaze locked onto mine, a glint of something unreadable flickering in his lone eye. "I've informed the Timehunter leader in Anatolia about your possession of the sun and moon daggers. They know your wife and her friends are Timebornes and Timebounds. They will soon be on their way here."

His words hit like a thunderclap, reverberating through the chamber. My jaw tightened, fury and dread battling for dominance within me.

Raul leaned back against the wall, his face cast in shadows, his voice a bitter whisper. "My job was to do what I needed to do. And now, I will die. I'm done."

The glimmer in his eye faded, leaving only a man stripped of everything—power, loyalty, and life itself—awaiting the inevitable end.

"You're despicable, you know that? What kind of man kills his child by poisoning it?" I spat the question at him, my voice trembling with rage. "You told me your first child was killed. And then you claim you had a child with Alina. But where is that child now? The child you begged Alina to bear? Why would you kill him? You're a disgusting monster, Raul."

Raul's gaze remained fixed on me, his expression unreadable. When he finally spoke, his voice was barely above a whisper. "You know nothing."

I knew enough to understand the monster before me. I knew enough to feel the burning need for justice—for Olivia, for his child, and for all those harmed by this man's twisted mission. Whatever Raul's endgame was, whatever dark purpose drove him and Mathias, I made a silent vow then and there: their kind would find no quarter in this world. Not while I still drew breath.

"You Timehunters were supposed to be the healers of our people," Balthazar interjected, his voice rising with unrestrained fury. "Your purpose was to bring relief and aid to those suffering from diseases and sickness. Instead, you've become a poisonous species. Without hesitation, you kill any human, Darkness,

Timeborne, or Timebound, with your alchemy. You, who were once revered as guardians, have become monsters—vicious villains hiding behind the false facade of a virtuous society."

As Balthazar spoke, his eyes flickered with emotion, his gaze distant, as though chasing a memory that eluded him.

Raul's lips curled into a sneer, his voice sharp and taunting. "Well, Balthazar, if you hate Timehunters so much… why did you choose to ally with me?"

Balthazar worked his jaw, his expression calculating as he weighed his next words.

"Because Marcellious married my daughter Emily," he replied evenly, "and I wanted to know where she was, you fucking idiot. Do you think I was truly helping you with Marcellious? No, I was using you to get to him. And when he finally broke and revealed Emily's location, I left your wretched company. You were always the loser in our little game, Raul. And now look at you—shackled, broken, and sharing this dungeon with me."

"Shut up!" Raul roared, his voice raw with rage, his bound body trembling with futile resistance.

I had no time or patience for their petty squabbling. Their words were poison, seeping into the already suffocating air of the dungeon.

"I'm leaving," I said coldly, my tone reverberating off the damp stone walls. I turned to go, eager to escape the oppressive weight of the confrontation.

As I moved toward the exit, a figure emerged from the shadows of the corridor. Alina. Her presence was like a ghost conjured from the past, her wide eyes locking onto Raul with a mix of recognition and disbelief.

"Is that you?" she whispered, her voice trembling.

Raul's face twisted into a mask of unbridled fury, his

body straining against the ropes that held him. His lips curled into a snarl as he spat venom at her.

"You fucking filthy whore!" His words rang out, dripping with malice. "Look at you—you're a fucking liar and a serpent. Every time you told me you loved me and cared for me and our child, it was just a game. You're pathetic. Your daughter has more beauty and respect than you'll ever have."

Alina flinched as though struck, her face losing all color as she stumbled back a step. The venom in Raul's words was a wound sharper than any blade, cutting through whatever strength she had mustered to confront him.

As disgust roiled within me, I stepped around her, barely sparing her a glance as I moved toward the exit. My heart pounded with unanswered questions, the weight of Raul's hateful glare pressing against my back. The darkness in this accursed place seemed to seep from the very walls, but I had no intention of lingering any longer.

The dungeon's oppressive air clung to my skin as I stormed away from the vile scene, my mind a turbulent sea of disgust and unease. Each step upward felt heavier than the last, the weight of Raul's venomous words and the darkness of that place threatening to pull me under.

As I ascended the stairs, the stench of dampness and decay gave way to the faint aroma of lavender, a scent that always lingered in the halls. It was Olivia's scent. It wrapped around me like a whisper of hope, spurring me on, each step bringing me closer to her still, fragile form.

Mathias' silhouette loomed at the end of the corridor, framed by the warm glow of the sconces. His posture was rigid, his presence imposing, as though he had been waiting for this confrontation.

"What happened to Olivia?" he asked, his voice measured

but laced with curiosity. "Do you know why she's unconscious?"

I said nothing, my silence thick and deliberate.

His tone sharpened. "Did you find the dagger?"

A surge of anger surged through me, hot and unrelenting. Lazarus' warning echoed in my mind—*Trust no one but Olivia*.

I clenched my fists, barely containing the fury that sought to break free. I would get no answers from this man.

Without a word, I turned away, my resolve solidifying with every step. They wouldn't get anything from me—not a word, a hint, or the slightest clue. I silently vowed to protect the blades with my life, no matter the cost.

My thoughts shifted to Gaius—Lazarus—who had hidden his true identity from me in Rome. I had always known him as Gaius, a figure of strength and wisdom, tirelessly watching over me and urging me to persevere. His whispered words of encouragement had been my guiding light during my darkest moments, and now, after so many years, he had returned. Every person I'd encountered, every fragment of my past, seemed to hold a deeper meaning waiting to be unraveled. My life was a puzzle, and piece by piece, it was beginning to take shape.

Gripping Olivia's dagger tightly, I quickened my pace. Its weight was a steady reminder of my promise, a drumbeat that echoed in my chest, urging me forward. I would protect what mattered most, even if it cost me everything. But as I clung to my resolve, a quiet unease crept into my mind. The real tests that would challenge not only my strength but my soul were still to come—and they would arrive in ways I could never foresee.

CHAPTER SIXTEEN

OLIVIA

Agony rippled through my body, each breath a searing reminder that I was still tethered to life. An invisible weight pressed against my chest, heavy and suffocating, as if the air itself sought to crush me. My limbs felt tangled in unfamiliar linens, foreign fabric against my skin.

I gasped, my eyes snapping open—or so I thought. Darkness enveloped me, a disorienting void that left me grasping for certainty. Candlelight flickered faintly at the edges of my vision, its warm glow casting restless shadows on stone walls and towering ceilings. This was not the sanctuary of my bedroom, but an alien place cloaked in an eerie, castle-like grandeur.

My gaze landed on the massive four-poster bed dominating the room, its dark wood frame intricately carved with swirling patterns that seemed to writhe in the shifting light. The canopy above was draped with flowing silk curtains, their translucent elegance a sharp contrast to the harsh reality of my confusion.

Overhead, an ornate crystal chandelier glittered like a

constellation, its cascading light illuminating the room in a golden haze. Flanking the bed stood two elegant bedside tables with gilded legs and smooth marble tops, each supporting a flickering candle that painted the mirrored surfaces with trembling reflections. Heavy velvet drapes veiled the windows, allowing only slivers of muted light to seep into the room, adding to its opulent, yet haunting, atmosphere.

"Where am I?" The words escaped my lips in a whisper, a fragile plea swallowed by the oppressive silence.

The dim glow of the candles highlighted lavish tapestries that hung like silent sentinels and velvet drapes that whispered secrets I could not understand. The air felt thick with strangeness, the unfamiliarity pressing against me as if the room rejected my presence. It was like I had been plucked from reality and cast adrift in medieval fantasy.

Instinct screamed at me to rise, to search for my baby, for Roman—but they were absent, swallowed by the opulence that mocked my longing. I ached to rub the confusion from my eyes, to blink away the fog and find clarity. But the chilling truth settled over me like ice—my eyes were already open, yet my family, my world, remained beyond reach, lost in the shadows of this unfamiliar place.

I pushed myself up from the plush bed that had cradled my disoriented slumber. My legs ached with a dull protest as I swung them over the edge, my bare feet meeting the icy chill of the floor. The air was thick, carrying the faint scent of aged wood mingled with the delicate aroma of unseen blooms.

I steadied myself against the intricately carved bedside table, its unfamiliar design a reminder that this was no place I recognized. The open door ahead beckoned, spilling dim light into the room and revealing a corridor shrouded in shadows.

Tentatively, I stepped forward, the cool air brushing against my skin like an unwelcome whisper.

The hallway stretched long and foreboding, the walls adorned with grand tapestries and paintings that spoke of wars, victories, and triumphs that felt utterly foreign. Sculpted into serpentine dragons, candle sconces clung to the stone walls, their flickering flames casting eerie shapes that seemed to slither and shift with the shadows. The silence pressed down like a living thing, heavy and watchful as if the air held its breath.

I walked forward, each step hesitant, my bare feet brushing against the polished stone floor. The grandeur of this place was overwhelming, like stepping into a forgotten world of kings and queens, where alliances were forged and broken behind heavy doors. The absence of voices or foot-steps amplified the strangeness, a chilling void in an ornate space.

Ahead, movement caught my eye—a woman ascending a staircase with a fluid grace that seemed almost surreal. Her gown shimmered with the glow of candlelight, a fabric too rich and regal for a servant. Threads of moonlight seemed woven into the folds, whispering of secrets and silken decadence.

"Excuse me," I called out, my voice a fragile thread in the vast stillness. "Where is everyone?"

The woman halted mid-step, her poised form illuminated by the flickering light. She turned with the precision of a dancer; her movements were calculated yet effortless. As her gaze met mine, she dipped into a deep curtsy, her dress pooling around her like liquid silver.

"Whoa, what are you doing?" I stammered, my mind racing with confusion.

"My lady, I'm sorry," she murmured, her eyes dropping to

the stone steps as if they bore the weight of an apology she couldn't fully express.

"Sorry for... what?" I asked, but the maid remained silent, her lips pressing into a thin line.

Swallowing the knot of apprehension tightening in my throat, I forced myself to speak again. "Where's my husband?" The words felt foreign on my tongue, like fragments of someone else's life spilling from my lips.

The maid's brows furrowed, and she fidgeted with the hem of her gown, her discomfort palpable.

"He's with the Shadow Lord in a meeting. He's with Lazarus," she replied, her voice laced with an odd mix of reverence and dread.

Lazarus? The name clawed at the edges of my memory, familiar yet shrouded in obscurity. A disquieting ache settled in my chest as I struggled to connect the fragments of recognition.

"Who is that?" I asked, feeling the question's absurdity even as I spoke it.

The maid's expression shifted, pity mingling with disbelief. "Oh, dear, that fall you had must have been terrible if you don't remember who Lazarus is."

Fall? The word clanged in my ears, foreign and disorienting. My fingers gripped the banister tightly as if holding on could steady the swirling void where my memories should have been. Before I could demand an explanation, the footsteps descending from above echoed through the hallway, their cadence steady and purposeful.

A figure emerged at the top of the staircase—a man whose presence seemed to command the air. My breath caught in my throat. It was Balthazar, yet not as I had known him. His skin was unmarked, its smoothness free of the lines that had once told the story of his years. His hair, now darker and longer, carried no trace of the silver streaks I remembered. He looked... impossibly younger, vibrant, and ageless.

"How is this possible?" I whispered, my voice barely audible over the drumbeat of my heart. I stepped back instinctively as if creating distance could protect me from the impossibility. "He looks twenty years younger."

A flicker of concern—or confusion?—crossed his features. Balthazar moved with the same commanding authority I knew, yet now there was an undeniable vitality about him, as though the years had been peeled away, leaving a man in the prime of his life.

The air trembled with a silent question as Balthazar approached, his eyes swimming with a concern I didn't trust.

"How are you feeling?" he asked.

I recoiled, pressing my back against the cool stone wall. The sight of him, younger and unmarred by time, was a riddle wrapped in an enigma.

"You—you were imprisoned," I stammered, my voice betraying the terror that clawed at my insides. "How did you escape?"

His brow furrowed deeply. "Imprisoned? My lady, what are you talking about? You must have hit your head harder than we thought. You should still be resting."

My pulse thrummed in my ears, a frantic beat screaming danger.

"No," I protested, the taste of fear sharp and bitter on my tongue. "I'm not imagining this. You were in prison after—after you tried to kill me." My voice broke, and panic spilled out in a torrent. "You're here to take my baby girl. You're going to hurt her!"

Balthazar's expression shifted the confusion on his face, deepening into something more profound, almost troubled. "What are you talking about? There's no baby, my lady. You managed to escape Mathias, but you were riding so fast your horse lost control and threw you to the ground."

"Mathias?" I whispered, the name spinning through my mind like a splintered echo. "What are you talking about?" My voice sounded small, fragile, and lost amid the overwhelming grandeur of the unfamiliar castle.

"Mathias attacked you," Balthazar explained, his tone slow and deliberate as if speaking to a frightened child. "But you don't need to worry. I've imprisoned him. It seems he was betraying us all along. Now Salvatore has emerged from the shadows, hungering for destruction." His eyes narrowed, and his voice dropped. "He wants to destroy you."

"None of this makes any sense," I said, shaking my head.

"I can take you to see Mathias if you don't trust me." As if to prove his peaceful intent, Balthazar reached for his belt and stripped away his sword and dagger. They clattered to the floor, echoing hollowly through the vast corridor.

"Salvatore," I murmured, the name stirring a distant echo of dread deep within me. My thoughts swirled with fragments —faces, names, memories—all just out of reach, like trying to grasp smoke with bare hands. It was a futile struggle, and the harder I tried to piece them together, the more fragmented they became. Everything felt wrong, twisted, and unfamiliar.

"This doesn't make sense," I repeated, stepping away from the disarmed figure. "Balthazar, stop toying with me. Stop these games. You are a dangerous, psychotic, and insane monster who tried to kill me. You took my unborn baby away from me and brought nothing but pain and misery into my life!"

Balthazar's expression contorted into genuine bafflement, his brows knitting together as if I had spoken in a language he didn't understand. "My lady, I would never hurt you. *I would die for you.* I am your faithful and loyal protector. I would never harm you. I don't know what baby you're talking about. You and your husband just wed a few months back."

His words hit me like a slap, the implication unraveling everything I thought I knew. The reality I clung to seemed to slip further out of reach, leaving only a hollow void. My breathing quickened as fear threatened to consume me.

"Take me to my husband," I said, my fear sharpening into resolve. I needed answers, and only Roman could provide them—Roman was always the lighthouse in my stormy sea of doubts.

"First, I want to show you where Mathias is," Balthazar said. "So you believe me."

His tone held a note of urgency that tugged at my trepidation, igniting the embers of dread that had settled in my chest.

Reluctantly, I followed him, each step heavy with foreboding. We went deeper into the castle's bowels, the air growing colder with every turn of the spiraling stone staircase. The echoes of our footsteps reverberated around us, mingling with the faint, rhythmic drip of water somewhere in the distance. My grip tightened on the banister, the chill of the iron biting into my skin.

The dungeon loomed before us, its entrance a gaping maw. It reminded me of the Hypogeum, its eerie aura steeped in history and death. Torches lined the walls, their flames flickering weakly against the oppressive darkness. The elongated shadows danced in a macabre waltz, painting the stone walls with the shapes of nightmares.

We came upon a cell, and there he was—Mathias shackled and barely a shadow of the man I once knew. His youthful face, unmarred by time, was a jarring contradiction to the grim surroundings of the dungeon. He looked like a ghost, his spirit fractured as the chains that bound him.

"What's going on?" I whispered, my voice trembling

under the weight of confusion. "Are you both playing some kind of twisted game?" Fear clawed at my chest, and I felt reality slipping through my fingers, unraveling far too quickly for me to catch.

Mathias lifted his head, his desperate eyes meeting mine. In the hollows of his gaze, I saw a man on the edge of madness—a predator caged but still dangerous.

"Well, well, well," he began, his voice rasping with a dry, mocking chuckle. "Look who's come to visit me... none other than Balthazar and the woman I was supposed to kill."

His words struck me like a blow, but his tone unnerved me. Usually composed and commanding, Mathias' voice cracked with something raw, almost unhinged. He let out another low chuckle, his eyes glinting with malice.

"You're a fool, Balthazar," he sneered, the chains rattling as he leaned forward. "Fighting for the wrong side. You and I —together, we could've been unstoppable—a formidable team."

Balthazar clenched his jaw, his fists clenched at his sides. His gaze never wavered from Mathias, his presence as steady and unyielding as a mountain.

"I would rather die with honor than fight alongside a traitor like you," Balthazar said, his voice steady and resolute. "I will always be loyal to Isabelle."

Isabelle. The name hit me like a cold gust of wind. *I used to be Isabelle.*

Mathias shook his head, his frustration rattling the chains that bound him. "One day, you'll regret this, Balthazar," he said, his voice tinged with venom. "And when you do, it will be too late."

Before I could process the gravity of their exchange, heavy footsteps echoed down the corridor, cutting through the tension like a blade. Roman emerged from the shadows, his figure materializing as if from the very walls themselves. He stopped short when he saw me, his brows knitting together in concern.

"Why are you out of your room? You should be resting," he said, reaching out as if to shepherd me back to safety.

"Resting?" I echoed, my heart pounding against my ribs. "Why is Balthazar not in prison? Why is Mathias in prison?"

"I don't know what you're talking about," he said slowly, as though trying to make sense of a puzzle with missing pieces.

In a rush of desperation, the words burst from me. "I just had a baby in the cave."

"No, my love, you didn't. You couldn't have. We just got married. I hope we're having a baby soon." His gaze searched mine as though willing my chaotic thoughts to align with his reality. "You must have hurt your head."

With a swift turn, Roman addressed Balthazar, his voice carrying the weight of command. "Balthazar, stay here and keep watch over Mathias. I need to tend to my wife."

The world tilted, my legs unsteady beneath me as my thoughts spiraled further into disarray. Roman's arm wrapped securely around my waist, grounding me as he guided me out of the suffocating darkness of the dungeon.

"Stay and rest," he said softly, settling me onto the plush bedding of our chamber. The room's opulence, with its gilded frames and flowing silk drapes, starkly contrasted with the grim cell I had just left. "I'll fetch the healer."

With a final worried glance, he disappeared, leaving me alone with the swirling chaos of my mind.

Soft footfalls preceded the entrance of Amara, the healer whose skills now seemed more crucial than ever.

"Amara!" I gasped, relief washing over me like a tide. "I'm so glad to see you again."

I watched in mute fascination as Amara's skilled hands moved over my body, her touch gentle yet precise as she conducted a trauma exam.

"Please tell me I'm not crazy," I murmured. "I don't know where I am or why everything is different than when I was last conscious."

Amara's gaze flicked toward the room's corners, her eyes scanning for unseen ears. Satisfied we were alone, she leaned in, her breath warm against the room's chill. The sharp, sterile scent of antiseptic on her hands mixed with the earthy tang of aged stone walls as she whispered, "You have a child in a different life. But here, you don't."

"Here?" My voice trembled, echoing slightly off the cold marble floors. Confusion twisted in my gut. "Where is *here*?"

She stood upright, her posture rigid. "I can't tell you. You must remember your past." Her eyes searched mine with an intensity that bordered on pain. "Remember Rome—when I was dying, I told you that you had a great destiny ahead of you? That time is now."

Fragments of cobblestone streets and whispered promises stirred at the edge of my memory, but they were fleeting, like smoke slipping through my fingers.

"A lot of people are trying to thwart you. You must find allies you can trust." Her voice was a low hiss. "Salvatore will do everything he can to keep you from remembering who you are. Right now, your greatest weakness is that you've forgotten the past. It gives him the upper hand."

I gripped the bedding. The weight of forgotten lifetimes bore down on me, threatening to splinter my resolve.

"We've come so far on this mission." Amara's hand settled on my shoulder with conviction. "It's time for you to remember and fulfill your destiny."

A vein throbbed at my temple as I pressed the heels of my

hands against my eyes, trying to coax forth images from the shadows of my mind. "I can't remember."

Amara's hand brushed against mine, her touch warm and grounding, tethering me to the present. "You're afraid of the truth," she said softly, her words carrying the weight of unspoken secrets. "You had a relationship with Malik. And Balthazar... he wasn't just anyone. He was your loyal protector."

Her words felt like pieces of a puzzle that refused to fit, their meaning just out of reach.

"Loyal protector," I whispered, the term alien and yet oddly familiar, as though it belonged to a story I had long forgotten.

"Indeed," Amara said, her gaze piercing, locking onto mine with an intensity that made me squirm. "I know it's hard to believe, especially after the pain he caused you. But you have to understand—you must remember. My main purpose in Rome was to bring you and Roman together. It wasn't easy. Now, we're too far in to lose you again."

Desperation clawed at my chest, my hands trembling as I reached for her. "Why can't you just tell me who I am?"

She shivered, wrapping her arms tightly around herself as though warding off an unseen chill that seeped through the castle stones. "That's part of the curse. You have to remember on your own."

"Amara, please," I pleaded, my voice breaking under the weight of my panic. "Help me. What do I do? How do I break through this fog?"

"I can't tell you; only you can remember." She leaned closer, her breath a whisper against my ear. "Trust Roman. Only Roman. You don't know who's telling the truth and who's lying. And Balthazar..." Her voice faltered. "He's lost too. He needs to find his way back."

"Roman..." His name was a lifeline, something solid amidst the quagmire of confusion.

"Once Balthazar and you remember who you are," Amara said, her voice so faint it was almost lost in the vastness of the chamber, "everything will change."

"Change how?" I questioned, but Amara only shook her head.

"Remember, Olivia," she said, stepping back into the shadows. "Before it's too late."

Amara's silhouette dissolved into the twilight, her presence lingering like an echo in the vastness of the chamber. Her final words struck like a hammer against the stone.

"You found the sun and moon daggers," she said, her voice carrying the weight of forgotten ages. "You have to remember the rest."

Her words hung in the air like a challenge, a key dangled just out of reach, waiting to unlock the prison of my mind. I grappled with fragmented images, shards of a life I couldn't imagine. The dagger... I could almost feel the cool metal in my grasp, the intricate handle, the perfect balance of the blade. But the rest—meaning and memories—remained obscured, shrouded in a fog I couldn't penetrate.

"Remember," Amara said, but her voice was fading, blending into the echoes of the grand hall.

I blinked, and the world shifted beneath me, time folding in on itself like an unseen tide. A gasp escaped my lips as I stumbled forward, the castle's grandeur dissolving into a room less opulent but rich with its history. Tapestries adorned the walls, their stories woven in vibrant threads, yet they offered no answers, only questions.

"Olivia!"

Roman's voice tethered me to the present, and I turned to see him by my bedside, his face drawn and tired, eyes rimmed with red but alight with something akin to joy. He was a disheveled shadow of the man I remembered, yet the sight of him was as refreshing as rain after drought.

"Roman?" My voice sounded distant, foreign.

As I struggled to make sense of my surroundings, my eyes slowly adjusting to the candlelit room, Roman threw himself at me, wrapping his arms around me with a fierce urgency. His embrace felt like home, a warm sanctuary after a long journey.

"I thought I'd lost you!" He pressed his lips against mine, pouring all his emotions and fears into the kiss.

His intensity took me aback, but my own emotions flooded to the surface. Tears fell from my eyes as I clung to him, grateful to be in his arms once again. We stayed locked in each other's embrace, our hearts beating in unison.

Roman pulled back, cupping my face, his eyes searching mine.

"We need to talk," he said, his voice breaking slightly. "I need to know what happened to you."

"I...I don't know." Disoriented, I tried to piece together the *hows* and *whys* of my state. "How long have I been unconscious?"

"Several days," he said. "You sipped water and slept. We were worried..."

"Days..." The word lingered on my lips, foreign and heavy. It intertwined with the fragmented images of dreams— or memories—that flickered just beyond my reach, stirred by Amara's cryptic words.

"Rest now," Roman said. "We'll find the answers together."

His assurance was a balm, and I clung to it, hoping we could piece together the puzzle of my identity and our entwined destinies.

A pang of discomfort clawed at my chest, a sharp reminder that reality was not just about memories and mysteries. The physiological evidence of motherhood made itself known in the bloated tenderness of my breasts, swollen with milk.

As I struggled to form a coherent thought, my eyes locked onto Roman's.

"I had the most bizarre dream," I said, my voice trembling with confusion and frustration. "It was about my past life… as Isabelle. She knew Mathias and Balthazar in the dream, but it didn't make any sense. I'm trying hard to remember, but something is blocking me—like a wall I can't get through."

The memories were fragments of glass scattered on the floor of my mind, glittering with importance yet impossible to piece together without bleeding for them. Despite the pain, I knew they held the key to understanding everything.

My breath hitched with the effort of thinking beyond the present moment, my mind straining against the weight of forgotten memories. "I need to speak with Malik and Balthazar."

Footsteps echoed in the hall. Malik appeared in the doorway. "Olivia, my darling. You have awoken."

Roman and I exchanged glances, his eyes conveying a silent message—trust in Malik's loyalty and discretion. I shared a trust, but I needed more than silent assurances. I needed answers.

"Malik, please," I said, my voice shaking. "I need you to tell me more about Isabelle and her connection to Balthazar and Mathias. She seemed to know them, and I had such a vivid dream, but the pieces refused to fit together. Please help me understand. Who was Isabelle? How did she know

Mathias and Balthazar? You've spoken of your attraction to her before—surely you know more."

A flicker of sadness and regret passed over Malik's face before he quickly masked it with a neutral expression.

"I'm sorry, my love, but I cannot help you," he said softly. "I've told you everything I know about our past—about Roman, about you—but your connection to Balthazar and Mathias is something you must uncover for yourself. It's not my story to tell. Forgive me, darling."

His words felt like a weight pressing down on my chest—the frustration of unanswered questions and unspoken truths clawing at me. I wanted to scream, to demand more, but before I could speak, Roman's hand gently squeezed mine, grounding me.

"Olivia, my love, you've been through so much already. Rest now. We will figure this out together—I promise."

Before I could protest, he stood and crossed the room. When he returned, he cradled a bundle in his arms, wrapped snugly in a blanket the color of dawn. Seeing the bundle stirred something maternal and primal within me—my baby.

"Look at her," Roman said softly, a note of wonder in his voice as he placed the infant in my arms. "She's our precious gem."

Her tiny face peeked out from the soft folds of the blanket, wisps of reddish hair framing her features like the faint glow of firelight. As her delicate eyelids fluttered open, revealing a pair of clear, piercing blue eyes that mirrored Roman's gaze, an overwhelming wave of love and wonder swept through me.

Together, we cooed over her, the sound of her soft breaths and the warmth of her tiny body grounding me in the present. A profound and fierce love surged through me, ancient yet immediate, as if I had carried this devotion across lifetimes.

Her rosy cheeks and bright eyes radiated an innocence illuminating the room, a beacon of joy amidst the shadows of uncertainty. She was more than just our child—she was a Timeborne, a gift beyond measure. I vowed then and there to protect her with every ounce of strength, to shield her from the darkness that loomed beyond these walls.

A bittersweet ache stirred deep within me as her tiny hand curled around my finger. The fragmented memories of past lives haunted the edges of my mind, whispering truths I couldn't yet grasp. Who was I, truly? What had I lost—and what was still waiting to be found? The questions pressed down like a heavy shroud, but I pushed them aside for now. Roman's steady presence by my side and the miracle of our daughter in my arms was enough to anchor me in this fleeting moment of peace.

Yet, even as I allowed myself to bask in their love, the turmoil inside me raged. The vivid and haunting dreams clawed at the corners of my consciousness, demanding answers I didn't yet have. And though I tried to stay in the present, a quiet voice whispered that this calm would not last —that the truth, once remembered, would change everything.

CHAPTER SEVENTEEN
OLIVIA

I restlessly roamed the expanse of my bedroom, my mind racing with fragments of haunting dreams. Each step I took on the cold marble floor echoed with the weight of my frustration. The lavish tapestries adorning the walls, meant to bring comfort, only deepened my sense of unease and disconnection. Despite the opulence surrounding me, peace felt like a distant memory.

The first dream lingered like a shadow, vivid and inescapable. I had been fleeing Salvatore's relentless pursuit, the twin blades heavy in my hands, their weight tethering me to a reality that felt just beyond my reach. The second dream jolted me awake in a grand, unfamiliar castle-like room—a world drenched in luxury that suffocated more than it comforted.

In the present, Roman stood nearby, cradling baby Luna. His laughter and soft coos directed at our daughter clashed with the storm inside me. Though my heart swelled with love for them both, my joy as a mother was tainted by the ever-present fear of the enemies lurking just beyond the edges of our fragile sanctuary. I smiled and nodded, doing my best to stay present for my husband and child, but the gnawing unease of my dreams refused to be silenced.

Roman and I had hidden the blades in a secret place deep in the woods beneath a well-placed boulder where even the shadows seemed unaware of their existence. They were our lifeline, perhaps the only leverage we had left, and we could not afford their discovery.

"Hand me the baby, would you please?" I asked softly. Roman gently placed baby Luna in my arms, her delicate form molding perfectly against my chest. Holding her close, I traced the elaborate frescoes on the bedroom ceiling with my eyes, their artistry starkly contrasting with the storm brewing in my mind.

It had been two weeks since I'd brought her into this world—a world riddled with shadows and deceit. My lips hummed a lullaby, but my thoughts were elsewhere, ensnared by the fragments of dreams that refused to let me rest.

In the hallway, I caught sight of my mother, her eyes locking onto mine with an urgency that made my stomach churn. Since uncovering the truth about her—the vile layers of deceit and manipulation hidden beneath her maternal facade—I had steered clear of her. Her presence was a storm cloud, dark and menacing, and I refused to stand in its path.

"Olivia, honey," she called out, her voice sickly sweet.

"Close the door, please," I murmured to Roman, avoiding her gaze. "And let's go outside. I need some air to clear my thoughts."

He nodded without hesitation, always my steadfast protector. As he placed himself between me and the woman who had birthed me but no longer held any claim to my trust, I felt a flicker of gratitude. We stepped through the French doors onto the balcony overlooking the lush gardens below.

The cool evening air kissed my skin, a temporary balm to

my frayed nerves. For a moment, amidst the soft rustling of leaves and the fragrant scent of roses, I imagined peace. But peace was fragile, and it had no place in a life built upon treachery and blood. Roman and I were an island of two in a sea of uncertainty, our vigilance the only shield against the tides of betrayal.

Behind us, the heavy creak of the bedroom door shattered the illusion of solitude. Malik entered, his presence a reminder that we were never truly alone, even in the quietest corners of Mathias' estate.

Roman placed a steadying hand on my back, guiding me and baby Luna back inside. I kept my gaze fixed on the window, the reflection of the garden my only anchor. I didn't want to speak to Malik. I didn't want to face anyone except Roman. Trust was a fragile thread, and mine had been severed too many times.

"Olivia, why have you been skulking in shadows, avoiding me?" Malik's voice broke through the silence, his words edged with hurt. "We're family. I miss our conversations."

Turning away from the window, where the last rays of daylight struggled to pierce the encroaching shadows, I met Malik's gaze.

"Family." The word tasted like ash on my tongue. "How can we speak of family when trust is such a fleeting ghost?"

Pain flashed across Malik's features.

"I know you found the moon dagger," he said quietly, moving closer but respectful of the space between us. "I know about Luna, about her being Timeborne. And Lazarus... I know you've met him."

My breath hitched, my eyebrows shooting up as I stared at him in bewilderment. "But... how?" I stammered. My thoughts raced, tangling in confusion. "No one is supposed to know about that," I added, my voice dropping to a near whisper.

Malik and Roman exchanged a look that seemed to carry unspoken words. "Roman told me while you were unconscious." He tamped the air with his hands. "Before you react, love, remember this—I have always been your ally and protector. I gave you my word before, and I'll give it again. I will *always* care for you, Roman, and Luna. I will protect all of you until my last breath."

He paused, letting his words sink into my paranoid brain.

"I understand why trust is hard for you, but I'm on your side. I may not be an angel, but trust isn't beyond us."

His sincerity tugged at something deep within me, loosening the knots of doubt strangling my heart. Despite the suspicions raging, I whispered, "I want to trust you, Malik."

"Then let's start with honesty," he said. "Ask me anything."

Inhaling a slow, steadying breath, I steeled my nerves and grasped onto the opportunity before it slipped away. "I've asked you before, and you refused to tell me. How is Isabelle connected to Mathias and Balthazar? I told you about my dream, where Isabelle seemed to know them. But you've stayed silent. Why? I have to know."

Malik's lips curved into a secretive smile as if amused by a private joke. "You are starting to remember, Olivia. Not completely, but it's there, somewhere in the depths of your mind."

"Then tell me how they're connected," I said, my frustration mounting.

He shook his head. "Some paths you must walk yourself to understand the journey. But I will say this—Balthazar wasn't always the monster we now know."

"Wasn't always evil?" I couldn't hide the skepticism in my voice.

"No," Malik said. "He was flawed, yes, but not inherently malevolent. He made grievous mistakes—trying to kill you, trying to burn you alive. Unforgivable acts. It was Mathias who made Balthazar the way he is, and Alina as well."

My heart raced with fear and curiosity. The web of our past was complex and dark, and I ached for clarity. I turned back to the window, needing space.

"Olivia?" Roman's voice pulled me back from the precipice of my thoughts, his hand warm on my shoulder.

I looked up at him, the worry in his eyes mirroring the turmoil within me.

"There are so many secrets around us," I said, shifting Luna to my other arm. "So much is coming to light. And speaking of my mother… There's something I overheard before Luna was born."

Roman's posture stiffened, his gaze sharpening like a blade ready for battle.

"What is it?" he asked quietly, aware that walls might harbor more than ornate tapestries.

"Mathias and my mother..." The words tasted bitter, and Luna stirred restlessly against me as if sensing the tension. "They spoke in hushed tones in the living room when I was heading to the kitchen."

In the corner of the room, Malik leaned against the doorframe, his presence nearly forgotten. A soft tut escaped him, a sound that seemed to carry skepticism and curiosity.

"They didn't see me," I said. "I heard them plotting—against us, Roman. They spoke of control, of power... and of treachery."

I shared the exact details of the conversation with him.

Roman's jaw clenched, his eyes darkening with the rising

storm of betrayal. "We knew we couldn't trust anyone, not truly, but to hear your mother is involved..."

"It's troubling but not surprising," Malik said. "Mathias has always been a master of games, and your mother is nothing short of evil."

"Or perhaps the other way around," Roman muttered.

Luna cooed softly, blissfully unaware of the tangled webs threatening to ensnare her future. Her tiny breaths filled the room with an innocence that felt almost fragile against the heavy tension pressing down on us.

"Either way," I said, tightening my hold on my daughter, "we need to be prepared. For Luna's sake."

Roman stood by the window, his silhouette framed by dusk's dim, fading light. The shadows cast by his figure stretched long across the room, a silent reflection of the storm brewing within him.

"Olivia," he said, returning to me. His eyes held a solemn depth as he reached for my hand. "Marcellious spoke of dark omens in his fevered state from the Belladonna. He raved about Lazarus coming to destroy Salvatore."

A chill slithered down my spine. It was one thing to suspect a threat, another to hear it spoken aloud with such certainty.

"We're in a lot of danger," I whispered, the truth settling over me like a shroud.

"I know. Lazarus—Gaius, as he once was to me—warned us in the caves. I've been vigilant ever since." His voice dropped, a note of something akin to fear lacing his usual confidence. "When Marcellious was lost to the Belladonna's grip and foretold of Lazarus' intent, Mathias gripped my arm so tightly it left marks. As if the very thought of Salvatore's destruction terrified him."

My heart pounded in my chest as I processed his words. If

Mathias had feared Lazarus, the threat would have been graver than we had realized.

"Then it's true. No one can be trusted." I glanced at Malik, who watched us with wary eyes. "Except for you, Malik."

"Exactly," Roman said. He stood resolute, a fortress against the uncertain storm brewing beyond these walls. "We stand alone, Olivia. The three of us. But we stand together."

A silent vow passed between us, unspoken yet as binding as the ancient spells that once wove destinies and bloodlines together. Whatever darkness loomed ahead, we would protect our family, our Luna. The room seemed to hold its breath as if acknowledging the weight of our commitment.

Outside, the fading dusk stretched long shadows across the ground, twisting them into shifting shapes that seemed to conspire in silence.

"What about Reyna?" I asked hesitantly, doubt creeping into my voice. "Can we truly trust her and Osman? Yes, they've helped us—Reyna during my contractions, Osman at the tavern—but they suddenly entered our lives. How can we be certain of their true intentions? Their true identities?"

The fear of betrayal lingered, its roots entwined with the memory of my mother's whispered conspiracy with Mathias. Their treachery had painted the world in shades of suspicion and unease.

"What if they're plotting against us too?" I continued, my doubts clouding every thread of thought.

Malik shifted uncomfortably. His eyes flickered with something inscrutable before returning to their usual stoic glint. I watched him closely, trying to decipher the secrets lurking beneath the surface.

"Olivia, my love," Roman said gently.

My attention snapped to Roman.

"I believe we can place our trust in Reyna and Osman," he said, his voice carrying a sense of conviction. "While you were unconscious, I carried you out of the cave. It was treacherous—Raul and his men had surrounded us. But Reyna… she dealt with them all, Olivia. Swiftly and with precision. She fought as though she were born for battle."

"No!" My voice rose in disbelief. "She looks so slight, so fragile. Like a bookworm. Angelic, even."

"Angel or not, she's far from being a mere bookworm," Roman replied firmly, a hint of respect edging his tone. "I asked her who taught her to fight, and she said it was her father."

"We don't know if she's telling the truth," I said. "She might be an ally, but we can't be sure. What if everyone is trying to kill us?"

Gently, I placed Luna in her crib, smoothing a hand over her tiny form before stepping back. The weight of exhaustion pressed against me, but I forced herself to focus on Roman.

"Don't get ahead of yourself, Olivia," Roman said. "Let's take this one day at a time. I'll tell Mathias that I intend to step away from the search for the blades, at least for now."

His gaze drifted to the crib where Luna lay peacefully asleep, her tiny chest rising and falling in rhythm. Oblivious to the chaos surrounding her existence, she seemed like a beacon of serenity amidst the storm.

"I'm a new father," he said, "and I don't want to leave your side or baby Luna's."

I looked into Roman's eyes, finding solace in their depths.

"Maybe you should go to the future, Olivia," Roman said. "You'd be safe there."

"Not without you, Roman. I would never leave you behind."

"Even if that were an option," Malik interjected, his tone

solemn, "you can't time travel. Not with Luna. She's Time-borne and the risks..."

A chill crept over my skin as I brushed my fingers against the smooth surface of the armoire.

"You're right, Malik," I muttered. "If we time travel, it could awaken her darkness. Only we three know of Luna's gift, which must stay that way."

My gaze drifted to the cradle. "But staying here isn't safe either. We can't keep hiding within these walls."

Malik leaned against the doorframe, arms crossed. "Then what do you propose?"

"Let's tell them we're taking a hiatus from searching for the blades," I said, facing him. "We need space to breathe, to plan our next move without prying eyes on us."

"Mathias will grow suspicious if the excavation team stops now. He's anxious to find the blades," Roman said, his brow furrowing.

"Obsessed is a better word," Malik said.

"Then we'll be careful with our words," I said, clasping my hands together to steady their trembling. "We'll make them believe it's a strategic retreat."

Malik nodded, though doubt flickered in his eyes.

"And what of Isabelle and Armand's connection to all this? Does Balthazar know who they are?" I asked, recalling the fragmented pieces of my dreams that tangled with reality.

"You will have to ask him yourself, Olivia," Malik replied, his voice steady but evasive.

"Then take me to see him." I stepped forward, determination setting my jaw. "I need answers, and if Balthazar has them—"

"No." Malik raised a hand to halt my advance. "It will be difficult to get answers from Balthazar. Mathias would never allow it. You know how closely he guards his secrets, especially those concerning Balthazar."

"Damn Mathias' rules!" I said, frustration boiling over. "How am I supposed to piece together my past when everyone keeps it out of reach?"

"Patience, Olivia," Malik said, his tone as calming as the cool touch of his hand on my shoulder. "There are other ways to uncover the truth that don't involve alerting Mathias to your intentions."

"Then we must find them before it's too late," I said. "We also need to find how to activate these daggers."

A sly smile tugged at the corner of Malik's lips as though he held some hidden knowledge. "The scholars in Anatolia are renowned for their expertise in ancient artifacts. Perhaps Osman could provide insights about the blades and their power. From there, a journey to Anatolia might be our next step."

His expression darkened, turning serious. "However, we can't ignore that Raul is imprisoned in the dungeon, and he claims to have alerted the Timehunter leader about our location. Traveling to Anatolia could be dangerous. But staying here isn't safe for you either, Olivia. With Mathias and Alina hunting for the blade, every moment here is a risk."

A sense of urgency built within me.

"We have to leave this place immediately," I said, my decision firm. "With the Timehunter society possibly after us and the constant threat from Mathias and Alina, staying here is no longer an option. And with Lee, Emily, and Marcellious leaving, we'll soon be completely alone in this house—vulnerable to all sorts of threats."

My heart raced as the dangers lurking within these human and supernatural walls came to mind.

"This house is crawling with monsters," I shivered.

"Patience," Malik said, his gaze never leaving mine. "We'll get you out of here in a few weeks. But we must concoct a solid story before we make our move."

"Stories won't protect us from betrayal," I said. "I'm angry that my mother is so evil, hiding secrets and truths out of reach. I despise her, Malik."

"Indeed," Malik said, his emerald eyes glinting thoughtfully. "Appearances can be deceiving, and allies are scarce. Trust must be earned, even among those who have proven themselves in battle."

"Then we'll watch and wait," I said, my resolve hardening. "We'll keep our friends close and our secrets closer."

"Agreed." Roman took my hand, the warmth of his touch a silent vow of solidarity.

A knock echoed through the heavy wooden door. Malik pulled it open, revealing Emily. She rushed toward me, arms outstretched, and enveloped me in a tight embrace.

As she released me, her words spilled out in a trembling rush. "I'm going to the future with Lee to heal Marcellious, and I'm scared."

I placed a reassuring hand on her shoulder, willing confidence into my voice despite the uncertainty of everything around us. "It's going to be okay," I said. "I'll miss you terribly, but it's for the best."

The weight of her impending absence settled in my chest like a heavy stone.

Emily hesitated. "Olivia, I'm hearing rumors that Marcellious and Reyna had an affair. I don't know what to think."

"From what little I know, Reyna holds her secrets close," I said. "She wouldn't break them. Strict values are her armor."

"Do you think that?" Emily said, clasping my hands.

"Yes, I do. Have peace in your heart when you travel to

the future. My father will be good to you, and I believe you'll find happiness beyond this madness. I hope to meet with you all soon."

"Promise me," she whispered.

"I promise," I said, my heart echoing the sentiment, even though promises felt easily shattered in our uncertain world.

As Emily exited the room, leaving behind the faintest trace of her perfume, a heavy foreboding settled over me, unshakable.

Osman stepped into the doorway with an air of defeat. His eyes, usually sharp as a hawk's, now carried a burden that seemed to pull down his broad shoulders.

"Still no sign of the missing blade," he said. "It's just as well that we don't have it."

I leaned against the wooden bedpost, the polished surface cool against my back, doing little to calm the fire within me. "Why do you say that?"

He sighed. "Because only the scholars of Anatolia can translate the dagger script. And the people of Anatolia? They are brutal and unforgiving. Extracting their secrets would be perilous."

The weight of his words pressed against my chest, but the need to understand the daggers overpowered any fear. Unlocking the past and safeguarding Luna was worth every risk.

Roman stepped beside me, his presence a reassuring warmth. His hand brushed against mine, grounding me.

"I think we can survive," he said, his determination slicing through the uncertainty. "Once we find the dagger, we will travel to Anatolia, learn how to decipher the blades, and destroy all the evil and danger around us."

His confidence bolstered my own. Together, we faced the road ahead—a path fraught with peril and the promise of answers. We could not allow fear to dictate our actions when so much was at stake.

But as his words settled in the air, a shadow passed over his face—brief but unmistakable. He glanced away as if sensing something I couldn't see. A chill crept up my spine, and I realized that the real battle had already begun long before we set foot on the path to Anatolia.

The danger wasn't just ahead of us—it was closing in faster than we could prepare for.

And then, in the silence that followed, a single thought pierced my mind—*We might already be too late.*

CHAPTER EIGHTEEN
OLIVIA

My body jolted upright, tangled in the silk sheets of my luxurious bedroom. Through misty eyes, I watched Emily dart back and forth in the hallway, her arms wrapped protectively around baby Leo as she checked and double-checked their meager belongings. Marcellious, still pale and fragile from the poison that had nearly claimed his life, staggered down the hallway past my door, each step an arduous task. Lee walked beside him, one hand gripping his arm to steady him.

"Olivia," Emily called out, her voice strained. "We're almost ready. It's time to say goodbye."

I nodded, swallowing the lump rising in my throat. She couldn't see me nod from where she stood, but I didn't trust myself to speak. The weight of the moment pressed heavily on my chest. How could I say goodbye to family when time itself was an unreliable force? Emily and Marcellious were stepping into the unknown, a future from which there was no guarantee of return.

"Be safe," I whispered, though my words felt inadequate against the magnitude of our reality.

Emily paused and offered me a smile that didn't quite reach her eyes. "We will."

I gazed down at Luna, my precious daughter, who lay sound asleep in my arms. Her tiny lips pursed and moved as if nursing the air. I couldn't help but run my fingers through her soft, silken curls that framed her angelic face. As I whispered my love for her, the candlelight danced across her delicate features, making her seem more ethereal than ever before. She was not just my child but a magical being capable of traveling through time. Every moment with her was a gift, and I cherished each with all my heart.

Lee appeared in the doorway, his jaw set with determination, though his eyes betrayed a hint of sadness. "We'll see each other again. This isn't goodbye."

I fought back tears and said, "I-I know."

But the reality was murky and uncertain.

The faint scent of beeswax and honey lingered in the air as Lee stepped into the dimly lit room, igniting a fragile sense of safety within me. Before I could form any words, Luna and I were wrapped in the warmth of his embrace. The rough texture of his cloak brushed against my skin, a contrast to the delicate softness of Luna's blanket, snugly wrapped around her tiny form.

"Olivia," he said, his voice a deep rumble that resonated in the quiet chamber. His battle-scarred hands, strong yet gentle, cupped Luna's small head as he leaned down to press a kiss to her forehead. "You are a strong and fearless warrior, and I've trained you well."

The weight of his trust anchored me to this moment.

"I wish I could tell you more," Lee said, his voice quieter now as his eyes darted toward the walls with a warrior's caution. "But the walls have ears. You should uncover the past alone—with Roman by your side."

His words struck a chord deep within me, sparking a surge of determination. The shadows of uncertainty had ruled my life for too long. It was time to face the truth, to step into the light that waited beyond the veils of secrecy.

"I think I have an idea about the secrets of the past, Lee," I said, my voice steady despite the storm of emotions whirling inside me.

Holding Luna closer, I let my love for her flow freely, wrapping around her like a protective cocoon.

"I love you so much, Little Moon," Lee whispered. "And I promise you and I will see each other soon."

The words were a vow, an unbreakable bond forged in the fires of our shared history.

Lee's expression softened. "I wish I could stay longer, Olivia, but Marcellious needs me. Malik and Roman will remain by your side to protect you and Luna."

Tears welled up in my eyes, blurring the steadfast figure before me. I blinked them back, not wanting to cloud this farewell with the salt of my sorrow. But they came nonetheless, slipping free to trace paths down my cheeks.

"You've always been the anchor in my chaos," I whispered, kissing his cheek.

His skin was warm beneath my lips, the fleeting touch brimming with the tenderness of our unspoken bond.

I wrapped my arms around him, holding on for an eternal second. In that embrace, I poured every ounce of gratitude and love I had for this man who had been more than a mentor —he was the compass that guided me through the darkest nights. "Stay safe," I murmured against his shoulder, knowing full well the perils that awaited us all beyond the safety of our walls. My heart clenched at the thought, but I pushed away the fear. Lee was as unyielding as the mountains, as relentless as the tide. He would return to us. He must.

With one last squeeze, I released him. I had been forged in the fires of his teachings, and for Luna, for all we held dear, I would not falter.

Emily entered the room.

"Olivia." Her voice was a choked sob as she closed the distance between us. She wrapped her arms around me and baby Luna, desperately trying to condense a lifetime of sisterhood into one heartfelt touch.

"Safe travels," I said, my lips trembling against her ear.

"Always," she breathed out, pulling back just enough to look into my eyes. "You, too."

I nodded, unable to trust my voice again.

Rosie, bright and small, scampered in, her feet pattering on the wooden floor, reminding us all that life persisted with an innocent vigor even in our darkest moments.

"Bye-bye, Emily," Rosie said with a lisp, wrapping her little arms around Emily's leg. Emily bent down to lift Rosie into a hug, her tears falling freely.

"Goodbye, brave little one," Lee said. He managed a weak smile for Rosie, who reached out to pat his cheek, her tender gesture threatening to unravel me completely.

"Tell Marcellious to feel better!" she said, her voice filled with hope and love.

Lee nodded, the emotions in his eyes threatening to spill over. He quickly wiped away the tears gathering in the corners of his eyes and whispered, "I will."

Their farewells were a montage of embraces and whispered promises, each a thread sewing the fabric of our bond tighter, even as they prepared to unravel it by stepping into a future unknown. And then, with a final glance laden with love and worry, they were gone, leaving the hallway outside my room hauntingly empty.

The settled silence was oppressive, a marked contrast to the flurry of activity moments before. A lump formed in my throat as I gently laid Luna down in her cradle. The soft rustle of her blanket and the sweet scent of her skin were small comforts in the vast emptiness of the estate.

I kissed her forehead. "Sweet dreams, my little moon."

Lying on the bed, I closed my eyes and let a few tears escape, rolling silently down my cheeks. Everything here was so complicated. Roman and I lived among monsters, and I couldn't shake the gnawing unease that haunted me. I felt unsafe —like a cornered animal pretending it had somewhere to run.

A heavy hand came to rest on my shoulder, and I turned to find Roman's solemn gaze upon me. His presence had always been a source of strength, but it only reminded us of what we all stood to lose.

"I need to check on the men in the caves," he said, his voice rough. "I'll take a horse and return as fast as possible."

The thought of being alone, even momentarily, sent a shiver down my spine. "Roman..."

He squeezed my shoulder. "You stay in your room. Rest with baby Luna. Malik will stay behind and watch over you."

The command was gentle yet firm, bearing the weight of a man who knew too much of danger.

Reluctance clawed at me, the urge to cling to him almost overwhelming. But I knew better than to argue when lives were at stake.

I nodded, taking a deep breath that did little to steady my nerves.

"Good girl," Roman said with a small, sad smile. "I promise I'll be back swiftly."

He leaned down, his breath warm against my skin, and pressed his lips to mine. The kiss was tender and full of longing, a silent promise that he would return. His lips moved softly against mine, urging me to open, and let him in. I moaned when his tongue slid inside. As our tongues danced together, our mouths molded perfectly as if they were made for each other. Time seemed to stand still as we lost ourselves in the heat of our embrace.

When he finally pulled away, his eyes glistened with unspoken emotion. My heart fluttered with both happiness and aching desire.

"Stay safe," he whispered.

He leaned down to kiss Luna's tiny head before leaving the room.

I watched his retreat, feeling the threads of my family unraveling with each step he took. His footsteps echoed down the long corridor toward the stairs.

Alone in the quiet of my room, with the shadows lengthening and the sounds of departure fading into silence, I prayed for the safety of those I loved, for Roman's swift return, and for the strength to face whatever darkness awaited us.

Night had fully settled, draping the room in darkness when the door creaked open. My mother entered without invitation, her silhouette rigid, an omen in itself.

"I don't want you in my room," I said, my voice steady despite the tremor of anger I fought to suppress.

"Listen," she snapped, her tone brittle, like thin ice cracking underfoot. "I'm your mother. Show me some respect. You've been too harsh to me, always pushing me away."

Her words clawed at the air between us, but I refused to flinch. How could I respect someone who felt like a coiled serpent in the shadows, waiting to strike? Every instinct in me screamed to push her away, to shield Luna from whatever poison she carried.

And yet, there was no escape. For Luna's sake, I had to stand my ground.

The room was barely lit by the flickering glow of a candle, its wavering light casting shifting shadows along the walls. Her presence made the air thick and stifling as if her essence was a miasma poisoning the space between us.

"Wow," I whispered, my voice hoarse but laced with disbelief and outrage. "After everything I've heard about you —trying to kill me—and you stand here, acting righteous? How can I show respect to a monster? A vicious, lying serpent?"

She tilted her head, feigning innocence with a practiced ease. "Why do you assume I'm a monster?"

A bitter laugh escaped my lips, a sound devoid of humor. "Cut the bullshit, Mom. We're adults. Face me like a woman." My fists clenched at my sides, knuckles whitening as I struggled to contain the storm within. "You've always wanted to get rid of me. I heard the conversation with Mathias—how you questioned him about me seeing snakes and talking with Lazarus. You want to dismember us one by one."

I stepped closer, my gaze never wavering, even as her eyes flickered with something dark and unreadable. "You destroyed Marcellious. You poisoned Balthazar against us all. You're a monster. A poisonous bitch."

Every word was a dagger, each syllable laced with venom drawn from years of pent-up anger and betrayal.

"The only reason you've returned is that you want the blades." My voice dropped to a whisper, sharp and cutting.

"But let me tell you something—you'll never have them. Not ever."

The silence followed was a battlefield, tense and crackling with unspoken threats.

My mother's posture shifted, shoulders squaring like bracing against an unseen gale. The facade of maternal concern melted away, leaving a cold, hard visage that seemed alien to our room.

"You know what? I'm done with pretenses," she spat.

I stared at her unflinchingly, my heart hammering against my ribcage.

"I *am* a monster, and I'm tired of hiding it," she said. "I know you found the blade. Lazarus told you to return to the cave and retrieve the moon dagger. You're hiding it somewhere."

She took a deliberate step closer, her presence casting a chilling shadow over the cradle where Luna lay.

"If you want your precious little daughter alive, you'll give me the blade."

Her words snapped something inside me. My hand flew out, connecting with her cheek in a resounding slap that echoed through the room.

"I swear to God, if you so much as lay a finger on my child, I will rip out your goddamn heart and feed it to you." Veins bulged in my neck, and my eyes blazed with fury. "Get away from me before I make good on that promise."

The door swung open with a sudden force, revealing Mathias. His dark eyes swept over the scene, his expression twisting into a mask of feigned disbelief. "How dare you harm my daughter. Where's the respect for your mother?"

"Stop with the act, *grandpa*." My words cut straight to the heart of the matter. "I know your true colors and intentions, Mathias. You're a monster pretending to be this honorable and hospitable host when, in reality, you can't wait to kill me."

I was acutely aware of the danger I was courting by provoking Mathias and my mother. They were dark, dangerous, and unpredictable beings. Yet, something deep within me —perhaps pride, perhaps defiance—compelled me to press further, to push them toward the breaking point. It was a toxic cycle, one I couldn't seem to escape.

It was a declaration, not just to him but to myself, a reminder of the reality I faced.

Mathias' lips curled into a cruel smirk as he stepped fully into the room, shutting the door behind him with an ominous finality. The heavy walnut panel clicked into place, sealing us in. It felt like a tomb, and I knew there would be no easy way out of the looming confrontation.

"What can I say?" Mathias drawled, leaning casually against the doorframe. His shadow stretched long across the dimly lit room, cloaking us in an oppressive darkness. "Your mother and I were cut from the same cloth. Like father, like daughter."

His voice raised the fine hairs at the back of my neck. The air seemed to thicken with tension.

I squared my shoulders, trying to steady my trembling hands.

"So you admit that you're a ruthless monster?" I asked though it was more of a challenge than a question. My heart was racing, but I couldn't let fear cripple me now.

"Yes," Mathias said, his tone clipped and laced with malice. His eyes gleamed with a sadistic glint that made the air feel heavier. "The facade is over. Now, my darling, it's time to make a decision. Hand over the Blade of Shadows, and I'll spare your pathetic life. And, as a token of my generosity, I'll even gift you my grand estate before we part ways. It's that simple... unless, of course, you'd prefer to see just how far my sadistic tendencies can go."

I met his gaze, defiant despite the dread twisting like a vice in my stomach.

"I don't have the blade," I lied. "The men are still looking for the moon dagger in the cave."

"You're lying." His voice was like a steel trap. "I know you have the blade, and those men in the cave are just pawns in your little game."

My heart pounded as I stood my ground. "I don't have it."

He scoffed, extending his hand, palm up, as if demanding tribute. "Don't waste my time with your lies. Hand over the moon dagger now."

"Even if I did have the dagger, giving it to you would be a death sentence." Venom dripped from my words as I stared him down. "You'd kill me without hesitation...just like you killed everything else between us."

Mathias' expression darkened, the thin veneer of civility crumbling away like ash in the wind. As he stepped toward me, his slow, deliberate movements rang out like the ominous drumbeat of an execution march. With each step, he loomed larger, an unstoppable predator closing in on his prey.

His voice lowered, each word rolling out like a lethal promise. "I've reached my breaking point. There will be no limits to the cruel things I can do to you and your precious little daughter."

The air around us felt electrified, the weight of his threat coiling tightly around my chest like a snake ready to strike. I stood frozen, every instinct screaming to run, but my legs refused to move. I couldn't show weakness—not now, not ever.

His voice dropped to a menacing whisper. "I don't want to take your family away from you like I did before."

My breath hitched, the suffocating weight of his words pressing heavily against my resolve. This man, this monster, had already destroyed so much. He could destroy everything I held dear with a single move. But I couldn't let him win. Not again.

A realization slammed into me like a freight train, rattling my very being.

"You..." I gasped, my voice trembling with fear and anger. "You were the one who killed Isabelle and Armand, weren't you?" The memories of that life were still vague, but I clung to fragments.

Mathias' posture stiffened before he erupted into a cackle that sent shivers down my spine.

"How clever you are," he said with vitriolic sweetness. "You figured me out. What's the point of keeping secrets anymore?"

I felt the blood drain from my face as he continued, his words like venom sinking deep into my soul.

"Yes, I killed your family in your past life," he admitted with cruel satisfaction. "I killed you, Armand, your children —all but Rosie." His voice was a serrated blade, slicing through the fragile threads of my hope.

A sob caught in my throat, raw and aching. "So, it's true —you sent the Timehunters after us."

"Indeed," Mathias confirmed, his laugh reverberating in the room, a sound more terrifying than any scream. "And it doesn't end there. I killed Balthazar's family, too. His wife, his children—they all met their end by my hand. It was my actions that broke him, that turned him into the monster you despise. I created him."

I staggered back, the weight of his revelations threatening to crush me.

"As for you," he said, leaning in closer, his breath hot and foul, "I've resisted the urge to kill you so many times in this life. Do you know why? Because I needed you. I needed you to recall the location of that cursed weapon from your previous existence. But now that you have it—and refuse to give it to me—I'll make sure your death is slow and agonizing."

He stepped even closer, his eyes dark and void of humanity. "Last time, I killed you too quickly. It was a mistake, and I had to wait for you to be reborn. This time, there will be no mercy. Unless, of course, you wish to fight me. But you won't win, Olivia. You'll never win."

My mother stood motionless in the shadows, her silence more haunting than anything Mathias could say. Her betrayal and complicity felt like a blade twisting in my gut.

Mathias went on. "I won't allow you to take what's mine —not this time. It ends now, once the dagger is in my hands."

"Did you follow me to Rome?" My voice broke, a mix of anger and despair giving it an edge.

A twisted smile curled his lips. "Of course I did. I sent the darkness after you. I sent Dahlia. You thought it was Balthazar, didn't you?"

A gasp escaped me, the horrifying truth settling like ice in my veins.

"And Amara, too," he added casually, though her name carried no weight. "I had her killed."

The room spun. Each revelation was a hammer blow, each word a nail in the coffin of the life I thought I knew. Stunned by his confessions, I clung to the only certainty I had left— the steady warmth of my daughter slumbering peacefully in her cradle, blissfully unaware of the monsters surrounding her.

A soft whimper escaped Luna's lips as I lifted her.

Cradling her close to my chest, I edged toward the door, desperate to escape this madness.

Mathias stepped into my path.

"Where do you think you're going?" he growled, leaning in close until his hot breath fogged my face. "You think you can just walk away without giving me what I want?"

His fingers dug into my arm like sharp blades, drawing blood as he squeezed tighter. "You will tell me where the daggers are, Olivia," he growled, his eyes blazing with a dangerous obsession. "*Now.*"

I struggled against his hold, shielding my crying baby as best I could. But his fingers tightened with unrelenting force, and I felt the sharp press of a blade at my neck, its cold edge threatening to draw more blood. My vision blurred as panic surged through me. Mathias was willing to kill me to get what he wanted.

I glanced at my mother lurking in the shadows, her face in a hard line.

"We need to apply more pressure to get her to talk," she hissed, stepping forward. "Move aside, Father. Let's see how she deals with this." She reached for a candle from the dresser, the flickering flame casting ominous shadows across her features. Without hesitation, she thrust the flame against the heavy drapes.

"Stop it!" I screamed as the fabric caught fire, flames licking upward hungrily. "What are you trying to do?"

"That was your last chance, honey," my mother sneered, her gaze locking on mine as the room filled with smoke. "No one's coming to save you. The household won't wake— they're all sedated. Now, tell me where the blade is."

The air thickened with suffocating heat. The room closed in around me.

"I swear, I do not have the blade," I said, my grip tightening around my newborn daughter.

"You would sacrifice your flesh and blood rather than reveal the whereabouts of the Blade of Shadows?" My mother's eyes flashed with wild, primal hunger. "Give us the blades. We'll vanish. You'll be free of us and never see us again."

Overwhelmed by the crackling sounds of the spreading fire and the stifling heat, I repeated desperately, "I don't have the blades!"

The fire spread rapidly, consuming the gilded wallpaper. Sparks ignited the rug, flames leaping higher.

Mathias and my mother blocked the exit, shielding their noses and mouths with their arms.

Tears streamed down my face, mingling with the sweat dripping from my forehead. I coughed violently, the acrid smoke invading my lungs. Luna's cries pierced the air, high and terrified, and I clutched her closer, trying to shield her from the inferno.

"Please," I said, my voice barely audible over the crackle of the flames that danced closer with every passing second. "I want to stay alive. I don't have the moon dagger."

If my life was ending, I at least wanted answers. Answers to the conversation I had overheard between Mathias and my mother. Answers to the confusion swirling around who my mother was.

"All those memories I have of you and the journal you wrote...they were all lies, weren't they?"

"Yes, Olivia," she said with chilling finality, her tone as cold as the fire was hot. "That journal was fabricated to lead Balthazar astray and make you believe I was leaving an abusive relationship. But the truth is, I've been the true villain all along."

She stepped closer, her eyes burning with malice. "And now, you will suffer and die in this room with your daughter. Unless..." She leaned in, her voice a venomous whisper. "You tell us where the dagger is."

Weakness seeped into my limbs, my arms trembling as they clutched Luna to my chest. The heat was unbearable, and Luna's screams pierced through the thick smoke, drilling into my skull and pushing me to the edge of reason. I could feel my resolve crumbling, the secret threatening to spill from my lips. I wanted to protect my daughter. I had to protect Luna.

"Fine," I choked out, the word blistering against the suffocating air. "I'll tell you—"

Before another syllable could escape, an inky blackness surged into the room, swirling with tendrils of dark energy. It slithered through the smog like a living, breathing force, cocooning around me and Luna. The oppressive heat vanished as the shadowy mass pushed back the flames, carving an eerie stillness into the chaos.

A woman's voice, achingly familiar, filled the space.

"Miss me?" she taunted my mother.

My mother glared at the woman. "Zara?"

"It's been a long time," Zara purred. "Give Salvatore my regards."

The presence of the energy ball and the sudden interruption felt surreal, a momentary respite from the hellish reality around me yet charged with a new kind of danger.

Then, everything went dark. This mysterious Zara woman was gone, and so was I.

CHAPTER NINETEEN

ROMAN

As I tightened the final strap on my horse's saddle, the moon climbed higher into the night, casting a cool, silver glow over Mathias' estate. Soon, our friends would harness its lunar influence to traverse into the future. Silently, I wished them safe passage.

The leather creaked under my hurried grip, a protest against my urgency. Time, however, was a luxury I couldn't afford. A shadow stirred in the periphery, gradually solidifying into Lee, his strides purposeful and heavy with intent.

"We're heading to the caves," he called out, his voice tinged with caution that mirrored my unease. "I want to be away from this place before we time travel. I don't trust the vipers inside to let us leave unscathed."

I nodded, securing the saddlebag with a sharp tug. "I'm heading to the caves, but I must move swiftly. I'm afraid I won't join you as you plod along with the wagon."

I glanced toward the darkened windows of the estate, feeling the weight of unseen eyes upon us. "But Lee…" My voice caught in my throat, emotion overflowing and making speaking difficult.

"What?" Lee's eyes searched mine, concern etched in his features.

I took a deep breath, trying to steady myself. "Safe travels," I finally managed to say.

Lee's face softened, his usual tough demeanor giving way to a gentler expression. Our gazes locked as we shared a moment of understanding and appreciation for each other. "You, too, my friend. Stay safe," he replied.

We embraced, the weight of our impending separation heavy on our hearts. Tears threatened to spill from my eyes as we pulled apart, and I could see that Lee was also fighting back emotion. Our friendship had never been more evident than in this tender embrace.

"What will you do with the wagon when you time travel?" I asked, genuinely curious about his plans for the cumbersome vehicle.

"The men in the caves can use it," Lee replied with a dismissive wave. "Mathias insisted they have another means of transportation. They won't notice our departure—we'll leave outside the caverns. They're used to us coming and going."

"Right," I murmured, my mind already leaping ahead to the tasks awaiting me.

Together, we walked out into the open yard bathed in silver moonlight, the gravel crunching beneath our boots. I led my horse by the reins, her breath visible in the chill night air as Lee kept pace beside me. Reaching the wagon, I peered into its shadowed interior, where Marcellious lay in a fragile state, pallor painting his once robust features. Emily beside him, cradling their baby, her eyes reflecting the fear and hope that battled within her.

"Marcellious," I said softly, climbing into the back of the wagon.

My brother's eyelids fluttered, revealing the glassy sheen of pain beneath. Crouching beside him, I took his hand, its coolness sending a shiver up my spine.

"I will miss you," I whispered, the words catching in my throat. "I'm sorry I wasn't here for you. I was too consumed with caring for and protecting my wife. Lee will take care of you in the future."

A tear slipped down my cheek as I pressed my brother's hand, carving a warm path through the grime of the day's worries. I hoped against hope that the journey ahead would grant him the medical attention he needed, and that the future would be kinder than the past.

"Miss Emily," I said, acknowledging her respectfully. "Safe passage. Be good to your man."

Emily sniffled quietly in response.

With one last look at the faces that had become an important part of my world, I stepped away from the wagon. My horse nickered, sensing the urgency of our departure, and together, we set off into the night—toward the unknown that awaited us at the caves.

As I galloped toward the caves, the steady rhythm of hooves pounding against the earth mirrored the chaos in my mind. The moon's pale light spilled over the path, guiding me through the darkness.

The men toiled relentlessly in the damp, musty air inside the caves. Their frustrated grunts and muffled curses echoed off the stone walls as they chased shadows, following leads I had intentionally misdirected. They would never find what they sought. The elusive moon dagger was already ours, hidden where no prying eyes or greedy hands could reach it.

The cave walls rose around us like silent sentinels, their rough, glistening surfaces seeming to hold their breath, waiting for a discovery that would never come. I gave the workers their final instructions; my voice was calm yet resonant against the oppressive quiet. Sweat streaked their faces, their dedication evident in every weary movement. I offered them my thanks, expressing gratitude for their unwavering efforts. The silence, broken only by the occasional drip of water from stalactites, felt timeless as if the cave existed outside the bounds of the world above.

Leaving the dimly lit caverns behind, I strode toward the entrance, eager to reunite with Olivia. But as I reached the hill leading back to the estate, the horizon burned with an ominous orange glow. Dread twisted in my gut.

Malik emerged at the crest of the hill, his silhouette framed by the fiery backdrop. He sat astride his steed, a dark figure against the flames.

"Malik! I told you to stay with Olivia!" I shouted, my voice thick with disapproval.

"I know, my brother," he called back, urgency lacing his tone. "I had to feed. I dispatched someone quickly into the woods and regained my strength. I'll ride back with you."

Before I could voice my frustration, my eyes locked onto the inferno consuming Mathias' estate. Flames licked hungrily at the sky, devouring the grand structure like a beast unleashed. Panic gripped me, my blood running ice-cold.

"My god—my wife, my baby!" I screamed, spurring my horse forward in frantic desperation.

"Rosie!" Malik's cry knifed through the air, tethered to a name that meant everything to him.

We charged toward the estate, the fire swelling into a monstrous inferno, devouring everything in its path. The horses screamed, sensing the danger, but we urged them forward, driving them to their limits until we reached the roaring blaze.

Dismounting in a flurry, we tied scarves around our

mouths, bracing ourselves for the smoke and cinders. The house was a living beast, its fiery jaws open wide, consuming everything I held dear. Without hesitation, we plunged into the part of the manor not yet claimed by the fire, my eyes scanning desperately, my heart pleading for a sign of life amidst the chaos.

"Olivia!" I screamed, my voice barely cutting through the crackling fury around us. The oppressive heat pressed down like a vice, every breath searing my lungs as if the air burned.

"Rosie!" Malik called out, his voice carrying the same desperation. He moved ahead of me with the grace of a predator, even amid destruction.

No answers came, only the relentless howl of the fire. There was no trace of Olivia's laughter, no sound of my baby's cries, no sign of Rosie's gentle presence—only silence and smoke.

We stumbled upon a horrific scene—bodies of maids, their uniforms charred, lives stolen too soon. Malik clenched his fists, his jaw tightening with grief and fury.

The house groaned and trembled, a behemoth in its death throes, ready to collapse and take its secrets to the ashes.

"Olivia!" I shouted again, my voice raw and ragged, a plea carved from the depths of my soul.

Malik pushed forward, room by room, relentless, his voice hoarse from calling Rosie's name repeatedly—a prayer, a demand, a cry.

But there was nothing. No one. Only fire, death, and the bitter taste of despair.

"Maybe they're in the dungeon," I said suddenly, the thought cutting through the suffocating smoke and grief.

Malik nodded, his eyes reflecting the frantic hope surging through us both. Together, we stumbled toward the stairwell leading down to the bowels of Mathias' estate. The heat began to abate as we descended, but the thick and suffocating darkness closed in around us.

The dungeon loomed before us, its iron gates ajar, gaping like the maw of a great beast. We swept inside, our steps hurried and hearts pounding.

Raul's lifeless body lay in gruesome disarray across the stone floor, his severed limbs scattered like discarded remnants of a broken man. Deep gashes carved through flesh and bone, his torso split open in grotesque butchery. But the most harrowing sight was the absence of his manhood—cut away with merciless precision—a final, humiliating punishment. Every jagged wound stood as a brutal testament to Balthazar's unrelenting savagery.

"Balthazar is gone," I choked out, the realization freezing the blood in my veins. He had vanished, leaving behind only destruction and death.

Malik's expression hardened. "We have to find the others."

We raced back upstairs, dread weighing heavily on every step. The house groaned and wailed around us, timbers snapping and splintering under the fiery onslaught.

Then, a faint cry pierced through the cacophony: "Help me! Someone, help me!"

The voice came from the library.

"Osman!"

As I approached the library, creaking wood and shattering glass filled the air. The heavy wooden door hung askew, barely clinging to its frame, one hinge broken. Through the gap, I saw Osman lying on the floor, his lower body pinned beneath a massive beam. His face twisted in pain, every attempt to move etched with pure agony.

"Roman..." His voice was weak. "I won't make it. Go! Protect your family. Protect my Reyna."

"No!" I dropped to my knees at his side, coughing as smoke clawed at my throat. My hands shook as I grasped the timber, desperate to lift it. But when I heaved, Osman screamed—a sound so raw and visceral it tore through the chaos around us.

"It's too late for me, Roman!" he rasped, his words final, a sentence I refused to accept.

"Damn it, Osman, I won't let you die!" My voice was fierce, defiant, a command hurled at the encroaching inevitability of death. I braced myself again, muscles straining against the weight, my world reduced to the task.

The fire roared closer, flames devouring the room with insatiable hunger. Smoke blurred my vision, but I refused to look away from Osman. His once strong, commanding voice had faded to a faint whisper, resignation shadowing his features. The light in his eyes flickered, a flame on the verge of extinction.

"I'm beyond saving," he gasped, blood bubbling at the corners of his lips. "The fire will consume me, and death's icy grip tightens around my heart. But you must flee this cursed place. Seek out Pasha Hassan in Anatolia. He holds the key to the blades' history... Only he can guide you on this perilous path."

His voice faded into a guttural rasp, each word laced with an urgency that demanded to be heeded.

The weight of his plea struck me harder than the sweltering heat enveloping us. "No, Osman, I won't let you die," I cried out, shielding my face from the encroaching flames with my arm.

"Roman, save yourself," he whispered, the light in his eyes dimming. "I am grateful for our time together. It was an honor to meet you." Though meant as solace, his words felt like knives against my soul. There was no honor in abandoning a man to die amidst the ruins of a demon's home.

Above us, the ceiling groaned ominously, a harbinger of imminent collapse. I hesitated, caught between the impossible's pull and the inevitable's weight. My survival instinct surged at that moment, overpowering my defiance of fate. I lunged backward as burning timbers crashed where I had been seconds before. The debris fell upon Osman, silencing his final cry in a devastating instant. For a moment, I stood frozen, staring at the motionless silhouette of a man who had fought until his last breath. The image seared into my mind, an indelible mark of guilt and sorrow. With a heavy heart, I turned away, each step weighted with the unbearable truth of what I was leaving behind.

"Olivia!" I called hoarsely, my voice frayed and raw. Panic clawed at my chest, relentless and savage, as the fear of losing her and our child consumed me. Room by room, I searched, but hope withered with each space, flickering like the final embers of a dying flame.

Up ahead, Malik emerged from the haze, a dark silhouette against the inferno's backdrop. His expression mirrored my own—a blend of desperation and unspoken terror.

Without words, we understood each other. We were kindred souls amidst the chaos, clinging to the fragile hope that those we loved had escaped the fire's merciless wrath.

"Help me find her!" I yelled, my voice cracking under the strain.

We navigated the smoldering maze together, shouting names swallowed by the roaring inferno. The foundation shuddered violently beneath us, a dire warning that the end was near. It was a choice between fleeing or perishing.

"Go!" Malik shouted, gripping my arm with a strength born of desperation.

We raced toward the exit, the fiery glow casting elongated shadows ahead of us as if even they sought escape. The ground trembled beneath our feet, and with a deafening roar, the house gave way, collapsing into a smoldering heap of ruin and ash.

We staggered to a safe distance, breathless and beaten, watching the once-grand estate crumble into nothingness. The air was thick with smoke, stinging our lungs and coating our mouths with the acrid taste of despair.

"Olivia," I whispered, the name breaking from my lips like a prayer. My heart clenched painfully. She was my world, my soul. And our baby—where were they in this hour of devastation?

Malik stood silently beside me, his eyes reflecting the sorrow deeply on my face. His presence was not a comfort but a shared acknowledgment of the grief and dread that clung to us like the smoke swirling in the night.

Ashes danced on the wind, cruel specters of what had been illuminated by the cold silver of the moon. The bitter stench of charred memories hung heavy in the air. Malik and I stood among the ruins, two helpless figures in a scene of unspeakable loss.

Silence reigned where life had once thrived. Balthazar had vanished into the chaos, leaving only betrayal in his wake. And Raul—his mangled, lifeless body—remained a grim testament to the horrors unleashed. The sight gnawed at my soul.

Malik's face mirrored my horror, etched with lines of grief, disbelief, and quiet rage.

"I don't know what to do." His voice sounded hollow against the backdrop of destruction. "How did this happen? Is it déjà vu?"

"What do you mean?" My words came out more as a

demand than a question, fueled by the adrenaline still coursing through my veins.

Malik's eyes, rimmed red and hollow, locked onto mine as we stood in the shadowed stillness of the abandoned farmhouse. The air between us felt thick, weighted with memories neither wanted to confront. His voice dropped to a whisper, raw with emotion. "Do you remember your past lives as Isabelle and Armand? The fire that destroyed everything?"

His voice cracked, splintered by the unbearable pain of centuries past.

A shiver of unease coiled through my body, tightening like a noose.

"I don't want to think about the past," I snapped, pushing away the unwelcome intrusion of lives long gone. "We must focus on finding Olivia, Reyna, Rosie, and Luna."

Even as the words left my lips, my heart sank, weighted by a sea of doubt swirling inside me. It was as if my resolve was a fragile ship battered by waves of uncertainty.

With every step, the world's weight pressed heavier on my shoulders. The ground beneath me was a graveyard of ash and ruin, the smoldering remnants of a monster's domain. The cold gnawed at my bones, though I wasn't sure if it was the chill of the air or the relentless grip of dread tightening its hold on me. I pushed forward, Olivia's name echoing like a desperate mantra in my mind. She and our baby had to be out there. Somewhere. Waiting for me. But with every passing moment, the fear inside me grew, gnawing at the fragile hope that kept me moving. *My dear Olivia... my little Luna... where are you?*

CHAPTER TWENTY

OLIVIA

I awoke to the soft nuzzling of horses and the sharp cries of baby Luna in my arms. The mingled scents of hay and ash filled my nostrils, the acrid sting an unrelenting reminder of the chaos we had barely escaped. My eyes fluttered open, struggling to adjust to the dim moonlight that filtered through the barn's wooden slats.

How did I get here?

Fragments of memory clawed at the edges of my consciousness—my mother and Mathias, their faces twisted into cruel masks, the very embodiment of betrayal. The pain of that moment resurfaced, sharp and suffocating.

"Shh, it's okay, little one," I murmured to Luna as her wails pierced the oppressive silence. Her tiny body trembled against mine, hungry and terrified. We were all coated in ash, grimy remnants of a nightmare that lingered. Nearby, Reyna huddled close, her face etched with exhaustion and despair. Beside her, Rosie clutched a ragged doll to her chest, clinging to the only comfort she could find in this hellish aftermath.

I tried to stitch together the fractured pieces of how we had ended up here in this fragile refuge. A woman... Zara.

Her name whispered in my mind like a fleeting shadow. She had pulled us from the flames, her presence elusive, more specter than savior. "This woman... she saved us," I mumbled, the words tumbling out as if saying them aloud would make it all more real. "But who is she? Why would she help?"

Panic began to swell in my chest, clawing its way up as names surfaced in a desperate litany. "Is Roman alive? Malik?"

Luna's cries crescendoed, drawing me back to the present. Her needs, simple and urgent, reminded me of my purpose. With trembling hands, I guided her to my breast, offering the only comfort I could. Slowly, her sobs quieted as she latched on, her tiny body relaxing in my arms. I held her close, my heart aching, torn between boundless love and paralyzing fear.

When Luna finally drifted into a peaceful sleep, her breaths soft and steady, I pushed myself upright. My limbs felt like lead, my head heavy with exhaustion and the weight of unanswered questions. But I couldn't stay still. I needed to move, see, and piece together the full scope of our nightmare.

As I staggered into the yard, the sight before me stole the breath from my lungs. Where a grand home had once stood, only a burnt husk remained. The blackened and skeletal ruins stood eerily against the pale light of dawn, a cruel echo of Costa's house... and Emily's. The fire had consumed them all, reducing everything to ashes and memories.

The devastation laid bare before me was a silent, damning testament to the monsters my mother and Mathias indeed were. They had tried to erase us, to wipe our existence from the fabric of this world. But they had failed. In my arms, I held the most precious part of our future. Luna, blissfully unaware of the ruin surrounding us, slept peacefully, her small, warm body anchoring me to a single purpose. I vowed to protect her from the horrors of our reality, no matter the cost.

Driven by a frantic need to find Roman, I searched the rubble of what was once our sanctuary. He had to be alive. I knew he had left before the fire started—but Malik… Malik might have stayed behind to protect me. I had no way of knowing. I clung to the hope that they had escaped. They had to.

Each step sent clouds of ash swirling around me, stinging my eyes and filling my mouth with the bitter taste of despair. My heart clenched at the silence, every hollow corner and lifeless space where hope should have existed.

"Roman?" My voice cracked, barely audible over the sound of my ragged breaths. I stumbled over a charred beam, the remnants of our haven now reduced to obstacles in a graveyard of memories. Once hidden and fortified by thick walls, the dungeon now lay open to the sky, its secrets spilling out like a fallen beast's entrails.

Descending the cracked stone steps, I braced myself against the cool dampness in the air below. Shadows danced across the broken walls, remnants of the fire's wrath.

Raul's lifeless body lay sprawled on the cold stone floor, his end written in the stillness of his form. The sight turned my stomach, but I forced myself to look, to take in every grim detail. There was no sign of Balthazar—he had escaped or been taken. The thought of him out there, free, sent a shiver of dread down my spine.

Anger and panic swelled within me, thick and suffocating like the smoke that still clung to the air.

"Everyone's dead," I whispered, my voice trembling with fury and heartbreak. My chest heaved, my heart hammering against my ribs. "I fucking hate my mother! She tried to kill me. She tried to kill my daughter."

Images of Mathias and my mother slipping away like shadows at dawn flickered in my mind, haunting and unshakable.

"Where's Osman?" Reyna asked, her voice brittle. "And Malik? Did he need to feed?"

Hope, fragile and tenuous, whispered that they might still be alive. I clung to it like a drowning man grasping for driftwood.

"Roman went to the caves..." I said, my words uncertain but clinging to the possibility. "I don't know where Malik is, but you could be right. Let's hope so."

The weight of loss and the oppressive silence became too much to bear. Turning away from the tomb-like dungeon, I sought the solace of open air. Outside, the sky stretched cruelly clear, a soft expanse of pale gold and lavender, the last traces of dawn giving way to daylight. Their tranquil light mocked the devastation below, an indifferent beauty against the backdrop of ruin.

Reyna stood beside me, her face a mirror of the destruction surrounding us. Rosie's small hand slipped into mine—a tiny, grounding presence in a world gone mad.

Then, through the haze of destruction, a flash of hope. Two figures emerged from the distance, running from the stables—Roman and Malik, alive. Relief surged through me, a burst of energy that drowned out the weight of despair. They had defied death, survived the inferno, and now sprinted toward us like salvation incarnate.

"Roman!" I shouted, my voice finding strength.

With Reyna and Rosie at my side, I ran toward them, toward the promise of reunion, toward the men who had refused to let destruction be the end of our story. Dust swirled around us as the distance between us closed. My heart thundered in my chest, my steps quickening with every beat.

Roman's figure sharpened through the haze until, finally, his arms were around me, pulling me close in a desperate embrace.

"Oh, my darling, you're safe," he breathed, his voice trembling with relief.

His kisses fell like soft raindrops on my forehead; he found baby Luna's peaceful face. Each word that followed wrapped around me like a lifeline in the aftermath of chaos.

"Both of you... I've been so worried," he murmured between kisses, his voice a low rumble, thick with emotion.

"My mother started the fire," I said, the words bitter and jagged on my tongue. "She locked me in my room. A woman saved me—someone I don't even know."

Roman's hold tightened, a growl rising from deep within him. Fury radiated off him, burning as hot as the smoldering ruins around us.

Nearby, Malik cradled Rosie, pressing his lips to her small face and head in tender, protective gestures. Though both bore the scars of our ordeal, their reunion was a quiet, poignant reminder of what we had managed to save amidst so much loss.

Reyna stood apart, her silhouette lonely against the backdrop of destruction. Her voice was barely a whisper but carried the crushing weight of dread. "Have you seen Osman?"

Roman's grip on me loosened as he turned to face her, his features shadowed with sorrow.

"I'm sorry, Reyna," he said, his voice low and heavy with finality. "Osman didn't make it. I tried to save him... but it was impossible."

Reyna's knees buckled beneath her, her face contorting in

a silent scream as she collapsed. Malik darted toward her, his arms outstretched just in time to catch her crumbling form. The sound that finally escaped her was raw and guttural, the keening wail of a soul torn apart, reverberating through the quiet devastation around us.

The ash beneath my feet seemed to whisper of betrayal and loss with every step as I moved closer to her. Reyna's silhouette was a broken shadow against the night, her pain an almost tangible weight pressing against the air.

"I'm so sorry. I'm so sorry," I murmured, resting a hand gently on her trembling shoulder. Her grief enveloped her like a suffocating shroud, an aura of despair that seemed to drain the very life from the air around us.

"It's all my fault," Reyna choked between heart-wrenching sobs. "I should never have brought him here."

"Reyna, there's nothing you could've done differently." The words felt hollow even as I said them. "I'm sorry you have lost him."

Her sorrow-filled eyes met mine briefly before looking away, the weight of her grief palpable.

"He was my best friend," she whispered. Malik hovered a few steps back, his towering presence a silent well of strength. His fierce and unwavering gaze rested on Reyna with a protectiveness that mirrored the resolve hardening in Roman's expression.

As if our collective grief summoned a shared purpose, Roman and Malik stepped closer, their postures radiating determination. Roman's sharp and unyielding voice cut through the stillness like a blade.

"We will protect you, Reyna," he vowed, his words brimming with fury. "And we will make Alina and Mathias pay for what they've done."

Reyna shook her head, wiping away the remnants of her

tears. A flicker of her old defiance returned, sparking in her eyes. "I should never have left Anatolia. I left my home to find the moon dagger... and look where it's brought me."

Malik's low and measured voice broke through the tension. "And where are Alina, Mathias, and Balthazar?" he muttered darkly. "I can't find them anywhere."

"Fare thee well, and may we never meet again," Reyna spat with a sudden venom that surprised us all. Her tears were gone, replaced by a blazing fire—not one of destruction but of unrelenting determination. "But they cannot hide from us forever."

I held Luna closer, steadying my breath as the weight of the conversation pressed against my chest.

"Mathias admitted to me," I began, my voice quivering with a mix of fear and resolve, "that he killed Armand and Isabelle in a fire. He destroyed Balthazar's family. He's a pure evil monster. Both he and my mother... they've dropped the facade. They've shown me their true faces."

Roman clenched his jaw with barely contained rage.

"Olivia," Malik said. "We must leave this place and travel to Anatolia. It's unsafe here, especially since you now possess both blades. We need to move, and we need to move now."

I nodded, absorbing the weight of his words, though sorrow still tethered me to the ruins of what we had lost. Reyna sat on the scorched earth, her spirit as fractured as the charred remains that surrounded us. I knelt beside her, rocking Luna gently in my arms.

"We must bury Osman," Reyna murmured, her tears falling unchecked, a river of grief that seemed unending.

"Reyna," Roman interjected softly, kneeling beside her, "he was crushed and burned in the fire. I don't want you to see him like that. We can honor him without..."

"Without what?" Reyna's voice cracked, eyes searching

Roman's face for answers none of us could provide. "Without seeing the remains?" she whispered, her pain raw and unfiltered.

Roman hesitated, choosing his words with care. "Without seeing him like that. We'll hold a ceremony. For Osman. To honor him."

Rosie, so small amidst the ruins, tugged at my skirt, her innocence a fragile light amid our devastation. She looked up at me, her wide, uncomprehending eyes brimming with questions.

"What do we do next?" she asked, her voice soft, her hope aching in its simplicity.

I glanced at Roman, his steady presence grounding me.

Taking a deep breath, I answered, "We will remember Osman as he lived, not as he died," I whispered, though the words felt as much for myself as they did for Rosie. "Then we gather our strength, and we move forward. Together."

As I shifted Luna in my arms, the air was thick with the lingering scent of char and sorrow. Roman's gaze found mine, a storm of resolve darkening his eyes.

"When Osman was dying," Roman began, his voice cutting through the oppressive stillness. "He told me we had to find a man named Pasha Hassan. Only he could help us decipher the ancient scriptures of the blades and bring their power back to life."

My heart clenched at the mention of a new quest. Even amidst the ashes of our despair, a flicker of hope kindled— fragile but alive.

"How do we find him?" I asked, the practicality of the task already weighing heavily on my mind.

Her face streaked with ash and tears, Reyna slowly pushed herself to her feet. Though emotion thickened her voice, determination cut through it like steel. "He lives in

Anatolia," she said, her resolve unshaken despite the grief hanging over her like a shadow.

"I understand that," I replied, my voice a soft murmur. "I have searched for people before, which can be difficult. And many times, they are dead or, if they are alive, they refuse to help."

"No, Pasha Hassan is alive and is one of the last scholars who knows the blades' history." Reyna's voice held a reverence that underscored the gravity of the man's knowledge.

"Then that's the next plan," Roman declared, his voice firm and resolute. "We head to Anatolia."

"It's dangerous," Reyna interjected, her gaze flickering with unease. The loss of Osman lingered in her eyes, but something else—something darker—shadowed her expression. "The most powerful Timehunter society resides there."

"I don't care," Roman replied, his jaw set with unyielding resolve. His eyes moved between Luna and me, then to Malik and Rosie, his family, and his responsibility. "We'll tell them we're explorers. A family. If that doesn't work, we'll say we're Timehunters from England."

Luna stirred in my arms, her tiny body shifting as she let out a soft sigh, blissfully unaware of the dangers her existence had already defied. My heart clenched as I glanced at her peaceful face, the fragility of her life sharpening my focus. We needed to decipher the ancient script on the sun and moon daggers—for her, for all of us.

Roman's plan settled over us like a beacon, lighting the way through the darkness surrounding us. Together, as a family, we would face the unknown.

CHAPTER TWENTY ONE

ALINA

My consciousness flickered like a dying flame as I came to, the stench of decay and damp stone assaulting my senses. A cold shiver ran down my spine, and I froze as something crawled across my skin. Panic surged as I jerked against the chains binding me to the wall, the clanking of metal echoing through the oppressive void. A tingling sensation spread, and I looked down in horror to see dozens of tiny white maggots swarming over my flesh. They writhed and squirmed, some creeping up my legs, others brushing against my face. Their slimy, relentless movements made bile rise in my throat as I frantically thrashed, trying to dislodge them.

I screamed a raw, throat-tearing sound that reverberated through the darkness, returning to me like a taunting echo.

"Where am I? Someone help me!" The words ripped from my lips, soaked in desperation.

"Alina, my daughter, are you alright?" Strained with pain and concern, the voice cut through the suffocating blackness. My father. Mathias. His presence was a cruel paradox—

comfort in the reminder that I wasn't alone but despair in knowing he was trapped in this waking nightmare.

"Where are you?" I croaked, twisting toward the direction of his voice, my vision swallowed by the impenetrable ink of our prison.

"A dark place, my dear," he said, his tone muffled, struggling as if to break through some unseen barrier. Then his voice hardened, laced with bitter reproach. "You fucked up. You knew the plan. But you got impatient. You revealed yourself to Olivia. And in the heat of it all, I followed suit. Now, here we are, in Salvatore's torture chamber."

The words struck like a hammer, and I groaned at the weight of our shared fate. Salvatore. The darkest of the dark. The very father of shadows. What cruel horrors awaited us in his lair?

Guilt coiled in my gut, a knot heavier than the chains biting into my wrists. We had fallen into the snare we had so carefully laid for others, undone by my recklessness. My tempestuous impatience had shattered the delicate balance of our scheme, and now we were paying the price.

I clawed at my skin, desperate to rid myself of the writhing maggots that clung to me, their slimy forms a relentless reminder of my downfall. Revulsion churned in my stomach, threatening to overwhelm me, when an eerie light flickered to life. It cast long, grotesque shadows across the damp stone walls of the dungeon, distorting the space into something far more sinister.

Salvatore's silhouette filled the doorway, his presence as oppressive as the chains that held me. His wicked laugh—a mocking cackle—ricocheted off the walls, a sound that carried the promise of pain and despair with it.

"You fucking idiots," he snarled, his voice dripping with

contempt. "Everything we worked for—everything—went to shit in just a few months."

I shuddered, the cold chains rattling as I instinctively tried to pull away from him, wishing I could shrink into nothingness. His presence was a suffocating weight, and every step he took felt like it pressed that weight further into my chest.

"Why is it," Salvatore continued, pacing like a predator savoring the moment before it struck, "the moment I released you to your daughter, Mathias, you managed to screw everything up? I should have handled things myself."

His footsteps echoed menacingly as he turned to face my father, his tone darkening with each word. "Your job was simple—keep Olivia alive. Not scare her half to death. You were supposed to make her feel safe. Comforted. Trusting." He stopped, his piercing gaze boring into us both. "But what did you do? You scared the shit out of her and showed her exactly who you are—a goddamned villain."

His words struck like a razor, slicing through the fragile remnants of my resolve. The careful facade we had built over years of manipulation lay in ruins at our feet, destroyed by our hubris. What was once within our grasp now felt impossibly distant, Olivia's trust as unreachable as a star in the night sky.

"Olivia wasn't supposed to fear you," Salvatore hissed, venom dripping from every syllable. "She was supposed to find solace, safety, in your presence. But instead, you threatened her life and the life of her innocent child. You didn't even try to earn her trust. You forced her to see the truth about who you are. And now?" His voice dropped, cold and final. "There is no going back."

His tone was final; his words were a judgment without appeal.

As Salvatore's gaze shifted, I followed it to where my father, Mathias, was bound. Belladonna branches coiled tightly around him, their toxic embrace a grotesque mockery of tenderness. The flowers brushed against his cheeks, their deadly scent a taunting reminder of their lethality. My father's agony was etched deeply into his contorted features, each twist of pain a grim testament to Salvatore's cruel sense of justice.

I watched helplessly, swiping at the vermin crawling over my skin, their numbers seeming to multiply with each passing second.

Salvatore's voice sliced through the suffocating air again, sharp and cutting. "You let Malik see your true nature. I listened to your pleas and allowed you to reunite with your daughter, and you've done this with that chance. Now Malik knows you're a liar. He sees through your facade and knows the darkness you've tried to conceal."

Mathias' agony was palpable, yet he remained silent under Salvatore's condemnation. Hopelessness settled like a stone in my chest, but I couldn't tear my eyes away from the horror unfolding before me.

"I have been watching you both," Salvatore continued, his voice thick with anger, "observing as Olivia stumbled upon your conversation and overheard your sinister plans. Until you obtained both blades, your sole duty was to remain the gracious Count Montego, the doting grandfather who earned Olivia's trust. Instead, you allowed your wrath to boil over, terrifying Malik and shattering the fragile illusion you were supposed to uphold."

Salvatore's words cut deeply, each a scathing reminder of how completely we had failed.

"You should have made Olivia feel safe," he snarled, pacing like a predator in a cage. "You should have shown her a united front, made her believe that you and Alina were her allies, that you were on the right side of this war. Instead, you revealed your true colors, and now everything is in shambles."

He was right. We had cloaked ourselves in a pretense of kindness, weaving a facade of warmth and familial bonds. But beneath that carefully constructed lie lay a festering darkness we could no longer conceal. Now, it threatened to devour us completely.

"She felt something was not right about you, yet she would still have been an ally if you had done what I asked," Salvatore hissed. His words were a damning litany of our failures, each one a nail in our collective coffin.

"Now," he said, clasping his hands behind his back and fixing his malevolent gaze on me, "let's move on to the next question. Where the fuck is Balthazar?"

The question hung in the air, weighted and sharp, with the unspoken promise of more torment.

Mathias remained silent, his silence a testament to our shared ignorance. We didn't know. We were adrift, tangled in the web of our own making, with only the certainty of Salvatore's wrath to drag us deeper into the abyss.

The stench of decay clawed at my throat, choking any words that might have bought us time.

"We don't know," I gasped finally, my voice hoarse, each word scraping against my dry tongue. The taste of rot and fear mingled as I struggled to force the truth free. Maggots writhed at the corners of my eyes, mouth, and ears, their slimy bodies crawling across my skin. I clawed at my face in frantic desperation, smearing their remains in streaks across my flesh. "We went to the dungeon to retrieve him, but… he was gone."

Salvatore's roar erupted, filling the chamber with a sound that was more beast than man. It reverberated through the dank space, shaking more maggots from the ceiling loose.

"We had everything in play!" he thundered, his fury a living, breathing thing. The shadows seemed to swell and tremble, conspiring to amplify his wrath. "And you both ruined it!"

Desperation raked its way up my spine, and a fragile, feigned courage came with it.

"Forgive me, Salvatore!" I begged, my voice trembling, the words hollow even to my ears. "I promise—I'll fix it!"

Salvatore closed the distance between us, striking my cheek with the force of a thunderclap. The taste of iron flooded my mouth as his fist followed, slamming into my jaw. The pain was sharp, immediate—a jarring reminder of my reality. I was nothing more than an animal, perhaps always had been to him. My skin crawled, still alive with the remnants of the creatures that had clung to me upon waking. Now, my spirit squirmed under his gaze, equally repulsed by his touch and the weight of his contempt.

"I'm so sorry. I promise we'll make this right. Please, let us go," I begged, even as self-loathing coiled in my gut. My words felt like bile, and whatever respect I had once held for myself had long since been buried under centuries of servitude and sin.

"Pathetic," he spat, his disgust dripping from the single word as he turned from me and stalked toward Mathias. With each step he took, the belladonna branches constricting my father tightened further, slicing into his flesh like serpents coiling around their prey. The flowers and berries trembled, their movements eerily synchronized, like a death rattle heralding its victim's demise.

Mathias gasped for breath, each ragged exhale a testament to his suffering. His face was contorted in agony as if his very skull were in the grip of some invisible vice. His chest rose and fell in erratic, shallow bursts—a heart seizing under the weight of terror, not disease.

"We'll make it up to you. We'll regain Olivia's trust," he rasped, his words pushed out through clenched teeth.

Salvatore's laughter rang hollow, devoid of humor. "If my sons were older, I wouldn't have needed you."

His scorn was sharper than any blade, cutting deeper than my father's visible wounds.

"I promise to make it right," I said again, my voice barely a whisper, knowing the futility of my words. "We'll regain Olivia's trust."

"Nonsense," Salvatore snapped, leaning in so close that his breath seared my skin like venom. His eyes burned with cold determination. "You are done with Olivia. You've ruined that path for good."

He straightened, his commanding presence filling the room as he delivered our sentence. "You will find me the scrolls to reunite the blades. You will scour the far reaches of the earth to retrieve those scrolls before Olivia even has a chance to lay her hands on them."

I swallowed hard, my heart sinking under the weight of his words. Our fate was no longer our own.

"Here's what's going to happen," Salvatore continued, his tone chilling in its deliberate calmness. "You will find the ancient scrolls, or I will kill your son, Angelo. Then, I will cut you to pieces and throw you into my poisonous fire."

The threat hung in the air like a guillotine poised to strike. Failure would mean more than death—it would mean obliteration, a gruesome end too horrifying to comprehend fully.

Tears welled in my eyes, blurring the dim light of the chamber. The chains binding me clinked softly as I shifted, their cold, unyielding embrace a stark reminder of my captivity.

"Not my son," I choked out, my voice thick with anguish. The heartache constricted my throat, each word a struggle to force past the lump of despair lodged there. "How dare you stand there and threaten him?"

Salvatore's icy gaze bore into me, his voice as cutting as a blade. "Who saved your boy from Raul's twisted hands?" he demanded, his words dripping with venom. "Me. And yet you dare to question my rights? He has power now—power that *I* gave him. That makes him more mine than yours."

The casual cruelty in his tone was unbearable, each word stripping away the last shreds of my dignity. Anger flared within me, desperate and raw. It surged to the surface, burning away my fear for a fleeting moment.

"If you're so strong and powerful, why not go after Olivia yourself?" I spat, defiance lacing every word. "Why are we your pawns? I'm sick of being your puppet!"

Salvatore arched an eyebrow, a slow, cruel smile curving his lips. "Why do people have servants?" he said with disdain. "Because they are far more important than those who serve them." The weight of his contempt was suffocating, pressing down on me like a physical force. "You're so stupid," he added, his voice filled with derision. "You were good for one thing only—a quick fuck. Release. A fleeting spurt of pleasure, nothing more. Thank the gods, my sons came from nobility, unlike you."

A sob caught in my chest, but I forced it back down, refusing to give him the satisfaction. The sting of his words cut deep, but I clung to what little strength I had left.

"I thought there was love between us," I murmured, the lie bitter on my tongue. The words felt hollow even as I spoke them, an echo of a long-buried hope.

"Love?" Salvatore's laugh was a blade, scornful and cutting. "You're nothing but a whore."

The words struck like a slap to my already battered soul. A reckless fury rose within me, and before I could stop myself, I blurted out, "Maybe Lazarus is a stronger and more powerful Shadow Lord than you. Maybe you're just scrambling in his shadows, desperate to prove your worth."

The air grew heavy and thick with an oppressive menace. Salvatore's hand moved in a lazy wave, and suddenly, serpents materialized on the ground. They slithered toward me, their movements deliberate and predatory. Cold scales scraped against my skin as they coiled around my limbs, their intimacy sickening and terrifying. I clenched my jaw, trying to suppress the scream clawing its way up my throat.

"Stop, Alina!" Mathias' voice broke through, strained and pleading. "Don't provoke him!"

"Provoked?" Salvatore's eyes darkened, the storm within them threatening to break. "You think I'm merely provoked?" His voice dropped, ice lacing every word. "I should bring your son here now and slice him up while you watch."

Fear sliced through my bravado like a knife. I cowered, my reckless courage dissolving. "I'm so sorry, Salvatore," I stammered, trembling. "I made a mistake."

The maggots smeared across my skin began to dry, hardening into a grotesque mask that pulled my features into a distorted grimace. My humiliation was complete.

"Indeed, you did," Salvatore said, his voice as cold as the dungeon walls. "Had you not revealed yourself to your daughter, you'd be basking in luxury instead of rotting in this pit. Find the ancient scrolls, or your life—and your son's— are forfeit. She must not succeed. Correct?"

"Right," I whispered, the word tasting of ashes and defeat. "I'll find them."

Salvatore's eyes gleamed with a cruel light, his satisfaction unmistakable. He strode to the center of the room where a massive cauldron sat, its contents unnervingly still.

"You know how important this mission is," he said, echoing ominously off the damp walls. "We will stop at nothing until I possess those blades and rule the world with darkness and claim ultimate power—forever."

With a single gesture, he conjured water within the cauldron. The liquid swirled unnaturally, its surface rippling despite the still air. Salvatore's hand shot out, grasping my wrist in an iron grip. The chains tugged and tore against my raw skin as he pulled me forward. Without warning, a blade flashed, slicing across my palm. Blood welled up and dripped into the cauldron below.

I screamed as Salvatore's guttural chant filled the chamber, the ancient, unholy syllables resonating like a malevolent hymn. The water's surface shimmered and rippled, light and shadow weaving together to form an image.

Olivia.

Her form emerged slowly, like a delicate watercolor painting bleeding into life. Her auburn curls cascaded down her shoulders, her eyes bright with the same spark of mischief I remembered from her childhood. A faint, knowing smile played on her lips as though she held a secret she dared no one to uncover.

She traveled through unfamiliar lands with Roman, the baby cradled protectively in her arms. Malik, Reyna, and Rosie flanked her, their expressions a mixture of determination and unease. The backdrop of their journey shifted—a dense forest, a windswept plain, the ruins of an ancient stronghold.

Salvatore's finger grazed the water's surface, tracing Olivia's image with unsettling tenderness.

"You're so beautiful, my love," he murmured, his voice softer than I had ever heard.

A surge of jealousy roared through me, hot and venomous. He had never looked at me that way, never spoken to me with such reverence. His gaze on her cruelly reminded me of everything I had never been to him.

Snapping back to the present, Salvatore's expression hardened.

"I need a darker minion," he mused aloud, his voice filled with quiet disdain. "You two have been useless. Balthazar would have been perfect for this," he added, almost as if speaking to himself. "He's consumed by revenge."

Mathias' chains rattled violently as he lunged forward, the slender belladonna branches constricting his arms and torso straining against his movements. His voice broke through the tension, desperate and raw.

"No! I can do the work," he pleaded, his words echoing through the chamber like a prayer begging to be answered.

"Quiet!" Salvatore snarled, turning on him with a dangerous glint in his eyes. "I know you can, Mathias. But remember this—Balthazar is nothing now. He doesn't have his memories. I returned those to *you*." His words were a blade, cold and cutting. "He remains lost, trapped within the fragments of his mind."

"Salvatore, my lord, listen," I interjected, struggling to keep the tremor from my voice. My chains rattled faintly as I shifted, trying to steady myself. "Mathias and I will find the scrolls. We'll outpace them all. We'll succeed."

"Will you now?" Salvatore's dark eyes bore into mine, heavy with scrutiny and disdain. The weight of his gaze pressed down on me like a smothering shroud. "If you don't, Alina," he said, his voice dropping to a venomous whisper, "I will slaughter everyone you hold dear. And I'll come for you when you're alone in your grief."

The threat hung in the air, sharp and suffocating. Though spoken softly, it roared louder than any shout, each syllable reverberating through the chamber with chilling finality.

"Understood," I replied, the word barely escaping my lips. My voice was low, but within me, a silent vow flared to life—I would endure for my son. For Angelo. For the flicker of hope that stubbornly refused to be extinguished.

The cold stone beneath me leached the warmth from my body, a cruel reflection of the chill that seemed to permeate my soul. Desperation gripped me as my mind raced for any edge, any chance of survival.

"We need to find Lazarus' weak spot," I said, my voice steady despite the storm raging within me. "Does he have children?"

Salvatore sneered, his disdain palpable in the dimly lit chamber. "No. Once upon a time, he had a wife, Amara, and a daughter, Theadora. But I saw to their demise myself. They've been dead for centuries, by my orders. The only things Lazarus cares for in this forsaken world are Olivia and Roman."

I summoned what little resolve I had left, my voice trembling but determined. "I promise we will get what you want. We will find the scrolls."

"Of course you will." Salvatore's reply slithered through the air like a serpent coiling around its prey.

Pain erupted across my body as snakes materialized seemingly from the shadows, their scaly bodies slithering around my limbs. I cried out, my struggles futile as they coiled tighter with each frantic movement. Their crushing weight drove the air from my lungs.

"Silence!" Salvatore yelled.

Before I could fully comprehend the command, a cloud of wasps materialized from thin air, descending upon Mathias and me like a nightmare. The wasps crawled across my skin, their tiny stingers puncturing me repeatedly, injecting venom that burned like fire. My face, neck, and limbs swelled grotesquely with throbbing pain, each sting amplifying the agony.

They burrowed beneath my clothing, their stingers finding the most tender, vulnerable places. I writhed helplessly, unable to escape their relentless assault. Beside me, my father let out a guttural sound of pure agony as the wasps inflicted their torment on him as well.

Time blurred. I didn't know how long we endured the torture, the searing pain making seconds stretch into eternity. And then, as suddenly as they had appeared, the wasps vanished, leaving me drenched in sweat and gasping for breath. My skin pulsed with pain, every inch of me swollen and raw.

Salvatore turned his back on us, his cloak billowing dramatically as he strode toward the dungeon's heavy iron door. It creaked open, and three small figures stepped into the oppressive chamber.

"Come, my sons," Salvatore called, his tone chillingly calm.

The boys couldn't have been older than seven or eight, yet their eyes held a darkness that defied their youth—a reflection of their father's malevolence. They moved silently, their small forms eerily composed amidst the chaos.

"Did you see, children?" Salvatore asked, his voice calm but filled with menace. "This is how we treat those who defy us."

He gestured grandly toward Mathias and me, our broken, bloodied forms serving as a grim exhibit. The boys' gazes flicked to us, unblinking, their expressions devoid of pity or fear.

Satisfied with the lesson, Salvatore and his sons turned and departed, their footsteps echoing faintly down the stone corridor. The heavy door groaned shut behind them, leaving us alone in the suffocating silence of the dungeon. I sagged against my chains, my body trembling as I tried to gather what little strength I had left. My mind raced with dread, wondering what horrors awaited us next in this chamber of doom.

CHAPTER TWENTY TWO

OLIVIA

The rhythmic clop of horse hooves against the dirt road was a lullaby, one I wished could soothe away the tangled complexities of my life. Inside the carriage, I cradled Luna to my chest, adjusting the light blanket over her as she nursed. The warmth of her small body grounded me, but it was a stark contrast to the chilling truth that our journey was no serene family outing—it was a perilous quest to unravel the mysteries hidden within the dagger's hilt.

"Another kilometer or so, and we'll stop," Roman called back from his mount. His sharp eyes scanned the horizon, his vigilance an ever-present reminder of the dangers that stalked us. Malik rode beside him; his brow furrowed in concentration as his mind likely churned with strategies to keep us ahead of any unseen threat.

The carriage creaked with each dip in the uneven road, its wooden wheels spinning tirelessly. Roman had insisted on bringing it along, reasoning that its speed outmatched a wagon's plodding pace.

"You need to rest, love," he'd said gently when I'd

protested. His hands, firm yet tender, had settled on my shoulders, grounding me in his unyielding determination. "And Luna needs you well."

He had been right. The carriage offered me the privacy to nurse and the rare chance to stretch out my aching, weary body. Our belongings, bundled in modest packs, were tied securely to the top of the carriage—a testament to our effort to travel lightly and inconspicuously.

"We don't want to draw attention," Roman had explained as he fastened his pack to his saddle. "We'll stop at taverns, but we can't linger. We're in a time crunch. Mathias and Alina could already be hunting us. We don't know. We have to be swift, and we *must* find Pasha Hassan."

His words echoed in my mind with every passing kilometer. Swiftness was our ally, secrecy our shield. Yet, as Luna's tiny hand wrapped around my finger, a bittersweet ache settled in my chest. I longed for the life we'd been torn away from—a life filled with simple joys, untouched by the specter of danger that now shadowed every mile, every whisper of tomorrow.

Yet, here we were—Roman, Malik, Reyna, Rosie, baby Luna, and me—together in flight, bound by a cause greater than any individual desire. My body had regained its strength, but the lingering exhaustion remained, every jolt of the carriage a stark reminder of the trials I had endured. Yet my heart hammered with determination, an unyielding resolve to protect this makeshift family we'd become.

"Rest now," Roman said, his voice soft but firm. His eyes found mine in brief, tender glances that carried promises unspoken. "I've got you."

And in those fleeting moments, beneath the canopy of the vast sky, I believed him.

The weeks dragged on, each day blending into the next as

we pressed forward. The weight of our shared purpose tempered the monotony of the journey. I reached out to Reyna, trying to offer solace in her grief. Since losing Osman, she had withdrawn into herself, her pain an impenetrable barrier. Malik, too, sought to console her with gentle words and protective gestures. Yet, I could sense something deeper within him—a simmering desire to be closer to her, to use his strength to shield her from further heartache.

The carriage jostled over the uneven road, its wheels groaning in protest as Roman urged the horses to maintain their grueling pace. I shifted in my seat, trying to ease the persistent ache in my back. Strapped against my spine, the sun and moon daggers pressed into me, their jeweled hilts catching the light like fragments of captured twilight. Below them, the familiar weight of my time-traveling dagger and Glock hugged my thighs—a dual reassurance of my ability to defend and protect should the need arise.

Luna lay nestled against my chest, her tiny breaths warm and steady. At only six weeks old, she already bore the weight of a fugitive's life, her innocence a stark contrast to the dangers that surrounded us.

My thoughts drifted to Mathias—my grandfather turned evil adversary—and my mother, whose relentless desire to kill me twisted like a knife in my heart. Yet, what perplexed me most was the newfound absence of fear toward Balthazar. Where dread once loomed, a peculiar sense of tranquility had taken place. In the swirling chaos of our lives, perhaps the only clarity I could grasp was the singular focus of finding the scripture to awaken the blades.

As we emerged from the dense woods of France, the landscape unfolded into a breathtaking panorama. Vast farmlands stretched endlessly, their golden grains swaying in the gentle breeze. Lush vineyards and vegetable gardens scattered across the countryside, vibrant-green and deep-red bursts contrasting the blue horizon. Sheep, cattle, and goats grazed contentedly while diligent farmers toiled under the warm sun, their hands shaping the land with tireless devotion.

Along the road, groups of travelers trudged steadily, all heading in the same direction as us. Roman, as fluent in French as I was, approached one of the groups to inquire.

"Where are you headed?" he asked.

"We are making our way to Vézelay," a man replied, his weathered face alight with purpose. "It is a major stop on the pilgrimage route to Santiago de Compostela. We will pay homage to the Basilica of Saint Mary Magdalene. See it there?"

Following his outstretched arm, I caught sight of it—a majestic town perched on a hill, crowned by the towering silhouette of the Basilica. Its grandeur beckoned us closer, an unspoken invitation laced with the promise of discovery.

"*Merci,*" Roman said, tipping his head before urging his horse onward.

As we crested the hill, the scene before me stole my breath. The Basilica of Saint Mary Magdalene stood resplendent against the azure sky, its weathered stone walls radiating strength and faith. Sunlight spilled across the clay-tiled roof, painting the structure in warm, golden hues. The murmur of pilgrims and travelers drifted toward us on the breeze, their voices mingling with the rustle of leaves, creating a harmony that seemed to belong to another world entirely.

Beyond the Basilica, the dimly lit sign of a tavern swung in the evening breeze. The soles of my feet ached with every jostle of the carriage, and my back protested with sharp twinges. Every muscle in my body cried out for relief, for the sweet reprieve of a soft mattress and a warm blanket. Heavy with exhaustion, my eyes threatened to close, their weight greater than my resolve to push forward. The promise of rest became my only thought, far more enticing than any prayer or forgiveness the holy sanctuary could offer.

The tavern was tucked between two timber-framed houses, its creaking wooden sign illuminated by the glow of lantern light from its windows. The warm, golden light promised comfort and respite from the biting chill of the evening air.

When we dismounted, my arms instinctively tightened around Luna, her small weight grounding me amidst the weariness. Roman led the way, his shoulders squared and strong, carrying the silent burden of protecting us all. Behind him, Malik dismounted, his gaze lingering on Reyna with a tenderness he tried and failed to hide.

Pushing open the heavy door, we were greeted by a wave of heat and the mingling aromas of roasting meat, ale, and burning pine. The sound of lively chatter and the strumming of a bard's lute filled the air, a sharp contrast to the somber silence of the road. My stomach growled audibly, reminding me how long it had been since we'd eaten anything more substantial than dried bread and cheese. The tavern's low ceiling and exposed wooden beams gave it a cozy, intimate feel, and the flickering candles on the tables added to the inviting atmosphere. It felt like a sanctuary where the world's weight might be momentarily set aside.

"We need three rooms," Roman said to the tavern keeper, a plump woman with shrewd eyes squinted at us over her ledger.

"Three rooms?" she repeated, a smirk tugging at her lips. "What kind of place do you think this is? Pilgrims are every-where, seeking refuge for the night. I only have two rooms, and you'll have to share. *Comprenez-vous?*"

"*Oui,*" Roman replied with a curt nod. "I understand."

Malik shifted uncomfortably beside me, his eyes darting toward Reyna. The infatuation he felt for her was clear in every glance, every lingering moment where his attention strayed to her. She, however, met his gaze with wary distrust, her grief and guardedness forming an invisible barrier between them.

"I'll take the floor," Malik offered quickly, his voice steady despite the faint flush on his face.

Roman handled the arrangements with his usual calm resolve, though the tension in his jaw betrayed his frustration. Coins clinked against the wooden counter; a small fortune was exchanged for a chance at rest. He always seemed to carry the weight of our survival with unflappable grace, and I admired him for it.

"Thank you," he murmured, his voice low and steady, carrying the unspoken promise that he would bear the weight of our world—a world teetering on the brink of chaos.

As I followed him to our assigned quarters, Luna cradled in my arms; I wondered what the morning would bring. For now, we had shelter, and we had each other. That would have to be enough.

The room was modest, dimly lit by the flickering glow of a solitary candle. The walls, weathered and uneven, seemed to echo the weariness in my soul. Luna, my sweet anchor in the storm, stirred gently against me as I shrugged free of my heavy cloak. Roman set our belongings in the corner, his movements deliberate as he arranged the cloak into a makeshift nest. I carefully placed Luna onto the soft fabric, tucking the edges around her small form to shield her from the world's weight beyond these walls. My heart ached for the life we deserved—a life unmarked by fear, pursuit, and shadows that loomed too close.

"Olivia," Roman murmured, breaking into my reverie, "I ordered you a bath. I will give you a massage afterward."

His words were simple, yet they carried a tenderness that contradicted the steel we needed to survive these past weeks. His eyes, filled with quiet devotion, were a balm against the raw edges of my heart.

"Thank you," I whispered.

He nodded, the corners of his mouth lifting in the faintest of smiles, and slipped out to check on the bath.

Alone with my thoughts, I yearned for more than survival. I longed for his touch—not out of necessity, but as a reminder of life and love amidst the encroaching shadows.

"My love," Roman called softly from across the hall.

The sight that greeted me was a rare luxury. Steam rose from the surface of a large copper bath, swirling in lazy tendrils like fingers beckoning me closer. The warmth reached out, easing the ache in my weary muscles before I even stepped inside.

"Is it not custom for the men to bathe first in this era?" I teased, a weak attempt at humor as I approached the bath. "Women and children get the dirty water, don't they?"

Roman's lips curved into a wry smile. "Perhaps," he said.

"But we are not bound by time, my love. Social customs are for those who obey them—not us."

Our own rules and our own needs bound us.

"Of course, you come first. You and the baby are the most important things in the world," Roman murmured, his voice low and steady as his warm hands reached for me. Rough yet gentle, they were the hands of a man who had weathered countless storms, and I melted into his touch.

With practiced ease, he began unfastening the buttons of my woolen traveling overgrown, letting it slide to the ground in a soft heap around our feet. His familiar scent enveloped me, a heady mixture of pine and leather, washing over me like a soothing balm. It had been far too long since we had shared such moments, and I reveled in his hands gliding over my skin, grounding me in a world that so often threatened to tear us apart.

The woolen kirtle followed, its earthy tones and comforting texture slipping away, leaving only the cool air to brush against my skin. My linen chemise was the last barrier, and Roman removed it with deliberate care as if unwrapping a treasure he had long sought to claim. I felt an intoxicating mix of liberation and vulnerability with each layer shed. My senses heightened, every breath and movement becoming part of an intricate, intimate dance.

He untied the straps securing my blades with reverence, his fingers steady as they worked. It was as though he were peeling back the layers of our shared struggle to expose the woman beneath—the woman he cherished above all else.

"So beautiful, my love," he murmured, his voice deep and rich, like velvet draped over molten gold. His heated gaze roamed over me, igniting a warmth that spread from my cheeks down to my very core. My hands instinctively went to my stomach, still soft and bearing the marks of motherhood. A flicker of self-consciousness crept in, but before I could speak, he stepped closer, his voice a raw mixture of tenderness and desire.

"So fucking beautiful," he repeated, his words dripping with admiration and longing as if daring me to see myself as he did.

I pushed past my self-consciousness, allowing the tidal wave of desire to consume me. Every fiber of my being was deeply, madly in love with this man. His mere presence sent my heart racing and my hands trembling. I couldn't resist the pull toward him. This love was all-consuming, saturating every inch of my soul until nothing remained but the raw, aching need for his touch, his presence.

He kissed my jaw, neck, and collarbones while caressing my bare skin.

"We'll get to the connection we both ache for," he murmured, his voice thick with hunger and restraint. "But first, I need you to rest. Rejuvenate. Restore yourself—for me."

His words dripped with unspoken promises, and I obeyed, letting him guide me into the bath. The steaming water rose around me like a lover's embrace, licking at my skin, soothing every ache and stirring every nerve. For a fleeting moment, I closed my eyes and imagined a world where his touch wasn't fleeting—a life where every inch of my body was his to explore without fear or interruption.

The quiet clink of copper broke through the haze, drawing my gaze to him. Roman stood at the bath's edge, his powerful body backlit by firelight, the pitcher in his hands steaming with heat. His eyes darkened as they raked over me, and a slow smile curled his lips—predatory, possessive.

He tipped the pitcher, letting the water flow in a slow, deliberate cascade. Steam curled into the air like a seductive whisper, warming my skin.

"Let me," he said, his voice deep, commanding, yet impossibly tender.

I turned toward him, my body languid and exposed, and watched as he peeled away his clothes. Each piece dropped to the floor with a quiet thud, revealing inch after inch of flaw-less, bronzed muscle. Firelight kissed the ridges of his body, highlighting every line, every curve, every sinfully carved detail. My breath caught as my eyes roamed over him, lingering on the hard, thick length of him that stood proudly between his thighs, a testament to his arousal.

"Roman," I breathed, the sound trembling with desire.

"You're breathtaking," he murmured, stepping into the water with a grace that belied his size. "My greatest temptation."

He moved behind me, his chest pressing against my back, hard and unyielding, a stark contrast to the soft curve of my body. His hands found my hair, threading through it with a gentle tug that sent a jolt of heat straight to my core. The herb-scented soap lathered under his hands, and he began washing me, his touch reverent yet teasing.

The scent of wildflowers and rain wrapped around us, but it was his touch that consumed me. His hands moved over my shoulders, down my arms, across my breasts. He lingered there, his fingers kneading the sensitive flesh, his thumbs brushing over my aching nipples until I gasped, arching into him.

"God, Roman," I moaned, my voice heavy with need.

He tilted my head back, his lips finding the sensitive curve of my neck. He kissed me there, his tongue flicking over my skin before his teeth scraped in a way that made me shiver. His hard cock pressed against my lower back, the heat of it branding me even through the water.

"Do you feel what you do to me?" he growled, his voice rough with desire.

"Yes," I whispered, my thighs parting instinctively under the water.

His hands slid lower, tracing the curve of my waist, and my hips, before slipping between my thighs. His fingers found me slick and ready, and he groaned, the sound low and guttural.

"You're soaked for me," he murmured against my ear, his fingers sliding inside me with deliberate slowness. "So tight... so perfect."

I cried out as he began moving his fingers, his strokes unhurried but devastatingly precise. His thumb found my clit, circling it in a rhythm that had my breath coming in ragged gasps.

"Roman," I moaned, reaching back to grasp his thigh, desperate for more.

"Not yet," he said, his voice a sinful tease. He withdrew his fingers, earning a whimper of protest, only to turn me to face him.

The water rippled as he pulled me onto his lap, the hard length of him pressing against my core, tantalizing but just out of reach. He cupped my face, his thumb brushing over my bottom lip before he kissed me—a kiss that was all-consuming, devouring.

His lips moved from mine, trailing down my neck, my collarbone, until they found my breast. He took the swollen peak into his mouth, his tongue flicking over it before his teeth grazed just enough to make me cry out.

"You're addictive," he murmured against my skin, his voice rough, raw.

His hand found its way back between my legs, and this time, there was no teasing. His fingers plunged into me, deep and demanding, curling to find that perfect spot inside me that made me see stars.

"That's it," he growled, his thumb pressing against my clit, his pace quickening as my body arched into him. "Come for me, Olivia. I want to feel you shatter."

And shatter I did. My climax hit me like a wave, powerful and all-consuming, leaving me trembling in his arms, my cries echoing in the steamy air.

As I slumped against him, breathless and boneless, he cradled me, his lips brushing over my temple. But the hard, insistent press of his cock against my belly told me he wasn't done.

"We're far from over," he whispered against my lips, his erection pressing insistently against me. "This is only the beginning."

Lifting me from the bath with the ease of a man accustomed to wielding both blade and love, Roman cradled my still-quivering body against his own. Rivulets of water cascaded down our skin, mingling as if reluctant to part from the warmth of our touch. With one arm securing me, he reached for the sun and moon daggers, their hilts cool against his fingers as he gathered them from the nearby stand. His gaze swept through the foggy tendrils of steam filling the room, ensuring our privacy remained intact before carrying me toward the door.

"Okay, it's safe," he murmured, his voice a low rumble that heightened my senses. He carried me out of the washroom and back into the seclusion of our chamber. The door clicked shut behind us, and I felt the distance between us and the world widen with every step.

Baby Luna lay in peaceful slumber, her tiny chest rising and falling rhythmically, undisturbed by our return.

Roman laid me on the bed, our damp, heated bodies imprinting the sheets like a brand. With deliberate care, he set the sun and moon daggers on the floor beside us—close enough to reach, yet forgotten for now. His eyes burned with a wild mix of mischief and feral hunger, his body hovering over me like a predator savoring prey. The weight of his gaze alone was enough to send a pulse of heat straight to my core, my thighs parting instinctively in invitation.

Without a word, he lowered himself between my legs, his lips grazing the sensitive skin of my inner thighs, his stubble leaving the faintest, tantalizing burn. His hands slid up my legs, spreading me open with firm, possessive confidence. His breath ghosted over my center, the anticipation alone enough to make me tremble.

"You're already soaking for me," he murmured, his voice thick and approving. "I could devour you all night."

And then he did. His tongue darted out, the first touch soft and teasing, like the flick of a flame. He circled my clit, slow, deliberate, his lips closing around it to suck lightly, then harder, pulling a broken moan from my lips. His mouth was relentless, his tongue alternating between gentle strokes and fierce, insistent laps that sent bolts of electricity shooting through my body.

"Fuck, Roman," I gasped, arching off the bed, desperate for more, desperate for him to push me over the edge.

He didn't relent. His fingers joined the assault, sliding into my wet heat with ease, curling upward to find the spot that made me see stars. His thrusts were deep, precise, in perfect harmony with his tongue against my clit.

The pleasure built in waves, cresting higher and higher until I shattered beneath him. My orgasm tore through me, fierce and all-consuming, my cries muffled only by the need to keep our sleeping child undisturbed. My thighs trembled against his head as he held me there, his tongue still working me gently, drawing out every last shudder and whimper.

Before I could catch my breath, I tugged him upward, my hands fisting in his damp hair, dragging his mouth to mine. I tasted myself on his lips as I kissed him with feral desperation, biting at his bottom lip, sucking it into my mouth until he groaned, deep and guttural.

"Inside me," I whispered, my voice hoarse, my body still trembling from the aftershocks. "Now."

He didn't hesitate. Roman positioned himself between my thighs, the thick head of his cock pressing against my entrance, teasing, stretching. He slid into me with one slow, deliberate thrust, filling me completely and making me cry out in pure, unbridled ecstasy.

"God, you feel perfect," he growled, his voice a low rumble that vibrated through my entire body.

He moved inside me, his rhythm slow at first, deep, agonizingly thorough, until my hips bucked against his, demanding more. And then he gave it to me. His thrusts turned fierce, desperate, each one harder and faster, hitting that spot inside me that made me scream his name like a prayer.

My nails dug into his back, raking down his skin, and he groaned in response, his head dipping to claim my mouth in a kiss so raw, so consuming, it left me breathless. His teeth grazed my neck and my collarbone before his lips found my nipple, biting and suckling in a way that sent jolts of pleasure straight to my core.

The room was filled with the sounds of us—our moans, our gasps, the slap of his hips against mine, the wet, sinful noise of him driving into me again and again.

"You're mine," he growled, his voice ragged, his eyes blazing as they locked onto mine. "Say it."

"I'm yours," I cried out, my body tightening around him as another orgasm built within me, threatening to consume me whole. "Always yours."

He groaned, his rhythm faltering as he thrust into me one last time, his release triggering my own. I shattered beneath him, my body clenching around him as waves of pleasure crashed over me, pulling me under, leaving me gasping, trembling, and utterly spent.

Roman collapsed beside me, pulling me against his chest, his body still warm and slick with sweat. His arms wrapped around me, holding me close, his lips brushing against my temple in a soft, reverent kiss.

There was only us for a moment—our bodies still tangled, the outside world forgotten, and the storm of passion between us finally calmed. But as I lay there, wrapped in his warmth, the weight of our reality began to creep back in, cold and unforgiving.

"Roman," I whispered, my voice barely audible, "what if the Timehunters find us? What if they take our baby?"

My fingers traced invisible patterns across his sweat-slicked chest the repetitive motion a futile attempt to calm the storm brewing within me. His steady presence grounded me, but even that couldn't stop the chaos in my mind. My anxiety surged, my thoughts racing faster than the heartbeat pounding in my chest.

"These dreams," I murmured, my voice trembling under the weight of unspoken fears. "They keep haunting me. I can't shake the feeling that something is holding me back, blocking me, keeping me from remembering."

The memories of my past—the ones that were supposedly the key to my destiny—hovered just out of reach like a foggy mist obscuring the truth. Frustration and fear warred within me, leaving a hollow ache in their wake.

"It's fear. You're afraid," he said softly, brushing a stray lock of hair from my forehead, his touch warm and reassuring.

"What could I be afraid of?" I asked, though deep down, my heart whispered the answer before the words left my lips. "I think… I think it's because I had a relationship with Malik, and maybe—just maybe—I had a connection to Balthazar that wasn't based on fear or mistrust. What if I find out my destiny is bigger than me? Too big to handle?"

Before he could reply, a small whimper cut through the

room, breaking the tension. Luna's tiny fists flailed in the air, her face scrunched in the early signs of hunger. Her cry, though soft, was insistent, a reminder of the life we were fighting for.

I rose and scooped her up, cradling her against me as she latched on eagerly, her soft suckling the only sound in the quiet night. Roman watched us, his lips curving into a playful pout.

"You know," he said with mock grievance, "I am quite jealous of Luna. She gets to nurse all the time from your lovely breasts."

A laugh bubbled up from within me, breaking through the heaviness that had settled over my chest.

"Luna will share," I teased, a smile tugging at the corners of my mouth. The lightness in our exchange was a small reprieve, a moment of normalcy amidst the chaos of our lives.

As Luna's eyelids fluttered closed once more, leaving her sated and content in my arms, I met Roman's gaze. In his eyes, I found not just love but an unwavering resolve that steadied my trembling spirit.

"We will get through this together," he said, his voice low but filled with determination. His words wrapped around me like a protective shield, each syllable a vow.

He leaned closer, his lips brushing softly against my neck, leaving a trail of feather-light kisses that sent shivers down my spine.

"No matter what obstacles come our way, I will always be by your side, protecting you and our daughter," he murmured. "Together, we'll face whatever challenges arise. And together, we'll overcome them."

As his words settled over me, the edges of my fear began to soften, melting into a deep sense of security and love. For a fleeting moment, the heavy weight of uncertainty lightened, and I allowed myself to lean into the comfort he offered, taking whatever reprieve I could find.

Yet, beneath the warmth of his assurances, I could feel the looming presence of the trials ahead. The challenges waiting for us grew more daunting with each passing moment, like invisible barriers tightening their hold. Fear gnawed at the edges of my resolve, but I clung to the determination that flickered within me, bracing myself for the road yet to come.

CHAPTER TWENTY THREE

MALIK

I tucked the rough woolen blanket around Rosie, her small form barely denting the straw mattress beneath her. She was nearing that magical age of seven—when the world should be full of wonder and discovery. Despite the relentless dangers stalking us at every turn, I was determined to shield her delicate innocence from the harsh realities pressing in. Yet, it often felt like trying to light a fire amid a raging storm—futile and nearly impossible. The shadows of deceit and betrayal loomed constantly, threatening to consume us. And still, I persisted, my resolve unyielding.

Her eyelids fluttered like moth wings near the flickering candlelight, casting faint, dancing shadows across the room. The mingling scents of woodsmoke and the distant murmur of tavern patrons seeped through the floorboards, grounding us in the fragile sanctuary of the moment.

"Are we going to be okay?" she mumbled, her voice thick with the pull of sleep yet tinged with a fragile innocence that tugged painfully at my heart.

"Always," I whispered, brushing a kiss to her forehead. "I will protect you until my dying breath."

It was a promise as solid as the ancient stones forming the walls of Vézelay, unshakable even in the face of our precarious reality.

She burrowed deeper into the covers, her tiny hand curling around mine. "I miss my bedtime stories," she mumbled, the wistful longing in her voice like a blade to my chest.

A small, bittersweet smile crept onto my face, defying the heaviness in my heart. "When we're safe, my little rose, I'll tell you a million stories. Each one will be filled with wonders and adventures beyond anything you could dream."

"Promise?"

"Promise."

Across the room, Reyna sat by the window, her silhouette framed by the soft, fading light outside. She hugged her knees tightly to her chest, her posture a silent testament to her grief. The space between us felt vast and cold, a chasm carved from her pain and self-imposed isolation. She had built an invisible wall brick by brick, keeping everyone at bay since the tragedy that had shattered her world.

I longed to bridge the gap, to offer solace or even just understanding, but in her eyes, I remained a stranger. The distance between us wasn't merely physical; it was a void filled with heartbreak, broken trust, and the jagged remnants of a love fiercely given and just as fiercely lost. She glanced at me briefly, her gaze skittering away like a frightened bird, refusing to linger.

I watched her with a quiet sadness that seemed to mirror the creaking timber of the old tavern. Yet, I understood her withdrawal with a painful clarity. To her, I was little more than a shadow passing through her life, unable to mend what had been irrevocably broken.

As Rosie's breathing evened into the rhythmic cadence of

sleep, I smoothed the creases in her blanket. Serenity clung to her small form, a fragile peace I was determined to protect. Casting one last glance at my daughter, I turned back toward the evening, knowing Reyna's silent vigil would continue—ever watchful, always tense, bracing for life's next cruel blow. All I could do was respect her space, standing guard from afar, hoping time would heal what seemed irreparable.

A knock shattered the stillness. I strode across the wooden floorboards, their grain rough beneath my boots, glancing back at Reyna. She didn't stir, her gaze fixed somewhere beyond the window, lost in her thoughts.

I lifted the latch, the door creaking as it opened to reveal a stout woman, her cheeks flushed from exertion or perhaps the bite of the evening chill. She bustled into the room, her gaze darting briefly toward Reyna before settling on me. A faint tension hovered in the air, amplified by the hurried energy radiating from her.

"Good sir," she began, her voice breathless yet tinged with urgency. "I have an important message for you."

Her eyes flickered back toward Reyna, then returned to mine, laden with an unspoken gravity. Sensing the significance of her words, I stepped into the dimly lit hallway, leaving the door slightly ajar behind me.

The woman leaned closer, lowering her voice to a conspiratorial whisper. "You are to meet someone named Zara on the next floor up. Third floor. She says it's important."

"Zara," I repeated, the name slipping from my tongue like a secret code. It carried a gravity that sent a chill down my spine despite the lingering warmth of the tavern.

"Indeed." The woman nodded emphatically, her expression underscoring the urgency of the message.

"Thank you," I murmured, my mind already racing with the possibilities of what this summons could entail.

The woman turned and descended the corridor, her steps muffled by the thick rug underfoot, leaving me alone with the weight of this revelation.

When I re-entered the room, Reyna remained unmoving by the window, her silhouette etched in quiet defiance against the dim light. The mention of Zara's name would mean nothing to her, yet everything I held dear seemed to hinge on this clandestine meeting. Our destiny may rest in the hands of the figure waiting just one flight above.

"I'll be back," I said, infusing my voice with reassurance, though the unease gnawed at me.

Her gaze remained fixed on the world beyond the glass.

"You don't need to check in with me. I'm nothing to you," she replied, her tone devoid of emotion, her words sharper than I cared to admit.

I hesitated, struck by the cold indifference in her voice.

I'm a fool to care for her. She lost her true love four weeks ago.

And yet, some foolish part of me yearned for a hint of concern, a trace of a connection.

Shaking the thought from my mind, I turned and stepped into the hallway. As I climbed toward the third floor, the wooden stairs creaked underfoot, the shadows lengthening with the waning light of day. Each step echoed the tension coiling inside me, a prelude to the unknown that awaited.

When I reached the third floor, I paused. Through an open doorway, I saw Balthazar lying on a bed, his body writhing as he muttered incomprehensible phrases. His voice was strained, threading through the dimly lit space like a fractured melody.

Without hesitation, I crossed the threshold, my focus

narrowing to the figure before me. In the corner of the room, Zara stood silently, her presence steady and watchful. Her eyes caught mine, and with a subtle nod, she gestured toward Balthazar, permitting me to approach.

"How are you, old friend?" I asked softly, though the words felt hollow as they left my lips.

Balthazar's eyes fluttered open, flickering between recognition and turmoil. His features twisted with pain and despair.

"Why did you save me from Mathias' dungeon?" he rasped, his voice a hoarse whisper laden with anguish. "You should have let the poison and fire consume me."

Every syllable pierced through me like a knife, stirring up memories and emotions I had long buried.

"I saved you because you're fighting for the wrong side," I said firmly, my voice steady despite the storm of emotions. "You're not the despicable man you pretend to be. Alina and Mathias—they're the ones who twisted your mind and corrupted your soul. Alina, with her insatiable hunger for power, and Mathias, with his endless desire to destroy you. But before all that, before Alina came into your life, you were different." My voice softened, carrying the echoes of old wounds and unresolved pain. "After you destroyed Mathias' school of darkness, you were like a father to me. You took me in, nurtured me, and molded me into who I am today. You made me strong. You made me powerful. And then, one day, you turned against me. You abandoned me."

The words cracked as they left my lips, a tremor betraying the tears that threatened to spill. The memory of betrayal was a fresh wound, raw and unhealed even after all these years.

The room fell silent, the weight of our shared history pressing down on us. Balthazar's labored breaths punctuated the stillness, a stark reminder of the fragility of the moment.

The air between us grew heavy with unspoken truths, the tension thickening like a gathering storm.

The tension coiled tighter.

"Don't let this go to your head," Balthazar growled through clenched teeth, his piercing gaze boring into mine with an almost physical intensity. He was a broken shadow of the man I once knew, yet his will remained unyielding. "Thank you, Malik, for saving me and pulling me from Mathias' clutches. I despise that fucking man who took everything from me."

His gratitude, twisted and cloaked in bitterness, left a sour taste in my mouth.

"You shouldn't have gone after Olivia all these years," I said, my voice slicing through the charged atmosphere like a blade.

Balthazar's face contorted into a vicious snarl, his eyes blazing with fury. "I will not rest until every last descendant and offspring of Mathias and Alina, including Olivia, lies in ruin at my feet!"

"Then you'll have to kill your daughter, Emily, too." The words fell from my lips with deliberate precision, sharp and unforgiving.

The fire in Balthazar's eyes faltered for a moment, replaced by a flicker of horror. His body recoiled, shrinking under the weight of his monstrous vendetta. The realization struck him like a physical blow, stripping away the veneer of rage to reveal something far more human—anguish.

The room's shadows shifted, and Zara stepped forward, her presence emerging from the gloom like a specter-made flesh.

Balthazar's eyes widened in disbelief. "Why do I keep seeing this ghost? She's dead!"

Zara's hand moved with the swiftness of a striking

serpent, the crack of her slap resounding through the room. "I have never been a ghost," she said, her voice laced with authority and exasperation. "I am very much alive. Flesh and blood. And I have been for centuries, you idiot."

"Impossible!" Balthazar's voice cracked, his words trembling under the strain of his fragmented psyche. "I saw Mathias kill you all those years ago!"

"You're wrong," Zara said, her voice unwavering, her gaze fierce and unyielding. "I'm not dead. I've always been here, always tried to reach you, even when you refused to see the truth. When Alina left you and poisoned you, it was me who set your house on fire. I took Malik from your dungeon and healed him when you thought he'd died in the flames."

A sliver of hope dared flicker within me. There may still be a chance to salvage what remained of the man who had been my mentor and tormentor. With Zara's return, there may still be a chance to salvage the broken man before me. Maybe redemption wasn't as far out of reach as it seemed.

Balthazar's trembling fingers rose, pointing at Zara with a mixture of shock and dawning comprehension. "It was you? All those times you appeared to me—comforted me during the darkest moments of my life—it was always you?"

Zara nodded, her eyes locked onto his, unwavering. "Yes, Balthazar. But how could you bring so much pain and suffering to Olivia and still want to kill her when you and her share a history and past together?"

"She's Alina's daughter and Mathias' granddaughter!" Balthazar spat; the words were venomous, his face contorted with years of ingrained hatred.

"Enough of this revenge!" Zara's voice cut through the charged air like a blade. "You need to wake up and remember who you were before this madness consumed you!"

Balthazar flinched as if her words had struck him physically. His voice rose in a roar, laden with anguish and fury. "How dare you speak of betrayal? You, who slept with Mathias and turned away from your husband? You betrayed me—us—everything we had together. He was our enemy! He took our family from us!"

The accusation hit Zara like a blow, her resolve crumbling under the weight of his words. Her body trembled as she fought to suppress the sobs threatening to overtake her, but the dam broke, and tears streamed down her face, her pain raw and unrelenting.

I couldn't remain silent any longer. Stepping forward, I met Balthazar's furious gaze with one of my own.

"Everything Zara did with Mathias was for you, Balthazar. She sacrificed herself for you. And you turned your back on her."

The weight of the truth hung heavy in the room, laden with sorrow for the years lost to betrayal and vengeance. Zara tried to speak, her lips parting, but the words caught in her throat. Tears streaked down her face as she choked on her anguish.

"I can't do it! I can't get the words out," she cried, her hands clenched into fists.

"I'll tell him," I said, stepping closer to Balthazar. His breathing was ragged, his wild eyes flickering between rage and confusion. "The only reason Zara slept with Mathias— one time, not continuously as you've imagined—was to uncover the truth."

Balthazar's chest heaved, his fists tightening at his sides. I pressed on, my voice steady.

"You were right about Mathias. He killed your family. He sent the Timehunters to destroy everything you loved. In the middle of his pleasure, Mathias confessed it to Zara."

The sound that erupted from Balthazar was primal, a

guttural howl rattling the room's very walls. His body trembled with unrestrained fury.

"I knew it! I fucking knew it!" His voice was a storm, his eyes blazing with rage and betrayal. "All those times in his stupid, sanctimonious school, preaching about only killing bad people—it was all a ploy. It was a manipulation to make me believe he was some savior. But I see him now. For what he truly is. He'll pay for what he's done. They all will. I'll make sure anyone who stood by and let this happen—they suffer for betraying me!"

His rage was unbound, a beast clawing into the dimly lit room. The flickering candlelight seemed to waver with the intensity of his fury, and for a moment, the hope of redemption flickered dangerously close to extinguishment.

"But you will not touch Olivia," Zara said, her voice steady, cutting through the tempest of his anger. Her tone carried a resolute authority, her tear-streaked face now calm. "You and she share a history that even your fractured mind cannot erase or ignore."

Balthazar froze, his hands clawing at his temples as though trying to unearth memories buried deep within him physically. His frame quivered under the weight of the unspoken truth.

"This is preposterous!" he growled, his voice laced with frustration. "How can I not remember something so important?"

"It's part of the curse placed when the blades were separated," I explained, my gaze fixed on him, willing him to see the truth. "I hope that you and Olivia will soon remember who you truly are. Only then can we stand stronger in our war against Salvatore."

The room seemed to contract under the weight of those words.

Balthazar turned to Zara, his voice dropping to a desperate whisper. "Tell me, how did you cheat death? I saw you crumple, lifeless, like a corpse. I held your cold body in my arms."

His eyes darted over her as if searching for any sign of deception.

"Lazarus, the Shadow Lord," she said calmly. "He saved me. Just as he saved our beloved Freya in the snow centuries ago."

Balthazar lurched upright, disbelief etched across his features. "My baby... Freya... she's alive?"

The hope that ignited in his eyes was raw and untamed, almost childlike in its purity.

"Yes," Zara said with a steely glint in her eyes. "But she's all grown up now. And she's betrayed us. She's become an ally to the other side." Zara's voice faltered for a moment before she pressed on. "All of our other daughters... they've perished. Their lifeless bodies remain as haunting reminders of our failures. Our last hope is up to the blades to restore their lives and bring them back from the dead."

A flicker of realization passed across Balthazar's face, and his shoulders sagged under the weight of this revelation. "That's why I've been after the blades," he said quietly, his voice rough with emotion. "That's why I've been pursuing Olivia so relentlessly. It wasn't just for vengeance on Alina and Mathias. It was because she was hunting for them, too. The journal was a crucial piece in finding the blades."

His resolve hardened like iron, a determined light replacing the shadows of his burning desire for revenge.

"No more going after Olivia," Zara said firmly, stepping closer. "You're supposed to be her protector. That was your duty from the start. You've lost sight of that, but it's time to remember who you are, Balthazar."

"Protect Olivia? Preposterous." His hands flailed as if trying to swat Zara's words away like bothersome flies. "And who are these people? Who is Lazarus? Salvatore?" Confusion laced his questions, his voice rising to a crescendo of frustration.

My heart grew heavy with sympathy for the man grappling with phantoms of a past just out of reach.

Zara stepped forward and slapped him, the sound echoing sharply in the small chamber. "Violence is the only way to get through to you. You must wake up and remember!"

"Stop hitting me," Balthazar growled, rubbing his cheek, yet there was a glint of something new in his eyes—perhaps recognition or the dawning of understanding.

I stood silently, observing the scene unfold. With a resigned sigh, I finally turned toward the doorway, prepared to leave them to reconcile their fractured history.

But Balthazar's voice stopped me. He turned to Zara, his expression softening into something raw and unguarded—a look of profound relief as if her presence was a miracle he scarcely believed.

"I'm sorry, Zara," he said, his voice thick with emotion, each word trembling sincerely. "For turning away from you, for becoming this... evil monster. I missed you—your wisdom, your guidance. I missed everything about you. And to know you're alive... to know Freya is alive too..." His voice cracked, and he let the words hang heavy in the air.

Then, slowly, he turned to face me. His gaze, filled with remorse and hope, met mine for the first time without malice.

"Malik," he said, addressing me directly, "I know I've done terrible, despicable things. The road to redemption is long and difficult, but with both of your guidance... I hope to return to being the man I once was."

Upon hearing Balthazar's words, my chest tightened with

mixed emotions. My eyes, usually steady and unwavering, flickered with hope as I absorbed the weight of his confession. The air between us seemed to crackle with vulnerability, the sincerity in his voice—a voice that once commanded fear and respect—cutting through the layers of darkness. Despite our tumultuous past, a sliver of belief stirred within me, fragile but persistent, whispering of second chances and redemption.

"I'm leaving. Zara, is there anything I need to know before I go?" I asked, my tone brisk, though my heart was heavy.

"It's about to get dark and dangerous," she said, her voice low but fierce. "We're going to lose people. Protect Olivia and Roman. Protect your heart. Don't let your emotions get in the way."

Her words landed like a weight on my shoulders, a burden I hadn't fully realized I'd accepted.

"You're in good hands," she added. "Pasha Hassan is a good man. You're going to like him."

"Okay," I replied, with a nonchalance I didn't feel. The corner of my mouth twitched into a wry smile. "Have fun with Balthazar. I'm sure you both have a lot of catching up to do. Maybe having sex with him will help him remember."

The words were meant to break the tension, a thin veil of humor to mask the unease in my gut.

Zara's expression hardened, her lips pressed into a thin, disapproving line. "No. He doesn't deserve to share intimacy with me."

Her rebuff was a cold splash of reality.

Without another word, I stepped out into the corridor, the door closing behind me with a resolute finality. The weight of what I'd left behind lingered, the revelations and pain sealing themselves away in the confines of that chamber.

Darkness enveloped me as I stepped into my room, the worn tavern floorboards muffling my cautious footsteps. My eyes had barely adjusted to the absence of light when a presence whirled around me. From the shadows, Reyna's silhouette emerged with fluid precision. Cold steel kissed my throat —the unmistakable sharp edge of her dagger, wielded with deadly accuracy by her delicate hands.

"It's just me," I said, my voice steady despite the blade at my neck. "Why the sudden attack?"

"I'm protecting Rosie from intruders," she said.

"Is that what you think I am? An intruder?"

She didn't answer, her silence more telling than any words.

"You're fast," I said, a hint of admiration slipping into my tone. "How did you get to be so skilled?"

Her breath was ragged, the tension between us thick in the stillness. "How are you connected to Zara?"

"Zara?" I echoed smoothly, masking my reaction. "I don't know what you mean."

She pressed closer, her chest rising and falling against my back, her breath hot and uneven. The heat of her body, the subtle curve of her frame pressing against me, sent a dangerous thrill coursing through my veins. My body betrayed me—my cock hardened, and a wicked smile curved my lips. I leaned imperceptibly into her, savoring the illicit contact. In one fluid motion, I spun on my heel. The blade grazed my skin, leaving a whisper-thin line of warmth as a bead of blood traced its path. I faced her now, our proximity electric.

"What are you doing?" she whispered, her breath unsteady.

"What does it look like I'm doing?" My voice dropped, laced with seduction, as I brushed my finger along her cheek.

She shoved my hand away, her defiance as sharp as the blade she still held. "Trying to seduce me?"

Her voice was cutting, but beneath it trembled something unspoken, unguarded.

"Can you blame me?" I murmured, my hand trailing to the nape of her neck, my fingertips seeking the rapid thrum of her pulse.

With unexpected strength, she shoved me back, her ferocity commanding. "I see what you're up to, Malik," she sneered, a smirk playing at her lips as she stepped away, but her eyes betrayed a flicker of uncertainty.

"Stay away from me. Don't delude yourself into thinking I have any interest in you." She paused, her voice hardening. "Have you quenched your thirst for blood yet?"

"Thank you for asking," I said, grinning as I stepped closer. "Quite enough."

Reyna wasn't fooled. She stepped closer, pressing her hand against the hollow of my chest.

"You're lying to me," she said, her voice low, a mix of concern and suspicion. Her eyes locked onto mine, searching for the truth that danced out of reach. "You haven't killed a soul tonight. You never left the tavern. So, I'll ask again—where were you?"

"Drop the knife, and I'll tell you," I said, extending an open palm toward her, my tone laced with a false gentleness. It was bait, and I waited to see if she'd take it. With feline quickness, she recoiled, brandishing the blade before her like a talisman against evil. The dim light of the room glinted off the knife's edge, mirroring the sharp determination in her eyes.

I couldn't suppress the grin that tugged at my lips. This dance between us was as exhilarating as it was dangerous. I lunged, not to harm her but to disarm. She dodged gracefully, retreating a few steps, keeping the distance between us. Each move she made was measured and calculated—traits of a predator or perhaps prey determined not to be caught.

With a swift motion, I cornered her against the rough-hewn wall, clamping her wrists before she could react. The knife slipped from her grasp, the cold metal clattering to the floor with a metallic song. I leaned in close, inhaling deeply, taking in the intoxicating mix of her fear and defiance.

She aimed a knee at my groin, a calculated strike, but I sidestepped it with a smirk as laughter bubbled up from my throat.

"You're feisty," I said, relishing her spirit.

Drawing back slightly, I studied her face, the contours sharpened by shadows and resolve. Her chest rose and fell rapidly, but her eyes never wavered, burning with fierce determination.

"I know you're not who you say you are," I murmured, my voice dropping to a dangerous whisper. "I know you're a skilled assassin. It was you who killed Raul and chopped him into bits in that dungeon."

Her chest heaved with ragged breaths, the intense stare in her eyes never faltering. "That vile man deserved every ounce of pain I inflicted upon him. After all he had done to me and Marcellious in that wretched prison, he knew what consequences awaited him. He attempted to rape me, subjected us to brutal forms of torture, and continued to be a loyal member of the ruthless Timehunter society. But I promised myself and my father that I would bring down their corrupt empire and every last Timehunter who supported it. It was a matter of survival for me, drawing on my background and instincts as a fighter to defend myself against that monstrous creature."

"Defend yourself?" I threw my head back and laughed, the sound ricocheting through the dimly lit room. "The way you carved up Raul, severing his manhood like some grotesque ritual—it wasn't just survival. You, Reyna, might wear the face of an innocent angel, but there's a darkness in you that's impossible to ignore. It calls to me. You need someone like me—someone who thrives in violence and danger—someone who can unleash the wild desires you keep locked away."

My voice dipped lower, laced with a dangerous seduction.

Her expression twisted, not with longing but pure revulsion. "You're the very embodiment of darkness," she spat. "I swore to my father I'd never give my heart or body to a man like you." Her words landed sharp, but her eyes betrayed her. Beneath the disgust, a flicker of something unspoken danced —fear, doubt, or perhaps curiosity.

"Darkness, am I?" I murmured, leaning in until our foreheads nearly touched. Shadows danced across her face, weaving us together in an intimate web of light and shadow. "And what about you? The woman who butchered a man into unrecognizable pieces, who took down opponents like it was second nature, who freed Marcellious and escaped that fortress with him—all that doesn't make you dark?"

The words rolled off my tongue like a caress, dripping with eroticism.

I leaned in closer, my gaze fixed on hers, searching for every flicker of emotion. She didn't flinch, but her voice came like a dagger, laced with defiance.

"I don't care where you were or who you were with," she said coldly. "You could've been with a lowly whore for all I care. It's your business. Now, let me go."

Her controlled tone couldn't hide the raw anger simmering just beneath. The hurt that bled into her words only deepened my amusement.

"Who are you, Reyna?" I asked, my tone a mix of

mockery and genuine intrigue. "How do you know so much about the darkness? And what's your vendetta against the Timehunters?"

"My blood is dark and dangerous," she murmured, a seductive whisper laced with ice. Though her hands were trapped, she didn't struggle—no, she leaned in, pressing against me, her body fitting against mine like a slow-burning challenge.

Her lips brushed my jaw, barely there, her breath hot and teasing—a slow, deliberate game. I clenched my teeth, grip firm, but the smirk curling at the edges of her mouth sent a dangerous thrill through me.

I loosened my grip. A single hesitation. That was all she needed.

With a swift, fluid motion, she twisted against me, feigning surrender, her body pressing closer as if yielding. Her fingers skimmed down my waist, featherlight, and in a heartbeat—the dagger was hers.

Cold steel pressed against my chest, but I was faster. My hand shot out, seizing her wrist, forcing her arm back as the blade hovered between us, the deadly tip trembling in her grasp.

Her breath hitched. Not in fear—but in exhilaration.

Her chest rose sharply against mine, our bodies flush, her pulse as wild as my own. The dagger stayed tight in her grip, caught between our struggles, her fingers refusing to loosen.

She didn't flinch.

"If you don't let me go," she said, her voice steady, edged with dark amusement, "I'll use this blade to kill you—and control you."

"Well, my love, I'm your perfect match." The words lingered in the air, electric, like the moment before lightning strikes. The tension between us snapped, and I closed the distance, claiming her lips with a hunger that bordered on savage.

The kiss wasn't gentle—it was a storm, fierce and consuming, a clash of need and chaos that left no room for hesitation. My hands gripped her waist, pulling her flush against me, our bodies fusing as if trying to erase the space that had dared to separate us. Her taste was intoxicating, a dangerous blend of sweetness and fire that sent heat coursing through my veins.

Her lips parted beneath mine, inviting my tongue to delve deeper, to explore, to conquer. The soft, wet friction of our mouths was maddening, each movement igniting a new blaze of desire. My hands roamed her body, desperate to claim every curve, every inch of her as my own. Her nails raked down my back, sharp and unyielding, sending a jolt of pain laced with pleasure straight to my cock.

This wasn't just a kiss—it was a reckoning, a volatile explosion of passion that blurred the line between ecstasy and destruction. Every touch, every bite, every breath we shared was charged with the unshakable knowledge that we were playing with fire. And yet, neither of us could stop.

Her moans vibrated against my lips, fueling the primal need surging within me. I pressed her against the wall, my hands threading into her hair, tugging just hard enough to tilt her head back, exposing the vulnerable line of her throat. My lips trailed down her neck, tasting her skin, biting just enough to leave a mark—a declaration that she was mine and mine alone.

Our spirits collided like stars exploding in the night sky, a violent, beautiful chaos that defied reason. She was everything I shouldn't want and couldn't have, and yet I was incapable of letting her go.

As her hands tangled in my hair, pulling me closer, my

mind warred with itself. I'd loved and lost before—lovers consumed by the darkness I carried. But with her, there was something different, something dangerous. A fragile ember of hope flickered in the storm of my thoughts.

Could she survive me? Could we survive this?

And yet, as I deepened the kiss, pouring every ounce of longing, fixation, and desperation into it, I knew it was already too late. I'd claimed her, sealed her fate. Whether it ended in salvation or tragedy, I couldn't care. At that moment, nothing else mattered but the taste of her, the feel of her, and the dangerous, unrelenting hunger that bound us together in a tempest of unbridled desire.

CHAPTER TWENTY FOUR

The cobblestones of Skopje's ancient streets, worn smooth by the weight of countless footsteps, echoed beneath the hooves of our weary horses. The air was alive with the reverberations of history, whispering tales of conquest and coexistence.

We had arrived at the heart of the Ottoman Balkans, where cultures intertwined as intricately as the vibrant kilims draped over the market stalls. The Vardar River meandered through the city like a silver thread, its waters sustaining the thriving commerce and life. Minarets stretched skyward alongside the domes of Orthodox churches, symbols of a delicate balance between tradition and change.

"Stay vigilant," Roman murmured beside me, his voice low but firm. His sharp gaze swept over the bustling crowd, his wariness a shield honed by years of battle. Ever the silent protector, Malik nodded, his hand hovering near the hilt of his sword hidden beneath the folds of his cloak.

We moved carefully through the city, threading past the crowded bazaars and narrow alleys. Leaving Skopje behind without incident, we pressed onward, the weight of our journey pressing heavily on our shoulders.

Beyond the city, Bosnia's lush hills stretched endlessly, offering beauty but no respite. The road demanded sweat and perseverance, each mile forward hard-earned. And now Serbia's sprawling terrain lay before us, a land of promise and peril. The end of the month loomed closer, each passing day a reminder of the urgency of our mission.

"Anatolia is still far," Malik said one evening as we set up camp on the outskirts of a Serbian village. His voice carried the weariness of the road but also a quiet determination. "But if Reyna is correct, Pasha Hassan will have the answers we seek."

I nodded, the enormity of our task pressing against my chest. The scriptures we sought were more than words—they were keys to a fate none of us could fully grasp. Each of us carried the burden in our way, our reasons for seeking them as varied as the stars overhead.

The gods had granted us a rare reprieve. Luna, wrapped snugly in a woolen blanket, slept soundly in my arms, her tiny form serene and still. Since leaving behind the bustling remnants of Skopje, her cries had been few, and her appetite was robust. With her boundless curiosity, Rosie embraced the journey with a resilience that filled me with quiet pride. And Reyna—bless her stubborn soul—was slowly emerging from her cocoon of grief. Though still present, the shadow of Osman's loss seemed to lift in fleeting moments. I caught her exchanging glances with Malik, their eyes meeting with an understanding that hinted at something unspoken. The tension that had once thrummed like a taut bowstring between them was easing, replaced by a tentative camaraderie.

With each passing night, Roman and I were consumed by an overwhelming passion that carried us through the next day's journey. We couldn't resist stealing moments to bathe each other in adoration and affection at every rest stop. The warmth of his touch and the taste of his lips lingered on my skin long after we parted, leaving me breathless and yearning for more. Our love was a blazing fire that sustained us in this wild, unpredictable world.

"Everything is going smoothly," I murmured, a silent prayer that it might continue that way.

The next day, the carriage rocked gently beneath me, its steady rhythm a lullaby that promised rest and respite. As I leaned back against the worn cushions, my thoughts wandered to Mathias and my mother, conspicuously absent from this leg of the journey. It was too much to hope we'd never see them again, but a girl could dream, couldn't she? For now, it was just the six of us—Roman and me, Malik, Reyna, Rosie, and Luna—bound together by purpose and necessity.

"Almost too smooth," I mused, watching Luna's chest rise and fall steadily.

Without warning, the carriage jolted to a sudden stop. The abrupt motion roused Luna from her peaceful slumber, her tiny features scrunching in protest as she wriggled in my arms. She grew so quickly at nearly five months old, her wide eyes bright with curiosity as she looked around. I hushed her gently, rocking her back to sleep. The soft light from the window fell across her delicate face, highlighting every perfect detail—her button nose, rosebud lips, and impossibly tiny fingers curled into fists. Even with the interruption, she settled back into the safety of my arms as if she knew she was protected.

"Stay inside, Olivia," Roman's voice cut through the peace.

His silhouette filled the narrow space between the

carriage door and the curtain before he stepped away. The knot of unease in my stomach tightened. I clutched Luna closer, her warmth comforting against the prickling uncertainty that crept over me.

"Could be anything," I whispered to Rosie, who was staring at me with wide, expectant eyes. "A fallen tree blocking the road? Or maybe a cart needing a bit of help."

But even as the words left my lips, I felt the tension in the air, an unspoken warning. Something wasn't right. I took a steadying breath, my gaze flickering to the curtain. Every instinct screamed for me to stay put, but curiosity clawed at me, relentless. Ignoring Roman's orders, I edged closer to the window and pulled the heavy curtain back just a sliver. The sight beyond sent a cold shiver coursing down my spine.

An army of shadows surrounded us—hundreds of black-hooded men on horseback, their turbans as dark as ink against the encroaching night. The faint gleam of moonlight on their mail coifs cast an eerie shimmer, the interlocking metal rings glinting like distant, restless stars.

The only visible part of their faces were their eyes, as sharp and unyielding as shards of obsidian, staring out from behind layers of steel and cloth.

Malik sat atop his sleek black horse, his posture rigid, his expression unreadable. Surrounding him were several fierce warriors, their curved swords drawn and pointed directly at him. They formed an impenetrable barrier, a living wall of cold steel and deadly intent.

Fear coiled tight in my stomach, and for a moment, the world seemed to narrow to the scene outside the window. The sunlight glinted off the warriors' weapons, each gleam a reminder of the danger we faced. My chest tightened, and terror and disbelief washed over me.

"Just my luck," I muttered, sarcasm barely masking the

dread that laced my words. "When I thought everything was finally going right."

Beside me, Reyna leaned forward to peer out the window. Her expression shifted, darkening like a storm cloud. Whatever she saw mirrored the bitterness settling in my chest as if the sour taste of old lemons had coated her tongue.

"Olivia, what is it?" Rosie's small voice trembled with unease, but I had no words of comfort to offer her.

"Stay down," I whispered, the protective instincts of a mother surging within me like a tidal wave.

Reyna's hand found mine, her grip tight and grounding, her unspoken solidarity an anchor in the chaos.

I couldn't sit idle, shackled by fear and Roman's command. Slipping my feet into my shoes, I moved toward the door, flustered but resolute. Reyna and Rosie watched me, their wide, frightened eyes like mirrors reflecting my unease. Handing Luna to Reyna, I stepped down from the safety of the carriage, defiance sparking in my every movement as I braved the unknown.

Roman stood a few paces ahead, his posture unyielding, his face a mask of stoic calm. "Is there a problem?" he asked, his voice cutting through the charged silence.

Not a word came from the sea of black-clad figures. Their silence was heavier than any shouted threat, a quiet that pressed against the air and set my nerves on edge.

Then, cutting through the oppressive stillness, a solitary figure emerged. His mount, black as a moonless night, moved with a deliberate grace, its hooves stirring small clouds of dust that lingered like foreboding whispers. The rider himself was cloaked in layers of dark furs, their opulence speaking of rank and wealth. Obsidian accents adorned his armor, catching the faint light and adding to his commanding presence. He exuded an air of authority, wearing it as naturally as the royal finery draped over him.

"Finally, someone to talk to," Roman said, a flicker of relief crossing his features before his composure snapped back into place. "We don't want trouble. We ask for safe passage."

The warrior dismounted with an air of cold majesty, his movements deliberate and assured. He stood tall, his piercing gaze sweeping over us, lingering just long enough to leave a shiver in its wake. Then he spoke, his voice as smooth and calculated as the steel at his side. "Raul Costa has informed me that you possess the sun and moon daggers," he said, his words falling like stones into the stillness. "And we've come to collect them."

My heart stuttered in my chest as Roman stood his ground, though the tension in his jaw betrayed the storm brewing beneath his calm exterior.

"Forgive me, but I have no idea what you are talking about. We don't have any daggers, and I have never heard of a man named Raul Costa," Roman said, his voice teetering between frustration and incredulity.

The air grew heavy and thick with unspoken threats, the kind that prickled at the skin and promised violence.

With an almost unnatural grace, the royal warrior closed the distance between himself and my husband, each step deliberate, a silent declaration of power.

Roman's hand hovered near the hilt of his sword, his muscles taut and ready to strike.

As the warrior reached Roman, he unfastened the interlocking metal that shielded his face, revealing features as unyielding as the rugged terrain we'd traversed. In a single, fluid motion, he drew his blade. The weapon caught the fading light, its sharp edge glinting with lethal intent. Before I could fully comprehend the movement, the cold steel grazed Roman's neck.

Roman's body jolted, his eyes wide with shock as though an electric current had coursed through him.

I sucked in a gasp.

"Be mindful," the warrior said, his voice smooth but edged with malice. "This blade is smeared with poison. One nick is all it takes to end your life."

A primal instinct surged through me—a desperate need to protect Roman, to shield him from the danger that loomed. I stepped forward, but the silent warriors surrounding us moved in unison, their weapons whispering against their sheaths as they drew them. The sound sent a shiver through me, freezing me in place.

"I'll make this simple," the royal warrior continued, his tone mocking civility. "Hand over the sun and moon blades, and I will leave you and your family unharmed."

Roman, ever the fighter, refused to yield. He lunged at the warrior with a sudden burst of movement, his blade flashing in the twilight. The warrior moved with a predator's grace, sidestepping Roman's strike with effortless precision. In one swift motion, he seized Roman's outstretched arm and used his momentum to hurl him to the ground. Dust rose in a choking cloud as Roman landed hard, his body sprawled against the unforgiving earth.

"The more you fight, the worse it will be," the warrior said coldly, looming over Roman with an air of finality that made my stomach churn. He placed a booted foot over my husband's chest and pressed down.

Roman grabbed the man's ankle with a vice-like grip. The warrior sneered, brandishing his dagger in a slow, mocking wave.

"Don't you dare try anything foolish," he warned. "My

aim is flawless. One small nick from this blade will end your life."

Roman froze, his muscles tense with fear as he weighed his options.

Panic clawed at my insides as I watched my husband pinned beneath the stranger's boot, our fate hanging in the balance. My voice, though trembling inside, emerged steady. "We don't know a man named Raul Costa," I said, my tone firm. "And we certainly don't have any daggers. You have the wrong people. You've attacked us, accused us of lies, and we don't even know who you are."

A few stars began to pierce the darkening sky, their soft light an ironic contrast to the menace that loomed over us. The horses, oblivious to the tension, nickered softly, their innocent sounds swallowed by the oppressive silence.

"Such bold words." The royal warrior's voice dripped with malice as his gaze shifted to me. He stroked his dark beard, his eyes lingering on my face with a calculating leer. "A woman who speaks so freely could easily be imprisoned for treason. And yet..." He tilted his head, a cruel smile curling his lips. "Your beauty is unparalleled. It would be a waste to lock you away when the Sultan's concubines could always use another gem to their collection."

My blood turned cold, but I refused to flinch under his gaze.

The sky had darkened to a deep indigo, the first stars glimmering in the vast expanse above. The warrior finally shifted his attention back to Roman, extending a hand toward him.

Warily, Roman accepted the gesture and pulled himself to his feet, his movements slow and deliberate. Dirt clung to his clothes and hair, but his composure remained intact as he squared his shoulders against the man who had humiliated him.

The royal warrior bowed deeply, a gesture both formal and intimidating.

As he straightened, his voice, low and commanding, reverberated through the tense air. "I am Pasha Hassan, leader of the Timehunters."

My heart skipped a beat. This was the man we had set out to find—the one with the knowledge of the daggers and the scriptures. But instead of being the ally we had hoped for, he stood before us as a threat, his presence no blessing but a curse.

My hands trembled as the gravity of the situation settled over me. Pasha Hassan wasn't just any man. He was the leader of the most ruthless Timehunters in existence. We were standing before one of the most feared figures in the land.

"Give me the daggers," Pasha Hassan demanded, his cold, unyielding eyes locking onto mine.

He was supposed to be a guide, a beacon on our treacherous path to Anatolia. Instead, he was a predator circling its prey.

"I don't know what you're talking about," I said, forcing my voice to remain steady as I met his gaze. Trusting him didn't feel like an option—not after the threat he posed or the venom in his words. How could I hand over something so powerful to a man who had already threatened my husband's life?

Pasha Hassan's lips curved into a cruel smirk. "Then you won't mind if we search your belongings."

Before I could respond, Reyna stepped down from the carriage, her sudden appearance drawing Pasha Hassan's attention. His eyes widened slightly, surprise flickering across his face before his expression hardened.

"What's this? If it isn't my beautiful Reyna," he said, his voice dripping with mockery. His hands came together in slow, deliberate applause. "Well, well, well. My daughter, the one who ran off with her betrothed and bound herself to this lot, has betrayed me."

Reyna stiffened, the color draining from her face. "Father, it's not what it seems," she said, her voice laced with desperation.

The revelation hit like a thunderclap. Roman stood frozen, stunned into silence. Even Malik, usually unreadable, looked alarmed. The air grew thick with tension, a suffocating weight pressing down on all of us.

"Your father is a Timehunter? Let alone the leader?" I demanded, my voice trembling with disbelief as I turned to Reyna. Betrayal coursed through me, sharp and unforgiving. "Why didn't you tell us?"

Pasha Hassan's piercing gaze swept over his sea of warriors. "Do you see? My beloved daughter has betrayed us. She turned against her blood, her people."

His voice, laced with venom, carried an edge sharp enough to slice through the whispers of the wind.

Reyna shrank back, trembling under his condemnation. The fear in her eyes was unmistakable, and anger surged hotly within me. She had led us into a trap, and now we were caught in its vicious jaws.

Pasha Hassan turned his darkened expression toward Reyna. "My daughter, how dare you defy me," he said, his hand rising with the intent to strike her.

"Don't you touch her!" Malik's fierce, protective roar cut through the tension like a blade.

He dropped to the ground in a fluid motion, bracing himself as if ready to lunge. His fists clenched at his sides, muscles coiled, prepared to fight for Reyna despite the overwhelming odds.

In an instant, the warriors surrounding him pressed their blades against his throat and torso, their movements swift and unyielding. Malik didn't flinch. He held his ground, defiance blazing in his eyes, but I could only watch helplessly.

Pasha Hassan's presence loomed over us like a storm cloud, his ominous aura spreading a chilling gloom. He gestured toward Malik, his voice calm but commanding.

"Bring him here."

The warriors seized Malik and escorted him forward, stopping within Pasha Hassan's reach.

His movements were slow and deliberate, but the tension in his posture betrayed his readiness to fight back. Pasha Hassan stepped closer to him, his piercing eyes narrowing as he leaned in. The air around them seemed to still as Pasha Hassan inhaled deeply, as though he could decipher Malik's secrets from his very scent.

"I smell darkness. My, my," Pasha Hassan drawled, his voice low and mocking. "My little girl, who has sworn never to succumb to the darkness, is now aligned with this man. What happened to the man I chose for you—Osman?"

Reyna's voice trembled like a leaf caught in a storm. "He died in a fire."

"Did he? What a shame. He was a good man and would have made you happy. "

"We found her betrothed in a tavern," Malik interjected defensively. "Raul was attacking her. We tried to save her and Osman."

Pasha Hassan's laugh was devoid of humor, cold as the steel in his hand. "Do you think I am so easily fooled? I am not an idiot. So stop with your stupid stories."

Little Luna's wail pierced the tension, and Rosie's whimper followed, a haunting echo. The sounds roused a primal fear that had lain dormant. Pasha Hassan's eyes gleamed with ruthless calculation as he seized upon our vulnerability.

"I am sure you want your children to live. You either hand over the daggers, or I will slaughter your kids." His voice was chillingly casual, as if discussing the weather rather than threatening innocent lives.

To my disbelief, Roman chuckled—a sound so out of place it bordered on hysteria. I shot him a glare sharp enough to cut. What was he doing?

"It's about time we come clean and reveal our true identities," Roman said, his laughter subsiding into a cocky grin. "We are Timehunters. This is my clan."

He placed a protective arm around Malik. "Yes, Malik is darkness, but he's part of our little band of Timehunters. He comes in quite handy when it comes to torture."

"Really?" Pasha Hassan arched an eyebrow, his sneer a cruel slash across his face. "Which Timehunter society do you come from?"

"We are the powerful Timehunters from England," Roman said with an air of bravado that made my skin crawl. "We run that society."

Pasha Hassan scoffed. "That society was destroyed many years ago by a man named Amir."

"Not everyone. Some of us escaped," Roman said smoothly.

Pasha Hassan glared at Roman, his piercing eyes narrowing. "Timehunters, you say. Then you must prove to me that you are Timehunters. If you can prove it, I will not seize the sun and moon daggers, and your children will be safe."

The hollow promise did nothing to ease the vice grip of dread tightening around my heart. How could we convince this man of our allegiance when deception was the only currency we had to barter with?

"We don't have the blades," I said, trembling. The night stretched endlessly, the stars cold and distant, offering no mercy.

From the corner of my eye, I saw the carriage door swing open, and men dressed in black emerged, their hands clutching the hilts of the sun and moon daggers.

"We've got them!" one of them shouted.

Luna's wails shattered the silence, her cries piercing the heavy atmosphere like shards of glass. Beside her, Rosie's small form trembled, her wide eyes glistening with terror.

"No!" a scream erupted from deep within me, wild and untamed.

Pasha Hassan merely raised an eyebrow, his expression disturbingly serene amid the chaos. His calm demeanor only fueled the storm of emotions within me.

"I will forgive the lie," he said, his voice smooth, almost condescending. "You did what anyone would have in your situation. But now… You must prove you are a Timehunter, or your life and your precious children's lives are at stake." His tone was as casual as if he were discussing the weather, as if such negotiations were commonplace for him.

Fury boiled inside me, directed at Roman. What had he done? His reckless words had placed our children in harm's way, turning their innocence into pawns in this deadly game. My chest heaved with the effort to contain my rage.

With a swift, desperate movement, Roman reached into the carriage, pulling Luna and Rosie into his arms. They clung to him, their cries mingling into a haunting, heart-wrenching chorus.

Sixteen warriors moved with precision, closing ranks around him and blocking any avenue of escape. Their weapons gleamed in the dimming light, a silent but deadly threat.

"Men, gather up," Pasha Hassan commanded, his voice cutting through the tense stillness as he turned to address his legion. "We have been here long enough. The children shall stay in the carriage with your wife and Reyna. We have a long way to go, so saddle up."

The warriors moved with chilling efficiency, mounting their horses and forming a grim procession that stretched into the dusk. Their presence loomed like shadows, heavy and inescapable. I turned to Reyna, the sight of her filling me with a venomous rage. Her eyes brimmed with turmoil, her lips trembling as if she were grasping for words that might bridge the chasm she had created.

"I am disgusted with you," I spat, each word like a shard of ice. "You set us up. I want nothing to do with you. You are nothing but a liar."

Betrayal burned through my veins, eclipsing fear and grief. I could barely look at her without the fury boiling over.

Reyna reached out, her hand shaking, but I recoiled as though her touch were fire. "I will explain everything," she whispered.

But there was no time for explanations. Pasha Hassan's men were already in motion, their steely grip dragging Roman and Malik away. My stomach churned as I watched one of the warriors bind Malik's wrists with slender belladonna branches—a cruel irony, given the plant's deadly reputation despite its beauty.

"Stop! You're hurting my daddy!" Rosie's piercing scream shattered the night, her plea for Malik heartbreakingly innocent. Her small voice, filled with raw emotion, cut through the suffocating tension, a reminder of the stakes we faced.

Rage surged through me like wildfire—rage at Reyna, at Pasha Hassan, at this cruel world that allowed such darkness to thrive. My family, once my fortress, was crumbling before my eyes, splintered by betrayal and the iron grip of power.

The warriors' hands were firm as they shoved me back into the carriage with the children. I clutched Luna tightly against my chest, her small, fragile body grounding me in a sea of chaos. Rosie nestled close, her sobs resonating with the aching helplessness in my own heart. Outside, four warriors took up positions beside the carriage, their silent vigilance a grim reminder of the peril that stalked us.

As the carriage lurched forward, the wheels creaking against the dirt road, I felt the weight of an uncertain future pressing down on me. It was as if we were being dragged deeper into an intricate web—a trap from which escape seemed impossible.

CHAPTER TWENTY FIVE

ROMAN

The rocky earth crunched under my boots as I approached the carriage. Olivia's silhouette trembled, her anger rippling like an electric storm. A sea of black-clad warriors surrounded us, their presence a menacing shadow across the grasslands near Sofia, nestled in the northwestern part of the Ottoman Empire within the Balkan Peninsula.

"Olivia," I whispered, my shadow merging with hers as I stepped closer, blocking the faint glow of starlight that dared to soften the darkness of our situation.

Her eyes burned with wildfire fury, consuming any trace of warmth or affection that might have lingered. The weight of her anger struck me harder than any blade ever could.

"I know you're angry with me," I began, my voice low and guilty. "But please understand—I had no choice. These Timehunter tests are necessary for our survival."

My voice cracked under the burden of my uncertainty. I wanted to sound confident and resolute, but the truth weighed heavy on me.

"How hard can it be?" I added, forcing a note of defiance

into my words. "I've faced countless trials and challenges before. My time as a gladiator in Rome taught me to endure unimaginable pain and suffering. I've killed without hesitation. Surely, these tests won't be beyond me." The words hung in the air, hollow and unconvincing, even to myself. Deep down, I knew these trials would push me to the brink—and if I failed, the cost would be unthinkable. Yet I couldn't let Olivia see my doubts. Not now, when we needed to be strong.

Her voice, sharp and cold as steel, cut through my thoughts. "Why did you open your mouth? We could have gotten away."

"No," I replied, steady but gentle, forcing the courage I used to know back into my tone. "They would have killed us anyway. I can prove to them that I'm a Timehunter."

It was as much a plea as a statement. I needed her to believe in me, to trust that this was the only path forward.

The fragile calm shattered, and the warriors converged around us like vultures circling a dying prey. Pasha Hassan pointed at Olivia, his command unspoken but undeniable. With a heavy heart, she climbed into the carriage, little Luna nestled on her hip. Reyna and Rosie followed her, their movements hesitant, shadows of dread etched into their faces.

I mounted my steed, a creature of sinew and muscle, its strength mirroring the determination coursing through me. The warriors surged forward, a dark tide rolling over the rugged landscape. Their vast numbers, though formidable, did not intimidate me as much as the memories of foes I had faced in the bloodied arenas of my gladiator days. Those battles had forged a hardened will, but now, with my family at risk, the stakes were infinitely higher.

We rode in silence, the rhythmic pounding of hooves, a somber drumbeat echoing the dread clawing at my insides.

The anticipation of violence simmered, a tempest waiting to erupt. For now, it remained a distant storm, its thunder muted by the inevitability of fate's cruel design.

As we approached Anatolia, the sun dipped below the horizon, its shadows surrendering to the glow of torches that lined a path leading into the earth. What awaited us was unlike anything I had ever seen. The entrance revealed a sprawling underground palace carved into the ancient bones of the land. Its grandeur mocked the rugged terrain above, an opulent secret hidden from the world.

"Impossible," I whispered, my breath stolen by the sight of towering pillars etched with stories of time and conquest. They supported a ceiling adorned with intricate designs, from which chandeliers hung, their crystals scattering light like stars across the gleaming marbled floor.

"Keep moving!" one of the warriors barked, shoving Olivia and me forward.

We were thrust into a chamber that could have rivaled the courts of any surface monarch. The walls were adorned with tapestries woven with silver and gold threads, depicting the chronicles of Timehunters—men and women whose lives were intertwined with the eternal dance of power, sacrifice, and bloodshed. Every thread told a story, every detail a testament to their ruthless legacy.

Before I could absorb the splendor, the air shifted with a cruel finality. My attention snapped to Olivia, whose arms were suddenly empty. Baby Luna and Rosie were spirited away by two impassive warriors, their movements as precise as they were unyielding.

"No! Please, they're my babies—they need me!" Olivia's voice broke, each word laced with a raw, desperate anguish as she lunged forward, arms outstretched toward our daughters.

"Silence," the lead warrior commanded, his eyes void of empathy.

The door slammed shut, sealing us in an isolation that was as suffocating as it was deafening. Olivia's choked sobs filled the silence, a haunting symphony of despair.

We stood frozen, enveloped in the weight of what had just transpired, the air thick with unspoken fears. Then, with a loud creak, the massive doors parted once again.

Pasha Hassan stepped into the room, his presence as commanding and sharp as a blade.

"You knew the bargain," he said, gaze locking onto mine. "You know you must prove yourselves as Timehunters—even you, Olivia."

I stepped between him and my wife, my protective instincts flaring.

"No, that's not how it works in England," I countered, though my voice betrayed the gnawing anxiety within me. "The wives don't need to be Timehunters."

Pasha Hassan's lips twisted into a cold, mirthless smile. "The society you speak of was destroyed long ago. But perhaps you are of a distant bloodline. Prove it to me—both of you."

His words lingered in the air, heavy with challenge and threat, weaving an inescapable trap around us. There was no denying the finality in his tone, no room to argue or plead.

"Guards," he commanded, gesturing to the men around us. "Bring them to my office."

Without another glance, he spun on his heel and strode away, his footsteps fading into the echoing corridor.

The guards closed in, their expressions stoic as they herded us down a narrow hallway lit only by flickering torches—the oppressive silence pressed against my ears, each step a resounding reminder of our peril. When we reached the end, the guards shoved us unceremoniously through a heavy wooden doorway.

Inside, Pasha Hassan's office gleamed with an unsettling grandeur. The walls were draped in crimson velvet, bordered with shimmering gold inlays, the lavish decor glinting under the light of crystal chandeliers. At the room's center, an ornate desk stood as a testament to his authority, its surface carved with intricate depictions of Timehunter conquests. Behind it, Pasha Hassan stood with arms outstretched, his expression disturbingly welcoming as though hosting honored guests at a grand feast.

"Let me offer you some refreshments," he said smoothly, gesturing toward a side table piled high with decanters of wine and platters of exotic fruits. Given the stakes of our presence, the casual offer was grotesquely out of place.

I shook my head, swallowing the bile rising in my throat.

"No, thank you. What are the tasks? Let's get this over with." My words were sharp, flint against steel, slicing through the room's ostentatious silence.

Pasha Hassan chuckled softly, the sound dripping with condescension. "How very brave of you," he said, his dark eyes glinting with amusement. "If you were Timehunters, as you claim, you would already know what the trials entail. Every true Timehunter knows."

"Our society is different," I retorted, injecting every ounce of confidence I could muster into my voice. "We follow different rules."

"You are courageous indeed," he murmured, his gaze sharpening as it raked over me. "You must take after your father."

The mention of my father sent a jolt through my chest, but I unflinchingly met Pasha Hassan's scrutinizing gaze, refusing to let him see the cracks in my armor.

"Did you know Amir?" he asked, his question laced with quiet malice. "The man who destroyed the Timehunter society of England?"

The name hit like a thunderclap, dredging up the memory of Balthazar's revelation—the truth about my father's identity. The words tasted bitter as I forced them past my lips. "Yes, he was my father."

Beside me, Olivia's hand found mine, her grip firm, her silent support grounding me. She understood the weight of that name, the history it carried, the wounds it left behind.

"Then you know," Pasha Hassan said, his tone deceptively conversational, as though discussing trivial history. "You know how your father, Amir, dismantled and destroyed the Timehunters long ago."

A surge of anger washed over me, hot and unbidden. "I despise my father and have no connections to him."

Pasha Hassan studied me, his eyes alight with a calculating gleam. "And why is it that you despise your father? Is it because he destroyed your Timehunter society, which you claim still exists? "

I glared at him, feeling the sting of old wounds.

"I was raised alone," I said, my words sharp with resentment. "He abandoned my mother. He impregnated her and left."

The truth of my past, usually locked away, now lay bare between us—a vulnerable offering Pasha Hassan showed no inclination to respect.

His laugh was devoid of any compassion.

"Actions like that don't matter," he said dismissively, waving a hand as if brushing away an insignificant detail. "Let's move on."

His indifference to my pain stoked my fury, but I kept

composed. This was his game, and he relished watching me squirm.

"You're a powerful warrior," he continued, his voice smooth, almost mocking. "I'll negotiate. You know the Timehunters have ten tests, but I will only give you the five most difficult."

I clenched my fists, feeling cheated.

"How is this fair? Even one test seems like an insult," I challenged, though I knew fairness held no place in Pasha Hassan's twisted logic.

His gaze bore into me, unyielding.

"If you are truly a Timehunter, you can do this," he said, his tone devoid of doubt. "If you pass the tests, I will return the blades, and together, we can reawaken their power. And —" his voice turned sharp as a dagger, "I will safely return your children."

Anger flared within me, a burning desire to strike back at this man who held our fates so carelessly in his hands. But raw emotion would not save us; we needed control now.

"You will complete the five hardest tasks," Pasha Hassan continued, his sneer deepening. "If you fail, you will be given the worst death imaginable. But first, you will watch your children die."

Searing hatred for Pasha Hassan scorched through me, a loathing deeper than any I had ever known.

"I know you're Timebornes and are lying to my face," he added, his voice laced with mockery. "But I'm willing to let you plead your case. Pass, and I will help you unravel the blades' mystery. It's that simple. Your tests will begin in a couple of hours."

A heavy silence filled the room, each of his words reverberating with the weight of an impending storm.

"Stay here and prepare," Pasha Hassan said, his voice echoing off the ornate walls of the underground chamber as he turned and left, his shadow lingering long after he disappeared.

When the door shut behind him, Olivia's breath hitched, her wide, tear-filled eyes searching mine for answers I didn't have. Dirt streaked her cheeks, and her trembling hands gripped my arm tightly.

"We're not going to survive this," she whispered, her voice breaking. "What if we're asked to jump off a building? Why did you say anything to Pasha Hassan? Why on earth did you tell him we're Timehunters?"

I took her hands in mine, feeling the tremor that mirrored the dread in my chest. The cold knot of fear in my stomach threatened to overwhelm me, but I pushed it down, forcing steadiness into my voice.

"I promise we'll get through this together," I said, trying to infuse my words with conviction for both our sakes. I held her gaze, hoping she could see the strength I was clinging to. "You're a warrior, Olivia. We'll survive this. We have to—for Rosie and Luna."

She shook her head, fresh tears spilling over. "I am not the same woman I used to be. I've had a baby! Do you think we can pass these tests? We don't even know what they are!"

Her vulnerability struck me harder than any blow I'd endured in the gladiator pits.

"Yes, you had a baby, but you're still a warrior—a strong, courageous woman with whom I fell in love." I brushed my thumbs over the backs of her hands, willing her to believe not just my words but the unspoken vow within them. We were in this together—I wouldn't let our challenges end here without a fight.

Before Olivia could respond, the door creaked open, and Reyna stepped inside. Her presence was like oil poured onto the fire, reigniting our anger. The urge to strike mingled with the sting of betrayal.

Olivia lunged forward, but Reyna raised her hands in a gesture of surrender.

"I know you're mad at me. I can explain."

"Explain?" Olivia's voice cracked, her protest ringing through the room. "You led us into this! You put my children's lives in danger!"

"Look," Reyna began, urgency lacing her tone. "I risked my life sneaking in here. I came to tell you what the tests are."

"Do you think we'll believe you?" I spat, each word dripping with disdain. "You betrayed us. Your father is despicable."

Reyna's expression hardened. "That's why I'm here. You have the power to overthrow him. You have two hours to learn and strategize."

I locked eyes with Olivia, searching for a sliver of trust or willingness to listen. Our lives—and our children's—hung precariously in the balance.

"The first test is called the Venomous Chalice," Reyna said, and Olivia's grip on my arm tightened.

"Please don't tell us this has something to do with snakes," Olivia whispered, her voice laced with dread, echoing the tightening knot in my stomach.

Reyna nodded solemnly. "You must enter a snake pit, find the largest one, drain its venom, and pour it into a chalice."

Olivia's breath hitched in a silent scream. Instinctively, I wrapped my arms around her, drawing her close to my chest. My touch was meant to shield her from the terror of Reyna's words, though my pulse thundered at the thought of facing those serpentine horrors.

"We will face it together," I murmured into her hair,

trying to imbue the words with a confidence I didn't entirely feel.

Reyna continued, indifferent to the panic she was sowing. "The second test is the Alchemist's Crucible. Both of you will ingest a deadly poison. You'll have eight hours to create an antidote. Fail, and you die."

"Die?" Olivia echoed, her voice trembling. The color drained from her face, leaving her ashen. She was no stranger to danger, but this... this was different. The stakes were higher than ever before.

Reyna pressed on, as relentless as the trials she described. "The third is called the Labyrinth of Shadows—a darkened dungeon with no light. You'll hunt opponents you cannot see. The only way out is everyone inside must be dead before you can exit."

Olivia's body tensed in my arms, her fear so palpable I could almost feel it coursing through my veins. I tightened my hold on her, hoping to anchor her—and myself—in the face of the mounting horrors.

"We've walked through the darkness before," I said softly, trying to reassure her, though I knew these shadows would be unlike any we had ever faced. "We'll find our way out again."

But even as I spoke, the same unspoken question lingered between us—How could we survive when every step ahead promised a dance with death?

"Has anyone ever passed these tests?" I asked, my voice a mix of curiosity and desperation. My grip on Olivia's shoulders tightened as though sheer force could shield her from the truth.

Reyna's response was maddeningly casual. "Of course. How else would we have the most powerful Timehunters here?"

I weighed her words, searching for a glimmer of deceit in her expression. The odds felt stacked against us, yet there was something in how she carried herself—an underlying belief that these trials, twisted and brutal as they were, might not be impossible to overcome.

"Number Four is the Duel of Fates," she said, her voice cutting through my thoughts like a blade. "You will fight in a duel, but you will be tied to each other by your wrists. You'll each wield a sword in your free hand. Your opponents will be several trained, black-hooded warriors armed with weapons infused with poison. One cut, and you will die."

The words hit like a blow to the gut, and Olivia recoiled from me.

"No, Roman!" she cried, her voice laced with desperation. "This is madness."

"Olivia, my love," I said softly, stepping closer to cup her face. Her skin was cold, her fear radiating like a storm about to break. "We've faced the impossible before. Until our last dying breath, we will fight. Together."

Her breaths came in sharp bursts, her chest heaving as panic threatened to consume her. But slowly, gradually, she nodded, her trust in me holding strong despite the terror we faced.

"Tell us the last test," I said, steeling myself for Reyna's answer.

Reyna hesitated for the first time, a flicker of something —was it respect or pity?—crossing her features.

"The fifth test is the Pit of Death," she said finally, her tone devoid of emotion. "You must face the Executioner. He is the most powerful warrior in the world. You will fight him in the pit, and you may choose any weapon."

Her gaze faltered, dropping to the floor as if she couldn't bear to meet our eyes. "Those are the tasks."

"Thank you," I forced out through gritted teeth, the words bitter as bile.

Reyna gave a curt nod, then turned sharply on her heel and disappeared from the room, leaving us alone in the oppressive silence.

Every breath Olivia and I took seemed to cut through the stillness, sharpened by the anticipation of what would come.

"Roman," she whispered, her voice trembling like a fragile thread stretched too tight, "do you think we can survive this?"

I looked at her, the weight of her question pressing down on me like an unbearable burden. But I could only give one answer, even if it felt like a lie.

"We must," I replied, squeezing her hand with a conviction I wasn't sure I possessed. But for her, for us, I would believe in the impossible.

The sound of heavy boots against stone echoed down the corridor, each step a harbinger of doom. Pasha Hassan appeared in the doorway, his towering figure cloaked in an air of authority and merciless resolve. He surveyed us with a chilling calm, his presence suffocating the room like a storm cloud blotting out the sun.

"I trust you are prepared for your tasks," he said, his voice cutting through the silence like a blade. "You have a couple hours left. Make it count."

Olivia's grip on my hand tightened as his words settled over us. I turned to her, brushing a strand of hair from her forehead and cradling her face. My gaze locked onto hers, and I poured every ounce of strength into the next words.

"I promise we'll make it through this," I vowed, my voice steady despite the storm raging inside me. "For Rosie. For Luna. For us."

Her eyes shimmered with unshed tears, her vulnerability

exposed, but I met with the determination in my own. With every breath I had left, I kissed her forehead, a silent vow to fight for her, for our family. As Pasha Hassan disappeared into the shadows again, the oppressive silence returned, heavier than before. The weight of the coming trials pressed down on us like an iron shroud. I held onto Olivia, willing to believe we could defy the odds and emerge from the darkness. But deep down, I knew the road ahead would be more treacherous than I could ever imagine.

CHAPTER TWENTY SIX
OLIVIA

The grip of the black-clad warriors on our arms was unyielding as Roman and I were propelled through a maze of opulence, only to be thrust into a room utterly devoid of such splendor. The door slammed shut behind us, the echo bouncing off cold stone walls. We found ourselves in a barren cell, the air stale and suffocating. Harsh light slanted through a narrow-slit window, illuminating swirling dust motes but offering no warmth to the lifeless gray stones surrounding us. The room was empty, devoid of comfort, with nowhere to sit but the cold, unforgiving floor.

My heart thundered in my chest, each frantic beat a reminder of our peril. My fingers twisted together, knuckles white, betraying the fear I couldn't suppress. I pressed my back against the icy wall, hoping to draw strength from its solidity. Closing my eyes, I tried to find solace in the stillness within, a fragile attempt at meditation to calm the rising panic in my throat.

The minutes crawled by, each one stretching unbearably. As I sat in the damp, cramped cell, my mind wandered to my babies—Luna and Rosie. Were they safe? Did they know how much I loved them? The thought of them in this wretched place tore at me, shredding what little composure I had left.

The door creaked open suddenly, jolting me back to reality. Reyna's shadowed figure filled the doorway. Her presence, though familiar, stirred more unease than comfort. She stepped into our bleak prison, her movements hesitant, her eyes darting around as though afraid to be caught.

"What are *you* doing here?" Roman snapped.

"I came to help," she said, her voice trembling as she stood in the dim light.

Roman scoffed and turned away, his disgust palpable. "You've done enough. You brought us here, Reyna. You set us up."

"I didn't think it would go this way," she whispered, wringing her hands. "I didn't think my father would attack you."

"Spare me your excuses," Roman said bitterly, refusing to look at her.

Reyna flinched at his words, but before she could respond, I spoke up, my voice fragile but insistent. "Reyna." She turned to me, and I forced myself to meet her gaze. "Please, let me see my babies before we face these challenges. Just once. Please."

Her lips parted as if to reply, but she hesitated. Guilt flickered in her eyes before she shook her head, her gaze falling to the floor. "I can't do that," she murmured. "My father would kill me if he found out."

"Please," I said, my voice now edged with desperation. "I need to see my babies!"

My vision blurred as I fought back tears, unwilling to appear weak in front of this woman who held the keys to my children's safety.

"They are well," Reyna replied curtly, though her voice lacked conviction.

"Please, Reyna. We might not survive these tests. *Please*," I begged, the foreign tone of pleading staining my words. Pride was a small sacrifice for the chance to see Luna and Rosie.

Roman squeezed my shoulder gently, a silent gesture of support.

The silence stretched like an endless abyss, tension thickening with each passing second. Finally, Reyna's shoulders slumped ever so slightly.

"All right," she said, her voice barely above a whisper. "But it has to be quick. And if anyone finds out—"

"Thank you," I breathed out, relief washing over me for the first time since we'd been dragged from Pasha Hassan's office.

Hand in hand, Roman and I followed Reyna down the dimly lit hallway, our footsteps echoing softly against the cold stone floor. Roman's grip was firm, his warmth seeping into my trembling hand—a lifeline amidst the storm of fear and uncertainty swirling inside me.

Reyna led us through the dimly lit passageway to an ornately carved door, its ancient wood groaning softly as it swung open. The chamber beyond was a stark contrast to the cold, unyielding stone of the tunnels. Soft golden lanterns cast a warm glow over plush white carpets, while murals of enchanted forests and mythical creatures adorned the walls, their colors vivid despite the absence of natural light. The air carried the gentle hum of lullabies, a fragile peace that felt almost otherworldly in the depths of the underground.

Two women stood near the center of the room, their faces etched with a maternal kindness that momentarily eased the ache in my chest. One gently rocked a cradle, her voice a soothing melody as she sang. Inside, little Luna's chest rose and fell in a steady rhythm, her tiny form a picture of serenity.

"Rosie," I whispered, my voice swallowed by the sheer relief that flooded me.

At the sound of my voice, Rosie looked up from her play mat, where she sat amidst a legion of carved wooden horses. Her little fingers held a clay whistle. With a squeal of joy, she abandoned her toys and sprinted toward Roman and me, her arms outstretched.

"This place is wonderful," she said, wrapping her small arms around my legs. "I have new toys. I'm taking care of baby Luna." She looked up at Roman and beamed.

"That's wonderful," he said, his voice soft yet warm. "I have no doubt you're doing an excellent job." He crouched and tousled her curly hair, his eyes growing moist as he gazed at her.

Kneeling, I leaned over the cradle and tenderly kissed Luna's sweet face, feeling the warmth of her innocence against my lips. I turned and held out my arms to Rosie. Embracing her, I felt her tiny frame tremble slightly against mine, but her twinkling eyes and contagious giggle shielded her from the gravity of our situation. She hugged me fiercely, then pulled away. "Look at how fast my horse can run," she said, holding up the wooden equine and galloping it through the air with neighing noises.

"Your horse is like the wind," Roman said, sweeping his arm dramatically.

"She's so fast!"

"This one's a boy horse, Roman. You're so silly." Rosie giggled, her little nose wrinkling in delight.

"My apologies," Roman said, nodding solemnly. "It's obvious your horse is a boy."

Rosie's laughter rang out again, filling the room with a melody of innocence that momentarily drowned out the weight of reality pressing down on us.

Despite the gilded cage surrounding us, her laughter brought a fleeting moment of joy. Yet, beneath that facade of happiness, a chilling fear coiled in the depths of my heart, a reminder of the trials we would soon face. These precious moments with my children were as fragile as glass, threatening to shatter under the weight of the tests looming ahead.

"Promise me you'll take good care of Luna," I said to Rosie, my voice barely above a whisper, my heart heavy with the uncertainty of what would come.

She nodded earnestly, her curls bouncing. "I will, Olivia. I promise."

But then her little face scrunched with worry, and her innocent question struck like a dagger. "When will I get to see Malik?"

"Malik is on an adventure," I said softly, forcing a smile that felt as fragile as glass. "You'll get to see him soon." The words tasted like ash, but I pushed them out, desperate to comfort her.

Hope flickered in her eyes for a moment, but it quickly gave way to tears. "I want to see my Malik!" she wailed, her small frame trembling with sobs that echoed the fear I fought to suppress.

"Shh, love," I soothed, gathering her close and stroking her hair. "I promise you'll see him again."

The promise rooted itself deep within me, a vow to face whatever horrors lay ahead, no matter the cost. My determination solidified like steel, an unyielding armor to shield us from the dangers looming over our family.

"Olivia," Reyna interrupted, her voice urgent. "We have to get back."

I gently kissed Rosie's forehead, my heart weighed down by a sense of impending separation. My eyes swept over the peaceful nursery, taking in every detail one last time. Then I turned to baby Luna, nuzzling my nose against her tiny one and planting kisses on her soft, velvety cheeks. The quiet stillness of this moment would have to be my source of strength as I faced the difficult trials ahead.

We scurried down the dimly lit hall, our heads bowed in deference. Reyna guided us to the doorway of the dank room.

The children's memory was all I had to give me hope and the will to succeed. I reached for Roman's hand and squeezed it.

"Rosie and Luna look well cared for," Roman said.

"They do," I replied, my voice cracking.

The door burst open with a resounding crash. Three warriors cloaked in black swarmed into the room. Their heavy steps echoed on the stone floor as they advanced. The tallest among them gripped a large hourglass in his hand, its sand shifting and swirling ominously.

My heart lurched in my chest, knowing this was the final countdown. The air was thick with tension and the acrid smell of metal and leather.

It was time to face our first challenge.

One of the guards stepped forward, his voice a deep rumble that echoed through the chamber. His eyes, cold and unyielding, settled on us as he spoke.

"You must enter the snake pit, find the largest one, drain its venom, and pour it a chalice. Fail, and you will not leave this pit alive." The guard's smirk was barely noticeable, but the challenge was clear.

Roman's hand, rough and calloused from years of wielding a sword, felt like a lifeline in mine as we were ushered into the serpent's den deep in the bowels of the underground palace. The room was suffocating, the air heavy with an earthy stench that turned my stomach. Dull torchlight flickered against the stone walls, casting elongated shadows that danced macabrely across the floor—a floor that writhed and pulsed with the sinuous bodies of countless snakes.

My breath hitched at the sight of them, each creature a master of death in its own right. Memories of Seattle and Lee's teachings surged through me—spot the gleam of danger in an animal's eye or the subtle warning signs in their stance. Those lessons, once tucked away in the recesses of my mind, now resurfaced, sharp and vital.

My gaze locked onto the Inland Taipan, its scales a mesmerizing mosaic of brown and tan, blending seamlessly with its surroundings—a natural camouflage for a creature whose bite could unleash toxins potent enough to decimate a platoon. Every breath I took felt measured, like the air could betray me.

"Olivia," Roman murmured, squeezing my hand, "remember what I said about fear."

His voice was an anchor, steadying me against the rising tide of panic. He was right. My thoughts flashed back to the cave with Lazarus and the snakes guarding the dagger—the cold, damp air, the adrenaline coursing through my veins, the pulse-quickening terror. I'd been scared then, too, but I had survived. And survival now depended on the same principle —mastering the fear, taming it before it tamed me.

"Right," I whispered back. The cave before us wasn't just teeming with serpents—it was a living, writhing tapestry of neurotoxins, hemotoxins, and nephrotoxins, all coiled into lethal elegance. Coastal Taipans lay poised, their stillness as deceptive as their speed, while Black Mambas moved with an unsettling, serpentine grace. Each subtle shift, every flick of a forked tongue, was a deadly promise.

"Focus on me," Roman said, his voice a lifeline as my pulse hammered in my ears. "Don't let them sense your fear."

I nodded, fighting to steady my ragged breathing. Concentrating on the warmth of Roman's hand, I willed my body to relax, forcing the tremors threatening to betray my fright to still. Fear would be a beacon, an invitation to strike to these serpents. If they did, their venom would deliver a swift and excruciating death.

With every controlled breath, I banished the images of fangs sinking into flesh, of venom coursing through my veins. Instead, I conjured Rosie's laughter and Luna's serene slumber. They became my shield, my strength. For them, I would face this pit of horrors and emerge victorious.

"Steady," Roman said again. His unwavering calm spread to me like ripples on water, grounding me in the moment.

"Steady," I echoed, locking eyes with him. Together, we turned to face the writhing sea of death, determined to do whatever it took to survive.

The hourglass loomed before us, perched on a jagged stone podium like a throne of fate. Its slender glass walls encased a cascade of golden sand, each falling grain a grim countdown to our impending doom.

One of the guards, his English halting but his menace clear, pointed at us with his blade. "We watch the hourglass...and you."

The words lingered in the heavy air as he and the other warriors retreated, leaving us with the serpents and the weight of the task ahead.

Roman's gaze locked onto the largest serpent, a monstrous Inland Taipan. Her immense girth and the protective coil of her body told us she was guarding her brood—a queen among vipers. The torchlight gleamed off her scaled hide, an iridescent warning of the death she carried.

"We need her venom," Roman whispered, his voice steady but firm. "But be wary, Olivia. A single bite..."

"Is enough to kill you, me, and everyone in this palace," I finished, my eyes fixed on the serpent's dark, watchful gaze. My voice was calm, but my stomach churned. "I've got it."

The weight of our mortality pressed against me, suffocating and relentless, but I swallowed my fear. Failure was not an option—not when my children's lives hung in the balance.

Roman took a measured step forward, and the sea of snakes parted for him. It was as if they recognized the predator in him—a fearless warrior whose heart pounded with the rhythm of countless battles. Yet, some dared to challenge him, rising with menacing hisses that sent shivers down my spine.

I stood frozen, my heart in my throat, watching as he approached the Taipan, his movements slow and deliberate. Every step he took felt like a defiance of death itself.

From the corner of my eye, a sinuous movement caught my attention—a Philippine Cobra inching closer. Its hood flared wide, its body poised to strike, a glistening harbinger of the potent neurotoxin it harbored, capable of rendering its victims lifeless in moments.

Panic clawed at my insides, urging me to flee, to escape this pit and its lethal inhabitants. But then, Lazarus' words echoed in my mind—a lesson from a time that felt like a lifetime ago.

Face them without fear. They won't hurt you.

I sucked in a deep breath, steeling myself against the rising tide of terror. Squaring my shoulders, I forced my legs to move, taking a deliberate step toward the cobra.

"I command you to step away from me," I said, my voice steady despite the tremor of adrenaline coursing through me.

The cobra reared back, its fangs bared in a silent challenge, but it did not strike. For an agonizing moment, we were locked in a battle of wills. Then, as if conceding, the serpent lowered its hood and slithered away. Taking a cue from their fellow predator, the other snakes scattered, leaving a clear path between me and Roman. My chest heaved with relief, but there was no time to linger in this small victory.

"Good," Roman called out softly, his voice cutting through the tension. His focus never wavered from the Taipan, and his movements were precise and calculated. "Keep control, Olivia. We have to finish this—quickly."

"Quickly..." I repeated under my breath, forcing myself to focus on the task at hand rather than the perilous dance we performed with death. Each grain of sand slipping through the hourglass narrowed our window of opportunity. For Rosie, for Luna, for all of us—I would not falter.

"Olivia! Get the chalice!" Roman's urgent shout pierced the air, snapping me out of my thoughts.

I spun around to see him wrestling with the Inland Taipan, a writhing mass of scales and muscle. His grip on the serpent's throat was ironclad, but his arms trembled under the creature's violent thrashing.

"Where is it?" My voice wavered, barely audible above the cacophony of hissing and the frantic thudding of my heartbeat.

"How should I know?" Roman shot back, grimacing as he adjusted his hold on the Taipan, its tail lashing like a whip. "But I've got one mad mama in my hands, and I'm not sure I can hold her much longer."

My eyes darted across the pit, scanning the dimly lit space for the glint of metal that could only be the chalice. Time felt like a noose tightening around my neck. We had to find it—and fast.

My heart hammered against my ribcage as I cast my mind back to the sterile, controlled environment of Lee's makeshift lab. He had mastered many dark arts, including snake venom extraction. His steady hands had demonstrated the delicate process of milking venom—a skill reserved for experts. We worked with precision tools and safety measures, contrasting this dank pit in the 16th century. I could still hear Lee's voice —*Never forget, Olivia, respect the serpent, for its bite is swift, and its gift lethal.*

And yet, here we were, standing in the antithesis of that controlled environment—a pit swarming with serpents, each one a harbinger of demise. No gloves to shield our hands, no face shield to intercept errant venom sprays, and no lab coat to protect our skin. All the tools that should have been at our disposal were absent, leaving us with nothing but our wits and sheer nerve to rely upon.

"Focus, Olivia," I whispered to myself, forcing the tendrils of fear to recede into the recesses of my mind. Rosie and Luna, their faces embodying innocence and trust, hovered at the forefront of my thoughts, stoking the fires of determination within me.

I pivoted on my heel, carefully avoiding the sinuous tangle of vipers that carpeted the stone floor. Like polished onyx, their eyes tracked my every step, a silent audience to this macabre ballet.

As I wove through them, a cold coil brushed against my boot. My breath hitched. My foot came down hard on some- thing thick and squishy beneath the layers of scales. The snake beneath me jerked violently, its body contorting in a desperate escape bid. My muscles tensed, my balance wavering for a split second. But fortune favored me. I had pinned it just behind its venomous head, rendering its deadly fangs useless.

"Sorry, not sorry," I murmured through gritted teeth. With a grimace, I pressed down harder, feeling the creature's struggles weaken until it lay limp, another casualty in our quest for survival. My heart ached for the necessity of it, but there was no room for hesitation.

I continued to scan the pit, my gaze darting from shadow to shadow.

"Found it!" I exclaimed, spotting the chalice perched precariously atop a ledge carved into the wall. I hastened to retrieve it with renewed vigor, knowing full well that every second squandered brought us closer to the end of the hourglass' patience.

Fear coiled in my gut like the serpents that surrounded me. Their venomous hisses filled the air, a haunting symphony of danger. Each breath I took felt like a gamble, the weight of their menace pressing down on me, threatening to paralyze me.

"Move faster, Olivia!" Roman's strained voice sliced through the cacophony of hissing. "I can't hold her much longer!"

Beads of sweat trickled down his face as he grappled with the thrashing Inland Taipan. Its powerful body shimmered under the flickering torchlight, a deadly masterpiece of nature. His arms trembled from the effort, the sheer force of the serpent testing even his formidable strength.

I drew a shuddering breath, lifting my eyes to the chalice. Its ancient metal glinted in the dim light, an ornate relic holding the weight of our salvation—or our doom. The ledge it rested on seemed impossibly far, an island amid an ocean of venom.

"Olivia! Now!" Roman's voice, sharp with urgency, snapped me into action.

Determined, I scanned the pit for anything useful. My

eyes landed on a King Cobra nest—a mound of sticks and debris tucked into a corner. Swallowing my fear, I moved toward it, praying the cobras wouldn't stir. I pulled two sturdy sticks from the nest with swift, deliberate movements. My heart pounded, every sound amplified, every shadow a potential threat. I hurried to a nearby torch, igniting one branch. The flames roared to life, their crackling warmth starkly contrasted with the cold dread that clung to me. With the hem of my skirt, I fashioned a makeshift loop at the end of the second stick. My improvised tools would have to suffice.

Torch in hand, I brandished the fire at the serpents. They recoiled instinctively, their fear of the flames creating a narrow, fleeting path. Step by cautious step, I advanced toward the chalice. Every movement was deliberate, every muscle tense, my senses hyper-aware of the slightest flicker of danger.

"Olivia?" Roman's voice was quieter now, laced with fatigue and edged with desperation. "Hurry."

"I'm doing my best," I snapped, more to calm my panic than out of irritation at him. I knew the stakes.

Reaching the wall, I propped my torch against it, illuminating the stone with its flickering glow. My first attempt to snag the chalice failed, the fabric loop slipping off the smooth surface. Heart pounding, I tried again, adjusting the angle, my fingers trembling with every passing second.

On the third try, the fabric loop caught hold. I eased the chalice from its resting place, the ancient metal gleaming as it descended, inch by precarious inch. My breath hitched as it finally rested safely in my hands.

"Got it," I whispered, more to myself than Roman.

"Good," he breathed out, relief mingled with urgency. "Now, come here. Quickly."

Clutching the chalice tightly, I moved back along the narrow path I had cleared. The serpents slithered aside as if repelled by the relic I carried, their instinctive menace momentarily subdued. Reaching Roman's side, I couldn't help but notice the tremble in his hands, the sheen of sweat coating his skin as he wrestled with the Inland Taipan.

"Took you long enough," he muttered, though the gratitude in his eyes betrayed the gruffness of his words.

"Can you extract venom?"

Roman's question hit me like a slap, jolting me out of my momentary relief at securing the chalice.

"Sure, with the right tools," I replied, my voice heavy with sarcasm, "but I've never done it in... these circumstances." The sterile, controlled lab environment I'd trained in felt like a distant dream compared to this snake-infested nightmare.

"Okay, listen," I said, forcing my voice to steady despite the pulse thrumming in my ears. "We position the snake's head over the chalice like this."

I demonstrated with my hands, hovering over the artifact.

"I've got fabric from my skirt—we'll use that as a membrane." My fingers fumbled as I adjusted the knots securing the cloth to the branch.

"Membrane?" Roman frowned but nodded, his grip on the thrashing snake unyielding.

I stretched the torn fabric over the chalice's opening. "Then we coax the snake to bite down on it."

The words felt infinitely easier than the action they demanded.

"Coax how?" he asked warily.

"Light pressure on the jaw or... tap its nose."

"Tap its—" Roman blinked, incredulous.

"Yep, that's what I said," I shot back, though my hands

trembled at the thought. "I hold the chalice; you handle the snake. Deal?"

"Deal," he said after a brief pause. "But Olivia, you tap."

"Great," I muttered under my breath. "Snake charmer. Add that to the resume."

Roman adjusted his grip on the writhing Inland Taipan while I crouched low, carefully placing the makeshift venom collector on the cool stone floor. Around us, the pit seethed with danger, the torchlight forming a fragile sanctuary against the writhing darkness.

"Ready?" Roman's voice was clipped, laser-focused.

"Let's do it," I replied, sounding far braver than I felt.

Roman brought the serpent's head close to the chalice. My pulse raced as I leaned in, the weight of the moment pressing on my chest. With a deep breath, I tapped the snake's nose—quick and light. The serpent recoiled slightly, its sleek body tensing before lunging forward. Its fangs pierced the fabric membrane, releasing a lethal stream of venom into the chalice.

"Steady," Roman murmured, though I wasn't sure if it was directed at me or the snake.

Time stretched unbearably, each second an eternity as the liquid death pooled in the chalice. My hands trembled, and I tightened my grip, forcing the vessel to remain steady. Finally, the flow ebbed, and Roman began to ease the snake away, his movements slow and deliberate.

"Did we get it?" I asked, scarcely daring to hope.

"Enough to save our skins," he replied, a hint of triumph breaking through his grim tone.

Roman hurled the irate Taipan toward the pit's far corner. It hit the wall with a dull thud before slithering into the shadows, leaving us momentarily free from its lethal gaze. I let out a shaky breath, staring at the venom-filled chalice in my trembling hands.

"Olivia," Roman said, his voice steady yet tinged with awe, "we did it."

I looked at him, the flickering torchlight casting wild shadows across his sweat-slicked face. Our eyes met, and without a word, we embraced, the chalice carefully cradled between us. His heart pounded against mine, a rhythm that spoke more of relief than triumph.

"Let's not celebrate just yet," I said, glancing back at the chalice. "We still have to deliver this to Pasha Hassan."

Roman nodded, and together, we turned toward the exit. Behind us, the pit writhed with life, a deadly sea of serpents we had somehow navigated. Ahead, the sands of the hourglass trickled down to its final grains, marking the narrowness of our escape. The three warriors waited at the pit's edge, their expressions unreadable as they flanked us. Without a word, they led us through the labyrinthine corridors of the underground palace. The weight of the chalice grew heavier with each step, as though it carried not just venom but the burden of our survival. Finally, we reached the ornate door to Pasha Hassan's office. The guards opened it with a flourish, and there he stood, his gaze sharp and calculating as it swept over us.

"Timehunters," Pasha Hassan mused, a sinister smile curling his lips as he eyed the chalice. "Or just lucky fools?" His eyes gleamed with dark amusement. "You've brought me what I requested, but you don't seem shaken."

"Should we be?" I asked, keeping my voice steady, though the adrenaline from the pit still thrummed through my veins.

Pasha Hassan's sly grin deepened. "Well, well, maybe you are Timehunters. Or perhaps..." he trailed off, circling us like a predator toying with its prey. "A sorceress, maybe?"

He walked over to the desk, the rich fabric of his robes brushing against the floor with a quiet menace. "Let's celebrate your... success," he said, reaching for a decanter on his desk. He poured wine into three goblets, the deep crimson liquid swirling in the flickering torchlight. He handed one goblet to each of us before raising his own in a toast. "To the victors," he declared, his voice smooth, almost mocking.

Roman and I exchanged a brief glance, and we raised our glasses together. The wine was velvety and warm, starkly contrasting the icy dread pooling in my stomach. A metallic tang lingered on my tongue as I drank, but I dismissed it, chalking it up to my own nerves.

Then it hit.

A stabbing pain shot through my skull, as sharp and merciless as a dagger. My vision blurred, the world around me spinning into a distorted haze. The goblet slipped from Roman's trembling hand, clattering to the floor with a hollow ring. He staggered, clutching at the table for support.

"What's... happening?" I gasped, pressing my palms against my temples as if I could somehow push away the searing pain.

Pasha Hassan stood before us, his expression of cold amusement untouched by the chaos around him. "The next test," he announced, his tone calm and measured. "The Venomous Chalice was merely the beginning. Now, you must face the Alchemist Crucible."

His words hung in the air, chilling and final. "You have eight hours to concoct an antidote. If you fail, the poison will claim you both."

"Roman," I rasped, reaching out blindly until my hand found his. His grip was weak but steady enough to anchor me. "Stay with me," I pleaded. "We're not done yet—we have to fight this."

My knees buckled, and the stone floor rushed up to meet me. Roman crumpled beside me, his breaths ragged and uneven. One realization burned bright through the fog of pain and betrayal—we had escaped the snakes only to fall into an even deadlier trap. The venom in our veins was not just a test of survival—it was a test of our resolve, intelligence, and will to fight against impossible odds. And we would fight. We had to. For Rosie. For Luna. For us.

CHAPTER TWENTY SEVEN

ROMAN

My eyelids snapped open, panic surging through my veins as potent as the venom coursing within them. The room swam into focus, a dizzying array of blurred shapes and dim light. It resembled an apothecary, its shelves lined with vials and herbs, echoing the ancient healing chambers Amara once commanded in Rome —though her reassuring presence was absent.

"Amara?" I croaked, desperate for a lifeline, for the comfort her wisdom always brought. But the silence that followed was deafening, a stark reminder that she was not here. Only Olivia and I writhed on makeshift beds as the poison tightened its grip. My body was drenched in sweat, every nerve aflame with a feverish agony.

Beside me, Olivia convulsed. Her lips were tinged with an unnatural blue, her once-vivid complexion fading to a frightening pallor. Her eyes fluttered open, filled with a terror that mirrored my own. Then, from somewhere deep within the room, a voice echoed, cold and precise, as if spoken directly into our minds.

"The second test is the Alchemist's Crucible. Both of you

were given a deadly poison. You'll have eight hours to create an antidote. Fail, and you die."

"Roman," she gasped, her voice barely audible, trembling with the effort it took to speak. "They've poisoned us... we're not going to survive this. I—I don't know an antidote. I can't even think right now."

Her words hit like a hammer, but I kept steady. My heart clenched, a vice of terror and helplessness threatening to drag me under. Not now. Not like this. Not after everything we had endured. This was only the second test, and already, it felt like the walls of fate were closing in.

A cold shiver crept down my spine, defying the feverish heat consuming my body.

"Olivia," I rasped, forcing my voice to carry strength I didn't feel, "we're going to help one another. Together, we can solve this."

Her trembling hand reached for mine, her grip weak but determined. Despite the poison ravaging her, there was still a spark of resolve in her touch. It was enough to stoke the embers of my own will.

We had faced the impossible before. I refused to let this serpentine kiss of death claim us without a fight.

Gritting my teeth against the dizziness threatening to pull me under again, I forced myself to sit upright. The room shifted and spun, the walls seeming to breathe, closing in, then retreating as if mocking my disoriented state. I blinked hard, trying to stabilize my vision, the effort like clutching at sand slipping through my fingers.

My gaze swept over the wooden shelves, each lined neatly with containers of varying shapes—clay, glass, and metal—meticulously organized in a way that mirrored the sanctuary Amara had once created.

The air was heavy with the scent of dried herbs, mingling

with the earthy aroma of the clay brazier standing solemnly in the corner. Blackened remnants within its fire basket bore silent testimony to recent use. Beside it lay a tinderbox and a basket brimming with kindling, poised to breathe life into flames at a moment's notice. Shadows danced on the walls, cast by oil lamps and candles that flickered and sputtered, their warm glow holding back the encroaching darkness of night.

With unsteady legs, I pushed myself off the bed, every muscle screaming in protest. The floor met my feet with unexpected solidity, and I swayed, nearly collapsing before catching myself on the edge of a shelf. My trembling hands held me as my eyes scanned the labels etched into the containers—*Rosmarinus. Salvia. Papaver. Mel.* Each name whispered of a past steeped in healing and comfort when the world wasn't as heavy as it felt now.

Then my gaze landed on the unfamiliar, the esoteric—*Cicuta Malefica. Solanum Infernum. Mandragora Noxia. Aconita Sanguinaris.* The words curled and distorted before my poisoned sight, ominous and foreboding. Desperation clawed at my throat as I reached out, fumbling with the lids of clay containers, inhaling deeply in search of salvation—or even solace.

Some scents brought flickers of memory—Amara's gentle hands preparing poultices and elixirs—but others were vile enough to make bile rise in my throat. My knees buckled beneath the weight of the venom coursing through my veins, but I dragged myself upright, driven by a single need—to save Olivia, to save us both from this calculated execution.

"I'm coming to help," Olivia wheezed, her voice barely above a whisper. Her body swayed with each labored step as she crossed the room, faltering like a sapling caught in the relentless winds of a storm.

"Olivia, stay put. Let me create the antidote," I said.

She shook her head, locks of hair clinging to her sweat-slicked forehead. "We're in this together."

I couldn't argue; it wasn't our way. Together, we scanned the labels on the bottles, but our minds were as muddled as a sailor's after a tempest. My fingers brushed against the spine of the *Book of Alchemy*, its cover worn and cracked from years of use. The book fell open, its pages fluttering like the wings of a trapped bird, revealing scripts written in both Turkish and English. The letters danced before us, mocking our desperate need with their indecipherable waltz.

"Focus," I muttered, willing my eyes to stop swimming. The words on the page rippled and floated away like oil on water.

Olivia collapsed onto her knees, bracing herself with one arm while clutching her stomach with the other.

"I can barely stand up," she gasped, her breathing ragged and uneven.

Panic gnawed at my insides, spurring me into frantic action. I grabbed the nearest containers, my hands shaking as I combined their contents with reckless haste. Droplets of liquid splashed onto the wooden surface as I poured them into a vial, my thoughts a silent plea to any god who might be listening that I wasn't about to hasten our deaths.

"Drink," I said, pressing the vial into Olivia's trembling hands. She brought it to her lips hesitating.

Her eyes met mine, wide and questioning.

"What did you put in this?" she asked, the fear evident in her tone.

"Some *Aconita Sanguinaris*, some *Papaver*...and some *Cicuta Malefica*," I answered, my voice faltering slightly.

The vial paused an inch from her lips.

"*Cicuta Malefica*," she echoed, her voice hollow. "I

remember Amara telling me—it's called the Poisoner's Plant. Extremely potent neurotoxin...causing convulsions, severe pain, and rapid death."

My heart plummeted. In my blind attempt to play the healer, I had nearly sealed our fate. With a surge of clarity piercing through the poison fog, I snatched the vial from her weakening grip and hurled it across the room. It shattered against the stone wall, its deadly contents splattering harmlessly away from us.

"Forgive me," I whispered, my throat tight with shame and fear.

We were far from safe, but at least I hadn't been the one to extinguish the flickering flame of hope that stubbornly clung to life within us.

Olivia staggered forward. Her knees buckled, and she crashed into the ancient shelves with a clamor that resonated through my very bones. Bottles toppled and shattered, their contents bleeding out onto the cold stone like the lifeblood of some ethereal creature. The air thickened with an acrid stench so potent it felt like a tangible weight pressing down on us, making every breath a struggle.

"Oh, my God," Olivia cried. "Our chances at a cure are ruined. I've broken everything. I'm so sorry!"

I rushed to her side and lifted her with gentle hands. She looked so small and fragile, like a lost child seeking comfort. We had to remain strong and quickly find a solution.

"Hush now," I soothed, brushing away a strand of hair from her tear-stained face. "We'll think of something. We won't give up."

"Roman..." Her voice was a raspy whisper as she covered her mouth with her arm, fear lacing each syllable. "I wonder if we'll die just by sniffing whatever this is?"

She clutched her chest, her breathing ragged and shallow,

her body convulsing. Primal terror gripped me, constricting my heart with its icy fingers. We were fading fast, our bodies succumbing to the venom's relentless advance.

"Olivia, no," I said, barely above a murmur.

I watched in horror as dark, vein-like tendrils snaked up her arms. They were the harbingers of death, painting a grim tableau on her pale skin.

"Come, you need to lie down." My words were firm, but my hands trembled as I lifted her. She felt so fragile, like a feather caught in a storm, and I struggled under the weight of her poisoned body. Every step felt like a battle, but with a final heave, I managed to lower her onto the bed. Her once vibrant eyes were now clouded with pain, and her body slacked against the tangle of sheets.

"Rest," I said, though the word tasted bitter. Rest would not save us.

An onslaught of memories surged through my mind, relentless waves crashing against the fragile shore of my consciousness. I saw a battlefield stretched out before me, the dead and dying scattered like discarded chess pieces. Amid the chaos stood Isabelle, her face etched with determination, her eyes brimming with tears that mirrored my anguish. My attire was different, armor from another time, another life.

"Run! Get the blades to safety!" I had shouted, the urgency in my voice carving deep furrows into my soul.

Her scream pierced the veil of years, haunting and resolute. "No, Armand, I won't. If I separate the blades, terrible things will happen."

"Go, Isabelle! Separate them," I commanded, my desperation sharpening into steel. "Do as I say. We must do what's best for all. We'll find one another—in this life or the next."

"Roman!" Olivia's voice sliced through the memory, pulling me from the haunting echoes of the past. I blinked, the images dissolving like smoke in the morning sun, replaced by the harsh reality of her weakening form.

I ran to her side, my past and present colliding, both battles equally dire. Her trembling hand found mine, her grip faint but insistent. The blackness continued its slow crawl up her arm, snaking like sinister vines, a tangible representation of the poison's victory. Her breath came in shallow, desperate gasps as she looked up at me, her resolve flickering like a dying flame.

"Roman," she rasped, her voice barely more than a whisper but laced with urgency, "I won't survive. You can't let Salvatore win. He must never have the blades."

Her words were a chilling echo of my fears, her plea a desperate tether to the reality I wished to escape. Through the haze of poison and despair, her resolve stirred something deep within me—a fire that refused to be extinguished.

"Roman, we're idiots," she murmured, her eyelids fluttering, her voice breaking under the weight of resignation. "If only Amara were here... We're doomed. We can't... figure this out."

The resignation in her tone was a siren's call to despair.

"No! This can't happen again," I roared, the denial ripping from my chest. Yet, the venom spread relentlessly, mocking my desperation, painting Olivia's skin with death's unyielding palette. I turned my face skyward, pleading with an unseen deity for mercy, for intervention. "Please, not like this. Not now."

The air around us shifted, subtle but undeniable—a whisper of something beyond the tangible. It was then that I felt it—the presence of Amara. Ethereal, distant, yet vividly real. My heart surged, pounding like a war drum as I instinctively approached where I sensed her.

"Help me," I begged, my voice cracking under my desperation. "What do I need to do to save us?"

Her voice, clear and resonant, echoed within me, unshaken by the barriers of time and mortality. "You've done this before. In Rome, when Olivia was poisoned—you healed her."

The memory crashed into me like a flood. Rome. The iron blade. I had used it once to purge poison from her body. My hands moved instinctively, fueled by the fragments of hope reignited within me. I scoured the room with frantic energy, tossing aside bottles and jars until my fingers landed on the hilt of a petite knife. Its once-innocuous purpose now carried the gravity of life or death.

Fumbling, I seized the tinderbox and struck flint to steel, coaxing sparks onto the dry kindling piled in the brazier. Flames roared to life, their heat licking hungrily at the air, starkly contrasting the icy dread gripping the room.

I held the blade over the fire, watching as it glowed white-hot under the relentless kiss of the flames. The metal radiated with promise and peril, a final gambit against the darkness threatening to claim us.

"Olivia," I said, turning to her, my voice steady despite the storm of fear coursing through me. Grim determination carved itself into every line of my face. "I have to do this."

Her gaze locked onto mine, wide with fear yet tinged with an unspoken trust. She gave the faintest nod, bracing herself for what was to come. The searing blade met her skin, and her scream tore through the stillness, raw and primal, a symphony of pain and defiance. The sound reverberated in my chest, cutting deeper than the act itself, yet I pressed on, my resolve solidified by her courage.

As the venomous black veins began to recede from her skin, I inhaled sharply, feeling the knife's purpose extend to me. Without hesitation, I dragged the razor-sharp edge across my palm. The heat lanced through my flesh, pain blossoming like firecrackers behind my eyes.

Consciousness returned to me in slow, disorienting waves. My eyelids fluttered open to see Pasha Hassan standing over us, his face shadowed in the dim light. He clapped softly, the solitary sound echoing oddly against the stone walls, mocking our torment.

"What a fantastic idea," he mused, a wry smile curling his lips but never reaching his eyes. "No one has ever tried such an unusual method. You passed the Alchemist Crucible."

His words struck like a blow, and my foggy mind scrambled to comprehend them. Passed? The agony we endured, the desperate gambit with the heated blade—it had been enough? Beside me, Olivia stirred, her breaths shallow but steady. Relief coiled through me like a balm, but it was tempered by the lingering dread of what lay ahead.

"Rest up," Pasha Hassan continued, his voice smooth and lilting, each syllable dripping with calculated calm. "Tomorrow, you will face your next challenge. You'll be summoned to the Labyrinth of Shadows."

With those cryptic words, he turned and strode out, his footsteps fading into silence.

I sat up slowly, every muscle protesting, when I noticed a tray had been placed in the corner of the room. Its appearance seemed almost magical, laden with an overflowing bounty of food and water. The spread was meticulous, almost mocking in its care—plump grapes glistening like jewels, a loaf of crusty bread whose golden surface crackled beneath my touch, and a pitcher of clear water that gleamed like liquid salvation. I gingerly broke off a piece of bread, savoring the satisfying crunch as it gave way. The sweetness of the grapes burst against my tongue, a cool, welcome relief to the parched desert of my throat. Wordlessly, I fed Olivia first, watching as she nibbled at the food, her expression slowly softening with the nourishment. Then I indulged, the meal a symphony of textures and flavors that momentarily dulled the sharp edge of our reality.

After we'd eaten our fill, Olivia touched her hand to her chest, her brow furrowing with concern.

"I'm worried," she murmured, her voice tinged with quiet dread. "The poison... it might've destroyed my milk supply."

Her words struck a chord deep within me, a reminder of everything we were fighting to protect. But I forced a steady tone, masking the anxiety churning in my stomach.

"That's the least of your worries," I said, my voice gentle but firm. "We'll get through this, Olivia. One step at a time."

She looked up at me, her eyes searching. "How did you do it? How did you save us?"

"Amara came to me," I replied, the memory of her spectral guidance still vivid, a fragment of light in the abyss. "I remembered how I healed you in Rome."

The recollection was a beacon in the storm, a moment of clarity amid chaos.

Olivia furrowed her brow. "How did they know to create a room like that?" she asked softly, her voice laced with unease. "It's like they copied our memories of ancient Rome."

Her words sent a shiver down my spine. How much did our enemies know about us? Were they always one step ahead, weaving traps from the very threads of our past? I pushed the thought away. Dwelling on the unknown would serve no purpose—not now. For now, we needed strength, focus, and resolve.

I returned my attention to her, handing her another piece

of bread from the tray. "Eat," I urged. "You need to regain your strength."

Nourishment did little to soothe the aching fatigue that gripped us, but it stoked the fires of resilience within. We had survived the Alchemist Crucible and defied death once again. Still, tomorrow, the Labyrinth of Shadows awaited—a test that would likely demand every ounce of wit and willpower we possessed.

As the oil lamp dimmed, casting flickering shadows across the room, we lay side by side on the narrow cot. The silence between us was heavy, punctuated only by the occasional creak of the wooden walls and the distant murmurs of guards beyond the door. In the dim afterglow of the dying light, our hands found each other, a lifeline in the encroaching darkness.

"The Labyrinth of Shadows shouldn't be hard," I murmured, my voice low, as much to reassure myself as her. "But it will be dark. We must stick together, no matter what, and fight to the last."

Olivia's fingers squeezed mine. Her smile was weak yet determined, a sliver of moonlight cutting through the encroaching night.

"Back-to-back, like we've always been," she whispered.

I nodded, the weight of her words settling over me like armor. Our shadows would stand united, even against the darkness that threatened to consume us.

Her voice softened, barely audible. "Promise me something?"

Her pale cheeks carried the faintest hint of color as she gazed up at me, her vulnerability piercing my heart.

"Anything," I replied without hesitation, my voice steady even as my chest tightened.

"Promise you'll keep making those terrible jokes, like,

'Oh, hey, we're Timehunters,' no matter how dire it gets." A flicker of playfulness sparked in her eyes, a reminder of the woman I had fallen in love with.

I chuckled, the sound hollow yet genuine. "Only if you promise to roll your eyes and pretend not to laugh."

Sliding closer to her, I cradled her in my arms. Tenderly, I kissed her lips, pouring every ounce of love and determination into the touch. Exhaustion tugged at the edges of my mind, but the need to hold her, to feel her warmth, overpowered it. Olivia deepened the kiss, her arms winding around my neck, her body melting into mine. And then, with a soft sigh, her lips slackened. I pulled back, a small smile playing on my lips as I realized she had fallen asleep mid-kiss. Gently, I smoothed her hair and pressed a kiss to her temple. Pulling her closer, I allowed myself to savor the rare stillness, the momentary peace amidst the storm.

But peace was fleeting. The sanctity of rest was torn asunder by the arrival of dawn's gray fingers, creeping under the door and heralding the guards' approach. Their faces were grim, their silence heavy with unspoken urgency as they ushered us forth. We moved through winding underground corridors, the walls narrowing to squeeze the fight from our souls. My grip on Olivia's hand tightened as we were led deeper into the bowels of the palace. Finally, we came to a stop, standing at the precipice of...

A place that looked exactly like Balthazar's lair.

Balthazar's lair? I shook my head, dread unfurling in my chest. The detail was unnerving, plucked straight from my memories. How was this possible?

The flickering light of sconces cast trembling shadows upon the cracked walls, their wavering glow barely piercing the oppressive darkness. Beneath our feet, the chittering symphony of cockroaches filled the air, their tiny bodies crunching under our boots. The sound became a grim drum-beat with every step, marking our march into the unknown.

A warrior clad in black—his armor as dark as the void that threatened to consume us—emerged from the shadows, silent and imposing. He handed us each a sword, the cold steel heavy in my grip.

"You'll be in a darkened dungeon with no light," he said, his voice a deep baritone rumble that reverberated in the suffocating darkness. "You'll hunt opponents you cannot see. Everyone inside must be dead before you can exit."

He then pinched the flames between his thumb and fore-finger, snuffing out the light.

"You must begin," he added, his command leaving no room for hesitation. The tension in the air thickened, and the shadows seemed to pulse with the promise of an unseen battle.

"How can we fight these warriors? I can't see a thing," Olivia whispered.

"We fight back-to-back and face whatever comes," I replied, my words firm despite the erratic drumming of my heart.

With deliberate movements, we positioned ourselves, our spines pressed together, forming a living shield. My hand tightened around the sword's hilt, the worn leather digging into my palm.

In the ancient, decrepit chamber, time seemed to stretch endlessly, each second an eternity. The air hung thick with the scent of decay, making every breath challenging. Cobwebs clung to us as the lingering touch of ghosts, a chilling reminder of lives lost, and battles fought. Yet, amidst the suffocating gloom, our resolve remained steadfast.

Only the shallow breaths we shared betrayed our presence in the oppressive silence. Back-to-back, we stood as a united force—a duality of strength poised to face whatever lurked in the shadows.

The faintest scuffle—a mere whisper against stone—alerted us to their approach.

"Left flank," Olivia murmured, her voice barely a breath but resolute.

I nodded imperceptibly, trusting her instincts as if they were my own.

The brush of fabric, ghostlike, signaled danger closing in. Olivia tensed against me, a spring ready to uncoil. Then, with predatory precision, she pivoted, her blade slicing through the air. A silver streak in the blackness revealed our enemy too late. Olivia's strike met flesh with brutal finality, the heavy thud of a body hitting the ground marking her victory.

Above me, I felt the shift of movement—a downward arc aimed at my head. Instinct took over. Steel met steel in a shower of sparks as I parried the strike. The force reverberated through my arm, but my grip held steady. A quick thrust of my blade found its mark, and a pained grunt echoed before my assailant crumpled into the void.

We stood motionless, our breaths harsh yet synchronized. We were the lone flicker of defiance against the oncoming storm in this eternal night.

The shadows writhed around us, alive with unseen adversaries. Their movements were muffled, but their intent was clear. Each inhale felt like a dance with death; each exhale was a defiant challenge. The darkness grew denser, its oppressive weight pressing in from all sides.

Then, like clockwork, the battle surged forward. Metal clashed against metal, a symphony of violence in the abyss. Grunts of exertion and the occasional scream punctuated the cacophony. Behind me, I felt Olivia—an anchor and an ally, her movements perfectly tandem with mine. To those watching from the shadows, we must have appeared erratic. But it was a dance—calculated, deliberate, and deadly to us.

We became phantoms ourselves, striking from unexpected angles. The faintest tremor of the ground beneath us was a signal, an enemy advancing. Our blades moved as extensions of our will, cutting through the pitch-black as if guided by fate.

My face itched fiercely, cobwebs draping over me like a cursed veil. I shook my head, trying to rid myself of the sticky threads without losing focus on the chaos erupting around us. Beside me, Olivia swiped at a particularly thick web obstructing her vision.

"Watch out!" I hissed just as a blade arced toward her head. She ducked, narrowly evading the deadly swipe. Her sword flashed in retaliation but met only empty air.

A horde of cockroaches, roused from the corners of the dungeon, swarmed the floor in a clicking, scuttling chaos. The sudden movement added to the pandemonium, causing several of our opponents to falter, their footing unsure.

I stepped into the writhing swarm, my sword moving with precision. One by one, stumbling figures fell to my blade. The crunch of carapaces beneath my boots blended with the din of battle, each step a grim reminder of the squalor in which we fought.

"Stay close," I told Olivia, though I knew she needed no such command. We were bound in this fight, our shared resolve and an unspoken pact to endure whatever darkness surrounded us.

The rhythm of our battle became its language. The clicks of our tongues and the taps of our boots on stone communicated volumes in the oppressive dark. Each sound carried intent—a warning, a direction. My blade intercepted a blow aimed at Olivia's back, the clang of steel ringing like a desperate prayer. She pivoted, slicing low at the attacker's legs, sending him staggering into my waiting sword.

I clicked twice—a signal to move left—and Olivia immediately lunged, covering my blind side as another shadowy figure emerged. Our movements were a deadly choreography, each parry and thrust refined by necessity and sharpened by fear.

Then, the air shifted, heavy with a new urgency. The remaining warriors, whether emboldened by courage or driven by desperation, launched themselves at us in unison. I could hear their collective breaths, the pounding of their boots, the whistle of swords cutting through the stale dungeon air.

"Stand firm!" I said, bracing myself against Olivia's back.

"Always," she replied, her voice steel-edged with grim determination.

We became a whirlwind of steel and instinct, an unrelenting force refusing to be separated. Blades clashed against ours, sparks flying like fleeting stars in the oppressive darkness. I felt the brush of a sword against my tunic, close enough to send a chill racing down my spine—but not close enough to cut. With a feral grunt, I surged forward, my blade finding its mark. The warrior fell, his scream reverberating through the stone chamber before being swallowed by silence.

The room became a maelstrom of violence, each clang of metal a note in the discordant symphony of survival. Bodies thudded to the ground until the clamor ebbed, replaced by the harsh panting of the last souls standing.

This was no mere battle—it was a crucible, testing the mettle of our spirits, forging our resolve into something unbreakable. We were not just warriors; we were survivors, etching our defiance into the ancient stones that bore silent witness to our struggle.

The final gasp of the last adversary was faint, barely audible over the sound of our ragged breathing. His body crumpled to the ground with a muted thud, and then the room fell into an eerie calm. The only sounds were the labored inhales and exhales of two souls who refused to be conquered by the dark.

For a moment, we stood unmoving—Olivia's back pressed against mine—our sweat-drenched bodies trembling with exhaustion.

The air around us seemed to shiver as the chaos that had reigned moments before settled into an unsettling stillness. Now littered with the fallen, the stone floor bore the stains of conflict. The indifferent walls echoed faint scratching as cockroaches crept from their crevices, drawn to the remnants of turmoil.

"Roman," Olivia's voice broke through the quiet, heavy with fatigue yet tinged with the faintest edge of victory.

"Olivia," I replied, feeling her weight lean into me, seeking support. At that moment, we were unspoken equals, bound not just by battle but by the relentless will to endure.

We had entered this abyss with only flickers of hope to guide us. Whatever awaited in the shadows, we had proven that we could face it together. This trial was not merely about skill or a blade's sharpness—our unyielding bond, our shared refusal to yield to the darkness, that led us to victory. Together, we were unstoppable.

A single candle flame burst into existence, casting a flickering light that revealed the carnage around us. Bodies lay strewn across the floor, some still bleeding, others mangled beyond recognition. Severed limbs and decapitated heads painted a grotesque tableau of violence and death. The metallic tang of blood mixed with the sickly-sweet stench of decay assaulted my senses, clawing at the edge of my sanity. My stomach churned, yet my gaze remained fixed on the macabre scene, unable to look away.

With deliberate effort, we disentangled ourselves, the weight of the moment heavy in the air. My hands trembled as I gripped my sword tighter, not from fear but from the adrenaline that still coursed through my veins. The scrape of metal against leather was a small, jarring sound in the oppressive silence.

I turned to Olivia, meeting her gaze. Her eyes reflected the horrors we had just endured and the unspoken understanding that bound us. Whatever lay ahead in this labyrinth of shadows, we would face it together. There was no need for words; our resolve was a silent, unbreakable pact.

But the tests were far from over. Each challenge loomed larger and more insidious than the last, stretching our wills to their breaking points. The question lingered, unspoken yet ever-present—Did we have what it took to endure, or would the weight of the next trial finally shatter our spirits?

CHAPTER TWENTY EIGHT

ROMAN

The echo of our synchronized heartbeats reverberated in the cramped, barren chamber that had been our world for the past week. The room was devoid of comfort, its starkness broken only by the daily provisions slid through a small opening at the base of the heavy wooden door. Though the meals were decent, they did little to quell the gnawing anxiety that had taken root deep within me.

"The Duel of Fates is next, my love. Are you ready?" My voice sounded hollow, as if the stale air of our underground cell had leached the strength from it.

Olivia's eyes met mine, a flicker of determination cutting through the resignation etched across her delicate features.

"As ready as I'll ever be," she replied, her voice steady though her hands betrayed a slight tremble.

An imperious pounding on the door shattered our quiet conversation.

"It's time," a gruff voice bellowed from the other side.

Our gazes locked, a moment of shared fear passing between us—the weight of what lay ahead pressed down like the earth above our subterranean prison. Whatever awaited us, we would face it together.

Rough hands seized us, and I felt the coarse fabric of a blindfold being tied over my eyes. Darkness consumed my vision, and panic surged, threatening to unravel me. But I forced it down, my resolve firm. Olivia needed me to be strong. My fingers searched for hers, finding them and intertwining in a grip that conveyed all the words we couldn't speak aloud.

We were pushed forward, the hands of our captors firm on our shoulders as we stumbled through labyrinthine corridors. The walls seemed to close around us, their damp chill leaching into my bones. Each step echoed ominously, a haunting reminder of our captivity. My fear grew with every twist and turn in the tunnels, but so did my resolve. I would protect Olivia—no matter the cost.

"Stay close to me," I whispered.

Her hand tightened around mine.

Rough hands yanked away the blindfold. My eyes, adjusted to the darkness, took a moment to focus on the grandeur of our grim coliseum. Vaulted ceilings soared overhead, shrouded in shadows that danced amongst the ancient engravings etched into towering stone pillars. The carvings bore silent witness to battles long past, where heroes and monsters were locked in an eternal struggle, their victories fading into the myths they had become.

"Oh God," Olivia muttered beside me.

Still clasping hands, we stepped closer to the arena's edge, peering into the circular pit that promised violence and despair. The ground below was a mosaic of sand and dirt, dark splotches marking where blood had seeped into the earth, time and time again—a grim testament to the lives extinguished there.

Above us, balconies loomed, occupied by figures cloaked in black. They resembled crows perched in an eerie anticipation of a feast, their silence more unnerving than any roar of the crowd could ever be. Behind them hung opulent tapestries, scenes of regal splendor that mocked the savagery beneath. The spectators reclined in cushioned seats, their composure at odds with the primal chaos they had gathered to witness.

The air was heavy and thick, with the scent of bygone bloodshed mingling with the dampness of the underground. It clung to my skin, each breath reminding me of the arena's unyielding purpose—a place of death, spectacle, and survival. Here, forged from stone and sorrow, every shadow seemed to whisper of ancient power and the violence yet to come.

Olivia's grip on my hand tightened her presence, a small, fierce light against the encroaching dread. Together, we stood on the precipice, the world reduced to the pit's span and the watchers' silent gaze above.

I glanced at the bloodstained ground, each dark patch a story cut short, a life stolen by the cruelty of this place. I could feel Olivia's fear like a living thing between us, her tremulous breaths barely audible over the pounding of our hearts.

"I'm scared, Roman," she murmured, her voice barely a whisper amidst the roar of our racing hearts.

"Stay close," I said.

My eyes remained fixed on the treacherous terrain ahead. The uneven floor of the arena was riddled with subtle dips and jagged rises, all cloaked in shadows that could mask their true danger. One misstep could spell disaster—a twisted ankle or a fall that would leave us vulnerable.

A black-clad warrior stepped forward, his movements precise as he bound our wrists tightly together with coarse rope. The fibers dug into our skin, biting as if eager to draw first blood. They placed a dagger in Olivia's free hand, its blade glinting faintly in the torchlight. Into my hand, they pressed a sword, its reassuring and foreboding heft.

Without a word, they began leading us down, the cold stone floor echoing with each step we took. The air grew thick with the scent of sweat and anticipation as we descended, closer to the arena below. Finally, we were halted at the edge, standing above, gazing down at the arena where the trial would unfold.

"Remember," I hissed, my voice low and urgent, "one nick from our adversary's blades, and it's over."

The poison that laced our opponents' weapons loomed like an invisible specter, ready to claim us at the slightest misstep.

Above us, Pasha Hassan rose from his ornate throne, his commanding presence stilling the crowd's murmurs.

His voice rang out, amplified by the acoustics of the stone chamber. "This challenge is one of endurance," he declared, his words dripping with malice. "You will face warriors. Every seven minutes, new men will enter the fray. Their blades are laced with death. Few survive this trial... and I do not believe you will be the exception."

The spectators' silence was oppressive, their collective gaze bearing on us. The air felt charged with anticipation, each breath laden with expectation. Pasha Hassan's expression held a cruel amusement, his eyes gleaming as he awaited the spectacle.

I squared my shoulders, forcing myself to meet his gaze, defiance sparking within me.

"We will destroy them," I said, my voice echoing through the chamber. "Together, we are unstoppable. "

I leaned closer to Olivia and whispered, "Don't let them

scratch you. No cuts, no grazes—nothing. The poison is merciless."

Her nod was quick, resolute, though the grip on her dagger betrayed her tension.

She glanced down at the dagger, then up at me. "But I have a dagger. You have a sword."

Her words carried a flicker of something—resolve laced with the stark acknowledgment of our imbalance.

"Then we make do," I said, squeezing her hand tightly in ours, the rope biting into my skin. It was a signal of unity, a promise that whatever awaited us in the pit, we would face it together. "Together, we are unbreakable."

With those words, we steeled ourselves for the battle ahead—for the bloodshed that would either forge our victory or seal our fate.

A priest entered the arena, his presence commanding and otherworldly. His robes were worn yet regal, and his face bore the weight of countless battles witnessed. His eyes closed in deep meditation as he began chanting an ancient incantation, his voice a low, resonant baritone that seemed to reach into the marrow of the earth.

His words carried a melody that was both soothing and powerful, invoking a sense of reverence. The chant rose, crescendoing into a plea to the gods and ancestors to bless the coming combat.

A supernatural wind swept through the arena as his voice echoed through the stone chamber. It howled like a restless spirit, tugging at Olivia's hair and mine, making them dance around our faces as though even the elements bore witness to this moment.

The priest turned to us, placing a hand on our shoulders. His stern yet compassionate gaze pierced through the layers of fear and resolve, grounding us. His touch carried an inexplicable calm, a silent reminder of the gravity of our duel.

He stepped back, bowing deeply until his forehead touched the ground in a final gesture of respect. As he rose, I felt a fleeting sense of peace, fragile as it was.

The shadows at the arena's entrance began to shift and solidify, morphing into ominous silhouettes. Before I could fully prepare myself, two warriors emerged, clad in black. The flickering torchlight reflected off the sheen of their swords, and my breath hitched—the unmistakable glimmer of poisoned steel.

"Roman." Olivia's whisper broke through the tension, her tone carrying an edge of unspoken strategy.

I nodded, barely perceptible, as the attackers advanced, their eyes gleaming with a malevolence that seemed to chill the air around us. There was no time to adjust to the bindings cutting into our wrists, no moment to hesitate.

One adversary lunged, his blade slicing toward my heart with the precision of countless battles. I twisted, using the tension in our bound wrists to pull Olivia into position. At my side, she mirrored the movement with uncanny grace, dipping low and driving her dagger across the thigh of the second assailant.

"Good," I muttered as the first warrior faltered, thrown off by our unexpected coordination.

The two fell quickly, their forms crumpling onto the bloodstained ground. Their final breaths barely spent before more shadows loomed at the entrance, stepping forward with lethal intent.

"Stay close," I hissed, my words barely audible over the muffled roar of the crowd.

Three more warriors emerged, their movements fluid and synchronized. They were confident—perhaps too confident.

The cacophony of the spectators masked their approach, but Olivia and I didn't rely solely on sound. We moved as one, bound by the rope and trust forged through fire and blood.

The first strike came swiftly, a sword arcing toward me with deadly precision. I caught it with my blade, the clash ringing out like thunder. Beside me, Olivia ducked beneath my outstretched arm, her dagger slicing upward to find its mark in the attacker's side.

"Watch it!" I barked as another warrior feinted, his blade flashing toward the narrow opening in my guard. But there was no need for alarm—Olivia was already moving, her blade intercepting his with a sharp, metallic clang.

Her petite frame was deceptive, a fatal misjudgment many had made. She evaded a horizontal slash with a nimbleness that bordered on supernatural, her blade flashing upward to counter.

"Olivia!" I called out, not in fear but in affirmation. She was the storm, I was the tide, and together we were relentless.

We fought in the dim light of the underground cavern amidst the cries of the bloodthirsty audience. Not just for victory but for each other—for every precious second that allowed us to cling to life, hope, and defiance.

The ground beneath us erupted, spewing forth flames like the mouth of Hades itself. Olivia and I leaped back in unison. The sudden light blinded me, its heat searingly close to our skin. We stumbled but regained our composure as another threat whistled through the dimness.

"Arrows!" I shouted, though the warning was unnecessary—the sound was unmistakable.

We danced an erratic ballet, contorting our bodies desperately to make ourselves elusive targets. We were shadows, moving in concert, each twist and turn a testament to our shared will to survive.

An arrow skimmed past, grazing my shoulder—a sting that spoke of death had it struck deeper. I gritted my teeth, forcing the poison's threat to the back of my mind. Survival demanded focus.

"Stay close!" My voice was hoarse with exertion.

Spikes shot upward from the floor, transforming the ground into a forest of deadly steel. We twisted through the treacherous maze, Olivia's nimble form darting behind my bulkier frame. Each leap over the spikes defied the mortality they promised.

"Left! Now, right!" I called, our movements harmonized by necessity.

Our enemies surged forward, emboldened by the chaos of the arena's traps. One warrior lunged, his blade aimed to pierce the hearts of us both. My sword met his in a cold ring of metal on metal. I swung wide, pulling Olivia into a deadly pirouette. Her dagger arced through the air—a silver flash in the dimness—finding its mark in the exposed throat of another assailant.

Our bindings, meant to hinder us, became the instrument of our enemies' destruction. With each fluid movement, we leveraged each other's strength, spinning and striking in a symphony of survival. We were not just combatants bound together but a single, lethal entity fueled by love and an unyielding desire to live.

"Roman," she breathed, her voice steady despite the carnage, "we keep going."

"Yes," I said, our eyes meeting. "Together."

The oppressive heat of the flames encircling us was suffocating, a physical barrier as formidable as the warriors we faced. Sweat streamed into my eyes, stinging and blurring my vision. Olivia's grip on my hand was slick, our joined wrists slipping precariously as we brandished our weapons.

Another trio of adversaries advanced with chilling synchrony, their movements precise, their intentions murderous.

"Stay with me," I urged. Olivia's breath came in ragged pulls, her body weighed down by the relentless fight.

"Roman, the fire," she murmured, her voice distant, haunted. "It's just like that night at Mathias'… when she… when my mother… she burned everything…"

"Olivia, now is not the time!" I said, desperation lending force to my words. "Focus on the here, the now. Stay with me!"

A warrior feigned left. I pulled Olivia right. In that split second of separation, another lunged, his blade aimed straight for Olivia's heart. I stepped between them, my sword intercepting his with a jarring clash of steel. But while my attention was divided, the third combatant struck from behind Olivia. His dagger, its blade shimmering with a sickly purple hue of poison, sliced through the air with lethal intent.

She twisted just in time, her agility saving her from a fatal blow but not from harm. The poisoned dagger grazed her arm, and even amidst the chaos, I heard her sharp intake of breath. Pain etched across her face as blood began to seep from the wound. Tears blurred my vision—rage and fear colliding in a storm that overtook every thought. With a furious roar, I swept one attacker off his feet with a brutal slash across his chest. He crumpled, lifeless, as I turned to face the others.

"Roman!" Olivia's voice cut through the noise, laced with pain.

We were still in this together; her injury was a call to arms, not a death knell.

Seeing his fallen comrades, the last adversary hesitated, fear flashing in his eyes. He started to back away, but retreat was no longer an option—not for him or us. Pale but resolute, Olivia moved with a grace that belied her wound. She feinted with the dagger, a high arc that drew the warrior's gaze. Then, she dropped low and slashed. Her blade bit deep into the tendons of his leg, and he crumbled.

"Never again," Olivia whispered fiercely.

I pierced the warrior's chest with a final, decisive thrust of my sword. His lifeblood spilled onto the sand, joining the dark stains that told tales of countless battles before ours.

I knew our love had forged an indomitable force in the hush that followed. Together, against all odds, we had triumphed.

But even as relief surged through me, the sight of dark veins spreading from Olivia's wound sent a cold dread racing through my heart. Our fight for survival was far from over.

I knelt beside Olivia, my fingers shaking as I traced the poisoned line marring her arm. The veins around the shallow gash pulsed with an unnatural blackness, spreading like tendrils under her skin. Panic clawed at my chest, yet the steady pressure of her hand in mine anchored me to the moment.

"Stay with me," I said, my voice hoarse.

She nodded, her eyes fierce with a determination that belied the pallor of her face. But as her eyelids fluttered closed, panic clutched my soul.

A suffocating sense of dread gripped my heart as I watched her, knowing she might be slipping away before my very eyes. Terror tightened its grip on my throat as I realized the possibility of losing Olivia forever.

"We need an antidote," I said, more to myself than to her. The truth of our predicament hung heavy in the air. We had bested death in its cruelest form, but it lingered, biding its time within Olivia's veins.

My eyes were drawn upward to the looming balconies, where dark figures hovered like sinister specters, their silhouettes stark against the pulsing glow of torchlight. We were at the mercy of these orchestrators of terror, their every whim determining whether we would live or die. Our fates were tightly bound to their cruel games.

Desperation laced Olivia's trembling voice as she pleaded with the shadowy figures above. Her hand clutched mine so tightly it felt like my bones might grind to dust.

In a single, fluid motion, I drew my blade and severed the rope that bound us, the sharp edge flashing as it cut through the coarse fibers with a satisfying snap. I vaulted over the barrier, my boots hitting the sand with a resounding thud that echoed through the cavernous space. My eyes locked onto Pasha Hassan, perched smugly on his ornate throne, a king presiding over a pit of blood and despair.

"Save her," I demanded, my voice ragged but resolute. "I have fought and won."

Pasha Hassan's laugh was like gravel scratching across my soul. "She shouldn't have let her emotions get in the way. She's dying due to her stupidity."

His words ignited a fire within me, a blaze fueled by every injustice Olivia and I had endured since being thrust into this nightmare.

In a single motion, I scaled the wall separating us from our tormentor. Pasha Hassan's eyes widened as I stormed toward him, his smug confidence faltering. Before he could react, my hand closed around his throat with the precision born of countless battles and survival instincts.

"I have proven to you that I am a fucking Timehunter," I hissed, squeezing just enough to drive my point home without ending him—yet. "Now, heal my wife."

"You still must win the final challenge," he rasped, his

eyes gleaming with malice. "Your wife will survive until then. But I'll make a deal with you. If you win the final test, I will heal her."

"Deal?" My grip slackened as despair threatened to creep into my resolve. "What kind of sick fuck makes a deal when I'm faced with losing my wife to poison?"

"Oh, well." Pasha Hassan's indifference cut deeper than any blade. "You should hurry to your next challenge, then. The Executioner has never lost a fight."

"I have fought every kind of person and beast," I spat back, defiance surging through my veins despite the odds.

"We shall see," he replied, his smirk unwavering.

"I will kill you," I said, "after I kill the Executioner."

"Bold words." Pasha Hassan straightened his robes, his composure unshaken by my threat. "You will face the most powerful warrior in all the lands. If you win, I will keep my word. You will have your children back, and you will have the blades back."

My brow furrowed, confusion etching itself into the lines of my face. Why would he offer to return the blades? Didn't he crave their power for himself, to wield with unparalleled might? Questions clawed at my mind, suspicions forming a labyrinth of tangled thoughts and emotions.

My heart pounded, adrenaline and fury coursing through me. The stakes had never been higher, but I refused to falter. I would conquer this final challenge or die trying for Olivia, our children, and the life we yearned to reclaim.

CHAPTER
TWENTY NINE

ROMAN

I stood in the dim corridor outside the arena where the Duel of Fates was held. My heart hammered against the confines of my chest as I watched the black-clad warriors carry my wife away. The limp form of Olivia, my beloved, draped like a pallid cloth over the outstretched arms of silent guards. Her once vibrant eyes were closed, her skin an unnatural shade that spoke of the poison's kiss—its treacherous work coursing through her veins.

"Olivia!" Her name tore from my throat, raw and desperate, echoing in the oppressive silence of the stone walls. My legs threatened to buckle, but the weight of her suffering kept me upright. My hands trembled with the futility of my situation. The memory of her pain, the way her body writhed as the venom coursed through her veins, clawed at my mind. I had faced death before—on blood-soaked sands, in battles that left my blade stained and my soul scarred. I had crossed swords with Marcus in the Colosseum, clashed with Marcellious, and stood against impossible odds. Yet nothing compared to this. This wasn't just survival; this was my family, my Olivia, my world slipping through my fingers.

"Let me see Rosie! Let me see my baby girl!" I pleaded with the guards encircling me. Their faces remained impassive, emotionless masks betraying no hint of compassion.

The itch for action flared beneath my skin, the urge to fight, to do something. Anything. With a guttural growl, I lunged forward, desperation driving my every move. The guards met my fury with cold efficiency, their brutal training ensuring I was subdued before I could even get close. I hit the cold marble floor hard, the impact jarring every bone. Before I could recover, a heavy boot pressed down on my chest, pinning me in place and crushing the air from my lungs.

"We could kill you now," one guard said, his voice dripping with venom, "or you can face the Executioner. Either way, you'll die. But…" He paused, a sneer curling his lips. "We'll grant you one last look at the living. Go. See your daughters. Say your goodbyes."

My mouth twisted in disgust. I leaned forward and spat, the glob landing near his feet with a sharp finality. My narrowed eyes burned with defiance, but the unshakeable fear that coiled deep within me flickered faintly, betraying the resolve I fought to maintain.

Another guard leaned in, his breath foul and his words a dagger to my heart. "You'd better hurry, or the poison will kill your wife."

The threat hung heavy in the air, a noose tightening around my neck. They held the power, the control. But they would never understand the relentless force driving me—the unyielding determination of a man fighting for the very breath of those he loved.

Gritting my teeth, I willed my legs to move, each step echoing with the weight of desperation as I followed them down the dim, endless corridor. The journey felt like an eternity, the shadows whispering of an end I refused to accept.

The guards led me to the playroom—a mockery of sanctuary tainted by the bitter truth of what was to come.

Inside, my daughters' laughter struck me like a blade, piercing the fortress of dread surrounding my heart. Their innocence was a cruel juxtaposition to the storm raging within me. Luna gurgled, reaching for me with chubby arms, her tiny hands grasping at the air. I lifted her, cradling her warmth against my chest as if I could shield her from the darkness. Rosie, my fierce little warrior, clambered into my lap, her presence grounding me in a way nothing else could.

"Everything is going to be okay," Rosie whispered, her small hand patting my cheek with a tenderness that nearly unraveled me.

Her unwavering faith in me and us tightened the knot in my throat.

"Promise, Roman?" she asked, her wide, trusting eyes peering up at me, untainted by doubt or fear.

"Promise," I said, my voice breaking under the weight of the word. I kissed her forehead, then Luna's, their scents—innocence and love—flooding my senses. It was a cruel reminder of what was at stake. "I love you both more than time itself," I murmured, each syllable etched into the fabric of my soul. "I will protect you at all costs. Always and forever."

Rosie nodded solemnly as if my words were an unbreakable pact. And they were. I had made a silent oath, one the gods themselves could not break.

"Take me to the final battle. At once!" I commanded the guards as I set Luna down gently and rose to my feet. My armor was invisible, yet I wore it all the same. With every ounce of resolve and love fueling me, I stepped forward, ready to face the Executioner and whatever hell awaited beyond.

The guards led me back into the cold embrace of the stone corridors. The air was damp, the walls oppressive, and my boots against the floor echoed like a drumbeat, marking the seconds of my life. Pasha Hassan was waiting for me at the end of the passage, his grin a grotesque mask of malice that betrayed the cruelty simmering beneath.

Without a word, they ushered me into an arena—a space so disturbingly familiar that it tore at the fabric of my sanity. It was a replica of the Colosseum, where I had once fought as a gladiator. The blood-soaked sand, the weathered stone, and the pitiless air—every detail was a mirror to a life I had thought buried in the past. My stomach churned as I stepped onto the sand, memories of combat and survival clawing their way to the forefront of my mind.

The eerie silence of the space was suffocating. Hundreds of black-clad warriors stood as silent sentinels, their faces hidden, their gazes piercing. In another life, the roar of the crowd had been my soundtrack, but now, their silence was deafening, a void that gnawed at my resolve.

Olivia was right. It's like they're pulling these memories from our minds.

Above it all, Pasha Hassan sat upon his ornate throne, his chain metal mask gleaming like a faceless specter of doom. He was the puppeteer, and we were his marionettes, dancing to the strings of his cruelty. His voice cut through the quiet like a blade when he spoke, cold and devoid of humanity.

"Let's begin," he said, each word a harbinger of chaos. "You will only get one weapon."

The command was simple, yet it heralded a storm of violence that would determine the fate of everything I held dear. With grim determination, I stepped forward, ready to face the abyss.

A guard, his silence as heavy as his armor, guided me to a table with an arsenal fit for the gods. I scanned the collection—a dazzling array of death forged in steel. My hand hovered, indecisive for only a moment, before settling on the gladius. Its familiar weight in my hand was a comfort amidst the chaos, the double-edged blade gleaming under the torchlight like a sliver of hope. Its sharp point whispered promises of lethality, a promise I intended to fulfill. But there was no scutum to pair it with, no shield to protect me from the onslaught I was sure to face. Vulnerability gnawed at the edges of my mind, threatening to undermine my determination. I pushed the thought aside. Fear had no place here. Not now. Not with everything at stake.

With the gladius in hand, I turned back to the arena, stepping onto the blood-soaked sand with grim resolve. My grip tightened on the hilt as I faced the abyss. Whatever monsters lay ahead, I would meet them head-on.

The metal clinking echoed through the cavernous arena, harbingering ancient rituals and inevitable violence. From the shadows, a priest emerged, his presence somber and commanding. In his hands, a brazier glowed with smoldering coals, tendrils of incense curling into the air like ghostly whispers. The heady scent mingled with the metallic tang of blood, creating an oppressive atmosphere that pressed against my senses.

He motioned toward a stone basin filled with water, its surface dark and still as obsidian. "Purification is required," he intoned, his voice a solemn whisper that seemed to resonate with the stones themselves.

I knelt beside the basin, the chill of the water biting into my skin as I cupped it in my hands and splashed it over my face. Each droplet fell away, carrying with it the weight of doubt and fear, leaving behind only the hardened resolve of a warrior. The icy shock of the ritual steadied my breathing, grounding me for what was to come.

Closing my eyes, I silently prayed to Mars, the god of war. "Grant me strength, grant me courage," I murmured, the words barely audible but reverberating within the core of my being.

The priest's chant began low and rhythmic, an ancient hymn that awakened something primal within me. Memories stirred unbidden—sun-drenched battles, the clash of steel, the roar of distant crowds. The smoke from the brazier enveloped the gladius in my grip, the fragrant cloud seeming to imbue the metal with a weight greater than its own—a divine favor bestowed by forces unseen.

"May this blade strike true," I whispered, the words carried on a breath that hung suspended between the realms of man and myth.

The priest approached me, bearing pigments of red and black. He painted symbols across my cheeks and forehead with practiced motions, marks of strength, and lineage. The cool paint against my skin anchored me to the present, to the reality of the battle ahead. It was a stark reminder that while my heritage might be steeped in glory and honor, today, I fought not for the adulation of a crowd but for the very essence of my being—my wife, my daughters, my soul laid bare in the sands of this forsaken arena.

"Ready yourself, Timehunter," the priest murmured, stepping back to survey his work. "History and destiny collide within you."

With war paint marking my face and determination steeling my heart, I stood and faced the direction of the impending battle, the gladius firm in my grasp. Today, I would not falter. For Olivia, for Luna, for Rosie—I would conquer time itself.

The leather straps bit into my flesh as the priest wound them tightly around my wrists and forearms. I flexed against the binding, finding comfort in the added support. Yet, when I sought assurance in the priest's eyes, there was none—only the ghost of a smirk and a subtle shake of his head that chilled me more than any omen. A silent verdict resonated with grim finality—no one survived the Executioner.

I turned away from the priest's foreboding gaze, focusing on the arena's entrance. There, silhouetted against the harsh light, stood my adversary—a hulking figure cloaked in garments that concealed all but the feverish glint of his eyes.

He moved into the arena with an unnatural gait, every step pulsing with barely contained ferocity. Beneath the shadow of his hood, his eyes burned—not with calm precision, but with unbridled madness. They roamed the coliseum, unfocused and wild, painting the portrait of a man who had long severed ties with reason. His whites gleamed unnaturally, like moonlight skimming the blade's edge, while his pupils dilated with a hunger that promised destruction.

My attire was scant, just as it would have been in the days of the Roman Coliseum. A short tunic barely reaching mid-thigh clung to my body, exposing my muscular arms. On my feet were simple leather sandals, offering little protection from the jagged sand or the sharp edges of my opponent's blades.

Despite the simplicity of my garb, I felt a primal strength coursing through me, as if the weight of the past—the countless battles and bloodshed of gladiators before me—had settled into my bones. My eyes locked onto my opponents as we awaited the call to battle, a silent exchange of challenge and resolve.

The horn's blast shattered the silence, signaling the beginning of the fight. I lunged forward instinctively, prepared to meet brutality with equal ferocity. But then I stopped, my momentum halting as the Executioner began his strange and unnerving dance.

His body convulsed, spasms rippling through muscle and sinew with a grotesque rhythm. He paced erratically, each step etching an unhinged pattern into the sand. His lips moved, muttering incoherent words, fragments of thoughts carried away by the wind. Then, as if possessed, he arched his neck back and let loose a roar that seemed to shake the very foundation of the arena. It wasn't the battle cry of a man but the guttural scream of something primal, something not entirely human. It clawed at my senses, a sound that bridged the void between beast and warrior.

The roar was followed by a dissonant symphony of screams and growls, noises that should not have existed together. The Executioner tore at his flesh, leaving crimson streaks across his chest and arms. The sharp, rhythmic slapping of his fists against his skin echoed through the coliseum, a horrifying display of pain disregarded as if his body were merely a vessel for chaos.

Chaos—he was its embodiment, a living storm whose presence threatened to unravel the fragile order of the world. I tightened my grip on the hilt of my gladius, the leather biting into my palm as I steeled myself against the tempest before me.

The Executioner stilled momentarily, his head snapping forward, eyes wide and unseeing. He pointed into space, his finger tracing lines that only he could perceive.

"You, there!" he shouted, his voice cracking and descending into fearful whimpers. "No, no, no…"

And then, as if the fear had transformed, his expression contorted into twisted glee. A grin stretched across his face, grotesque and unnatural.

His laughter erupted like a rupture in the earth, spilling forth a cacophony of cackles, sobs, and guttural screams that grated against the ancient stones of the arena. The sound ricocheted through the space, amplifying its madness until it felt alive, creeping through the air and seeping into my skin. It crawled into my ears, twisting into a discordant melody that threatened to linger long after this nightmare ended.

"Focus," I whispered, forcing air into my lungs despite the weight of dread pressing down on me. The leather straps binding my wrists felt more like chains, tethering me to a grim destiny I had no choice but to face.

With a snarl that cut through his deranged laughter, the Executioner spun suddenly, his massive blade cleaving through the air. The weapon met nothing but shadows, yet the sheer force of his swings screamed unrestrained violence. Each motion was wild and erratic, a tempest given human form, leaving no room for prediction or strategy.

Adrenaline surged, sharpening my senses as I prepared for the inevitable onslaught. But to my astonishment, the Executioner's rage was not directed at me. Instead, he charged toward the arena's edge, his guttural roar echoing like thunder. The spectators recoiled in collective fear as his weapon crashed into the wooden barrier separating them from the pit below. The barricade splintered beneath his fury, sending shards of wood flying into the crowd like shrapnel. Cries of alarm rang out, but he paid them no mind, his maddened eyes shimmering with sadistic delight.

"By Mars…what have I stepped into?" I muttered under my breath, gripping the hilt of my gladius until my knuckles turned white. I had never faced an opponent so utterly consumed by chaos. He was a storm, an unrelenting force of destruction, and I was standing in its path.

The Executioner's eyes—two dark stones burning with an

unholy fire—fixed on me. In their depths, I saw death reflected, multiplied a hundredfold.

"Olivia," I murmured, my wife's name a prayer, a talisman against the madness I faced. The thought of her, of Luna and Rosie, anchored me. It reminded me why I had to survive, why I couldn't falter now.

The Executioner began to circle me, a predator stalking its prey. His mutterings transformed into low, guttural growls, each rumble resonating like a dark hymn. His massive frame coiled with tension, muscles twitching as though barely containing the storm of violence within. Every movement was deliberate yet unpredictable, the calculated chaos of a killer who lived for the dance of blood and sand.

Then, with a deafening roar, he brought his weapon—a monstrous, lethal scythe—crashing into the ground. The impact sent a tremor through the arena, dust billowing around us like a rising shroud. Shards of stone pelted my skin, sharp and relentless, like arrows fired from the earth. He clawed at his skull with clenched fists as though trying to douse the blazing fires of insanity that burned behind his eyes.

A hush fell over the arena, suffocating and unnatural. The warriors clad in black stood statue-like, their collective breaths held in anticipation. The silence was more chilling than the chaos that had preceded it. All eyes were fixed on the Executioner, a man untethered from reality, a raw spectacle of fragility and fury laid bare.

"Strength," I whispered, invoking Mars, though the god felt leagues away in this moment of terror. "Let me be strength."

As the dust began to settle, the Executioner raised his head. His primal gaze found mine, locking on with a ferocity that sent an icy shiver down my spine. His expression twisted into one of singular focus—an insatiable bloodlust, a hunger for pain and suffering that knew no bounds. He embodied war in its most brutal and unrelenting form, and I, Roman, the supposed Timehunter, was the only thing standing between him and his chaotic craving for destruction.

"Protect them," I thought, my mind filled with the images of Luna and Rosie. Their innocence and faith in me were an unwavering contrast to the brutality unfolding before me. Their trust was my fuel, their love my armor.

This battle was more than physical. It was a fight for sanity, for family, for my very soul—a soul that threatened to be consumed by the shadow of the man who raged before me.

The air thrummed with a tension so thick it felt alive. I watched, breath locked in my chest, as the Executioner unleashed a roar that shattered the silence of the coliseum like a thunderclap. He surged forward, less a man and a living storm of fury. His essence seemed distilled into raw, unrelenting chaos, as though he had abandoned his humanity to become a vessel for the ancient, dark spirits of war that had haunted our ancestors.

I braced myself, gladius raised, ready for the inevitable clash. This was no ordinary duel—a trial by fire against madness incarnate. The familiar weight of my weapon was a promise, a silent oath that I was not yet defeated.

The ground trembled under the berserker's charge, his spiked mace swinging in wide, deadly arcs. Its pendulum-like movements were as erratic as they were devastating, the wind from each swing biting at my skin. My instincts screamed for action. With a swift sidestep, I narrowly avoided the first strike, the mace slamming into the sand with enough force to send dust into the air.

As his weapon struck empty ground, I saw the flicker of frustration in his wild eyes. He swung again, faster this time. I raised my blade just in time, the collision jarring my arm and sending shockwaves. The strength behind his attack was a brutal reminder of how fragile flesh and bone could be.

"Focus, Roman," I told myself, shaking off the numbness creeping up my arm. There was no room for hesitation or error. I had to be faster, sharper.

I retaliated, my gladius cutting through the charged air. Each strike was calculated and aimed at the vulnerable gaps in his defenses. My blade met its mark with a satisfying bite, but the Executioner bore it all without faltering. Each blow seemed to fuel him further, the crimson streaks on his garb nothing more than decoration to his relentless assault.

Again and again, I struck, my sword a blur of motion. Blood speckled the ground, a grim testament to my efforts, yet he stood unyielding, a monolith defying the sea's battering waves. His body seemed to ignore pain, his movements as wild and unrelenting as before.

"Olivia... Rosie... Baby Luna..." Their faces flashed in my mind, a momentary reprieve from the carnage around me. For them, I could not falter. For them, my blade would sing until the bitter end.

The Executioner's silhouette moved like a marionette gripped by the strings of madness, his movements as erratic and unpredictable as a tempest. He feigned a strike to the left, muscles coiling with deceptive intent, only to unleash his fury in a lunge to the right. His eyes—a maelstrom of wild rage— locked onto mine, and he screamed. The sound was not human. It was the guttural cry of a beast dragged from the depths of a nightmare, a sound that clawed at the air and made the arena's walls shiver.

I braced, feet digging into the blood-stained sands, and met his charge. My blade absorbed the impact of his mace, the collision reverberating through my bones like the toll of a death knell. The force threatened to unbalance me, but I gritted my teeth, grounding myself with the thought of Olivia and our daughters. Each thunderous clash pushed me back, my boots scraping the ground as I fought to maintain my stance amidst his relentless assault.

It became painfully clear with every blow—I could not forcefully overpower this berserker.

Giving up was not in my nature, but survival demanded adaptation. I pivoted and retreated, circling the arena's perimeter to buy precious seconds to regroup. The Executioner pursued his run disjointed and staggering yet terrifying in its single-minded intent. He was chaos personified, a storm I had no choice but to weather.

I weaved through the debris scattered across the arena floor, remnants of past battles now serving as my refuge. Darting behind a pillar, I felt the rush of his spiked mace as it missed my head by inches, the force splintering the stone where I'd stood moments before. Dust choked the air, mingling with the metallic tang of blood and sweat. I reached down and scooped up a handful of sand, the coarse grains biting into my palm like tiny blades.

As the Executioner rounded the pillar, his howl splitting the oppressive silence, I flung the sand into his face. His roars shifted to cries of fury, the blinding particles rendering his swings frenetic and aimless.

This was my chance.

I stepped back, creating distance, while he clawed at his eyes, his frustration and rage palpable. My heart pounded against my ribcage, not from fear but from a grim determination. Observing him now, his vulnerabilities began to emerge —the slight limp from an earlier blow, the way his guard dropped when his swings grew too wide.

In the dance of death, I found his madness' rhythm. Now, it was time to make my move.

The Executioner charged with the force of a hurricane, but I was no longer a man caught in the storm—I was the calm in its eye. As he brought down his mace with the full weight of insanity, I sidestepped, my movements fluid and deliberate, my boots tracing familiar patterns on the blood-streaked sand.

"Is this all you have?" I taunted, my voice low but cutting through the din of his rage.

His growl was guttural, primal—a sound unshackled from reason. It was the confirmation I needed. With a swift arc of my gladius, I struck, the blade slicing through the air and biting deep into the exposed flesh at his side. Crimson erupted across his tattered garments, staining him with the undeniable mark of his mortality. Yet, he did not flinch or falter. If he felt pain, it was drowned in the abyss of his madness.

"Fight, then," I spat, circling him like a wolf stalking its prey. "Fight until the end!"

Each strike was precise, deliberate, and deadly. My gladius sang as it met flesh—one hamstring, then the other. His movements slowed, his towering form wavering like a crumbling monument to chaos.

A sudden, thunderous crack split the air. The ground beneath us gave way, a deep chasm tearing through the arena floor. I leaped back, and the displaced air rushing past brushed my skin as the earth crumbled beneath my boots. Shards of stone rained from above, each one a deadly projectile. I twisted and dodged, survival instinct guiding every move as the arena became a weapon.

The Executioner, oblivious or indifferent to the destruction around him, stumbled forward. His foot caught on a loose stone, and with a grinding rumble, the floor beneath him collapsed further. He staggered, a jagged rock slicing into his leg. His roar shattered the tense silence, agony, and defiance echoing through the arena like a dying beast's final cry.

"Watch closely," I whispered to the shadowy figures that lined the stands above.

My gaze never wavered from the Executioner. His erratic gestures, once terrifying in their ferocity, now painted a picture of a wounded animal—cornered, desperate, and lashing out in its death throes. The chaos of his being had finally met the precision of my resolve, and the end was drawing near.

"Your champion falters," I said, louder this time, though the arena remained silent. No one would answer, and I knew this fight was mine to finish. As the Executioner's breaths grew ragged and his steps faltered, I steeled myself to deliver the final blow—the culmination of the violent spectacle they had all come to see.

His silhouette wavered like a mirage in the heat of battle; the ferocity that had once defined him was now reduced to languid, unfocused swings. Blood dripped from the gashes in his legs, pooling in the sand beneath him. His breath came in labored gasps, each one a reminder of how far he had fallen from the monstrous force he had been.

My heart thundered in my chest as I surged forward, gladius in hand, every step a declaration of intent. The distance between us evaporated, and his massive arm arced feebly through the air in a last-ditch attempt to defend himself. But the effort was sluggish, the swing a shadow of the terror it had once inspired.

This was my moment. Years of combat had honed my instincts to a blade's edge, and I moved without hesitation. Ducking beneath his wild, clumsy swing, I felt the rush of displaced air against my skin. In one fluid motion, I drove my gladius forward, its sharp edge slicing through resistance until it found its mark—his chest, above the armored waistline.

The blade sang as it pierced his flesh, the note resonating in the arena's stillness. A gasp escaped his lips, more of a shock than pain—a warrior's realization that the end had come. His wide eyes, reflecting the flickering torchlight, burned with fading defiance before dimming into the resignation of a man confronting his mortality.

His knees buckled, and he fell, his massive frame crumpling onto the blood-soaked sand. I stood over him, my gladius still embedded in his chest, its hilt an unyielding promise that I would strike again if he dared rise. My every muscle remained taut, my senses attuned to any hint of deceit or final treachery.

But there was none. No last burst of strength, no defiant roar—only the rasping, uneven breaths of a defeated warrior. Slowly, his gaze turned inward, the madness that had consumed him retreating behind the veil of looming darkness. The Executioner's final moments were silent, save for the faint whisper of life leaving his body.

"Yield," I said, though it was hardly necessary. The outcome was clear. The Executioner lay defeated, his massive frame succumbing to the inevitable. The audience's silence pressed down upon us, their collective breath held in a suspended pause, awaiting the conclusion of this deadly spectacle.

Gripping the edges of the bloodied mask, I tore it from the Executioner's head with a mixture of fury and desperation. The face that stared back at me sent a jolt through my entire being—it was Pasha Hassan—the architect of my torment, his features twisted in pain but unmistakably his.

"Impossible," I whispered, my voice barely audible above my heartbeat pounding. My gaze snapped to the royal throne where I had seen him sitting, orchestrating this entire ordeal.

There he sat, still as stone, an unflinching observer of the violence. My eyes darted back to the defeated man before me, the bloodied face identical to the figure on the throne. A chill coursed through me, my mind struggling to reconcile the duplicity.

"Any last words, Pasha Hassan, before I kill you?" I hissed, my gladius poised to strike. But as I withdrew the blade from his chest, my resolve faltered. My breath caught as I watched in disbelief—the flesh, torn and bloodied from my strike, began to knit itself back together. Before my eyes, the mortal wound closed, leaving nothing but unbroken skin. My mind reeled. How was this possible? Pasha Hassan... a Timehunter. A being of darkness with powers I had only begun to fathom. But to heal so completely, so unnaturally, defied every law of mortality I knew.

"Indeed," the real Pasha Hassan said, his voice laced with an emotion I couldn't place. "I know you hate me. I know you despise me. But tell me, Roman—would you truly kill your flesh and blood? Would you honestly kill your father?"

My grip on the gladius wavered.

"My... my... my father?" The word tumbled out, bitter and sharp, scraping against my tongue like a blade.

A prideful smile flickered across Pasha Hassan's pained expression. "I have waited for this moment for many years, my son. Seeing the warrior, father, and husband you've become—makes me so proud of you. I never abandoned you, my boy. I never left your mother. Everything I did... it was to prepare you."

"Prepare me? For what? Lies? Deception?" I spat, my heart racing, torn between the impulse to end him and the shock that shackled my hands. I could not believe what I was hearing. This man—Pasha Hassan—was my father? The father I had desperately yearned to meet? My gaze drifted to his face, and for the first time, I saw it—the resemblance to Marcellious, my brother. The truth crashed over me like a tidal wave, relentless and suffocating.

My heart pounded, confusion and betrayal warring within me.

"If you are here, then who is on your throne?" I demanded, my voice a mixture of fury and desperation. I scanned the arena, seeking the man who had orchestrated this nightmare, the figure I believed to be Pasha Hassan.

"Roman." The figure on the throne spoke, his voice echoing through the massive arena. "I see that rage has not dampened your sharpness."

With a slow, deliberate motion, he removed his mask.

My jaw dropped in shock. Malik? How could this be? My mind reeled as I realized I had been deceived by the man I called my brother.

"You have fought with such bravery, Roman," Malik said, his tone laced with admiration.

"Malik..." I choked out, my voice thick with bewilderment.

"Yes, my dear brother," Malik replied calmly.

"You knew all along." I stumbled backward in disbelief.

"I did," Malik confirmed with a smirk.

My grip on my sword weakened until it fell from my hand with a resounding clang on the cold stone floor. My body trembled with an overwhelming mix of emotions—anger, hurt, and, above all, a deep sense of loss and betrayal at the hands of my flesh and blood.

"I know you have many questions, Roman," Pasha Hassan said, his words slicing through my mind.

But did he understand the weight of those words? Everything I thought I knew had been turned on its head. The truth was far more complicated than I ever could have imagined.

"Malik knew my identity all along," Pasha Hassan continued, pressing his hand over his chest, the motion almost contemplative. His voice remained calm, though there was an undertone of something unexpected—almost... tender. "He was bound by secrecy. Olivia was never given the poison. The blades used in the last challenge were coated with a sedative."

His eyes met mine, imploring me to understand. "I wanted the final battle to be with you... I wanted to fight my son, this great, strong warrior. And you won, Roman. You won in a fight to the death with the Executioner."

"Olivia!" Her name burst from me. "Where is she?"

"She is waiting for you in my chambers. Go get cleaned up," Pasha Hassan said, his voice softening in a way that caught me off guard. "Then, I will tell you and your wife everything you desire."

Turning from the enigma etched in the sand, a tumultuous wave of emotions engulfed me. The figure before me, my estranged father, a ghost from the past I had long resented for his absence. Yet, amidst this revelation, a labyrinth of perplexity entwined my thoughts, leaving me adrift in a sea of uncertainty. Questions swirled relentlessly in my mind like a windstorm—what intricate web of fate had led to this moment? Was Reyna now not just a traveling companion but kin? As I grappled with these disorienting truths, an unsettling shroud of ambiguity veiled my future, casting shadows upon the path ahead. How would this change things in Olivia's and my quest for survival against enemies too powerful to comprehend?

CHAPTER THIRTY

OLIVIA

I awoke to the scent of jasmine and myrrh, an intoxicating blend that seemed to swirl around me like a protective shroud. My head swam as I tried to lift it from the plush silk pillows, each embroidered with golden threads that shimmered in the soft morning light filtering through the lattice windows.

Tapestries of vibrant hues adorned the walls, depicting scenes of hunting and feasting, while the floor was covered with rugs so thick I knew my feet would sink into them like warm sand.

The canopy bed I lay in was a masterpiece of carved wood, swathed in diaphanous curtains that rippled gently in the breeze. Everything around me exuded excess and luxury —from the intricate inlays on the furniture to the ceiling painted with celestial motifs, gazing down like silent, watchful gods.

I struggled to sit up; every movement was sluggish, like wading through water. The door creaked open, breaking the stillness, and she entered—Zara.

Her face was seared into my memory, etched amidst

flames and chaos. She was the enigmatic being who had swooped in to save me when my mother sought my destruction. Zara's presence carried an unshakable calm, her hands steady, her sapphire eyes shimmered with an empathy that seemed to transcend time. She moved with an elegant fluidity, her steps deliberate and imbued with a quiet power.

Her attire—a blend of deep blues and purples that flowed like water—only heightened her aura of mystique, hinting at the shadows she navigated and the timeless journey she carried within her. Her golden hair cascaded like liquid silk, catching the light in an almost otherworldly way, framing her delicate features with an ethereal glow.

"You're the woman who saved me," I rasped, my voice cracking under gratitude and bewilderment. "From the fire, my mother set to force me to talk."

"I am indeed," Zara replied, her voice a soothing melody. "I transported you away from the burning building. And I made sure Reyna and Rosie were guided to safety."

"Oh, thank God," I murmured, taking a long breath.

"Be still, child," she said, pressing a cool hand to my forehead. Her touch was a gentle breeze, calming the confusion swirling in my mind.

"You are safe here."

"Safe?" The word felt foreign on my tongue, muffled by the lingering fog in my mind. How could I be safe when the last thing I remembered was the bite of steel and the certainty of death? "Is that a joke?"

"I do not jest. Your ordeal was but a charade," she said, offering me a cup filled with a liquid that smelled faintly of mint. "The blade that cut you—it carried no poison, only a sedative to dull your senses."

Confusion tightened its grip on me, and I pushed the cup away, desperate for clarity. "I don't understand. Are you telling me that every test my husband and I endured was all for show? Part of some twisted game?"

"In a sense, yes, but for reasons you will come to understand," she said, smoothing the bedding covering me with delicate precision.

"Who are you?" I asked.

She offered a small, knowing smile, her gaze locking onto mine with an intensity that seemed to pierce through my soul. "My name is Zara."

Her voice, soft yet firm, carried the weight of centuries, each word a testament to her enduring vigilance.

"I know," I said, my breath hitching as memories of my mother's venomous accusations resurfaced. "My mother said your name. But *who* are you? What are you? Where do you come from?" The words tumbled from my lips like water breaking through a dam.

Zara's eyes—dark pools of unfathomable depth—held mine with a steadiness that anchored me amidst the chaos of my thoughts.

"All your questions will be answered in due time," she said, her tone as gentle as the silk drapes lining the latticed windows.

My voice trembled as I asked, "Where is my precious child, Luna? And where is Rosie? I need to see them."

Zara's expression softened. "They are safe, my dear. In the nursery, surrounded by new toys for Rosie and a team of devoted nannies for Luna. You will be reunited with them soon, I promise."

With her tall frame and commanding presence, Zara embodied the essence of both a guardian and a warrior.

My heart ached to hold my children in my arms again.

"Please," I said, "I must see them now. I miss them more than words can express."

Zara smiled kindly, though there was a firmness in her gaze. "My dear, you need to rest and regain your strength. Trust me when I say you will see them soon enough. For now, take comfort in knowing they are safe, as are you and Roman."

I couldn't wrap my mind around the idea that everything we had experienced was just a facade. My stomach felt sick with confusion and betrayal.

Zara touched my shoulder, her hand warm and grounding. "I understand your confusion, dear. But it was all part of Pasha Hassan's plan. He wanted the final challenge to be against his son."

A chill shot through my body, leaving me frozen in place.

"Could you repeat that?" I asked, trying to make sense of her words.

Zara's piercing blue eyes locked onto mine, their unfathomable depths stirring something deep within me. "Pasha Hassan insisted on the final challenge being with his son."

"His... son?" The word caught in my throat, heavy and jagged, its weight sinking in slowly. It wove a tangled web of implications that I struggled to unravel. "What exactly are you getting at?"

"It's the truth," Zara said evenly. "Pasha Hassan is Roman Alexander's father.

"Every trial set before you, every challenge, was meant to shape you both for what lies ahead," he said, his voice unwavering. "Each one was drawn from your memories, shaping the path forward."

My heart hammered against my ribcage, the word "flabbergasted" barely scraping the surface of the storm raging within. How had the world tilted drastically on its axis while I remained oblivious?

"Who are you?" The plea tumbled from my lips, raw and edged with a burgeoning fear of the unknown.

"I am bound to protect you," Zara declared, her unwavering commitment resonating in every word she uttered. "For as long as breath fills my lungs, that vow shall never waver."

"But you are the darkness," I stammered. Images of our recent encounters flashed through my mind, her dark powers protecting and somehow transporting me to safety. "I saw with my eyes how you took me from one dangerous situation and brought me to safety."

Zara's expression hardened like a storm cloud gathering before a thunderous strike.

"Most darknesses have been poisoned and twisted by those who fear their power," she said in a low, ominous tone. "But Malik and I are different. He has been under my tutelage. He was taught to use his darkness for good, to fight for the right side."

Her words sent chills down my spine. The idea that not all darkness was inherently evil was foreign to me, yet Zara made it sound possible—convincing, even.

"Remember this, Olivia," she continued, her gaze unwavering, her voice like a blade carving truth into the silence. "Not all darknesses are born evil. Many are made evil by those who seek to control them."

"Thank you," I murmured, the memory of flames licking at my flesh and her timely intervention merging into one. "For rescuing me and my baby from the fire... and for ensuring that Rosie and Reyna made it out too."

"Think nothing of it," Zara said, her expression softening briefly. "It was both my honor and my duty. We stand on the precipice of something great. You're safe, Olivia—for now."

Her assurance should have brought comfort, yet it left me

with a fresh tide of unease. "Explain," I pressed. "Please, I need to understand. Everyone keeps holding onto these secrets, and I'm so tired of being left in the dark."

But Zara's lips sealed shut like the tomb of a long-forgotten sultan, her expression an impenetrable mask.

"Some truths," she whispered, a note of finality threading through her words, "are for another time."

Impatience clawed at my insides. "So, you won't tell me anything?

"I promise you, Olivia, everything will be revealed to you soon. Just stay patient for a little bit longer," Zara said, her enigmatic smile shielding her mysteries.

"I want to see my husband," I said.

"I will go and get him," she replied, her voice calm, before exiting the room with a rustle of her simple yet elegant garments.

I rose from the majestic bed, my legs still unsteady. My mind raced with confusion in the grand, lavish room. Zara's cryptic words echoed as I tried to understand it all. Roman and I had been under constant threat, yet now she claimed we were safe? My body still trembled from the fear and trauma of being captured by Pasha Hassan and his army. Could there be a new definition of safety that I was discovering?

I paced the opulent chamber, which felt more like a sultan's palace than a mere bedroom. My feet sank into thick, ornate carpets that muffled my restless steps.

The light spilling into the room captured my attention, drawing me toward its source. I couldn't fathom where it came from in a space seemingly shielded from the sun in this underground palace. Yet, the room was bathed in a warm, golden glow, casting everything in a hazy, ethereal illumination. I walked toward the light's source—a diffuse, glowing orb near the ceiling. It floated effortlessly, suspended in midair, radiating light and warmth. Shadows danced on the walls, alive with movement. I reached out to touch it, but my hand passed right through as if it were made of mist.

I glanced around, searching for any other light source, but there was none. There was only the orb, filling the darkness with its gentle, comforting, and strange glow. Pulling my hand back, I saw the fine attire adorning my body. The caftan I wore was a masterpiece of crimson velvet trimmed with intricate gold embroidery. Its hem was embellished with delicate pearls that whispered of wealth and status. The sleeves billowed gracefully, edged with threads of silver, while a sash cinched at my waist, studded with jewels that caught the light like stars. This was the garb of a noblewoman of the Ottoman Empire, far removed from anything I had ever owned or imagined wearing.

I turned toward the full-length, ornamental mirror standing against the wall. The woman reflected at me, draped in elegance, her posture regal. But it was her eyes—my eyes —that betrayed her. They were not the eyes of nobility but of a woman hungry for answers, yearning to piece together the fractured reality around her.

The hardwood floor vibrated under the weight of approaching footsteps, growing louder as they neared my bedroom door. Excitement rippled through me at the thought of Roman's imminent arrival. My heart thrummed with a heady blend of love, anticipation, and an unquenchable thirst for knowledge. The journey we'd embarked on together had transformed me and tempered me like steel forged in adversity. I hardly recognized the girl I once was in the reflection of this foreign world.

The mosaic of my experiences, each a piece of colored glass, had assembled into a vibrant picture of the person I had become—a warrior, a lover, a mother, a seeker of truths.

Standing on the precipice of revelation, I ached to share this new self with Roman—to see his reaction reflected in those deep eyes that promised solace and adventure.

The heavy carved door swung inward, and Roman stepped across the threshold. My breath hitched at the sight of him. His caftan fell in rich, cascading folds, the deep azure fabric embroidered with gold thread that shimmered like rivulets of sunlight. A sash encircled his waist, its intricate brocade speaking of wealth and power, while his boots, turned up at the toes, gleamed with a polish that rivaled the ornate silverwork on his belt.

His clean-shaven face revealed the strong jawline I had traced many times with my fingers. His normally unruly hair was brushed back neatly, framing his striking features. It wasn't just the clothes that made him seem princely—there was an aura about him, a commanding presence that filled the room as though he had always belonged to this world of splendor.

Without hesitation, I ran across the plush carpet, my heart galloping. With a few strides, I was in his arms, throwing decorum to the wind as I pressed my lips to his in a kiss that sang of desperation and relief. It felt like the end of the world and the beginning of everything, all at once.

Roman cupped my face with his hands, his thumbs brushing away the tears rolling down my cheeks.

"Oh, my love… I thought I lost you," he whispered, his voice thick with emotion. "You were so pale… You weren't breathing, Olivia."

The weight of those words bore down on me, yet they lifted a burden I hadn't known I carried.

"The thought of losing you darkened my world," he said, "but your presence now paints my days in the colors of dawn. I love you more profoundly with each sunrise."

Our eyes locked, and I felt the universe still for a moment.

"In every life," I whispered, "in every version of reality, it's you—my constant, my certainty. You are the dream from which I never wish to awaken."

His smile then was worth every trial we'd ever faced, every question still unanswered. It was the silent echo of my soul recognizing its counterpart in another.

Our bodies collided with a force fueled by an insatiable hunger for each other; each kiss was a fierce proclamation of our unbreakable bond and the wars we had waged to preserve it. My skin prickled and tingled under the scorching heat of his touch, igniting an inferno along my body as he traced a searing path down my spine through the delicate layers of my Ottoman attire. Every caress felt like a powerful thread binding our souls together, pulling us closer until there was no space between us.

"Olivia," Roman growled against my lips, his breath hot and irresistible like a raging wildfire consuming us both. "You will not believe what happened at the last trial. Pasha Hassan confessed to me that he is my father."

"I know. A woman named Zara told me." I tried to focus on the gravity of his confession, but it was like trying to grasp smoke. My senses were overwhelmed by his scent, the strength in his arms, and the taste of his kiss. My fingers danced up into his hair.

"The blades were never poisoned. It was a sedative," he said, voice husky as if each word was a struggle against the tidal wave of desire that threatened to sweep us away.

"A sedative," I breathed, utterly focused on him. "Zara told me. And I'm not dead, so I believe her." I tried to smile, my lips trembling as his gaze held mine with a tenderness that deepened the fire between us.

"*So* not dead," Roman murmured, his hands trailing up and down my back.

I could barely nod, let alone form coherent thoughts. Our connection was electric, consuming—every brush of skin against skin amplified by the revelations and mysteries enveloping us. We moved together, and words fell away. Only the language of touch and longing remained.

I gasped when his lips trailed from my mouth to the sensitive hollow of my neck. My hands roamed over the embroidered velvet of his waistcoat, feeling the solid strength of his chest beneath, the power of the man who had fought for us—for this moment of unguarded passion.

"Olivia, my love," he whispered, pulling back just enough to look into my eyes. The intensity in his gaze mirrored the fervor of our embrace. "We are entwined, you and I, beyond bloodlines and battles. In this life, and all others."

With a groan that vibrated through my very being, he captured my lips once more, his kiss a promise, a plea, a surrender. As we clung to each other, the world outside our cocoon of ardor ceased to exist. There was only Roman, only this moment, only the undeniable truth that whatever came next, we would face it together, hearts ablaze.

The sudden creak of the door sliced through the haze of our desire. A male servant entered, his eyes darting away as though the sight of our entwined bodies was too much to bear.

"I do apologize," he stammered, a deep blush creeping up his neck, "but Pasha Hassan is awaiting you in his study."

He retreated quickly, closing the ornately carved door with a soft snick.

I pushed away from Roman, trying to steady my breath and thoughts. The urgency in the servant's voice reminded me that there were matters beyond the walls of this opulent prison of passion.

"This is your moment," I said to Roman, clasping his hand in mine, feeling the calluses of many battles. "You've been waiting to learn about your father and who he is. Now, this is your chance to ask and learn everything about him. Hear your father's story before awakening the blades."

Roman's jaw tensed, and his eyes clouded with a fear I had seldom seen.

"I'm scared, my love," he admitted, his voice barely above a whisper.

"Why?" I asked, squeezing his hand tightly. "You've always wanted to know your father and your origins. This man is part of your creation."

The room thrummed with electric tension, the air crackling as though it could barely contain the moment's weight.

"I'm afraid of the truth," he said. "This man...He is powerful beyond measure. You should have seen him in the final battle against me. He was like a madman, consumed by a berserker rage that defied all logic. But it's not just darkness that drives him... there's something more to him, something mysterious and enigmatic."

I stepped closer, my voice steady yet filled with an urgent plea. "This is your moment, Roman. Ask him every question that haunts your mind. The truths he reveals may tear you apart, but you have to face them. Prepare yourself for raw reality, for brutal honesty. This is your moment, and I will stand by you through it all."

Roman stilled, his gaze distant, as though staring into the abyss of his thoughts. "I'm so tired of being trapped in this cycle of our parents' secrets and lies. Every revelation shatters what little sense of normalcy we've managed to hold onto. What if he had killed me?" His voice cracked, a rare vulnerability breaking through his resolute exterior. "He would have had to live with the knowledge of murdering his flesh and blood. And what if I hadn't won? Or worse…" He shuddered, his words catching in his throat. "What if I had slid my gladius across his throat and watched his lifeblood gurgle from his neck?"

I placed my hand on his chest, feeling the steady rhythm of his heartbeat beneath my palm. "We'll never know the answer to that, thank God. Perhaps he would have declared victory before plunging his blade into your heart. But Roman, your father didn't end your life. He challenged you, yes, but perhaps… just perhaps, he cares for you more than he dares to show. Maybe he wants to share his true story and finally give you the answers you deserve."

Roman's laugh was bitter, his lips curling in disbelief. "Deeply cared for me? You realize how ludicrous that sounds, don't you, my love?" His voice blended anger, sorrow, and a flicker of something softer—dangerously close to hope.

I shrugged, forcing a faint smile. "Just trying to find something positive in this madness."

"I wish I shared your optimism." Roman's voice softened as he brushed a stray lock of hair from my face, his touch both tender and grounding. "When he revealed who he was to me… seconds before I could have killed him…"

I could only imagine the storm of emotions Roman must have felt—shock and disbelief. It mirrored my own when I had first seen my long-lost mother, a ghost from the past resurrected before my very eyes. The surrealism of these revelations was almost too much to bear, yet here we stood, bracing ourselves for whatever came next.

"And Malik…" Roman said, his eyes haunted. "I feel so betrayed by Malik. He watched the fight like it meant nothing. He calls me his brother, yet he sat there, impassive, while

I fought for my life, imagining that you were dying. He hid behind that mask, watching. I feel like we're all pawns in some twisted game."

"We *are* pawns," I admitted softly, "but we also don't know the whole story with Malik. He swore to protect us, Roman. Maybe he's just following orders and playing a role we don't yet understand. We need to hear the truth, all of it. I'm just playing devil's advocate here. The first step is you discovering who your father is."

Roman exhaled deeply, the tension in his shoulders easing ever so slightly. His arms encircled me, pulling me close, his kiss silencing any lingering doubts.

"My heart beats for you," he whispered against my lips, his words threading through the fabric of my soul. "You and only you."

"Roman," I gasped, caught in the whirlwind of his love and longing, "if we don't leave right now, I'm going to..."

His eyes darkened, and a wicked grin played across his lips. "I'm going to strip you and ravage you until you're screaming my name."

A shiver ran down my spine, desire threatening to consume me. But with great effort, I stepped back, forcing my breathing to steady. "As much as I want that, we can't. Not right now. Your father has summoned us, and we need answers. Our desires can wait."

My voice trembled with the effort it took to resist him. We had to focus. The answers we sought were just beyond the threshold, waiting within the shadows of Pasha Hassan's study.

Hand in hand, Roman and I stepped across the threshold into Pasha Hassan's office. The room was a cavern of secrets, lined with shelves groaning under the weight of countless tomes, their spines as ancient and inscrutable as the man we sought. Dust motes danced like specters in the stray beams of sunlight piercing the heavy drapery.

Pasha Hassan stood with his back to us, his hair unbound and falling loosely around his shoulders. He was clad not in the opulent robes I had come to associate with his station, but in a plain, flowing shirt that hinted at the muscle beneath, tucked into loose trousers cinched at the waist. His feet were bare upon the rich carpets. Even dressed so simply, he exuded an authority that transcended mere clothing. His gaze was fixed on a painting across the room, his focus intense, as if the image held some secret only he could understand.

Pasha Hassan turned, and I caught my breath at the stark humanity in his dark eyes.

"I want you to know one thing, my son... if I may call you my son..." he began, his voice low but steady. "I understand you're angry. I was acting on orders."

"Why did you deceive us?" Roman demanded, desperation and betrayal lacing his tone.

"Because if I had revealed my true identity from the beginning, you would have turned away from me," Pasha Hassan said simply. "I needed you to learn and trust me before knowing the truth."

"Trust you?" Roman snapped, his voice rising. "You manipulated and endangered my wife and me, took our children, and put us through unimaginable trials. And above all things, you're a Timehunter."

Pasha Hassan's expression remained stoic, yet there was a faint flicker of something deeper in his eyes as he replied, "My son, I am many things—a teacher, a grandfather, a darkness. But most importantly, I am a father who would do anything to protect his children."

"Protect us?" Roman scoffed. "You speak of love as if it

were foreign to you. You never once showed up in my life or Marcellious'."

A pang of hurt cut through his words.

Pasha Hassan inclined his head. "I will tell you everything. All answers."

The door creaked open before another word could be spoken, and Malik entered. His presence was like a jolt to the room, his eyes flickering with regret and something else—shame, perhaps. Without hesitation, I closed the distance between us and wrapped my arms around him, the confusion he represented momentarily eclipsed by my instinct to comfort. Roman stayed back, his expression unreadable, the weight of his emotions etched into every tense line of his posture.

"I apologize for subjecting you to such torment," Malik said, his expression etched with pain. "You have every right to be furious with me, to despise me. But please know that I was merely following orders. I knew our path, the people we would meet, and the fate that awaited you and Olivia. I knew everything—the grueling examinations, the harrowing challenges, and even the revelation that Pasha Hassan was your father, Roman."

A heavy sorrow emanated from Malik's every word, deep remorse for all that had transpired. The weight of his confession hung in the air, heavy and oppressive.

The betrayal stung, but Roman stepped forward, his voice steady and resolute.

"I want to know the whole truth from you, Malik—once Pasha Hassan finishes. I'm done with the secrecy, the lies, and the betrayal from those I trusted the most."

Malik held his gaze, his voice unwavering. "I promise, Roman. You will hear everything."

Pasha Hassan interjected, his tone calm yet commanding.

"Let us settle this now. Sit, and I will tell you everything." He gestured toward the ornate seating area, his expression unreadable.

Roman's voice boomed with authority as he stood beside me. "We demand the truth. No more lies, no more secrets. We need to know everything—no matter how painful."

His piercing gaze bore into Pasha Hassan, an unspoken challenge laced with the weight of years of confusion and hurt.

"Only the truth, my son," Pasha Hassan assured as he motioned once more for us to sit and begin unraveling the tapestry of deception that had ensnared us all.

I couldn't wait to hear what he had to say.

CHAPTER THIRTY ONE

ROMAN

Pasha Hassan's study was a treasure buried beneath the earth. The domed ceiling was a celestial map, constellations picked out in gold leaf against a backdrop of azure. My eyes traced the patterns, feeling the weight of history pressing close, each star a reminder of the vastness of the secrets surrounding us.

"Roman, Olivia," Pasha Hassan's smooth voice broke the silence, pulling us back to the present. "Would you like some refreshments?"

Olivia nodded, her gaze lingering on a tapestry depicting a battle long past, its threads vivid and haunting. "Yes, thank you."

Silent as shadows, servants materialized with trays bearing cups of sherbet and plates of sweetmeats. The sherbet was a chilled pomegranate on the tongue, but its sweetness was short-lived. The urgency pounding in my chest turned the flavor bitter. Pleasantries could not mask the storm brewing within me.

Setting my cup down deliberately, I leaned forward, eyes locking on Pasha Hassan. "We need answers."

The room seemed to pulse with my declaration, the air thickening as if it awaited his response. Pasha Hassan regarded me with a measured calmness, his expression betraying none of the gravity of our meeting.

"I want you to know one thing," he began, his voice low and intense. "The Timehunters were never your enemies but your allies. They were once a noble society of healers, using their mastery of time to create tonics and potions to aid those in need. But along the way, Salvatore twisted their minds and made them killers, turning them against us darknesses, Timebornes, and Timebounds."

"Why?" I asked, struggling to make sense of his words.

Pasha Hassan's eyes blazed, his fury barely contained. "Who knows? Perhaps the seeds of corruption lay dormant in Salvatore until he could take no more. The Timebornes and darknesses were once allies, united in purpose. But Salvatore poisoned the Timehunter society, manipulating them into destroying us and weakening our powers."

I stared at him, disbelief surging through me. "But you're a Timehunter yourself, and you lead the society of Anatolia."

"I am a Timehunter, but I am not like the others. I use my abilities for good, not evil."

His statement left me momentarily speechless. "What do you mean?"

"The Timehunters were originally known as Timehealers," Pasha Hassan said, his voice tinged with sorrow. "The ruthless, dangerous, and corrupted Timehunters are Salvatore and Mathias. All the trials you have endured are to prepare you for what's to come. The formidable warriors you have faced were once wild and untamed, brought under my control. Each one, a fierce soldier for the Sultan, honed to be unbeatable in battle."

His voice carried a sense of pride as he spoke, his

piercing dark eyes locking onto mine with an intensity that demanded my full attention. The weight of his gaze was almost physical, bearing down on me, forcing me to confront the gravity of his words.

"I have been building your army," he continued. "An army not corrupted by Salvatore or Mathias. I've been here under disguise until I could meet you as my son. I have been waiting for this moment for a long time, Roman. Everything you have been told about the Timehunters being so powerful is true, except we are the rightful Timehunters—not the corrupted ones Salvatore created and trained under Mathias."

His words lingered in the air like smoke, curling into the recesses of my mind and muddling thoughts I had once held as unshakable truths. I leaned back in my chair, the wood creaking under my shifting weight, feeling unsettled and strangely vindicated. The search for clarity had brought Olivia and me to this gilded chamber, to this man who claimed both paternity and subterfuge in the same breath.

"Who is commanding you, then?" I pressed, my voice firm despite the unease creeping through my veins.

Pasha Hassan reclined in his ornate chair, his posture unbothered by my growing impatience.

"Lazarus has given me the orders," he replied with a nonchalant wave of his hand.

"Who is Lazarus?" I asked, my patience waning under the weight of riddles. "I knew him as a man named Gaius in Ancient Rome. He was a man who saved me from death many times."

"Yes, you knew him as Gaius, but his true name is Lazarus," Pasha Hassan said. My frustration simmered beneath the surface as he leaned forward, locking eyes with me.

"Let me start at the beginning. Listen carefully. I was a student at Mathias' school of darkness long ago."

His words slithered through the air like smoke, hard to grasp, harder still to trust. "Mathias is dangerous. Powerful and dangerous. He is under the guidance of Salvatore, the father of darkness. I was trained by Lazarus, who is the father of Timebornes. We are on the good side of things."

"What do you mean you're on the good side of things?" I asked, unable to mask the skepticism in my voice.

Pasha Hassan rose from his chair, pacing the room like a caged animal suddenly unleashed. His energy crackled with tension.

"My job," he said, turning to face a portrait of a stern-faced man that hung upon the wall, "was to spy on Mathias and watch him closely."

His gaze lingered on the painted eyes before he turned back to me.

"There was a time when Balthazar and I were good friends," he admitted, his voice softening as though he spoke of a cherished memory now twisted by time. "But then Balthazar went off the rails with his vengeance against Mathias. He became a different person. I destroyed Mathias' school of darkness."

He took a deep breath, his words heavy with the weight of his past.

"After his school fell, Mathias spread his influence, creating new Timehunter societies in every country with his army of shadows and twisted followers."

The dire implication made my heart race, painting a grim picture of an ever-growing force of evil seeping across the globe.

"Lazarus ordered me to destroy every Timehunter society

built by Mathias," Pasha Hassan said, his voice low but unyielding. "I destroyed them all."

The study seemed to shrink around us as his claim reverberated in my mind. The conviction in his tone made it difficult to dismiss the enormity of what he said.

I glanced at Olivia, whose scowl mirrored the same confusion gnawing at my insides.

"My partner who has helped me destroy these societies," Pasha Hassan continued, "is Zara."

"Zara! The one who saved me from the fire," Olivia exclaimed.

Pasha Hassan nodded.

"She is bound to protect you," he said kindly, acknowledging Olivia's bewilderment but not fully addressing it.

Olivia parted her lips, no doubt brimming with curiosity and burning questions, but Pasha Hassan raised a hand, signaling her to wait.

"My dear Olivia, I understand your need for answers and will provide them all. But first, Roman must know the truth about my past." His eyes held a glint of sadness, shadows of secrets yet to be revealed.

He turned back to me. "Raul Costa's society was the last I needed to destroy. So I sent Reyna and Osman to finish the job," Pasha Hassan began. His voice grew quieter, the calm before an emotional storm. "Your grandfather, Thomas Alexander—your maternal grandfather—was England's biggest and greatest Timehunter leader. He was despicable and deeply corrupt."

The world I once knew shifted again, slipping away like sand beneath my feet.

"My job was to destroy that society. I didn't expect to meet your mother," he said, and for the first time, a tremor seemed to ripple through his resolve. "Your mother slipped into my home one night and confided in me. She told me she was betrothed to someone evil, a Timehunter three times her age. I couldn't stand by and let that happen. I loved her too much. My heart ached for her and what her cruel father had arranged for her."

He paused, his hand instinctively clutching his chest as though the memory had lodged like a dagger.

I winced, the thought of my beautiful, kind mother trapped in such a situation twisting my insides. The image of her marrying a ruthless, evil Timehunter was unfathomable.

"We fell in love," Pasha Hassan continued, his voice heavy with emotion, "but I kept guarding my heart, knowing that my life was dangerous, and she deserved better. Yet, desire and temptation took over, and we began our affair. Then, you and your brother were conceived."

He stopped, his words hanging in the air like an unspoken apology.

"During our time together, we destroyed the society," he said, his voice firm but tinged with sorrow. "Everyone died, and your grandfather was left crippled."

The words struck me like a blow.

"But then, what about her being disowned?" I interrupted, the mismatched pieces of my past clashing within me. "When she was alive, she mentioned that to me."

Pasha Hassan's jaw tightened, his expression shadowed by old wounds. "When I destroyed the Timehunter society," he said, "your mother found out she was with child. Her father, already furious—his society destroyed, himself crippled, and her betrothed dead—could not handle another scandal. So he disowned her for shaming the family and for sleeping with the enemy—namely, me."

His voice carried an undercurrent of bitterness as he began to pace the room, his footsteps purposeful yet restrained.

"When I found out Elizabeth was carrying my child, I offered assistance and support. But she refused because of the dangerous life I carried. My life was always filled with danger and death, and I wanted to protect her from the brutality."

He sighed, his gaze growing distant as if he were peering into the tapestry of his memories.

"So I left and returned to my home in Anatolia to continue my duties. But my thoughts and heart were never far from Elizabeth," he said, his voice dropping to a whisper. "After I left her, I traveled to the Americas and met Dancing Fire. Little did I know that my best friend would fall madly in love with Elizabeth one day."

A small, wistful smile tugged at the corner of his lips. "But fate works in mysterious ways. Dancing Fire and I agreed that Elizabeth could be with whom she chose." His tone grew more somber. "Your mother birthed you in the Americas. Your twin brother and you were separated because Lazarus instructed the Great Chief to do so—to protect you both from Salvatore. Salvatore was always watching, searching for Timebornes to corrupt or destroy those who refused to follow his ruthless and vicious ways."

Pasha Hassan paused, his gaze heavy with emotion.

"Your brother was raised by Dancing Fire, safe from Salvatore's reach. You, on the other hand, returned to England with your mother.

A heavy sigh escaped him. "When she returned to England, I went back to her. We couldn't stay away from each other—she understood my dark nature. Our love was powerful, just like the love you and your wife share. I stayed with Elizabeth until you were one year old. Lazarus commanded me to return to my duties. I begged Elizabeth to come with me, but she didn't think it was safe."

I sat there, trying to absorb the flood of information, the weight of my unknown history washing over me like a relentless tide.

The air in the study solidified, pressing against me from all sides as Pasha Hassan's revelations unfolded. I reached out unquestioningly, my hand finding Olivia's, her touch a lifeline tethering me to reality as my mind threatened to spiral into disbelief.

Pasha Hassan's voice remained steady as he continued, but there was a subtle bitterness beneath his words. "Your mother knew. She knew of your true destiny, and that one day, it would be time for you to fulfill it. And when you came to her and said you were joining the army, ready to fight for your country in the late 1700s, she was afraid of losing you. You were her last hope, the only one left."

His eyes met mine, brimming with sadness stretching back through generations. "She was so upset when you had to go."

"Upset?" The word felt feeble, inadequate to describe the chasm of loss and deception that yawned open before me. My throat tightened as shock gave way to a deep-seated ache. "What about Reyna?"

"Everyone abandoned your mother," he said, lowering his gaze. "Reyna is your full-blooded sister. When you left for the Americas, I returned to comfort your mother. She and I rekindled our love for each other, and we had Reyna. Together, we raised her until things became dangerous."

His voice faltered momentarily, the weight of the past pressing down on him.

"You and your brother had time-traveled to the past in Rome. Olivia—your Olivia—was soon to enter our lives. And Salvatore... Salvatore was growing furious." Pasha Hassan paused, his expression darkening as if dredging up a memory too painful to voice.

"He killed your mother," he finally said, his voice breaking. "To save Reyna, I took her away."

My pulse thundered in my ears, drowning out the distant echoes of the opulent study.

"But Lee told me a different story," I managed to say, each word scraping raw the lining of my soul.

"Lee and I concocted that story," Pasha Hassan said, his tone heavy with guilt. "To protect you."

"Protect me?" I asked hollowly. "Lee said he married Elizabeth and then buried her when she died."

Pasha Hassan's face twisted in anguish, his voice strained and tense. "Lee and I have been your protectors for years, shielding you from Salvatore's grasp. We lied about our alliance with Lazarus because Salvatore has been watching Lee for some time now. He suspects that Lee is working with Lazarus—and he is—but Lee cleverly plays the role of an innocent pawn to divert suspicion. "Your mother meant everything to Lee. He loved her deeply, but she chose me. She was my wife, the love of my life. And it was Salvatore who took her life when his plans began to unravel."

His words punctured the last fragile thread of hope I had clung to, and the tears I'd held back broke through the dam of my willpower, flooding my vision.

I bowed my head, weeping for the goodbye I never had, for the mother I thought knew but didn't, and for the woman whose memory was now a fractured tapestry of truth and deception.

"Your mother is gone from this world," Pasha Hassan

said, his voice heavy with regret. "But she is now a prisoner in another world. One day, you may have the chance to see her again."

"Another world?" Confusion mingled with my grief, forming a maelstrom of emotions I could barely navigate. "What do you mean?"

"Time has layers, Roman," Pasha Hassan explained, his voice steady yet haunting. "Some battles are fought beyond the realms we see and understand."

Olivia's hand tightened in mine, grounding me as his revelations unraveled everything I thought I knew.

"I have always been a part of your life," he said, his tone unwavering, as though this admission carried the weight of a thousand hidden truths. "I have watched over you and your brother, ensuring your survival."

The room seemed to tilt under the weight of his words.

"Watched over me?" I managed, my voice strained, teetering between disbelief and yearning.

"Indeed," Pasha Hassan said, rising from his chair. "The original Timehunters were guardians of balance, sworn to mend the fabric of time torn by the Timebornes. But corruption seeped into their ranks, twisting their purpose. The darkness was never meant to harm their Timebornes. Yet power…" He paused, his gaze hardening. "Power corrupts even the noblest of intentions."

He strode toward the towering bookcase lining the study, his fingers brushing along the spines of ancient tomes as though searching for a forgotten truth. At last, his hand stilled. He pressed a hidden mechanism, and with a soft click, the bookshelf swung open, revealing a chamber suffused with an ethereal glow.

He stepped inside and emerged moments later, holding

two blades—one radiating sunlight, the other cloaked in the cool luminescence of moonlight.

"Here they are," he said, his voice reverent.

My hands trembled as he placed the sun and moon daggers in my grasp. Their energy pulsed against my palms, alive and charged with ancient power.

"And as you know," Pasha Hassan continued, his gaze locking onto mine with a gravity that chilled me, "I possess the knowledge to awaken them." The weight of his words settled over the room like an oppressive shroud. He paused, letting the silence stretch as if daring me to absorb their significance fully.

"I am grateful that you and your wife survived Raul Costa's masquerade ball and retrieved the sun dagger," Pasha Hassan said. "Balthazar did us all a favor by eliminating most of the Timehunters at that party. Only a few survived—Raul and ten others."

"Reyna..." I murmured, the name slipping from my lips like a plea.

"Reyna wanted to prove herself," Pasha Hassan said, leaning forward in his chair. "She is more involved than you realize."

The air in the room seemed to hum with tension as Pasha Hassan pressed on, unraveling the intricate web of events that had led to Marcellious' capture and Reyna's instrumental role in dismantling Raul's regime.

"Marcellious' capture wasn't a betrayal by Costa," Pasha Hassan said, his voice heavy with emotion. "It was all orchestrated by Mathias and Salvatore. Their ultimate goal was to dismantle your entire team, piece by piece."

His voice cracked as he continued, the weight of his revelations bearing down on us.

"Reyna stayed longer than was safe," he said, his eyes

shadowed with grief. "She risked everything to save Marcellious and ensure Raul's society fell. I know you and your wife have accused her of betrayal, of trapping you both, but that wasn't her intent. I sent her to England with Osman because I trusted her to guide you back to me. Losing Osman was a tragedy I will never forgive myself for, but I couldn't allow either of you to stay near Mathias and Alina any longer."

The words hit me like a physical blow, stealing the air from my lungs. Amid the swirl of revelations, one thought crystallized—the answers I sought—about my role, purpose, and very identity—were within reach. Was I a darkness? What was my place in this vast, tangled web of alliances and betrayals? Perhaps, at last, I would discover the truth.

"It all makes sense now," Olivia said softly, breaking the silence. "Why she saved Marcellious. He is her brother."

Pasha Hassan nodded, his gaze distant as he perched on the edge of his ornate desk. His fingers traced absent patterns across the polished wood; his voice filled with the weight of secrets too long kept.

"Malik knew," he said, his tone almost wistful. He glanced at the map pinned to the wall, its surface marked with the scars of battles fought and yet to come. "Your mother and Mathias are dangerous. Every move must be shrouded in secrecy, or they would have destroyed us before we could fight back."

His eyes shifted to the sun and moon blades resting in my arms, their energy thrumming against my skin like a heartbeat.

"We are ahead of the game right now. You possess the blades," he said as if to anchor me in the moment. "And I possess the knowledge that you seek."

He had an undeniable magnetism, an enigma that drew

me in, his words hanging in the air, tantalizing yet just out of reach.

"Forgive me, my son, Roman, for the trials and tests I put you through," he continued, his voice softening, tinged with a regret that seemed to ripple through the space between us. "It pained me to watch you and your wife fight for your lives, but I was following orders from Lazarus. My love for you and your brother knows no bounds, and it hurts me deeply not to be part of your lives. I longed to teach you how to fight, ride, and hunt, but my duty always came first."

The weight of his confession pressed against the room's stillness, filling it with sorrow and longing. His words were an unspoken apology, a bridge across the years of absence and distance.

"Do you know why these blades are so important?" he asked, his voice dropping to a whisper that seemed to echo in my very bones.

Olivia and I exchanged a glance, the gravity of the question pulling us into its orbit. Slowly, we shook our heads.

I turned to Olivia, who sat a few feet away, watching me with awe and quiet strength. She had been my guiding light through the darkness, helping me piece together the fragmented truths of my past and leading me to this very moment. Without her, I would still be lost.

Wordlessly, I extended the daggers to her, offering them with a small bow. She accepted them with a gentle smile, her fingers brushing against mine in the exchange, a spark of connection that grounded me. Then, I turned to my father—a man who had only existed in my imagination until now. Tears blurred my vision as I stepped forward, wrapping my arms around him in a tight embrace. It was a moment I had never dared to dream of, and now that it was here, I was utterly overcome.

"Thank you," I whispered, my voice trembling with raw emotion. "For everything."

For a fleeting moment, peace enveloped me, warm and comforting. But even as I held him close, the shadows in the corners of the room seemed to whisper of unfinished business, of looming dangers waiting just beyond the edge of this fragile reprieve.

This was far from over.

CHAPTER THIRTY TWO

OLIVIA

My gaze wandered across the family portraits that festooned the walls of Pasha Hassan's study. An unmistakable air of love seemed to emanate from them; the tender way Roman's mother was depicted, her smile serene and knowing—it was the same smile that now graced Roman's face as he stood beside me. Then my eyes fell upon the likenesses of Pasha Hassan's sons, Roman and Marcellious, their youthful exuberance frozen in time. It warmed something inside me, seeing how deeply rooted their bonds were.

"Olivia?" Pasha Hassan's rich, resonant voice pulled me from my reverie. "You seem contemplative."

I turned to him, the question gnawing at me finally spilling out. "Why are the blades so important? How are they so powerful? Why does everyone want them?"

Pasha Hassan leaned back in his ornately carved chair, his imposing frame dominating the space as he steepled his fingers thoughtfully. His deep-brown eyes glimmered with an ageless wisdom, as though he held the secrets of entire lifetimes within them.

"Why do *you* think they are so coveted?" he asked, his tone inviting yet enigmatic.

I hesitated, feeling the steady presence of Roman behind me. The sun and moon daggers had been a constant source of fear and wonder, their mysteries as vast as the cosmos.

"We don't know much," I admitted, my voice steady despite the uncertainty gnawing at me. "But we've heard they can destroy the darkness forever. They can cure even the most insatiable hunger for killing. And if they fall into the wrong hands..."

"Partly," Pasha Hassan interjected, his expression inscrutable. Rising from his chair, he moved toward the stone fireplace, picking up an iron poker against the hearth. The flames danced, their flickering light casting shadows across his features.

Roman and I exchanged a glance.

"Could it be... for immortality?" Roman ventured, his tone tinged with both skepticism and curiosity.

"Or is it the promise of ultimate power?" I added, thinking of the legends surrounding such artifacts.

"You are both close but not quite," Pasha Hassan said, his gaze sharpening as if challenging us to dig deeper into the well of our understanding. He stirred the fire to life with the poker, the embers glowing brighter, before placing it back where he found it and returning to his seat.

Frustration mounted within me like a wildfire, its heat and intensity growing with each passing moment. The puzzle pieces were tantalizingly close, yet they refused to connect. My curiosity burned just as fiercely, propelling me forward despite the uncertainty clouding my mind.

Taking a deep breath, I let my thoughts spill out, raw and unfiltered.

"Pasha Hassan," I began, my voice trembling slightly,

"ever since I first time-traveled to Ancient Rome, I've been caught in this relentless chase. Secrets, lies, and betrayal seem to weave through everything like an unbroken thread. With Balthazar and other darknesses hunting me at every turn, trying to kill me, I can't help but wonder... What is the truth about these blades? How did they come to be? And who exactly are Salvatore and Lazarus, these mysterious fathers of darkness and Timebornes? I need to understand. No more half-truths. I want the whole story."

Pasha Hassan's gaze narrowed, his dark eyes glittering like obsidian in the flickering firelight. A beat of silence stretched between us, heavy with unspoken truths. I sensed we were teetering on the edge of revelation, about to peel back a layer of this mystery that had remained shrouded for too long. Whatever he said next could illuminate the path ahead—or plunge us deeper into shadow.

Pasha Hassan leaned forward, his tall frame casting long, distorted shadows across the room. The firelight painted his features in a dance of light and shadow, accentuating the moment's gravity. He beckoned us closer with the crook of a finger, his voice low and deliberate. I scooted to the edge of my seat, my heart pounding with anticipation. Beside me, Roman took my hand in his, the warmth of his touch grounding me amidst the turmoil swirling within. The room fell utterly silent, save for the soft crackle of the fire, as we braced ourselves for the truths that would shape everything ahead.

"Let me tell you a story," Pasha Hassan began, his voice resonating like the toll of a distant bell. "Once, there was an ancient city called Ugarit. It was a jewel of its time, now lost to the sands of history—a place where chaos reigned. War, famine, and the despair of its harsh rulers gripped the land. Yet, it was also a major trading hub and cultural center during the late Bronze Age, famed for its early alphabetic script. The city thrived between 1450 and 1200 BCE, only to meet its ruin during the upheaval of the Late Bronze Age collapse. Invasions by the sea peoples, internal struggles, natural disasters, and the collapse of trade networks converged to seal Ugarit's fate. Ultimately, it was abandoned, its glory days reduced to whispers of memory."

Pasha's voice softened, yet it carried the weight of time itself as he continued. "King Cyrus and Queen Seraphina ruled Ugarit with compassion and wisdom, but their crowns were heavy burdens. The suffering of their people ate away at them, and desperation led them to seek an answer beyond mortal means."

He paused, his gaze seeming to pierce through the very walls of the study as if he could see the city of Ugarit in its prime. "In their despair, they turned to Lazarus—a powerful sorcerer whose command over time and magic was unmatched. His knowledge was vast, his power dark and enigmatic, a double-edged sword for those who dared to wield it."

The air grew heavy with his words, the fire in the hearth crackling softly as if the flames were listening. Dust motes danced in a beam of moonlight streaming through a crack in the ceiling, suspended in the weighty silence that followed.

"Cyrus and Seraphina asked Lazarus if they could travel back in time and alter the course of history to save Ugarit before it was too late," Pasha Hassan began, his voice steady but steeped in gravity. "Lazarus told them it was possible and agreed to help."

I gasped, unable to contain the incredulity bubbling up within me. The story Pasha Hassan wove seemed more than a myth; it carried a strange resonance as if some part of it echoed through the very fabric of our existence.

Pasha Hassan's voice grew taut with anger as he pressed on. "But Lazarus warned them that such a monumental and dangerous task required another—a sorcerer whose power rivaled his own. Salvatore, a name that even then struck fear into the hearts of many, was the only one who could match him. However, Salvatore had been imprisoned, his magic stripped away, and his tools destroyed. He was left to rot in a dark dungeon, yet even in his weakened state, his hunger for power burned with an intensity that could not be extinguished."

The notion of two such forces joining sent a ripple of fear down my spine.

"Lazarus understood the tumultuous history between Salvatore and the king and queen. He knew their fear of him and hesitation would make convincing them a challenge. But they had no choice. Their desperation outweighed their caution. The monarchs approached Salvatore with their offer —freedom in exchange for his assistance in making the time travel possible."

Pasha's hands moved as he spoke, weaving the story before us with the grace of a master storyteller. "Salvatore, with the cunning of a predator who knows the scent of weakness, demanded more than just freedom. 'I will help you,' he said, 'but only if I am guaranteed my freedom forever. I shall never be imprisoned again.'

"Faced with no other options, the rulers reluctantly agreed, releasing the sorcerer from his chains. Lazarus and Salvatore began their preparations, their combined power a force that even the gods might fear. Each step brought them closer to their goal, a feat that would alter the course of history itself."

Roman and I sat transfixed, spellbound by the unfolding saga. The warmth of the study contrasted sharply with the cold inevitability that Pasha Hassan's words seemed to carry. The weight of the tale pressed upon us, growing heavier with every detail.

"The preparations were not simple," Pasha Hassan continued, his voice now laced with reverence for the magnitude of the task. "Lazarus and Salvatore waited patiently for the perfect alignment of the sun, moon, and stars—the night of the first-ever solar eclipse in the ancient city of Ugarit. On that night, under the shroud of cosmic shadow, their combined power reached its zenith."

His gaze grew distant as though he were watching the events unfold before him in the flickering flames. "Together, they wove a spell of unimaginable complexity. It was more than mere magic; it was a reweaving of time itself, a bold attempt to reshape destiny's threads and save Ugarit from the grip of ruin."

A chill ran through me as Pasha Hassan's expression darkened.

"But when the celestial shadow crept across the sun, and their incantations reached a crescendo, there was...a dissonance. An unforeseen flaw within the heart of their magic." He paused, the silence stretching taut between us. "Instead of salvation, the spell unleashed devastation. Ultimately, volcanic wrath razed Ugarit to nothing but memory and ash."

Roman's grip tightened around my hand. We were ensnared by the gravity of Pasha Hassan's words, by the cataclysmic error that had set forth such a chain of unstoppable events.

Pasha Hassan stood abruptly, his movements mirroring the restlessness of his tale. He paced deliberately, tracing the intricate patterns of the Persian rug that graced his study floor with each step.

"From the ruins," he said, his voice quieter yet more resonant, "rose Solaris—a city untouched by the hands of Earthly architects. These blades created a realm parallel to ours, yet untethered from the reality we know. Everyone who had once lived in Ugarit now found themselves in a beautiful realm with a giant timepiece at its heart."

I pictured the survivors of Ugarit, waking amidst the rubble to find a sky dominated not by the familiar sun but by an immense clock, its face a mirror of the moon.

"They were cast adrift in a world unrecognizable, surrounded by the remnants of their lives and a truth too peculiar to grasp. The solar eclipse hadn't merely heralded destruction—it had torn open a passage to a new dimension of time. The women of Ugarit, whose birth was imminent, immediately went into labor during the eclipse in this new realm. Daggers appeared by their sides when the babies were born. These children became the first Timebornes, gifted with the ability to travel through time."

His voice deepened with a sense of awe. "And on that fateful day, two powerful blades were forged—the sun and moon daggers. Near the entrance to Solaris, a giant clock was discovered lying on the ground, its face bearing the passage of time like a silent witness to the chaos. As we later learned, the clock's hands were the Sun and Moon Daggers themselves. Their power was undeniable, yet shrouded in mystery.

"These Blades of Shadows hold unimaginable power," Pasha Hassan said, halting before the fireplace, the flames casting erratic shadows over his sharp features. "These two artifacts you possess created Solaris and opened this new realm of time." His voice dropped, tinged with reverence and caution. "And it was there that Lazarus and Salvatore, each nearly a hundred years old, found themselves not aging but growing younger—time itself reversing for them."

A strange tension hung in the air, the weight of his words

pressing against my chest. I could feel the duality of creation pulsing through every syllable—an essence born neither wholly malevolent nor benevolent yet inextricably bound to the destiny of the Timebornes.

"During the birth of the first Timebornes," Pasha Hassan continued, his voice heavy with sorrow, "their darknesses— beings meant to protect them—appeared alongside them. But Salvatore, in his ambition and hunger for power, corrupted those darknesses, imbuing them with a sliver of his malevolence. He twisted them into instruments of evil, meant to one day destroy their Timebornes and spread darkness across the world."

Roman tensed beside me, his hand brushing mine as though to anchor me. Pasha's next words brought a flicker of hope amidst the despair.

"But Lazarus intervened," he said, a spark of pride igniting in his dark eyes. "He tamed the darkness Salvatore had corrupted, training it to protect the Timebornes instead of harming them."

Roman's gaze found mine, concern etched deep into his features as I raised trembling hands to massage my temples. Pain blossomed like a dark flower in my skull, sharp and relentless.

"What is it, my love?" Roman asked, his voice gentle but laced with worry.

"I don't know," I murmured through gritted teeth. "I suddenly have a splitting headache."

The ache hammered against my skull, pulsing in time with my racing heartbeat.

Pasha Hassan gestured toward the door. "Shall I call for a healer?"

Even as the throbbing grew unbearable, the desire for answers burned brighter. I shook my head—regret flooding in immediately as the movement sent stabbing pain through my skull.

"No," I said firmly, though my voice was strained. "Please, continue with the story."

Pasha Hassan nodded, his expression flickering between understanding and hesitation. "Solaris flourished into a haven, a sanctuary for those on Earth seeking to correct their mistakes. People journeyed there for redemption and restoration—a chance to undo accidental crimes or heal from tragic losses. Under the rule of kings and queens, each adding their prosperity and growth, Solaris thrived."

He paused, his tone shifting to one of profound gravity. "But one queen in particular... She was the most powerful of them all. Her rule marked an era of unparalleled strength and prosperity. And yet..." His voice softened, barely above a whisper. "She vanished without a trace. History remembers her only as the lost queen of Solaris."

The ache behind my eyes grew unbearable, a storm clouding my thoughts and scattering my focus. Pasha's words blurred into the background as the pain drowned everything else.

"May I have something to drink?" I whispered.

Without a word, a servant seemed to melt from the shadows, carrying a cup filled with a steaming herbal concoction. The aroma wafted toward me—earthy with a hint of mint and something else, something soothing and unfamiliar. I took a tentative sip, the warmth spreading through me, coating my throat, and seeping into my system. Slowly, the vice around my head began to loosen its grip, the relentless throb easing into a dull ache.

"Thank you," I murmured, a breath of relief escaping me. My voice was steadier now, my resolve returning. I turned back to Pasha Hassan, ready once again to listen.

"In Solaris," he began, his tone measured and reverent, "the Timebornes were known as the guardians of time. They possessed a unique and profound ability to traverse through time itself, aiding those in need by correcting past mistakes that could cause harm to others. Their purpose was not just to alter events but to mend the fabric of destiny, ensuring that time flowed as it was meant to."

His gaze drifted toward the hearth, the flickering flames reflecting in his dark eyes. "With their unparalleled abilities, they could erase painful memories from an individual's life or allow those memories to remain lessons for personal growth. Their decisions shaped the very essence of humanity's experiences."

He paused, his voice softening as he continued. "The Timebounds served as the Timebornes' most trusted allies— steadfast companions who accompanied them on missions and cases, providing support and strategy when the path was perilous. And then there were the Timehealers," he said, his tone carrying an almost reverent admiration. "These remarkable individuals specialized in using Solaris' unique flora, crafting healing potions and antidotes that could mend not only physical wounds but also the fractures left behind by time."

As he spoke, I envisioned these revered beings, their hands deft as they mixed elixirs, their knowledge vast as the stars above. They were the menders of broken timelines, weavers of second chances.

"The darkness' biggest role in Solaris was to protect Timebornes and Timebounds at all costs," Pasha Hassan continued, his tone edged with pride and sorrow. "They were professional, skilled assassins—warriors who eliminated evil, shielded the kingdom, and defended the realm against those who dared to defy its laws."

I imagined these silent guardians, shrouded in mystery, their loyalty as unyielding as iron. They were the unseen force, the shield against the tide of time that threatened to sweep us all into oblivion. Their existence was both a promise and a warning, a delicate balance that preserved the sanctity of the realm.

As the weight of his words settled, I began to understand the gravity of what we faced—the delicate dance between light and shadow, past and present, memory and oblivion.

"But what of Salvatore? What happened to him?" Roman asked, his voice laced with an urgency that mirrored the pulsing of my own heart.

Pasha Hassan exhaled deeply, his gaze dropping to the richly woven rug under our feet. "Beneath the surface, Salvatore's malevolent influence grew. He despised the bond between the darknesses and the Timebornes. It enraged him to see the darknesses protecting and even loving their Timeborne counterparts when his vision was chaos, destruction, and domination."

He paused, his expression darkening as the tale unfolded. "Many darknesses fell in love with Timebornes, and their unions brought forth the Timebounds. Salvatore saw this as a betrayal of his ideals. He began to poison the minds of the darknesses, twisting their loyalty, controlling them, and corrupting them into weapons against the very Timebornes they were meant to protect. Like a cancer, his bitterness spread, unseen, until it was too late."

The room seemed to hold its breath as he spoke the final words, each syllable heavy with foreboding. "Salvatore cultivated an army of darknesses, loyal only to him, with a singular, devastating purpose—to destroy their Timeborne counterparts."

The idea of such treachery within Solaris' walls was enough to chill the blood.

"When his plan was uncovered, Salvatore was cast out of Solaris," Pasha Hassan said, his tone low and simmering with restrained anger. "But Salvatore was cunning. He evaded complete expulsion, secretly hiding in the shadows and continuing to corrupt the darkness, biding his time."

My breath caught as I envisioned this master manipulator, an architect of chaos weaving his web of deceit and vengeance from the shadows.

"And then what happened?" I asked.

Pasha Hassan's expression darkened further, his words like thunderclouds rolling across the room. "Many of the darknesses were once loyal to Lazarus, trained under his guidance to protect and serve the Timebornes. But as Salvatore's influence grew, many turned away from Lazarus, lured by Salvatore's promises of power, vengeance, and liberation from their perceived servitude."

The bitterness in his voice was palpable, each word steeped in resentment. "Salvatore knew he needed more than brute strength to achieve his aims. He needed an army—a force capable of destroying his enemies—the Timebornes, Timebounds, and even the loyal darknesses who opposed him."

He leaned forward, his gaze piercing through the flickering firelight. "So he turned his sights on the Timehealers. Their knowledge of Solaris' unique flora and their ability to mend physical and temporal wounds was unparalleled. Salvatore twisted their minds, manipulating them with promises of power and dominion over those who wronged them."

Pasha Hassan's upper lip curled in disgust, his eyebrows furrowing as though the mere thought of Salvatore's actions was enough to make his blood boil. His voice dropped, his words hanging heavy in the room. "With these newfound weapons—potions corrupted to harm rather than heal—Salvatore gained control over the darknesses, building himself a vast and mighty army that would obey his every command."

The room seemed to constrict around us, the air growing heavier with each word. Roman released my hand to rake his fingers through his hair, frustration radiating from him like a storm brewing beneath the surface.

"Then, what of the balance, the order of things?" he asked, his eyes locked onto Pasha Hassan's. "Salvatore created this army of vicious darkness, turned the minds of the Timehealers, and made them betray their people?"

Pasha Hassan's gaze darkened, his features etched with a sadness that seemed to span centuries. "The monarchy fell after countless kings and queens had ruled Solaris with happiness, joy, and success. What was once a unified kingdom splintered into separate factions—the House of Shadows, the House of Timebornes, the House of Timebounds, and the House of Timehealers."

Each name reverberated with power, carrying its gravity and purpose, as though their identities stitched together the very fabric of Solaris. Pasha Hassan's fingers traced an intricate pattern along the polished grain of his Rosewood desk, the hypnotic motion reflecting the delicate balance Solaris had once maintained.

"The peaceful realm was no longer at peace," he continued, his voice a low rumble. "Salvatore and Lazarus had once been allies, united by their shared vision for Solaris. Yet, Salvatore's greed for power corrupted him, leading him to turn the darknesses against their Timebornes secretly. Lazarus, a powerful sorcerer and protector of the realm, eventually uncovered Salvatore's treachery. He warned the leaders of Solaris of the growing corruption infecting their land. With an army of loyal darknesses, Lazarus set out to confront Salvatore and end his schemes."

Pasha Hassan's voice wavered, the weight of the tale pressing down on him. "But when they finally found Salvatore, it was too late. He had amassed an even greater army fueled by dark power capable of twisting and poisoning the minds of all who opposed him."

Roman's jaw clenched as the gravity of the revelation settled over us.

"And now," Pasha Hassan said, his tone grim, "Salvatore's ambitions had outgrown his hatred. His sights were set on the throne and the ultimate prize—the Blade of Shadows. The fate of Solaris teetered on the edge of ruin as this dangerous game of power and magic unfolded."

The finality in Pasha Hassan's tone left no room for doubt —Salvatore was an unparalleled threat to Solaris and the world beyond. As the echoes of his revelations faded into the crackling firelight, I realized that Roman and I stood at the precipice of a battle that would shape the fate of entire realms.

The shadows in the study seemed to stretch and deepen as if mourning the fractured history of Solaris. I sat stiffly in my chair, the weight of Pasha Hassan's words pressing down on me, chilling me to the core. A history marred by betrayal and conflict was now ours to confront.

"Salvatore's return from the shadows was like a plague," Pasha Hassan said. "Death and destruction followed him as closely as a shadow clings on a sunless day."

Roman leaned forward, his fists clenched tightly on his knees, his gaze fierce. His eyes burned like embers, radiating both frustration and disbelief. A low growl escaped him. "Those fools—King Cyrus and his queen—they should have listened to Lazarus instead of falling prey to Salvatore's deceit!"

"But they did listen," Pasha Hassan countered, his expression weighed down by sorrow and regret. The lines etched into his brow deepened, a testament to the burden of his knowledge. "Lazarus told them they needed Salvatore's help. He believed freeing him was the only way to save their city. They trusted Lazarus, but even the brightest stars can be obscured by the mists of time."

He shook his head, his voice dropping to a mournful whisper. "Salvatore was cunning. He knew how to play the role of the penitent. He knew when to bide his time and when to strike. The people who gave him a second chance could never imagine how deeply his thirst for vengeance ran. He mastered the art of masking his true nature, spreading dark lies with the precision of a blade to weave the chaos he craved."

A chill crept through me, settling in my chest as I imagined the harmonious realm of Solaris fracturing under the weight of Salvatore's schemes. I could almost see the realm tearing at its seams, its people divided by mistrust and fear, their unity shattered by the tendrils of his malevolence.

"And the daggers?" I asked, almost afraid to hear more.

"Chaos incarnate," Pasha Hassan said, his voice grave. "When they were separated, it was as though the very fabric of Solaris was torn in two. A great expulsion ensued, casting us away from Solaris, with our memories stripped bare as we were flung to this harsh Earth."

A heavy silence fell over the room, suffocating in its intensity. The enormity of what we faced loomed like a shadow, stretching across the fragile remnants of hope we carried. A legacy of strife and a battle unseen yet deeply felt now rested on our shoulders.

"Scattered like leaves in a tempest," I murmured, my mind conjuring an image of lost souls drifting aimlessly, their ties to Solaris severed but not forgotten.

Pasha Hassan nodded, his expression burdened with sorrow. "In this world, the darkness is cursed with a never-ending cycle of violence and survival, constantly seeking to kill for sustenance. And amid it, all are the Timebornes, hunted by both the darkness and the Timehealers, who have been twisted into ruthless Timehunters. Their sole mission is to eliminate all Timebornes, Timebounds, and opposing darknesses. Our once unified realm now lies fractured, its people adrift, clinging to fragmented memories of a peace that feels as distant as a dream."

Roman stood abruptly, his posture tense, his hands clenched at his sides. His gaze locked onto the dim torchlight flickering against the stone walls, shadows dancing like restless specters. His voice, when he spoke, was low and filled with resolve. "We must destroy Salvatore and his army of monsters."

The finality of his words settled like a lead weight in the room. The truth was undeniable—we were remnants of a shattered realm, bound by fate and loss, thrust into a quest that seemed impossible and necessary.

The weight of Pasha Hassan's revelation pressed down on me as though the air had grown heavier. I struggled to process the implications, my mind spinning with questions and doubts.

"These blades... they are to open the realm of Solaris?" My voice was barely a whisper, disbelief lacing every syllable. A chilling realization crept through me, twisting into my thoughts like an unsolvable puzzle. Could I be from Solaris? Or at least a descendant of someone who was? The thought gnawed at my consciousness, weaving its way into every corner of my mind.

But even more perplexing was my mother's role in all of this. Born on Earth, I couldn't reconcile how I—or she—fit into this ancient tale of realms and daggers, Timebornes and darknesses. The pieces of the puzzle seemed both tantalizingly close and impossibly far away.

Pasha Hassan nodded solemnly, his gaze weighted with centuries of untold truths. "That's right. Mathias has always been a devotee of Salvatore, harboring his memories of Solaris while we've all been wandering in the dark. He fears the union of the blades—not for the power they wield, but for the truths they will unveil.

"Everyone wants to return there," he said, almost reverent. "But our recollections are lost in the void. When the blades are reconciled, the veil lifts, and we begin to remember. Salvatore's defiance against Lazarus altered the very fabric of our existence.

"This world is not our home," Pasha Hassan continued, his voice softening with longing. "Our exile began here when the blades were separated. They possess the capacity to revive the realm of time, to mend what has been shattered."

Roman swallowed hard, his face a mask of conflict. "You seek to obliterate the darkness, yet that's not our ultimate goal. Salvation lies in Solaris. There, you can vanquish Salvatore himself."

"Everyone has their motives," Pasha Hassan said. "Balthazar yearns for the blades to reclaim his daughters and family—all prisoners within Solaris' confines. Lazarus pines for his beloved Amara and his children. Even Raul and your grandfather Thomas, tangled in their webs of desire, are ensnared. My beloved wife, your mother Elizabeth, is trapped there."

His voice softened further, carrying the weight of unspeakable loss. "Everyone who has died from that realm here on Earth is now a prisoner in Solaris. All of them—the good and the bad—wish to be released, to see Solaris restored to its former glory." I felt Roman stiffen beside me as the enormity of Pasha's words settled over us like a shroud.

"Nearly all of the Timebornes on Earth have lost their memories," Pasha Hassan continued, his eyes glistening with the light of hope and despair intertwined. "Yet a yearning to go back persists in their hearts."

A sudden chill ran through me as I caught Roman's eye. Our gazes locked, and in that moment, it was as if we shared an unspoken understanding. Memories of a distant world flooded my mind—a world I had never known until this very day. It was as though a piece of my soul stirred, yearning to return to that unknown realm. A shiver passed through my body, the color draining from my face as the realization sank in. Were we connected by something greater than ourselves? And why could I remember so little?

"I know when you originally learned about these blades from the Great Chief, your sole purpose was to destroy Balthazar and all the evil darknesses out there. But destroying Salvatore is paramount," Pasha Hassan said, his tone grave. "He plots to rule over Solaris, to twist it into a bastion of evil, creating destruction and chaos. Your mother covets dominion over that throne and wishes to rule alongside Salvatore. But once, life thrived there—it was harmonious and resplendent. We aided one another in unity until Salvatore sowed discord, turning us against ourselves."

We sat there, stunned into silence, the weight of the truth pressing heavily on us. Words failed as the enormity of our heritage and destiny bore down. The only sound in the room was the soft crackle of the fire, its warmth failing to chase away the chill that seeped into my bones.

"In the wake of the blades' separation and the banishment of our people from Solaris, Lazarus has been tirelessly piecing together a plan to regroup and build an army against Salvatore's dark forces," Pasha Hassan continued, his voice resolute. "We know that since those blades were torn apart, Salvatore has been actively seeking them out, harnessing his twisted powers to locate them and bolster his corrupted army of Timehunters. But now, thanks to Lazarus gifting us back our memories of Solaris, Zara and I have been working tirelessly to restore them and bring the lost souls back to where they belong—fighting for their true home."

"And with you, Olivia, now possessing both blades, it is time to bring them back to life," Pasha Hassan said, his voice filled with conviction. "Reunite our people, lead them back to their rightful place, and vanquish Salvatore and all his dark minions once and for all."

My veins pulsed with a newfound determination as I locked eyes with him. The weight of his words settled deep within me, igniting a fire I hadn't realized was waiting to be stoked. My voice was low, steely, carrying the promise of unwavering resolve. "Roman and I will stop at nothing to destroy him and restore Solaris to its former glory."

But even as I spoke, frustration churned within me, a storm of unresolved memories threatening to boil over. They lingered just out of reach—fragments of a life I couldn't fully recall. Why couldn't I remember the whole truth? Why couldn't I unleash the full fury burning within me? The pieces were scattered like shards of a broken mirror, and I was desperate to piece them together before it was too late.

CHAPTER THIRTY THREE

OLIVIA

Surrounded by the heavy scent of aged leather and copal-polished Rosewood, I perched on the edge of an ornate chair in Pasha Hassan's study, my mind swirling with a tempest of revelations. Every intricate carving in the room seemed to echo his regret and resolve. He loved his family deeply, yet he bowed before a cause greater than any bond of blood or affection. Pasha Hassan sought to protect what was left of his lineage just as fiercely as my father had endeavored to shield me.

I traced the cool metal of the mysterious blades across my lap, their engravings taunting me with secrets yet to be unlocked. I looked at him, his silhouette framed by the expansive tapestry behind.

"How do we decipher the scriptures on these blades?" I asked, hope threading my voice.

"You must wait, my dear. We all must rest and restore," he said gently. "Tomorrow morning, I will bring you the book. It contains the alphabet needed to decipher the scripture."

"Pasha Hassan—" I began, but he raised a hand, stopping me mid-sentence.

"I would like you to call me Amir," he interjected. "Not Pasha Hassan. And Roman, when you're ready, I would love for you to call me Father."

Beside me, Roman shifted uncomfortably, his posture rigid with unvoiced emotions. "I'm… I'm not ready to call you Father. You put me through too many trials. I respect you, but…" He faltered, his voice wavering with the weight of his pain.

"I understand. Take your time," Amir said, his hands trembling slightly, betraying his vulnerability.

"Even referring to you as Amir gives me pause," Roman admitted. "But I shall try."

"I hope that one day you will forgive me, Roman. I owe you my life," Amir said, his voice heavy with sincerity. "But I had to do what I did. I followed my orders. Salvatore will stop at nothing to destroy us all. These challenges… they are what Salvatore puts his warriors through. I am merely following orders."

A heavy sigh escaped him, laden with the weight of his regret. "Don't be upset with Malik and Reyna. I did this to you. I had to. It pained me more than you'll ever know. It pained me to take your children away. I did it selfishly… to be their grandfather."

The absurdity hit me like a rogue wave crashing into still waters. A startled laugh burst forth from my lips before I could stifle it.

"Good one, Amir. So, we were fighting for our lives, and you were playing Grandpa."

Beside me, Roman's lips curled into a wry smile, a silent acknowledgment of the bizarre truth we'd been served.

"But, speaking of the children…" I said, my voice softening as my heart swelled with longing. "Please, let me see them. I miss them so dearly."

"Of course," Amir replied, his warmth contrasting with the cold resolve of moments earlier. With a curt nod, he signaled to someone beyond my line of sight. "As you wish, my dear."

Measured footsteps approached, and a guard appeared in the doorway, clad in the ornate uniform befitting Pasha Hassan's service. The guard bowed slightly, then gestured for us to follow him. My heart raced as we moved down the dimly lit corridor, every step bringing me closer to the reunion I had yearned for.

Inside the sanctuary, the air was still and fragrant with the sweet scent of innocence. Moonlight streamed through cracks in the ceiling, casting a celestial glow over the two slumbering forms nestled in their cribs. Roman's hand tightened around mine, his grip conveying an unspoken torrent of emotions as we gazed upon our daughters, their small chests rising and falling with the tranquil rhythm of dreams.

"They look so peaceful," I whispered, tears pricking the corners of my eyes, the weight of the world momentarily lifted by their serene presence.

"Like they've never known a moment's distress," Roman replied.

Movement stirred from the corner of the room, and Reyna emerged from the shadows, her presence a silent yet commanding sentinel. A frisson of surprise jolted through me.

"Reyna…" My voice faltered as I stepped toward her, the earlier strain of doubt and suspicion giving way to relief. Without hesitation, I enveloped her fiercely, "I'm so sorry I accused you of treachery. You were just doing what you had to do."

Her arms tightened around me with equal fervor, and her

voice carried the weight of understanding when she spoke. "Our father never would have killed you, Roman. The trials would have stopped. But you passed perfectly. You are ready."

The tension within us unspooled, forgiveness knitting together the fractures in our relationship. Roman joined our embrace, his presence a grounding force that anchored us all.

As we stepped back, the flickering candlelight danced across Reyna's features, highlighting the undeniable resemblance to Marcellious.

"I saved Marcellious. He is my brother, after all, which means I am your sister, Roman," she revealed, her eyes holding a glint of pride.

The corner of Roman's mouth lifted in a bittersweet smile. "You carry the face of an angel like our mother."

Reyna's laughter was soft but tinged with darkness. "I might look like an angel, but I am dark and deadly."

"I've already seen that," Roman replied, his tone layered with both respect and acknowledgment.

"You have no idea how long I've wanted to meet you and Marcellious," Reyna said, her voice thick with years of yearning. "Mother and Father spoke of you both so often. Our mother would be so proud to see us together like this. I hope we'll free her from Solaris one day."

With those parting words, Reyna turned and disappeared into the shadows from which she had come.

Gazing upon Rosie's and Luna's slumbering forms, nestled in the soft glow of moonlight filtering through the fractured ceiling, our resolve solidified like the delicate threads of their well-worn blankets.

"We fought all our battles and challenges for them," I whispered, my voice barely more than a breath. "Look how angelic they are."

Roman reached for me, his fingers threading with my own as if drawing strength from the connection.

"I hope we can reunite the blades, help the people of Solaris, and finally become a peaceful family with all our children," he said, his gaze lingering on the serene faces of our daughters. "No more fear."

With one last lingering look that imprinted their innocence into our hearts, we silently agreed it was time to leave. Hand in hand, we retreated from the nursery. The same warrior who had escorted us there kept his watchful eyes on our backs as we navigated the dimly lit corridors toward our room.

Relief washed over me the moment we entered the chamber. Here, amidst plush pillows and silken drapes, Roman and I sought refuge—not just from the weight of the world but the overwhelming enormity of our destinies.

"Olivia," Roman breathed, his voice low and thick with desire as his hands cupped my face. His intense gaze burned into mine, his eyes darkened with lust and devotion, making my heart flutter wildly in my chest. Slowly, he leaned down, his lips capturing mine in a kiss that spoke of battles endured and victories claimed. The passion between us was unrestrained, raw, and electrifying.

Our kiss deepened, tongues tangling in a dance that was both primal and exquisite, ancient yet fresh with discovery. The way his tongue thrust into my mouth and retreated mimicked a rhythm so intimate it sent a wave of molten heat straight to my core. A long, breathless moan escaped me, vibrating against his lips as I melted into him.

Roman's touch was intoxicating, his hand sliding around my neck in a gentle yet commanding grip that sent a delicious shiver down my spine. His other hand found my hip, pulling me closer until there was no space left between us. The hardness of his cock pressed against my stomach its heat and insistence fanning the flames of my desire.

As his lips moved with mine in perfect harmony, his hand slid lower, cupping my ass, squeezing and kneading with a precision that left me trembling. Every touch sent electric shocks racing through me, my body instinctively pressing against him, seeking more, needing more.

Roman broke the kiss, his lips lingering close enough that our breaths mingled, the air between us heavy with unspoken need. Our eyes locked, his smoldering gaze holding me captive as our chests rose and fell in unison, the anticipation building like a storm about to break.

"There are too many layers keeping us apart," I whispered, my voice trembling with need.

A devilish grin curved his lips, his eyes gleaming with wicked mischief. "Allow me to fix that, my love."

He turned me toward the full-length mirror, positioning me so I could see every movement, every lingering touch. His strong hands gripped my hips as he pressed his body flush against mine, his heat searing through the thin fabric separating us. His breath was warm against my neck, his lips grazing the sensitive skin there, sending a shiver rippling down my spine. Roman's hands moved with reverence, untangling the sash of my long silk kaftan. The fabric slid from my shoulders and pooled at my feet, leaving me in the sheer entari beneath. His hands followed, sweeping across my curves with a touch so gentle it was maddening. His fingers worked the fabric away with deliberate care, baring the body I had tried to hide, the curves that still carried traces of Luna's birth within me.

He paused, his lips pressing a hot kiss to the nape of my neck, and I gasped, my head falling back against his shoulder.

"You're exquisite," he murmured, his voice a husky rasp as his eyes roamed over me in the mirror.

I lifted my head, catching sight of the damp stains spreading over the fabric of my gömlek, the evidence of my body's nourishment for our child. My breasts were full and heavy with milk, and Roman's gaze darkened further as it lingered on the wet patches that clung to my nipples.

"I see you have milk for me, my love," he murmured, his voice a sinful growl that sent a thrill racing through me.

His hands slid up to cup my breasts, the warmth of his palms igniting a fire in me that made me tremble. His thumbs grazed over my hardened nipples, teasing the damp fabric and sending shocks of pleasure straight to my core. "These are mine," he whispered, his lips brushing against my ear. "Every part of you, Olivia. Mine to love, to worship, to taste."

He slipped the gömlek down, baring my engorged breasts to the cool air and his heated gaze. Roman's hands molded to my curves, his thumbs circling my nipples, coaxing a soft, needy moan from my lips. His mouth found my neck, trailing kisses down to my shoulder, his breath hot against my skin.

"Look at yourself," he murmured, his voice low and commanding, thick with authority and desire. "See what I see. Look at how stunning you are. See how much I want you, how much I *need* you."

I met his gaze in the mirror, and the intensity there stole the breath from my lungs. His darkened eyes held a hunger so deep, so consuming, that it felt like his desire alone could devour every doubt I carried. His hands slid lower, their journey unhurried, savoring every curve. His lips followed, leaving soft, burning kisses along my shoulder and back, igniting a firestorm of need that consumed me entirely.

My fingers trailed over the faint stretch marks that curved

across my belly, their presence like echoes of the life I had carried within me. They felt like rivers etched into my skin—beautiful but stark reminders of how much I had changed. My body prickled under the weight of my insecurities, invisible eyes that seemed to judge me harshly. Shifting uncomfortably, I tried to silence the whispers of imperfection that crept into my thoughts.

Sensing my unease, Roman's grip on me tightened, grounding me in his touch. His lips pressed softer, more deliberate kisses to my shoulder, his movements unhurried, as though he knew he needed to pull me from my spiral.

"You've never been more beautiful," he rasped, his voice molten and reverent. "Every mark, every curve, every piece of you—it's ours, Olivia. They tell our story."

I glanced at the mirror again, catching the raw emotion in his eyes, the way he looked at me like I was the only thing that mattered. His hands slid back up to cup my breasts, squeezing just enough to make me gasp. His thumbs grazed my nipples again, this time slower, deliberate, sending sparks racing through my body.

"You're a fucking goddess," Roman growled, his breath hot against my ear. "These curves, this body, everything about you—it's mine. Every part of you is perfect, Olivia. Do you feel that?" His hand moved to cover mine, guiding my fingers to trace the stretch marks on my belly. "These marks? They're proof of your strength, of the life we created together. And they make you even more irresistible."

His words seeped into me, melting away the icy grip of self-doubt. Roman's lips returned to my neck, this time sucking gently, teasing, leaving marks of his own. The warmth of his tongue against my skin sent a moan spilling from my lips, louder this time, as my body responded to every stroke of his hands and every burning kiss.

"Don't hide from me," he murmured, his voice rough and

desperate. "Don't you dare. Let me see you. Let me worship you."

In the mirror, I saw myself through his eyes—strong, radiant, utterly desired. His hands slid down my hips, gripping firmly, pulling me back against his hard, unyielding body. The heat of him pressed into me, his arousal impossible to ignore. He rolled his hips slowly, teasing me, making my breath catch and my knees tremble.

"Let go, Olivia," he whispered, his voice thick with desire. "Let me love you. Let me show you how perfect you are to me."

Before I could retreat further, his hands were on me, pulling me close, his strong arms locking me against his chest. The solid heat of him, the steady beat of his heart, surrounded me, grounding me. His lips brushed my ear as he whispered, "Every inch. Every scar. Every curve. You're mine, Olivia. My fire. My everything."

His hands slid down my back, deliberate and slow, igniting sparks along every nerve ending. I let out a shaky breath, my body trembling as he worshipped me with his touch.

"God, I love you, Roman," I said, my heart swelling with raw emotion.

A sinful smile tugged at his mouth as his hands roamed lower, gripping me firmly. "Good, my flaming fire," he murmured, his lips brushing against my neck. "Because I adore you, every piece of you. Like the sun worships the dawn, I'll never stop loving you."

His hands moved deliberately, tracing a slow, torturous path down my sides, his touch igniting sparks that raced across my skin. My body arched instinctively into him, desperate for more as his fingertips teased the edges of my hips, just enough to leave me trembling. My breath came quicker, my heart pounding in my chest as heat flooded me. When his lips left mine, they began a searing descent down the length of my neck, lingering at the hollow of my throat, then lower, lower still, until I was sure I might combust beneath his touch.

I let out a soft, involuntary moan as his lips brushed along the curve of my spine, each kiss deliberate, scorching, leaving a trail of fire that burned through every last shred of restraint I had. He paused at the waistband of my salvar, his teeth tugging at the fabric, teasing, his breath hot against my skin. The ache between my thighs grew unbearable, and my hands reached back, grasping at his arms, silently begging for more.

"Olivia, my heart," Roman whispered, his voice thick with desire and devotion, the rawness of it sending a wave of heat through me. "I will love you through every breath, every moment, every lifetime. As rivers carve their way through ancient stone, so too will my love for you shape eternity."

He moved around to face me, his movements slow and predatory, his eyes darkened with a hunger that stole the air from my lungs. His hands slid up, cupping my breasts, his touch both reverent and sinful. A gasp escaped me as his thumbs brushed over sensitive peaks, the warmth of his palms spreading through me like liquid fire.

"In the dawn of every new day," he murmured, lowering his lips to trace the curve of my collarbone, "when the sun kisses the horizon, know this—my devotion to you burns brighter, hotter. And when the stars take their place in the sky, my love will guide you, a beacon that never wavers."

His words were a heady mix of poetry and possession, but it was his touch that undid me. His hands slid over the curves of my body, exploring me with a slow, deliberate reverence that set every nerve alight. His lips found mine again, this time with unrestrained hunger, stealing the last of my breath as he pulled me closer.

"Olivia," he growled against my mouth, his voice dripping with need, "in the tapestry of time, our love will be the golden thread—the fire that burns through the centuries. You are everything. My past, my present, my forever."

Tears pricked at the corners of my eyes as Roman's devotion enveloped me, raw and unrelenting. In that moment, the flaws I once saw in myself disappeared, replaced by the sheer power of his adoration. His love wasn't just tender—it was consuming, a force so primal it made me feel radiant, unstoppable, and entirely his.

My body trembled under his touch, the ache between my thighs growing unbearable with every deliberate brush of his hands. My breath came in shallow, erratic gasps as he cradled my face, his lips capturing mine in a kiss so deep, so carnal, it unraveled me completely. His tongue claimed me with an urgency that sent waves of heat coursing through my body, his hands roaming with possessive precision as though I belonged to him and only him.

I clawed at his clothes, my fingers frantic, removing each article in a desperate need to feel his skin against mine.

The satin şalvar slipped from my hips, sliding down my legs in a whisper of surrender. Roman groaned, the sound low and primal, as his eyes raked over me, darkened with lust. His powerful, naked form shimmered in the moonlight—a masterpiece of strength and desire. The sight of him, hard and ready, sent a fresh surge of heat pooling between my legs.

"You're incredible," he growled, his voice rough with hunger. In a single, effortless motion, he lifted me into his arms, his arousal pressing hot and insistent against my core as he carried me to the bed. His lips never left mine, claiming me with every step.

As he laid me down amongst the cushions, his mouth found my neck, trailing a blazing path of kisses that had me arching into him. His hands explored me with reverence and hunger, his touch igniting sparks that left me gasping. My body was his canvas, and he painted his love on every inch of me with lips, teeth, and tongue.

His kisses moved lower, his mouth lingering on the curve of my breasts before claiming a sensitive peak. I cried out as his tongue swirled around me, his teeth grazing the delicate skin just enough to send jolts of pleasure straight to my core. His hands slid down my sides, firm yet teasing, leaving me trembling and desperate for more.

"Roman," I whimpered, his name a plea as his lips continued their descent. He took his time, trailing fire from my belly to the curve of my hips, his hands parting my thighs with deliberate care. I lay there, exposed and vulnerable, my body burning with need as he settled between my legs.

His lips brushed the sensitive skin of my inner thighs, his breath hot and teasing as he inched closer to where I ached for him most. Every kiss, every flick of his tongue, sent shivers cascading through me, each touch building the fire that burned hotter and hotter.

When his mouth finally found me, I shattered. His tongue moved against my swollen flesh with deliberate, excruciating precision, alternating between soft, languid strokes and quick, teasing flicks that had me writhing beneath him. His hands gripped my hips, holding me steady as he drove me higher, the pressure building with every skilled movement of his tongue.

I moaned his name, my voice breaking as he pushed me to the edge of sanity. The heat, the intensity, the way his mouth worshipped me—it was too much and not enough all at once. My fingers tangled in his hair, pulling him closer as my body arched off the bed, desperate for release.

"Roman," I gasped, my voice breaking as waves of pleasure crashed over me, consuming me whole. His mouth didn't falter, his tongue relentless in its pursuit of my release, teasing and tasting until every shuddering cry escaped my lips. My body quaked beneath him, trembling as aftershocks rippled through me, leaving me breathless and light-headed. I floated in a haze of ecstasy, my mind spinning as he continued to worship me.

Roman withdrew, his tongue leaving me with a sinful ache, his hands gliding soothingly over my trembling thighs as I came down from the high. His grin was wicked, his expression a heady mix of satisfaction and pure, unfiltered hunger. "Don't think we're done, my beautiful flame," he murmured, his voice dripping with promise. "I'm just getting started."

Before I could catch my breath or even respond, his mouth returned with devastating intensity. His tongue was merciless, exploring me with precision and passion, driving me to the edge over and over again. Each time I begged for mercy, he pulled me back under, my cries filling the room as another orgasm tore through me. My body arched off the bed, trembling as I soared higher than before, my pleasure so raw, so consuming, it left me sobbing his name.

"That," he murmured, his voice dark and intoxicating as he pulled away, "was just a taste." His words sent a thrill through me, anticipation igniting deep within. "There's so much more I want to show you, Olivia. So much more I want you to feel."

His hand moved lower, gripping his swollen cock, and he slid it teasingly between my slick folds, coating himself in my arousal. I gasped, my back arching as the anticipation reached its peak. "Roman…" My voice was a whisper, a plea, as he pressed against me, the heat of him stealing what little composure I had left.

With one slow, deliberate thrust, he entered me, filling me completely. The sensation was overwhelming, his hardness stretching and claiming me in a way that stole the air from my lungs. Our bodies moved together, finding a rhythm that was as primal as it was perfect, a dance older than time itself. Each thrust was a masterpiece, a stroke of passion that etched itself into my soul, binding us together in a way that transcended anything I had ever known.

"Look at me," he growled, his voice rough with desire as his gaze locked onto mine. "You're mine, Olivia. Every inch of you belongs to me."

We moved as one, our connection unshakable, each thrust sending waves of pleasure crashing over us. My nails raked across his back, leaving marks on his skin, a physical declaration of the pleasure he gave me. His lips found mine, our kisses deep and ravenous, a battle of tongues and need that left me dizzy.

Laughter bubbled between us, soft and breathless, mingling with the moans and cries of ecstasy. Roman's teasing touches had me laughing one moment and writhing beneath him the next, his hands exploring every inch of me as though he couldn't get enough. The sound of my laughter blended with his low growls, a symphony of passion and joy that built into an unstoppable crescendo.

The pressure inside me built to a breaking point, each thrust amplifying the fire between us until it exploded in a tidal wave of bliss. "Oh, God, Roman!" I screamed, my body shattering around him as I reached my climax, the intensity ripping through me and leaving me trembling in its wake.

"Fuck, Olivia," he groaned, his thrusts growing erratic as

his release overtook him. With one final, powerful thrust, he spilled himself inside me, his warmth filling me as he growled my name. My body clenched around him, another orgasm tearing through me as my cries mingled with his, our voices echoing in perfect harmony.

When we finally collapsed into each other's arms, the world outside ceased to exist. There was no past, no future—only this moment, only Roman and me, tangled together in the aftermath of our passion. His heartbeat echoed against mine, our breaths mingling as we lay entwined, basking in the glow of what we had created together. In his arms, I was whole, loved, and utterly complete.

I sighed into the crook of his neck, my mind drifting to the shared dream that now tied us together. A future for us, our children, and the world we would rebuild together. The warmth of his body and the steady rhythm of his breathing became my anchor as I traced the inked patterns on his chest, each line and swirl a reminder of our journey.

"Roman," I murmured, my voice tinged with awe. "We finally have answers." My eyes sparkled with a radiant joy, a light that had been absent for far too long.

Roman pulled me close, his arms wrapping around me with a protective warmth that lulled me into a peaceful sleep. I was so sated—not just from our lovemaking but from the weight of the knowledge we now held.

The strange glowing orb in the corner of the room pulsed with dawn's calling, casting a warm, golden hue over our entwined forms. It felt like we had feasted on the universe's secrets, savoring each revelation as if it were the most sumptuous of meals. And yet, there was more—so much more—

the lure of unraveling the sacred scripture's mysteries awaited us.

As if on cue, the scent of freshly baked bread and strong coffee wafted into the room, heralding the quiet entrance of a manservant carrying a tray laden with breakfast. He set it down with practiced grace, offering a respectful nod.

"Master Roman, Lady Olivia," he said softly. "Breakfast is served."

Roman and I indulged in the comfort of our bed just a moment longer, letting the robust aroma of the morning meal envelop us. With each bite, the strength and vigor we needed for the day ahead returned to our bodies.

"Pasha Hassan awaits you in his study," the servant informed us after we had eaten our fill. His words were simple, yet they carried the weight of expectation.

"Tell Amir... tell *Father* we will be there shortly," Roman replied, his voice steady and resolute.

I nodded, bolstered by the prospect of what lay ahead. We were ready to unravel the mysteries enshrined within the sacred texts and begin weaving the future we had fought so fiercely to secure.

With hearts full and minds eager, we rose from the soft embrace of our bed, stepping into the light of a new day—one brimming with hope and purpose. Yet, beneath this fleeting sense of tranquility lurked shadows. The inevitable dangers waiting to test us were never far. We knew peace was but a temporary guest in our tumultuous world.

CHAPTER THIRTY FOUR

OLIVIA

Drunk on love and with our bellies full of nourishing food, Roman and I shuffled down the corridor, our steps muffled by the plush carpets sprawling like a sea of red velvet beneath our feet. The air was thick with the scent of sandalwood, copal, and old books —a fragrance that clung to the ancient walls of Amir's underground palace. Roman's arm brushed against mine as we walked, the warmth of our tangled sheets still lingering between us.

We were giddy, almost tipsy, on the heady blend of danger and desire that had consumed us just hours before. Along the path, we stole kisses like precious treasures, each promising more. Our insatiable hunger for one another remained a flame neither of us wished to extinguish.

As we neared the heavy oak doors, the gravity of our mission returned, pulling me back to the reality of what lay ahead. Yet, the glow of the night lingered on my skin, a radiant aftermath of being wrapped in Roman's embrace.

With a gentle push, the doors creaked open, revealing

Amir's study. He glanced up from an ancient tome, a knowing smirk tugging at the corners of his lips.

"I trust you slept well," he said, his voice laced with humor and a shrewd glint in his gaze. "Though I suspect sleep was not your primary indulgence."

Heat rushed to my cheeks at his words, painting them a telltale shade of crimson. There was no concealing the fervor that clung to us, as tangible as the morning dew on the palace's stone walls. Amid the embarrassment, though, a flicker of pride warmed me—pride for the connection Roman and I shared, a bond that was ours and ours alone.

"Indeed," I managed to reply, lifting my chin slightly. The blush remained—a banner of the love I bore for my husband—but I refused to let Amir's teasing diminish the beauty of what Roman and I had found in each other.

"Alright, let's get down to it," Amir said, his voice taking on a serious tone. He stood and meandered toward the same darkened closet where, just yesterday, he had unearthed the daggers.

Anticipation coiled within me like a spring as he disappeared into the shadows. Moments later, he emerged cradling a tome so ancient its very presence seemed to hum with the weight of bygone eras. The leather binding was cracked and weathered, the color of deep mahogany, and it bore intricate etchings that whispered of arcane knowledge and secrets locked away in time. Bound with robust cords, the edges of its pages gleamed faintly, tinged with gold that glinted in the study's dim light.

"Here," Amir said, extending the book toward me with a reverence that bordered on the ceremonious. I reached out and accepted the relic with equal care, feeling the cool brush of the leather against my palms.

"Behold, the book of the alphabet you need to decipher,"

Amir said. "You must figure out the words one by one. I can offer guidance if needed, but you should embark on this journey together."

His expression carried a conspiratorial edge as though he were privy to some secret jest at our expense. "Make yourselves comfortable in my study. I shall bring food and drink to sustain you while you work."

With that, his gaze lingered on us, amusement twinkling before he strode from the room. The door shut softly, leaving Roman and me with the venerable volume—a book that promised both enlightenment and enigma, its secrets waiting to be unraveled.

Settling into the plush loveseat tucked in the corner of the study, I playfully tugged Roman down beside me. He grabbed a nearby cushion with a mischievous glint and tossed it at me. Laughter filled the room as we engaged in a spontaneous pillow fight, the seriousness of our mission momentarily forgotten.

A sense of freedom and youthfulness washed over me, a feeling I hadn't experienced in years. The pillows flew back and forth in a playful flurry until we finally called a truce, both breathless and grinning.

"Let's not forget why we're here," I teased, though the warmth of his body beside mine made it tempting to ignore the work awaiting us. Roman's deep, soothing laughter echoed my sentiment before he leaned in for a kiss—a lingering reminder of our shared night.

"Work it is," he said.

Pulling himself away from our shared cocoon, Roman unfurled the leather bundle that encased the blades onto his lap. They shimmered with an ethereal light, their edges sharp and gleaming. The metallic sheen seemed to pulse with a life of its own, as if the daggers were aware of their imminent role in decoding the ancient script.

"I need something to write with," I said, unwilling to leave his side for even a moment.

My fingers brushed the polished surface of the desk as I searched, eventually encountering a stack of thick, luxurious paper. It was likely imported from Persia, and its texture was a testament to its quality.

"The finest paper for the most sacred of words," I mused, a smile curving my lips.

Beside the paper lay a Qalam, its reed body honed to perfection, ready to dance across the page. A small pot of black ink rested nearby, a concoction of lampblack, gum Arabic, and water—a perfect blend of artistry and precision.

"The tools of scholars and poets," I said, lifting the Qalam with reverence.

"Let's move to the desk," I suggested, carefully gathering the paper, pen, and ink. "We wouldn't want to risk staining the loveseat or letting our fervor for knowledge ruin the furniture. Pull up a chair, Roman," I added, my tone still laced with the playful energy of our earlier antics.

He dragged a chair to my side and carefully laid out the sun and moon daggers atop Amir's grand desk. The leather wrapping unfurled like an ancient scroll, revealing the blades' intricate designs and the enigmatic scripture carved into their surfaces.

"Let's make this interesting," I said with a sly smile. "For every word we decipher, a reward."

Roman's brow arched. "What kind of reward?" he asked, his lips curving into a grin. "Kisses, perhaps?"

I nodded, meeting his playful gaze. "Exactly."

"Sounds delightful," he said, his voice warm and full of anticipation.

We leaned close together, our heads nearly touching as we pored over the ancient text. The air between us crackled with a mix of concentration and an unspoken intimacy. Each time we unraveled a word, our lips met in celebration—a soft, fleeting kiss that left us craving more but kept us grounded in our shared task.

The hours slipped by in a haze of stolen glances, light brushes of fingertips, and the silent language of lovers united by a singular purpose. Our kisses became punctuation marks for our successes, each sweeter and more rewarding than the last. The afternoon melted into evening, the light outside dimming as our work brought us closer to the truth.

"Look, Roman!" I exclaimed, my pulse quickening as the final word fell into place.

The daggers trembled on the desk, their metallic surfaces shimmering as if alive. A low hum emanated from them, vibrating with a force that sent a thrill down my spine.

I reached for the blades, my fingertips grazing their glowing edges. They burned with an ethereal light, pulsing in time with my heartbeat. The ancient words I had deciphered tumbled from my lips, each syllable resonating with a foreign and familiar power.

"*iinani 'adeu qiwaa alsama' aleazimati, wa'atlub mink 'an tutliq aleinan linurki,*" I said, reading from the deciphered script on the paper. "*Biaistikhdam shafarat alquat alqadimat hadhihi, 'adeu alshams walqamar wazilal alliyl. 'arshad rihlatay eabr thanaya alzaman, hayth al'asrar alqadimat makhfiat ean al'anzari. dae hadhih alshafarat tashuqu hajb aleusur baynama 'usafir taht daw' alnujumi. 'anar hikmatak ealaa aldurub ghayr almatruqati, wamnahni albasar hayth yasud alzalamu. man lahib alshams aleanif 'iilaa lamsat alqamar albaridati, 'anr tariqi bialsalasil alsamawiati. fi hadhih alraqsat mae zilal alzaman aleamiqati, hayth tamtazij*

al'asda' watabqaa alhaqiqatu, makanani min aleuthur ealaa
almafqudi, warabt makasib almadi walmustaqbali."

As I recited the ancient text, I translated it in my mind. *I*
call upon the great forces of the sky; I ask you to unleash
your light. With these ancient blades of power, I call upon the
night's sun, moon, and shadows. Guide my journey through
the folds of time, where old secrets are kept from sight. Let
these blades cleave the veils of ages as I travel under starry
light. Shine your wisdom on paths untread, and grant me the
sight where darkness reigns. From the sun's fierce blaze to
the moon's cool touch, illuminate my way with heavenly
chains. This dance with time's deep shadows, where echoes
blend, and the truth remains, empowers me to find the lost
and to bind the past and future's gains.

As the incantation climaxed, the blades moved of their
own accord, sliding across the table like two celestial lovers
drawn by destiny. The sun embraced the moon in an ethereal
dance, their luminous forms merging seamlessly. The moon
cradled the sun in a perfect union, and a crescendo of radiant
light enveloped the room.

I gasped, exhilarated. We had done it. The ancient scripture had been deciphered, and now, before our eyes, the
blades had fused into one.

The glow dimmed slowly, the brilliant display fading into
a muted silence. The conjoined blades lay still, inert. Their
brief luminescence, which had filled the room with otherworldly energy, was replaced by an almost anticlimactic
stillness.

Roman and I held our breaths, waiting for a sign, a
continuation of the miracle we had witnessed. But nothing
came—only a pervasive quiet, punctuated by the faint crackle
of the oil lamps in the study. Disappointment settled over us
like fine dust, heavy and suffocating.

"Roman," I breathed, trembling, "why did it stop? Did we do something wrong?"

A wave of panic surged through me, threatening to drown out any rational thoughts. My breaths quickened, shallow and uneven. My mind raced with fear and uncertainty, my body stiffening as a suffocating sense of defeat closed in. It felt like falling into an abyss, the weight of helplessness pressing against my chest.

Roman's steady voice broke through my spiraling thoughts. "Let's go get my father and ask him."

Nodding, I clung to the sliver of hope in his calm resolve. Together, we left the study behind, our footsteps hushed against the rich carpets lining the underground palace's corridors.

The dining area awaited us, an opulent space that exuded a sense of grandeur. Gilded archways framed the doorways, their golden sheen catching the flickering light of the oil lamps. The walls bore intricate mosaics, vibrant depictions of conquest and splendor from the Ottoman Empire's storied past. Persian carpets softened our steps, their patterns a kaleidoscope of vivid colors and intricate designs. A long dining table carved from dark mahogany dominated the center of the room. Its rich, polished surface reflected the warm glow of the hanging lamps above. Cushioned divans surrounded it, their inviting fabric calling for relaxation and leisure.

Amir sat at the head of the table, commanding even in repose. An array of dishes was spread before him—honey-drizzled figs that filled the air with sweetness, the savory aroma of spiced lamb simmering nearby, and a bowl of jewel-like pomegranate seeds catching the light. A stack of fresh flatbreads lay within easy reach, their edges curling with steam.

"Father," Roman said hesitantly, the word unfamiliar on his tongue.

Amir looked up, his keen eyes immediately locking onto the blade we carried between us. A flicker of delight crossed his face.

"Ah! What is this?" he said, his voice brimming with approval. "I see you did not need my help. This is most excellent."

"Amir," I began, my voice tight as I fought to keep my frustration in check. "The blades—they're not..."

I trailed off, extending the conjoined sun and moon daggers. Their lifeless form felt heavier than before, a tangible reminder of our perceived failure. They lay cold and unremarkable in my hands, stripped of the light and power we had anticipated.

"I'm impressed," Amir said, leaning back in his chair to survey our work. His praise felt hollow against the weight of disappointment crushing my chest.

"They're dead," I blurted, my desperation slipping through my words. "Nothing is happening. Our daggers at least light up when awakened."

"You connected the blades, yes," Amir said, his tone maddeningly casual. "But now you need the Scrolls of Time."

"The Scrolls of Time?" I repeated, exhaling heavily. The thought of another obstacle, another hunt, when victory had seemed so tantalizingly close, felt unbearable. "What are these scrolls?"

"It's like a recipe," Amir said, reaching for a cluster of grapes and popping one into his mouth with infuriating ease. "They guide you on how to make the blades truly alive and powerful."

Frustration boiled over inside me, the heat of it rising to

my cheeks. "You should have prepared us. You should have at least mentioned there were more steps to the process!"

Amir's expression remained composed, his calm juxtaposed with my agitation. "Had I told you, would you have even learned the scriptures?" he asked, his voice sharp yet patient. "No. You would have given up."

"Where do we find these scrolls?" Roman interjected, his arm slipping around my waist in silent support.

"Your father, Jack, has them," Amir said, his piercing gaze landing on me.

My heart sank further. Another puzzle piece lay hidden, waiting for us to unearth it. The path ahead promised to be fraught with more secrets and trials than I had ever imagined.

"Are you kidding? My father has the scrolls?" I asked, my voice a mixture of disbelief and anger. The room spun slightly as Amir's revelation bore down on me.

"Yes, your father," Amir confirmed. "He is a man with many secrets. It's time for you to travel back to the twenty-first century and see your father, Jack James. The full moon is in a few days. You must all prepare. Only your father can help you because he is the keeper and protector of the Scrolls of Time."

"My daughter is a Timeborne," I said, the fear for Luna's future clawing at my chest. "If we time travel, her darkness will awaken."

Amir sighed, his tone softening only slightly. "There are far greater things to worry about, my dear. You must fear Mathias, Alina, Salvatore, and his army of darkness. Malik will come with you to keep you safe."

The reality of what lay ahead settled into my bones, heavy and unrelenting. Enemies were closing in, and our family's safety hinged on actions we had yet to understand, let alone master.

"Then we have no choice," Roman murmured, his hand tightening on my waist as he read the resignation in my eyes.

"None whatsoever." Amir stood, his form imposing as he pushed away his plate. "Make your preparations. Time waits for no one."

He dabbed his lips with a cloth napkin, his words like a solemn decree. "It's going to be a long journey. Prepare."

The weight of his gaze felt like chains around my wrists, binding me to the path I could not escape. I drew a deep breath, trying to quell the nerves fluttering in my chest like caged birds. Time travel was not new to me, but it had been an eternity since I last ripped through the fabric of time. The thought alone made my stomach churn.

With Amir's departure, a heavy silence filled the room. My mind reeled from his words, each a bitter pill laced with hidden truths and veiled intentions.

"Great. Now I have learned that my father has been keeping more secrets from me," I whispered. "Is there anyone in my life who has not deceived me?"

As I turned to face Roman, the ache in my heart eased. His eyes, steady and sincere, met mine, and a wave of warmth washed over me. In that gaze, I found an anchor in the storm that raged around us.

"Never," Roman said, brushing away the tear from my cheek. "You've always had me, Olivia, as your trusted companion, and you always will."

His simple vow cut through the lies and secrets that seemed to ensnare us. He was my constant, the one soul whose love and loyalty remained unshaken amid the turmoil of our lives. With him by my side, I could weather any storm, decipher any mystery, and face whatever darkness threatened to consume us.

"Let's prepare then," I said, finding strength in his unwavering presence. "Together."

We spent the day busying ourselves by gathering the necessary supplies for our upcoming time-travel journey. Meanwhile, we took every opportunity to spend quality time with the children. Rosie, in particular, was bursting with exuberance, bouncing from one corner of the room to the other as she helped pack and prepare for her next adventure.

"Malik will join us, won't he?" she asked, already envisioning all the wondrous places they would discover together.

"Of course," I said. "Come, sit now, and let me comb your hair.

Her lower lip stuck out in a pout, but she plopped before me on the carpeted floor. As she endured my attempts to tame her wild hair with an intricately decorated bone comb, she focused on the small wooden doll in her hands. The doll was dressed in a tiny kaftan, complete with delicate embroidery that mimicked the styles worn by the household women. Surrounding her were miniature pieces of furniture—a small bed with a quilted cover, a small table, and a set of polished metal cups and plates. She arranged her playthings carefully, creating a miniature world where her imagination could flourish.

Roman, who had disappeared some time ago to rock Luna for her nap, reappeared, his face soft with the triumph of a small victory.

"I got her to sleep, finally," he said, leaning over to kiss my head. "The staff has prepared us supper to eat before nightfall."

"Good," I replied, pulling the comb through Rosie's hair with finality. I tied her hair back into a ponytail with a silk ribbon.

"That will never last," Roman said with a chuckle.

"I know." I sighed, getting to my feet. "Let's go eat, Rosie."

Rosie slipped her small hand into mine, and we approached the dining room together.

The heaviness of the meal sat in my stomach as my mind churned with thoughts and worries about our upcoming time travel. It had been far too long since I had seen my father, and the anticipation was almost overwhelming. But amidst the excitement was a twinge of anxiety about the challenges ahead. We had already overcome so much on our journeys through time. Would we truly be granted safe passage to the 21st century? The uncertainty hung like an oppressive cloud, casting shadows over our plans and hopes for the future.

"I want to spend time with my father before we travel," Roman said, breaking through the labyrinth of my thoughts.

Rosie perked up. "Can I come with you?"

Roman glanced at me before nodding. "Of course."

"Enjoy yourselves," I replied, my voice steadier than I felt. "I need to get the kids' things ready. Then let's meet outside in the courtyard at nightfall."

One of Amir's guards escorted me up a twisting labyrinth of stairs and hurried me and Luna outside through a secret door. The sudden openness felt strange, almost surreal. A warm breeze teased my kaftan, making it ripple against my legs. The full moon cast its silvery glow over the underground palace, illuminating the courtyard in an ethereal light. I cradled Luna close, her small form both a source of comfort and a reminder of the fragility of the moment. As I approached the courtyard, my footsteps echoed softly on the cool stone walkway.

The shadows shifted unnaturally, forming into three hooded figures. In an instant, they lunged toward us. With one arm wrapped protectively around Luna as her screams pierced the night, I brandished my dagger in the other.

"Shh, darling, mommy's here," I whispered, my voice trembling as I parried a blow aimed at my heart.

My blade sang through the air, clashing violently against the steel of my assailants. The movements were sharp, desperate. I noticed a flash of red thread on their belts—different from the black insignia of Amir's guards.

"Traitors!" I spat, realization dawning as my heart pounded like war drums.

Every strike of my dagger was fueled by an unwavering resolve to protect Luna. Her cries, raw and terrified, were a fierce reminder of what was at stake. The moon bore silent witness as I fought, the deadly dance casting fleeting shadows across the stones.

One by one, the attackers fell, their bodies crumpling at my feet. But there was no time to process the victory. Clutching Luna tightly to my chest, I ran, my lungs burning as I pushed forward toward the safety of the courtyard. The air was thick with the scent of jasmine, mingling with the metallic tang of blood. Luna's cries echoed, a haunting, desperate melody propelling me forward.

A fourth figure emerged from the darkness, his blade catching the moonlight in a menacing gleam.

"Please, not my baby," I whispered, sprinting toward the great gong that loomed at the courtyard's edge. With every ounce of strength, I swung its mallet, unleashing a deafening clang that shattered the night's stillness and reverberated through the stone walls.

The attacker surged toward me, his blade slicing through the air. Pain erupted in my arm as his weapon found its mark, sending searing agony radiating through my body. I stumbled to the ground, the cobblestones cold and unforgiving beneath me. Desperate, I wrapped myself around Luna, shielding her tiny frame as I braced for the final blow.

The man raised his blade high, his intent unmistakable. Tears blurred my vision as I whispered a silent prayer, holding Luna closer than ever.

Suddenly, a wall of fire erupted behind him. The searing heat illuminated the night, casting long, flickering shadows. The man froze, a crimson stain blooming on his chest. He staggered, his blade slipping from his grasp before he collapsed lifelessly to the ground.

Behind him stood Balthazar, his imposing figure framed by the roaring flames, a look of triumph on his face.

He had saved us.

"Olivia, run, now!" His urgent voice shattered the paralysis gripping me. Adrenaline surged through my veins, propelling me to stand and move forward. Clutching Luna tightly, I sprinted away from the lingering danger.

Even as fear pounded in my ears, gratitude for Balthazar bloomed within me. He had risked his own life to save mine and my daughter's. This was not the same man I had once known—he was stronger, braver, transformed into a protector I hadn't expected.

"Run!" Balthazar's voice rang out again, underscored by intense heat. Daring a glance back, I saw another assailant, his terror-stricken face lit by the flames before he was consumed, his body vanishing into an inferno. It was a vision from a nightmare, but in Balthazar's hands, it became our salvation.

"Roman!" I screamed, blood trickling from my wounded arm as adrenaline pushed me onward. I pressed Luna closer, her cries muffled against my chest. The pain in my arm burned, but the need to protect her eclipsed everything else.

Roman and Amir stormed into the courtyard, Malik close behind with Rosie cradled in his arms. Their faces were etched with a volatile mix of concern and fury, their presence a fleeting beacon of hope. But relief was a luxury we couldn't afford—it vanished as quickly as it came.

The five of us moved as one, our feet pounding the ground, desperately trying to escape the lurking threat. But our flight was abruptly halted.

Mathias and Salvatore materialized before us.

I skidded to a halt, my breath coming in ragged gasps as my heart thundered in my chest. The full moon illuminated their forms, their presence casting a suffocating shadow over the courtyard.

"Excellent work vanquishing the men I sent to apprehend you," Salvatore drawled, his voice dripping with mockery.

A guttural scream of rage tore from my throat.

"Where are you running off to?" he asked, his sharp smile cutting through the night like broken glass. His gaze was icy and calculating, a predator savoring its cornered prey.

Roman's steady presence anchored me, his hand brushing my back as if to remind me I wasn't alone. I met Salvatore's gaze head-on, unflinching despite the storm of terror raging within me.

"I'm going to defeat you," I said, my voice hard with conviction.

"Are you now, my darling?" Salvatore's tone was laced with amusement.

"I will destroy you," I promised, though doubt coiled in the depths of my mind, whispering insidious uncertainties. But I stood tall, refusing to waver.

Salvatore's smirk widened, a cruel twist of his lips as he stepped closer.

"Go on then and time travel," he said, his voice laced with mockery as he advanced.

Confusion warred with fear within me. Why was he allowing us to leave?

"Your time travel daggers will no longer work since you connected the blades. Time travelers around the world are now stranded," Salvatore declared, triumph gleaming in his eyes like polished steel.

A knot of dread lodged in my throat. The merging of the sun and moon daggers—the victory we had clung to so fiercely—had inadvertently sealed our fate. Standing before Salvatore, the full extent of our peril unfurled like a storm cloud overhead.

"Fight!" Amir's command rang out like a thunderclap. From the shadows, Amir's army of black-clad warriors emerged in a haunting procession, their movements fluid and silent, like specters materializing from the void. They moved precisely, weapons gleaming under the moonlight as they surrounded us.

But Salvatore's power was overwhelming. With a mere flick of his wrists, the darkness engulfed them. One by one, Amir's warriors doubled over in agony, their anguished groans piercing the charged air. Balthazar fell to his knees, his eyes bulging with pain. Always so strong and proud, Malik crumbled under the weight of an invisible force. Even Amir himself—regal and commanding—was reduced to a writhing figure on the ground.

The earth trembled beneath us as the knees of his entire army buckled in unison, their bodies collapsing like marionettes whose strings had been severed. I stood frozen, my heart pounding like a war drum, clutching Luna to my chest as her cries echoed in the night.

Beside me, Roman gently took Luna from my trembling arms. His strength was my anchor, grounding me amidst the chaos.

Roman guided the knife over Rosie's and Luna's tiny palms, his hands steady despite the anguish in his eyes. He tried to make the incision as gentle as possible, but even with his delicate touch, Luna's piercing screams cut through the air, and Rosie wailed in pain. Their little hands trembled, tears streaming down their cheeks, each cry tugging at my heartstrings like a cruel melody. But I couldn't falter now. I couldn't let despair win.

"Watch me time travel," I spat at Salvatore, trying to mask the tremor in my voice. With a resolute glare, I drew my dagger across my palm, the sharp sting of a line of fire. Blood welled up, hot and vivid against my skin. I raised the blade, reciting the scripture with a fervor that bordered on desperation.

The words fell flat.

The air remained still, and the dagger in my hand was cold, lifeless—an inert weight dripping with my blood. A wave of panic surged through me as I stared at the weapon, my voice faltering. The dagger that had once been a vessel of power now felt like a cruel betrayal. How could this be happening? The world had turned against me when I needed it most.

From the shadows, Mathias' laughter joined Salvatore's, the sound intertwining into a cruel harmony that echoed like a mocking hymn.

"See? We know more than you," Mathias sneered, his voice dripping with contempt. "You're so very stupid, Olivia.

And where is your precious Lazarus now? In your moment of need, he is nowhere to be found. You're alone."

The taunt stung, each word slicing through my resolve like a dagger. Despair clawed its way up from the pit of my stomach, threatening to consume me whole. Salvatore's sneer, a twisted mask of triumph, was the face of my failure.

"I'm the most powerful sorcerer in the world," he declared, his voice heavy with finality. The air seemed to thrum with his dominance, pressing down on us with suffocating force. "Hand me the Blade of Shadows, Olivia. It's your only chance for a merciful death."

"No." The word escaped me as a growl, raw and defiant. Resolve hardened within me like steel tempered in fire. "I will prove to you that I can make this work. I can do this."

With fierce determination, I seized the sun and moon dagger, my grip steady despite the trembling of my heart. Without hesitation, I drew the blade across Roman's palm, then over the children's small hands, and finally across Malik's. Crimson lines etched across our skin, our blood mingling in a single, vivid bond—a unity forged in desperation.

"Hold onto the blade," I urged them, then repeated the scripture like a battle cry.

The blades began to hum, a low vibration that grew into a rustling sound, filling the night with a tangible sense of promise.

Unlike anything I had ever felt, a surge of power coursed through us. The blades ignited into a blaze of defiance, their light piercing the encroaching darkness. Heat radiated from their cores, illuminating our faces and casting stark shadows against the chaos surrounding us.

The world blurred, transforming into streaks of color and sound, a tempest cradling our existence. The scripture left my lips in a final crescendo, and then there was silence—a void that swallowed every echo of our defiance. The stillness pressed on my chest, heavy and unyielding.

With an explosive whoosh, reality snapped back like a taut string released. The air rushed into my lungs like I had been holding my breath for a lifetime. My eyes flew open at the sound of Luna's cries, her small wails cutting through the residual haze of the spell.

Had I done it? Had I time traveled to the future?

I looked around, my vision slowly clearing to reveal a verdant sea of green. The familiar woods bordering my father's home stretched out before me. The present—modern and overwhelming—hit me like a physical force. We stood out like misplaced echoes of another time, our Ottoman Empire attire with its heavy fabrics and intricate patterns stark against the simplicity of the modern world.

Rosie ran to Malik, clinging to his caftan as if he were her lifeline. Her wide eyes darted around, taking in the strangeness of our surroundings.

"Olivia!" Emily's voice cut through my disorientation, sharp and clear like an anchor in the chaos. She emerged from the trees, her eyes wide with shock and relief. "Oh my goodness, Olivia is here!"

I handed Roman our baby, the weight of Luna transferring from my trembling arms to his steady ones.

"Emily!" My feet pounded against the ground as I sprinted toward her, my dagger bouncing in its sheath at my shoulder. My breath came in ragged gasps as I drew closer.

It was startling to see her in modern-day clothes—a cherry-red sundress that flowed with every graceful step, accentuating her curves. Her hair was intricately braided, framing her face like a crown, and she seemed to glow in the sunlight. There was an otherworldly beauty to her, as though she both belonged to this time and simultaneously transcended it.

"Oh, Emily," I said, pulling her into a tight embrace. We rocked back and forth, the weight of time and separation melting away in those precious moments. When we finally withdrew, Emily's eyes shone with unshed tears.

"I've missed you so much," she said, trembling. "And by your look, you've been through hell."

"You have no idea," I replied, my voice breaking. "I have so much to tell you."

Together, we raced toward my father's house, the thud of our footsteps syncing with the frantic rhythm of my heart. A cold dread settled over me as the familiar structure came into view. The icy fingers of fear gripped me when I saw the scene unfolding at the doorway.

There, in the open entrance, stood my father, his face pale and ashen, a gun pressed to his temple. The hand holding the weapon was not unfamiliar—it belonged to my mother, Alina. Her eyes were cold, calculating, and filled with venom. Her finger hovered dangerously close to the trigger.

The memory of Tristan holding a gun to my father's head surged forward, but now it was my mother—the woman who had given me life—poised to end his.

The metallic glint of the gun caught the sunlight streaming through the trees, casting ominous shadows on my father's terrified face. He pleaded silently with her, his lips moving without sound, his eyes wide and imploring. My heart pounded like thunder in my chest, bile rising in my throat as I grappled with the horror of it.

"You stay the fuck right there," Alina shouted, her voice cutting through the air like a whip. "You come any closer, and I'll pull the trigger. I'll kill your precious father, and then I'll kill you."

"Mom!" The word burst from my lips, sharp and acidic. I spat the title like it was poison. "Salvatore has corrupted your mind!"

"Don't talk to me about Salvatore!" she sneered, her grip on the gun unwavering. Her eyes blazed with a fury that made my blood run cold. "Your father—this conniving, son-of-a-bitch man—was right under my nose with the scrolls. He played me for a fool! Acting like some helpless, depressed shell when all along, he knew exactly what he was keeping from me."

"Mom, please," I said. I was desperate to reach some shred of empathy within her, so she didn't kill my father. "This isn't who you are. Let me help you see that you don't have to do this. Put the gun down, and we can work together to defeat Salvatore. I know some humanity is still inside you, buried deep within."

She merely laughed a harsh and mocking sound that sent shivers down my spine. Her eyes were cold and unfeeling.

"I don't need you and your idealistic talk of working together." Her voice was the sound of winter through an empty hall. "Humanity? Ha! A meaningless concept to me."

Emily and I tensed, our bodies taut with the readiness to act. But before we could move, the air shifted—charged with an oppressive energy that prickled against my skin.

Mathias materialized before us like a shadow-given form, his tall stature and piercing gaze commanding the space. He bore a predatory grin that sent waves of dread coursing through me. The air around him seemed to ripple and distort as though reality itself bent beneath the weight of his presence. His silent entrance was more deafening than any sound, a thunderclap of power that froze me in place.

"Why the fuck are you standing there? Shoot her!" Mathias barked at Alina, his tone sharp as a blade. His gaze fixated on the sun and moon dagger trembling in my hand. When Alina hesitated, he stormed forward, his movements swift and deliberate. Before I could react, his iron grip wrenched the blade from my grasp.

"Mom, no!" I screamed, my voice cracking with desperation. But my plea was drowned out by the deafening blast of the gun. Time slowed as I watched in horror, the bullet tearing through the air straight toward me.

Suddenly, Lee's figure blurred into my line of sight, his body intercepting the bullet meant for me. The force of the impact jolted him backward, a sharp gasp escaping his lips before he crumpled to the ground.

In the blink of an eye, the sun and moon dagger disappeared—along with Alina, Mathias, and my father. The woods fell eerily silent, the haunting whisper of the wind the only trace left of their presence.

"Moon Lee!" Marcellious' anguished scream tore through the quiet, a sound so raw and heart-wrenching it reverberated in my soul.

"Oh, gods!" Roman bellowed as he and Malik burst through the trees, the children—Luna and Rosie—clutched tightly in their arms.

Panic surged through my body as I fell to my knees, pressing my trembling hands against the bullet wound in Lee's chest. Warm, sticky blood oozed between my fingers, staining them deep-crimson. My heart thundered in my chest as I desperately tried to stem the flow, each second feeling like a lifetime. The metallic tang of blood filled the air, sharp and bitter, as the weight of the situation settled heavily on my shoulders.

"Little Moon," Lee rasped, his voice a fragile thread that fought against the inevitable. Blood flecked his lips as he spoke, each word a monumental effort. "My time has come.

Fight for your destiny; fight for what is yours. We will see each other again."

Each word felt like a parting gift, a fragile ember of hope against the encroaching shadows. His eyes locked with mine, filled with unwavering love and a profound sacrifice that shattered every barrier around my heart.

"No, Lee, please!" I screamed, my voice raw and breaking under the weight of grief. My cries echoed through the forest, carried by the wind like a desperate plea to the universe. Tears streamed down my face in relentless torrents as I clung to him, refusing to let go as if my sheer will could tether him to this world.

My chest tightened as though being crushed by an invisible force, each beat of my heart resonating with the searing pain in my soul. It felt as if every fiber of my being was being torn apart, unraveled into fragments too broken to piece back together.

Roman and Malik knelt beside me, their faces etched with despair. Together, we encircled Lee, enfolding him in our collective embrace as if the warmth of our presence could stave off the inevitable. The atmosphere grew heavier with each passing moment, the weight of our sorrow tangible, pressing against us like a suffocating fog.

Despite our desperate grip, the vitality within him ebbed away, slipping through our fingers like sand. His final breath was a whisper, a fleeting moment that left a chasm of silence. As we clung to him, unwilling to release him to the void, the crushing reality of his loss descended upon us.

Without his steadfast mentorship and unwavering support, the trials ahead seemed insurmountable, the path forward a daunting void. Yet even in the depth of our despair, his words echoed in my mind, igniting a fragile flame of resolve—*Fight for your destiny; fight for what is yours.*

CHAPTER THIRTY FIVE
ROMAN

Lee's blood was warm on my hands as I cradled him in Olivia's father's overgrown yard. Marcellious' cries cut through the heavy air, a relentless keen that melded with the rustle of leaves and the distant calls of evening birds. Beside me, Malik stood rigid as stone, his features carved into an expression of grim resignation, his arms tightening protectively around Luna and Rosie.

"Lee..." I murmured, but it was useless. Lee was gone, snatched away by a bullet never meant for him. Hatred for Alina churned in my gut, a black tide that threatened to swallow me whole.

"Roman..." Olivia's voice broke through the fog of my anguish. "Roman, please..."

I rose, gently laying Lee's body down on the vibrant grass —a cruel juxtaposition to the loss we bore. Marcellious' screams of rage tore at my soul, each cry a mirror to my turmoil.

Why? How could this happen?

"I fucking hate my mother. I am going to kill her," Olivia

wailed, collapsing into my arms. Her body trembled as sobs wracked her frame. "My beloved friend and mentor is *gone!*"

Her words were raw, jagged edges slicing through the suffocating quiet.

"Shh, love," I murmured, though my voice was a fragile thread against the torrent of grief surrounding us. "We'll get through this."

My heart felt like it was being wrenched apart. The weight of her despair, the unbearable loss of Lee—it was too much to bear.

"Lee shouldn't be dead," Olivia cried, her voice cracking with every word. "He should still be alive, and it's all because of me."

Tears streamed down my face as I fought to reconcile the tragic reality before us. My mind raced, replaying every moment that led to this devastating outcome. Each misstep, each choice—it all felt like it had spiraled into this unbearable loss.

"I can't stand her, you know?" Olivia said, her voice thick with emotion. "It's like this never-ending storm inside me, tearing at everything good. All those years of letdowns and lies, threats that cut deeper than any blade, words that poisoned every memory... Mom's like a monster growing stronger daily, impossible to escape."

"But now isn't the time to mete justice," I said firmly. "Now is the time to tend to the dead. Your mother will get what she deserves."

Olivia's eyes bore into me, cold and distant, as though my words were empty air, unable to reach the tempest within her.

With a heavy sigh, Malik, Marcellious, and I lifted Lee's lifeless body together. The weight of him was more than physical—it was the weight of everything we had lost. We moved silently through the woods, shadows clinging to us like mourners in a solemn procession. Lee's shed loomed ahead, where he had breathed life into wood and thread, crafting symbols of hope and dreams with his hands.

Inside, we cleared his worktable, brushing aside intricately carved statues and delicate dreamcatchers that whispered of his spirit and talent. We laid him gently upon the wooden surface, and the world seemed to dim around us. The stark reality of his absence settled on my chest like a stone, threatening to crush me with its finality.

"Goodbye, my friend... my mentor..." I choked out, my voice breaking as I reached to close his unseeing eyes with trembling fingers. "You were the best of us."

Outside, the wind whispered through the trees, carrying our shared anguish to the heavens. It was as though the forest itself mourned with us, swaying in time with the rhythm of our grief.

The door to the shed burst open, and Olivia staggered inside, her chest heaving from the exertion of running. She had exchanged her elegant caftan for a simple, modern dress, its fabric clinging to her in disarray. Despite the change, her face was still a mask of raw emotion—grief etched into every line.

She dropped a bundle of clothing onto a chair. "Here. Emily provided us with modern clothes. There's a set for Malik, too. We can't go around looking like this." Her lip curled as she gestured toward my Ottoman attire, a hint of disdain slipping through her sorrow.

Wordlessly, I picked up a shirt and a pair of pants, stepping aside to replace my 16th-century garments with the familiar practical modern attire. The fabric felt different against my skin, a sharp reminder of how far we'd come— and how much we'd lost along the way.

"Emily's watching the kids," Olivia said in a rush, her

voice trembling. "I don't know what to do next. The clothes Emily gave me felt like busywork to distract me from my grief. It didn't work." Tears streaked her face as her words flowed out in a hectic, uneven stream. "We have to bury him. Can you... can you contact someone from his tribe?"

"Uh..." I wasn't sure how I was supposed to do that.

"You saw my dad use a phone when you were here before, right?" she pressed, desperation creeping into her voice.

"Uh..." I said again, faint recollections of strange 21st-century communication devices flickering in my mind.

"Lee has an old-school landline in his office. Look around his desk for ten-digit numbers—those are phone numbers. Then, you pick up the receiver thingie..." She mimicked, lifting something to her ear. "And stab the numbers onto the little squares on the phone."

Her fingers moved in quick stabbing motions, her exasperation growing. "Hold the handset—the receiver thingie—next to your ear. And listen. And talk."

"Can't you do it?" I asked, mystified and feeling overwhelmed by the task.

"I need to sit with Lee," she said, her voice softening. "I feel it's important not to leave him alone. You can do this, sweetheart." She squeezed my bicep, her grip firm with a misplaced confidence I didn't share.

I did not, however, feel reassured.

"If you can't figure it out, come and get me," she added, her expression softening as if trying to summon her faith in me.

How hard could it be? Nodding mutely, I stepped out of the dimly lit shed and into the unrelenting starkness of grief —a heaviness no sunlight could erase. The house loomed before me, alien in its familiarity, its walls steeped in echoes of laughter that now seemed like distant memories.

In Lee's office, amidst the chaotic remnants of his life's work, I found a name and ten hastily scribbled numbers on a crumpled scrap of paper—a breadcrumb left by fate. The note read, "Sioux Elder."

I rummaged through the cluttered desk, searching for any sign of this "landline" Olivia had mentioned. Jack and Lee once showed me modern communication devices—small, rectangular gadgets that fit snugly in their palms. Yet, there was nothing of the sort here. Instead, my eyes fell upon a squarish object made of what they called plastic. A wire coiled from its back, confirming my suspicion—this had to be the landline.

I lifted the unfamiliar object—the handset, I presumed—and pressed it to my ear. A strange buzzing sound filled the silence, making me doubt whether I'd chosen correctly. Recalling Olivia's instructions to "stab" the small squares in a specific sequence, I examined the device more closely. Each square bore tiny letters beneath the numbers, their presence turning the task into an exercise in deciphering ancient symbols.

Even in my fog of grief and confusion, I pressed the squares in the order scribbled on the paper. The buzzing hum ceased, replaced by a soft, melodic tone—tiny bells ringing in unison, clear and soothing.

My pulse quickened when a woman's voice pierced the silence, warm and inviting. "Hello?"

Her words flowed like sweet honey, embracing me in an unseen comfort. Though I could not see her, her presence was palpable, as if she had materialized from thin air. My throat tightened as I prepared to respond, uncertainty weighing heavy on my chest.

"Hello?" I stammered, quickly reading the name scribbled on the paper. "Talia Redfeather?"

The name felt foreign as it left my lips.

"Ah, Roman," she said, her voice carrying the weight of recognition. "I believe I know why you're calling."

"You do?"

"Yes. There has been a passing. It was Moon Lee, wasn't it?" She didn't wait for my response. "This morning, as dawn's first light kissed the sky, an unusual chill whispered through the air."

Her words carried a reverence that painted vivid images in my mind as if I were standing beside her, witnessing the scene she described.

"The bald eagle," she began, her voice soft and mournful, "with its wings spread wide—a blessing from the Great Spirit —rose gracefully from the east. It circled our village three times, each pass tugging at my soul a little more. And when it let out that final haunting cry, it felt as though sorrow was etched into the skies themselves."

She paused, the weight of her words settling in the space between us before she continued. "A white buffalo calf stood alone on the hill—a sacred messenger of change, purity, and peace. A sign of the great loss our people have suffered."

Chills crept up my spine, the room around me dissolving into the vivid imagery her words conjured. How could nature itself mourn so deeply?

"Lee was... he was much loved," I said.

"Indeed," Talia replied, her tone firm yet tender. "And now, I must speak with Olivia. She needs to know what must be done."

"How did you—"

The question faltered on my lips. Of course, they knew of Olivia through Lee.

"Lee spoke of you both," Talia explained. "You were no secret to us. Now, I must speak to your beautiful wife."

"I, uh… the thing I'm speaking on is affixed to the wall," I said, fumbling over the words. "She's in the shed."

Talia laughed softly. "This is all new to you. You are from a different era."

"Yes," I admitted, my ears burning with embarrassment. "I'm not familiar with these devices."

"Well," she said patiently, "set the handset on the desk. Please do not put it back on the phone, or we'll be disconnected. Go get Olivia, and I'll wait here."

Relieved by her calm guidance, I placed the handset carefully on the desk and hurried to the shed. "Talia Redfeather wants to speak with you," I called to Olivia.

She followed me back into the house, her hands trembling as she pressed a small button labeled "Speaker."

"Hello?" she said, her voice wavering slightly as it carried into the air.

Talia's voice filled the room, melodic and grounding, as though it danced with an unseen rhythm. We leaned in, hanging on every word, as she explained what needed to be done. "Take Lee to Paha Sapa," Talia instructed, her tone steady and reverent. "His shed—his favorite place. "Find his writings—his poems and thoughts," she continued. "Read them to him until we arrive."

"I will," Olivia said, though her voice quivered with hesitation. "But… we have children. They might interrupt us."

"A few teens from the tribe will accompany us," Talia reassured. "They will look after the children until the ceremony ends. You don't need to worry."

With those arrangements settled, we began our vigil—a time of preparation and remembrance. Together, we jotted down the prayers Talia recited over the line. It was a final act of devotion, a last gift for a man who had been more than a friend, more than a mentor—he had bridged worlds, if only for a fleeting moment. Then, we returned to the shed.

Olivia's hand brushed against mine as she took the paper. Her voice was soft, trembling like a leaf caught in the wind, as she read the prayer aloud.

"Grandfather Great Spirit, all over the world, the faces of living things are alike. With tenderness, they have come up out of the ground. Look upon your children with children in their arms, that they may face the winds and walk the good road to the quiet day."

Once a place of creation and dreams, the shed now held Lee's silent form like a sacred sanctuary. The thin veil between worlds seemed to quiver with each word, the air thick with reverence and loss.

"Teach them to walk the soft earth as relatives to all that live," Olivia read, her voice catching as tears welled in her eyes.

I knelt beside Lee, tracing the lines of his weathered hands—hands that had shaped so much and taught and guided. My voice cracked as I whispered, "May you find peace in the Great Spirit's arms." The rest of Talia's prayer stayed lodged in my throat, unspoken yet deeply felt.

Olivia leaned closer, her breath mingling with mine, bringing a fragile warmth to the shed's cool air. We sat together in silence, the prayer weaving around us like an invisible shroud, offering solace in the depth of our sorrow.

The soft cadence of Olivia's voice filled the stillness as she continued reading from the prayer. Each syllable was like a brushstroke, painting a vision of serenity—a place untouched by the grief that weighed so heavily upon us.

In the silence that followed, it felt as though Lee's spirit stirred, preparing to embark on its final journey. The air vibrated faintly, charged with the energy of his unspoken dreams and unfinished stories. I closed my eyes, granting myself a moment to escape the cruel certainty of death.

"May your journey be swift and your spirit soar," I whispered. Behind my closed lids, I imagined Lee's essence rising, weightless as the eagle's feathers that had circled overhead, ascending into an endless expanse of sky.

Tears glistened in Olivia's eyes, though her gaze remained fixed on the unseen horizon. Perhaps she, too, envisioned Lee's ascent, his spirit finding freedom beyond the boundaries of this mortal world. In that shared silence, there was a beauty—a wordless understanding that transcended speech.

Marcellious, who had known only the sharp sting of loss until now, drew a shuddering breath. His hand found mine, trembling yet firm, and we formed a circle of solidarity around Lee. United in our hope for his peaceful passage, we became anchors for one another.

The world outside the shed continued its indifferent spin, but within these walls, time stood still, reverent and unmoving, honoring the soul prepared to take flight from earthly bonds to the boundless skies.

The words slipped from my lips like a gentle stream. "In the land of the ancestors, forevermore."

As Malik quietly led the children home, Olivia and Emily settled on either side of Lee's body, their grief etched into their faces. They were statues of sorrow, unmoving save for the occasional tremble of a suppressed sob or the quiet trail of a tear they could not wipe away in time. Like the prayer itself, their stillness was a testament to love—a love that transcended the finality of death.

Marcellious had sunk to his knees beside me, his body shuddering with sobs that reverberated off the wooden walls of the shed. I placed a hand on his shoulder, offering what little comfort could be found in the warmth of human touch—a fragile connection in the vast emptiness of grief.

"Grandfather Great Spirit," I began, my voice steadying as I recited the ancient prayer, "look upon your children with children in their arms, that they may face the winds and walk the good road to the day of quiet."

We passed Lee's worn, leather-bound book of quotes between us, reading its cherished words as though each was a sacred offering. I turned to a page marked with Lee's hand, the underlined text of journeys through nature and the lessons it imparted. These were words he had lived by; now, they became the words we used to guide him forward.

As the hours stretched, the shed's light grew dim, shadows lengthening across Lee's carvings and dreamcatchers. They seemed to stand vigil with us, silent sentinels honoring the man who had given them form.

"May you find peace in the Great Spirit's arms," I whispered into the gathering dusk, the weight of the book grounding me to this moment even as Lee's spirit journeyed to a place beyond our reach.

"Where there is no pain, no fear, no harm," Olivia murmured, her hand seeking mine. She squeezed it with a quiet strength—born not from defiance but love and shared resilience.

"May your journey be swift and your spirit soar," Marcellious said, his voice cracking yet imbued with a fragile acceptance that began to thread through his grief.

"In the land of the ancestors, forevermore." We repeated the words together, their rhythm becoming a mantra, binding us in unity. We continued reciting the poems, our voices steady and reverent, until those who would help us carry Lee to his final resting place arrived.

The stillness settled over us like a gentle fog, and I felt the soft cadence of Olivia's breathing begin to align with mine. Our hearts beat in quiet harmony as we sat adrift on the sea of sorrow, suspended between the world of the living and the echoes of the spirit realm.

When dawn brushed the horizon with its golden hues, Talia arrived. She was flanked by two others whose faces bore the wear of a night spent in solemn vigil. Two teenage girls emerged from their vehicle, their youthful expressions tempered by grief. They moved with purpose, their footsteps respectful upon the earth that cradled generations of memory.

One of the girls spoke first, her voice steady yet gentle. "Where are the children? We're here to watch them while you attend the burial proceedings."

The other girl offered a reassuring smile. "Don't worry. We're great with kids. We've got more cousins than we can count."

"Thank you," Olivia said, her voice thick with emotion, her eyes swollen and red from hours of crying. "Thank you so much."

I guided them to Jack's house, where they could keep the children safe and comforted. Meanwhile, Talia, Olivia, and I turned toward the shed, joined by the other woman—Maya. I had only just learned her name, spoken in a hushed breath amid the chaos. The door creaked open, a solemn whisper in anticipation of what was to come.

Talia, Maya, and Olivia began the sacred rituals in the soft morning light. They washed Lee with water drawn fresh from the brook that whispered gently past the yard, its song a quiet lullaby for the departed. Each movement was deliberate, filled with care and devotion, as they prepared him for his journey.

They dressed Lee in traditional Sioux clothing, the intricate patterns woven into the fabric speaking of his heritage, his identity, and the stories that had shaped him. Every fold, every stitch seemed to hum with the echoes of a life lived with purpose. Carefully, they placed Lee's most treasured belongings by his side. His prayer pipe, its surface worn smooth from years of use, rested against him—a companion for his voyage into the afterlife. It was a poignant reminder of his connection to the spiritual and the eternal.

As the smudging ceremony began, the air grew thick with the earthy scent of burning sage. Spirals of smoke rose, weaving toward the rafters, carrying prayers in the Lakota tongue to the heavens. The rhythmic cadence of drums joined the sacred song; each beat resonated like the earth's heartbeat.

My chest tightened with emotion, my soul aching at the moment's beauty. There was a quiet, profound love in how Talia and her companions honored Lee, each gesture a testament to his place among us and passage to the next realm.

"Roman," Marcellious murmured beside me, his voice heavy with grief. His eyes glistened as he looked toward me, seeking strength amidst the overwhelming sorrow.

I clasped his shoulder, offering what little comfort I could as the women wrapped Lee's body with organic cloth, cocooning him in the fabric of the natural world.

"Come," Talia said softly, her voice steady and reverent. She beckoned us back to the circle where others had gathered to pay homage to Lee. "We must prepare for the journey."

I rejoined the vigil with a heart weighed down yet full of quiet wonder.

Lee's body, swathed in the soft fabric, was carefully placed in the back of his battered old truck. The scent of sage still lingered, a fragrant reminder of the prayers whispered in the shed. The silence enveloping us was heavy, broken only by the occasional wail of mourning carried on the breeze.

"I can drive," Olivia offered, her tone calm, though I

could see the turmoil churning behind her eyes. "I've done it plenty in this century."

"No way," I replied, my gaze set firmly on the horizon where the Black Hills loomed, waiting for us. "I'm driving."

"You, the guy whose transportation skills are best on horseback?" she countered, her eyebrow arching.

"I learned how to drive when I was here before," I said firmly, leaving no room for further argument. The tight press of her lips told me she wasn't convinced but chose to relent.

Nearby, Malik leaned casually against Talia's van, a wry smile tugging at his lips. "I'll ride with the others in the van," he said, gesturing with exaggerated caution. "Not risking my life with you, brother."

He guffawed, waving his hand over his head as he sauntered off. The sound of his laughter lingered for a moment, a fleeting contrast against the somber backdrop before fading into the night.

I climbed behind the wheel, gripping it with confidence and trepidation. The key turned with a loud grind, and the vehicle roared to life. The raw power of the engine thrummed beneath me, unfamiliar and unruly. The truck lurched forward, weaving erratically as I wrestled with its movements.

"Roman!" Olivia yelled, clutching the door for balance. "You'll shake Lee to pieces if you keep driving like this!"

Chastened, I eased off the accelerator, my knuckles whitening as I tightened my grip on the steering wheel. Slowly, I coaxed the vehicle into a smoother rhythm, balancing our speed with the solemn respect owed to the precious cargo we carried.

The road ahead stretched endlessly, unfurling like a ribbon disappearing into the horizon. Each mile brought us closer to the sacred ground, and each stop we made served as a somber reminder of the reality awaiting us at the journey's end. Talia's van led the way, a quiet guide through a landscape that grew increasingly foreign and reverent as we neared our destination.

"Google Maps won't help you here," Talia had warned before we set out. "It cannot speak the way. This is sacred ground."

"Google Maps?" I murmured to myself during one of our brief stops. Pulling Olivia aside, I asked quietly, "What is this... Google Maps? I've used maps before, but they were made of paper or leather. They didn't talk to me."

Despite the heaviness of our mission, Olivia laughed—a light, unexpected sound that pierced through the solemnity.

"Oh, Roman," she said with a gentle smile. "Google Maps is an app. It's like a map that's alive—it talks to you, gives you directions."

"An... app?" I repeated, the words strange and unfamiliar on my tongue.

"Yep, it's on a phone or a computer," she explained. "But it doesn't know everything, especially not the things that matter most."

Her words lingered in my mind as we climbed into the truck. I marveled at the layers of this world—how technology could bridge distances and connect people yet fail to guide them along paths steeped in spirit and history. With every mile beneath us, I was reminded that some journeys couldn't be mapped by devices or satellites. They required more than a physical guide—they demanded reverence, remembrance, and the wisdom of those who understood the sacred ways.

When we finally arrived at the small dwelling marking the end of our road journey, fatigue settled over me like a heavy cloak. The engine's steady hum fell silent as I turned off the ignition, leaving only the soft rustling of the wind through the surrounding trees. Olivia stepped out first, stretching as Malik emerged from Talia's van. His gaze met mine, filled with concern and quiet determination.

"Roman," he said, pulling me aside while the others gathered their bearings, "I'm heading back with you after the burial. They'll stay here and return in a few days."

He gestured toward Marcellious and Emily, who spoke softly a few feet away. "Marcellious wants to stay with the Sioux for a while. And let's be honest—there's no way I'm letting you drive again. Watching you in the rearview mirror was like watching a drunken fool navigate a minefield."

Olivia stifled a laugh, "Good call."

I couldn't argue. My earlier driving had been more a battle with the truck than a smooth journey, and Lee's body had endured more jostling than I cared to admit. Nodding, I placed a hand on Malik's shoulder, silently thanking him for looking out for all of us.

We joined the elders who had gathered to receive us. Their faces, weathered and serene, carried an air of solemnity and grace. I felt a grounding sense of purpose settle over me in their presence. Together, with careful reverence, we lifted Lee's body from the bed of the truck. The weight of our collective grief was as tangible as the physical burden we carried on our shoulders.

The ceremony began under the canopy of trees in a clearing touched by sunlight and shadow. The rustling of leaves and the whispers of the wind wove through the air like a sacred hymn. We laid Lee's body upon an animal hide draped over a sturdy litter, the frame lashed together with sinew and adorned with intricate beadwork and feathers. Each detail reflected respect and artistry, cradling Lee's form as if it were part of nature.

With steady, practiced hands, the elders wrapped Lee in

soft leather adorned with intricate symbols of spiritual significance. Their murmured prayers, ancient and melodic, carried the weight of countless generations. Each sacred word, spoken in the Lakota tongue, became a bridge between worlds, guiding Lee's spirit on its journey to the afterlife.

As they worked, the air seemed to hum with reverence. The elders infused the ritual with the essence of their beliefs, their hearts heavy yet unwavering in their sacred duty. The scent of sage and sweetgrass lingered, their smoke rising in soft spirals, purifying the space and offering blessings for Lee's passage into the unknown.

When the preparations were complete, the community gathered around the litter. Each of us took our designated position, muscles taut as we lifted the sturdy frame bearing Lee's body. The weight pressed down on us, but the strength of our determination carried us forward. The litter swayed gently with each step, like a vessel gliding over calm waters. The sun beat down on our backs, its warmth merging with the heat of our exertion.

The elders led us on foot toward Wakȟáŋheya Háŋska— Sacred Heights—a place of profound peace and ancient wisdom. Ponderosa pines stood tall and regal, their branches swaying as if whispering secrets of the ages. Weathered rock formations towered above us like sentinels, while the ground beneath our feet was soft with grass and speckled with wildflowers in vibrant hues. With each breath, the fragrant air carried a quiet solace, mingling with Lee's body's delicate, earthy scent—a blend of wildflowers and fresh grass that seemed to honor his final journey.

I glanced at Marcellious, his face a mask of sorrow. Yet, though grief weighed heavily upon him, his steps remained resolute. Beside him, Malik walked with quiet determination, his eyes fixed straight ahead as if seeking strength in the path before us.

Here, amidst the elements, we weren't just burying a friend. We were returning him to the land that had shaped him, a land that knew neither betrayal nor malice—only the eternal cycle of life, death, and rebirth.

As we approached Wakȟáŋheya Háŋska, a wooden archway rose before us, its surface carved with intricate Sioux symbols. The craftsmanship commanded reverence, a silent reminder of the sacred ground we now entered. Smooth river stones guided our path, leading us past towering totem poles and carved faces of ancestors who watched over this hallowed place. We laid Lee's body beside the prepared burial site, the leather wrapping around him snug as if cradling him one final time. The elders stood beside us, their presence grounding and solemn. Malik, Marcellious, and I joined them, our grief woven with the silent acceptance of this inevitable farewell.

Above us, an eagle soared across the sky, its wings slicing through the heavens with a graceful arc. It circled once, then twice, then thrice. Each pass felt like a benediction, a celestial sign of Lee's soul ascending. My eyes followed the eagle as it climbed higher, becoming a speck against the vast expanse of blue—a part of something infinite, just as Lee was now.

The Spirit Tree stood at the circle's edge, its ancient, gnarled limbs stretching skyward. Ribbons and prayer ties adorned its branches, fluttering in the breeze. Each strip of fabric carried a hope, a wish, or a memory offered up to the ancestors who listened from beyond the veil of time. The tree stood as a witness to our sorrow and reverence, a living monument to the connection between earth and sky, the living and the departed.

Olivia stepped beside me, her presence a quiet balm to the

ache gripping my heart. Together, we turned to face the beginning of the ceremony, united in purpose and bound by love—not just for each other, but for the man who had touched our lives in ways words could scarcely convey.

In the profound stillness of that sacred place, surrounded by the spirits of those who had walked before us, we prepared to say farewell.

A male elder's voice broke the silence, resonant and clear, carrying the weight of many winters. His words fell into the quiet like stones into a still pond, sending ripples through the gathered crowd. He recited the lines of an ancient poem, his tone imbued with reverence and wisdom. "Life is but a path we walk, a journey where we learn and talk."

I stood there, my hand clasped tightly in Olivia's. The roughness of her palm met mine, her grip trembling ever so slightly—a reflection of the unsteady rhythm of my own heart. The warmth between our hands seemed to defy the chill of loss that hung like a shroud over us all.

As the elder's words carried on the breeze, each one weighed heavily on me. Lee's life had been well-walked, marked by profound love and selfless sacrifice. Now, that path had ended, leaving only echoes in the wind and whispers among the leaves. Those memories would remain forever etched in my mind, a testament to a life lived with purpose and a heart that had shaped ours.

Beside me, Olivia cried quietly, her shoulders trembling as silent tears carved paths down her cheeks. Her grief was raw, but I saw an unspoken promise—a vow to honor Lee's courage and integrity in the days ahead to carry his legacy forward.

The elder's voice rose above us, unwavering and steady, a beacon steeped in tradition. The scent of pine and sage swirled around us as sunlight filtered through the canopy, casting dappled shadows over Lee's still form. "And now, you walk into the light," he intoned.

The phrase echoed against the hills, reverberating like a sacred whisper, promising freedom from the burdens of mortality. I closed my eyes and could almost see Lee—our friend, our mentor—stepping beyond the veil, his stride confident, his spirit unbound, his heart at peace.

The elder bowed his head, and the mourners followed, each offering a collective gesture of respect to the timeless rhythm of life and death.

The circle tightened around the grave as the elders stepped forward. Their voices rose in song, weaving a melody as ancient as the hills. The haunting tones danced with the rustling leaves and soared into the endless sky, a hymn calling out to the Great Spirit.

"*Tankashila Wakan Tanka, taku wicahpi kin yuhapi kte,*" beseeching the Creator to receive Lee's soul. The words wrapped around us, steeping the air with reverence and connection.

Marcellious clutched a weathered photograph of Lee laughing beside a roaring campfire. His hand trembled as he placed it atop Lee's chest, his expression blending sorrow and gratitude. Olivia stepped forward next, her eyes rimmed red but shining with quiet resolve. She carried a dreamcatcher that Lee had crafted—a web of sinew and beads meant to snare nightmares and let only the sweetest dreams pass through. She gently laid it on his abdomen, a final gift from her heart to his. One by one, we stepped forward to offer our tributes. A beaded necklace woven with care—a smooth river stone, polished by the flow of time. A hawk's feather as a symbol of guidance and protection. Each item held meaning, a fragment of our love for Lee.

Marcellious' voice broke the silence. "Lee was more

than a friend," he said, his words thick with emotion. "He was my best friend and my father. He taught us about life, respect for all beings, and the courage to stand up for what's right."

My throat tightened as I stepped forward, my voice emerging raggedly. "Lee was more than just a fighter to me. He taught me honor and integrity and, above all, led me to my wife. He stood by us through everything, but now we must say goodbye and lay him to rest." Beside me, Olivia nodded, tears shimmering in her eyes. I turned to her and whispered, "Your turn." She took a deep breath, her voice steady and unwavering.

"Lee was not only my mentor but my best friend," she said, her words carrying the strength of conviction. "He showed me how to survive in this harsh world and lifted me when I hit rock bottom. His soul will live through us, and I promise to avenge his."

A ripple of nods and murmured assent passed through the crowd. One by one, others stepped forward, their words weaving Lee's essence into the community's collective memory.

"His laughter was like thunder rolling over the plains," someone called out.

"His hands could soothe the most troubled souls," another added.

I listened, my heart swelling with pride and aching with loss. Each story painted a vivid portrait of a man who had lived fully, loved deeply, and left an indelible mark on all our lives.

As the ceremony neared its end, the sun dipped lower toward the horizon, casting us in a warm, golden glow. The elders gathered for a final prayer, their voices a soft murmur carried on the breeze.

"Mitákuye Oyás'iŋ," they intoned in unison. "We are all related."

Above us, an eagle appeared—perhaps the same as before —soaring high and solitary. It circled once, a silent witness to our grief, before vanishing into the vast expanse of the sky.

At that moment, I felt a profound connection that transcended grief and anger. It was a reminder that life, like the eagle's flight, was a series of countless beginnings and endings, each leading to the next in an unbroken cycle.

At last, the elders lowered Lee's body into the earth's embrace. We stood together, a silent congregation bound by shared sorrow and reverence, watching as our beloved friend was laid to rest.

"Travel well, my friend," I whispered, my voice barely audible above the whispering wind.

The earth received each shovelful of dirt with a soft murmur, a tender sound that seemed to beckon Lee to his final rest. As the grave filled, voices rose in song—a tapestry of sound woven from sorrow and solemn joy. The melodies carried the essence of the plains, speaking of the wind, the sun, and the enduring heartbeat of the land.

The final act was almost intimate. Together, we covered Lee with the earth, tucking him in as gently as one might lay a child to sleep. The soil seemed to cradle him, welcoming him back as one of its own.

As dusk painted the sky in deep purples and oranges, the scent of roasted meats and wild herbs filled the air. Fires crackled in the twilight, and the community gathered around them for a feast in Lee's honor. Stories flowed freely, laughter mingling with tears as we shared tales of his courage, wisdom, and the love he had sown among his people.

I sat close to Olivia, her presence grounding me amid the swell of emotions. We ate, we listened, and when our turn came, we offered our memories of Lee—the mentor, the warrior, the brother of our hearts.

"His spirit will guide us," Olivia said, her eyes reflecting the flickering flames. "Just as it always has."

I nodded, my resolve hardening with each passing moment. I would not let his death be in vain. Salvatore, Mathias, and Alina—they would answer for what they had done.

"Lee believed in balance," I told her, my resolve hardening like the ground that now held him. "And balance will be restored."

The feast continued into the night, celebrating a life that had touched so many. Yet as the stars began to emerge, the overwhelming emptiness left by Lee's absence pressed heavily on my chest one by one. But alongside the ache, a searing fire burned deep within me, unyielding and unrelenting. It was the fire of vengeance—a promise to see Alina and her vile allies answer for their heinous crimes. No matter the cost, justice would prevail.

CHAPTER THIRTY SIX

OLIVIA

After the funeral, Roman and I returned to my father's home, our hearts heavy and our faces streaked with tears. Grief clung to us like a physical weight, dragging us down with each step. Beneath the sadness, anger simmered—a deep, unrelenting frustration at the powerlessness I felt. Mathias had taken my father, and he could be anywhere, in any century, hidden beyond my reach. The sun and moon blade was missing, too, and with Lee's sudden death, the despair surrounding us grew like a suffocating fog. It felt like all the light and hope had been drained from our world, leaving only shadows behind.

We sat together in the sunroom—a space unfamiliar to my teenage memories of this house. It was a new addition, just as alien as the sorrow filling the air. I cradled the iced tea Roman had made, its tartness softened by a hint of sweetness. The soft ice clinking against the glass was a faint comfort in our silence—a silence brimming with echoes of loss and the unspoken fears of what lay ahead.

"He must have updated it since I was last here," Roman murmured, his gaze tracing the wooden beams of the ceiling and the expansive windows that invited the forest inside. "I don't recall it looking like this."

My father's simple home in the woods bore the unmistakable marks of change, just as we did. Once cramped and outdated, the kitchen now gleamed with stainless-steel appliances and smooth granite countertops. But the renovations felt hollow without him here to share the moment, to witness our reactions.

"Roman," I began, my voice breaking through the stillness, but the sound of crunching gravel cut me off.

Our eyes met, and without a word, we rose and stepped out into the cool embrace of the forest air. A beat-up van rattled down the narrow path toward the house, its worn exterior bearing countless stories of travel and survival. Behind the wheel was Marcellious, Emily beside him, their expressions unreadable as they approached.

As they stepped out of the van, exhaustion clung to Marcellious like a shadow. Dark circles under his eyes resembled bruises, remnants of battles fought silently. His hand kept drifting toward Emily—brushing her arm, encircling her waist—as if touching her anchored him to the present, to the fragile wholeness of their family in the aftermath of so much loss.

"How are you holding up?" Roman called out gently.

Marcellious managed a weak smile, though it didn't reach his eyes. "I'd just gotten him back," he said, his voice trembling. "Lee healed me, brought me back to life after Raul tried to break me. He meant everything to me, and now he's gone." The last word cracked as it left his lips.

A heavy silence followed, pressing on us like an unseen weight. The enormity of what had happened hung in the air, unspoken but deeply felt.

"I wanted to tell you something, Marcellious," Roman

said after a moment. "I met our father—in the Ottoman Empire, where we studied the scriptures and merged the blades."

The revelation struck Marcellious like a physical blow. He staggered back, his body tensing, his face a mix of shock and anger.

"The only father I ever had was Moon Lee," he spat, his words sharp and deliberate. "The man who gave his seed to our mother is dead to me—has been for a long time."

Roman flinched at the venom in his brother's voice. I stepped closer, placing a hand on his arm, hoping to offer comfort.

"I'm sorry, Marcellious," I said, my voice choked with emotion. "It's my fault Lee is gone. He took the bullet meant for me. He sacrificed himself to save my life. And now—he's gone because of me."

My confession ignited something deep within Marcellious. His face reddened with fury, and for a moment, I thought he might lash out. Instead, he gripped my shoulders tightly, his voice low and seething with determination.

"Do not blame yourself for what happened to Lee," he said, his tone a mixture of comfort and menace. "Your mother is the one responsible, and she will pay for her actions. I swear on Lee's memory—I will see to it personally that justice is served."

His words both comforted and unnerved me. I knew Marcellious would stop at nothing to avenge Lee's death, even if it meant putting his own life on the line. Yet, in that moment, I was grateful for his unyielding resolve. Together, we would face the painful truths of what had transpired. Our journey to find my father and seek retribution for Lee had only just begun.

Emily stepped forward, the strain on her face softening as

she addressed us. "I'm going to prepare us all a meal. Come on over in a while." Her gaze lingered on Marcellious, a blend of affection and concern shining in her eyes. "I'm going to let Marcellious rest while I cook."

I offered her a small, weary smile, my heart still aching with sharp pangs of loss. Yet, I felt a faint solace in her simple gesture of sharing a meal.

"Do you need help?" I asked, eager for the company and the understanding of someone who shared in our collective heartache.

"Thank you, sister, but no," she replied with a gentle shake of her head. "I'd like to do something to help us all heal. You remember, when you met me, I was an herbalist. The tribe sent us home with many healing herbs."

She wrapped me in a brief hug before turning to guide Marcellious back toward the van. Her steady and nurturing presence was a small balm for the storm that raged within us all.

When we entered Lee's humble abode, the air was rich with the scent of herbs and spices. Malik, his brow furrowed in quiet concentration from what I assumed was a recent return from the hunt, joined Roman and me. Emily busied herself in the kitchen, where the rhythmic sounds of sizzling and chopping filled the room.

The countertops were a vibrant display of tradition and care, lined with colorful vegetables and marinated meats. Savory roasted root vegetables were nestled beside a platter of cedar-planked salmon, its pink flesh glistening under a glaze of maple and Dijon. A quinoa salad flecked with cranberries and toasted pine nuts offered a refreshing contrast while the aroma of freshly baked rosemary bread wafted through the room, promising warmth and comfort.

"Food will be ready in less than an hour," Emily said, her

voice steady as she continued her work, the rhythmic chopping of vegetables punctuating the silence.

In Lee's front room, Marcellious sat slumped in a well-worn armchair, the weight of sleepless nights and relentless grief etched into his features. Malik stood beside him, a hand resting on his shoulder in quiet solidarity, murmuring words too soft for me to hear. In the corner, Leo, Luna, and Rosie played with blocks, their laughter a faint reminder of innocence untouched by the sorrow that enveloped the rest of us.

Roman and I leaned against the cool wall, finding a fragile refuge in each other's presence. The room felt both heavy and hollow, a space brimming with loss.

"I feel like a failure," I whispered, my voice trembling under the weight of my thoughts. "So much death has followed me since my travels through time began. Amara was killed. So many of the Native Americans lost their lives because of me. Tristan was beheaded. He was a terrible man, but even his death was horrific. My father's gone. He has the scrolls. What if Salvatore—"

"We will find Jack, my love," Roman interjected firmly, his voice cutting through the whirlwind of my despair. His steady gaze met mine, grounding me. "Don't worry. We will get through this difficult moment."

His words were a lifeline, yet they couldn't quiet the storm within me. The enormity of everything that had happened—everything that still loomed ahead—threatened to drown me.

"I can't believe Lee is gone," I murmured, the ache in my chest sharp and unrelenting. "I need some air. Let me know when Emily's dinner is ready."

Roman nodded, concern flickering in his eyes but allowing me the space I needed. I slipped out of the house and made my way toward the creek, my feet carrying me almost instinctively to the familiar sound of flowing water. The creek moved with a gentle insistence, its surface reflecting the golden hues of the evening light. Trees lined the bank, their leaves whispering secrets to the soft breeze that rustled through their branches. Kneeling by the water's edge, I let my fingers trail through the cool stream, watching as it slipped away, unstoppable and unyielding—like time itself.

A sudden chill brushed the back of my neck, making the hairs on my arms stand on end. I straightened, a sense of unease prickling my skin.

Then I felt it—a soft touch on my back. My heart lurched as I spun around, my breath catching.

Standing before me, her presence, as unexpected as it was undeniable, was Amara. Her gaze was calm, her expression serene, but her eyes bore the weight of something far greater. "I know the pain is strong in your heart," she said softly, her voice carrying a familiar warmth. "But now it's time to fulfill your destiny."

"Oh, Amara... You're not real," I spluttered, disbelief clashing with the evidence before me. "You died a long time ago. All because of me. My darkness killed you, and now your ghost is haunting me."

Memories flooded my mind, sharp and vivid—the impossible vision of her in the caves in Wales back when we were living at Mathias' estate. The weight of guilt pressed harder against my chest.

Amara's gaze didn't waver, steady and piercing. "My dear child, I may have died, but your father—my son, Jack—needs you. You must save him before it's too late and before Salvatore does his worst to him. It's time to pick yourself up and fulfill your destiny."

"What... what did you say?" I swayed where I stood, my knees threatening to give way.

"My son, Jack, needs you," she repeated firmly, her voice like a lifeline pulling me out of my despair. "I've already lost my other two children, John and Theodora. I can't lose him, too."

Her words echoed in the stillness, a call to action that quickened my pulse and steadied my resolve. With a deep breath, I braced myself for what lay ahead.

"Amara… you're my grandmother?" I stammered, the revelation striking like a bolt of lightning. The woman before me—so familiar yet enigmatic—nodded, her ethereal gaze clouded with sadness.

"Yes, child," she whispered. "In Rome, I knew, but the silence was my shroud. John James, Jack James, Theodora are my lineage, my children, my legacy."

Her words unraveled a knot in my mind, revealing threads of the past and present, intertwining into a tapestry too intricate to grasp fully. An uncle I had never known as such, a father in peril—all these fragments of knowledge spun within me, whirling like leaves caught in an autumn gale.

"Remember the words I gave you when I was dying," Amara said, her gaze intense, imploring me to search through the fog of my memories.

"Tell me," I whispered, desperate for clarity.

"You have a great destiny ahead of you," she said, her voice steady yet tinged with sorrow. "You have weathered countless hardships, trials, and losses, yet you remain a pillar of strength, a beacon of bravery. It is something I admire greatly. Despite the darkness that may surround you, never forget the shining light of your husband, your daughters, and your family. They are the fuel that propels you forward. And in your journey to find your father and reclaim what is rightfully yours, know that I will always be with you, supporting you from afar. My love for you knows no bounds."

Her form began to dissipate, the edges of her presence softening as though the very breath that carried her words was scattering her into the wind.

"No! Wait! Please stay!" My voice cracked as I reached for her, but my fingers closed around nothing but the cool evening air. She was gone, leaving behind an aching hollow where her presence had been.

Turning back toward the creek, I felt the world tilt beneath my feet, the weight of grief and revelation threatening to pull me under. Then, in the shadows of the trees, I spotted Zara. Without hesitation, I sprinted toward her and enveloped myself in the sturdy comfort of her embrace.

"Oh, Olivia," Zara said, her voice soft as she held me close. "I'm so sorry for Lee's passing, but don't worry. Stay strong. I will stand and fight by your side until my last dying breath."

Her words were a lifeline, pulling me back from the edge. Before I could respond, a shimmer in the air caught my eye. The space beside us seemed to ripple and coalesce, taking shape until a figure emerged—a figure I knew all too well.

Balthazar.

He materialized with a quiet grace, his every movement calculated yet humble. When he bowed low before me, it was not with the arrogance I had once known but with something far heavier—remorse. When he straightened, his eyes met mine, filled with a sorrow that seemed to reach into his very soul. "I hope you will one day forgive me," he said, his voice low and weighted with regret. "I have made many terrible mistakes. Let me make peace with you and help you fight your battles—against Mathias, Salvatore, and Alina."

His head hung low as if his guilt was too much to bear. "Once the blades are activated, kill me, and put me out of my misery. I want to reunite with my dead children. Make my death painful—for all the pain and torment I caused you."

The gravity of his request left me reeling. Did he deserve mercy? Redemption? What he asked was not something you'd request of an enemy but of someone you trusted— someone you loved.

I swallowed hard, trying to ground myself. "Let's focus on the now," I said, unable to process the enormity of his plea. "I believe you when you say you want redemption. We will face what comes together."

Balthazar nodded solemnly, his acceptance both comforting and unsettling. Looking at him, I felt the weight of destiny pressing on my shoulders. But I wasn't alone. I had allies—a family forged by blood, shared trials, and unwavering loyalty. Together, we would confront whatever lay ahead.

A sharp rustle cut through the solemn quiet of the creek side, sending a chill down my spine. I instinctively pressed closer to Zara, the warmth radiating from her a steady reassurance as she shifted into a protective stance, her body taut with readiness.

Shadows shifted and coalesced into figures, and from their midst, Roman emerged at the forefront of an imposing procession. Behind him moved a phalanx of black-hooded men—a fraction of Amir's formidable army of darkness. At the head of the procession stood Amir, with Reyna by his side, their commanding presence unmistakable.

"Roman?" My voice quivered with confusion and disbelief.

Before Roman could answer, another figure stepped out from the ranks—a man leaning heavily on a gnarled cane, his frail form belying the gravity of his presence. Lazarus.

"It's you!" I gasped, the shock of seeing him here robbing me of breath.

Lazarus lifted his gaze to mine, his voice heavy with a resonance that seemed to echo through the air. "Olivia," he said, his tone carrying an undeniable weight, "the time has come for you to remember."

I shook my head, a mix of weariness and desperation coursing me. "What exactly is it that you expect me to remember? I've told you and everyone else countless times— my past is lost to me. No amount of forcing will bring back memories that are no longer there. I've tried, but my mind refuses to cooperate. I've lost everything and everyone dear to me. Lee is dead. My father is in the clutches of Mathias and Alina. My mother tried to end my life. And now, even the blades that were once in my possession are in the hands of my worst enemies, all because of secrets, betrayals, and lies. My heart has endured too many losses. My soul has suffered greatly. How can you expect me to remember amidst all this chaos? And Lazarus, why do you keep secrets from me instead of just telling me about my memories?"

Lazarus' expression darkened, his voice grave as he replied, "But you did this to yourself. You knew the consequences."

"What are you talking about?" I demanded, my heart pounding with unease.

"You, Olivia, were the one who brought us all here from Solaris. It was your power that separated the Blade of Shadows," he said, his piercing gaze never leaving mine.

A wave of memories surged through me, unbidden and fragmented. I recalled the dream—the battlefield, Salvatore chasing me for the blades, my desperation as chaos reigned around me. The fragments blurred together, sharp and vivid, until I felt a chill run down my spine. Something slithered across my feet. I looked down in horror as snakes coiled around my legs, climbing higher, their scales cold and unrelenting against my skin.

"Please stop this, Lazarus," I shrieked, terror lacing my voice as the snakes tightened their hold.

"No," he said firmly. "I will not stop. Fear is what will trigger your memories and unlock the truth."

The fear inside me threatened to consume me as Lazarus' words echoed in my mind.

The snakes coiled tighter, their cold, unyielding scales pressing against my skin. They slithered around my arms, torso, and legs, their movements deliberate and unnaturally synchronized. Their sharp fangs pierced my flesh, a searing pain that sent a jolt through my body. I gasped for air, but the serpents continued their relentless advance, winding around my neck, covering my mouth, and suffocating me with their cold, unyielding grip.

With each desperate gasp, their constrictions mirrored an unnatural rhythm as though they breathed in tandem with my faltering lungs. Panic clawed at the edges of my mind as the crushing pressure mounted—a silent crescendo of terror. I tried to scream, to cry out for help I knew would never come, but the sound was trapped, swallowed by the serpents sealing my lips. Darkness crept into my vision, an encroaching tide that threatened to pull me into oblivion.

As my consciousness faltered under the weight of impending suffocation, a voice cut through the blackness. It was not a shout but a steady, calm presence—emanating from within, vibrating through my very bones.

"Are you ready to accept your destiny, Olivia?" The voice was authoritative, almost serene, and its resonance struck me.

Lazarus?

"Destiny." The word hung heavy, saturated with prophecies I had tried to ignore, battles fought in shadows, and secrets whispered in the dead of night. It was the legacy I had been running from, the birthright I had tried to deny. But here, in the clutches of darkness, with my breath stolen and my life slipping away, there was no room left for denial. There was only the unrelenting truth that acceptance was no longer a choice—it was an inevitability.

I could fight no longer. Fate's inexorable march had crushed my resistance. My heart pounded a confession in the silence—a surrender that echoed through the void.

Yes, Lazarus. No matter how dangerous or brutal the answer is, I am ready.

As if my silent vow had triggered some ancient mechanism, the serpentine coils began to unravel from my body. The crushing weight on my chest lightened, the constricting bands around my throat eased, and air flooded into my lungs in a ragged, life-giving torrent. My eyes flew open, and the world became focused with a sharpness I had never known.

A sudden, piercing pain lanced through my body as something bit into my flesh. Lazarus' hand descended upon my eyes, his fingers cool and firm against my temples. A blinding brilliance erupted within me, a light rivaling the sun, forcing my memories to emerge with an irresistible, searing power.

Balthazar and Zara appeared first, dark figures standing sentinel in the tapestry of my past life. Guardians—fierce, unwavering, and bound to me by more than duty. Their presence gave way to flashes of Armand, his lips meeting mine amidst a sea of wildflowers. Love bloomed in the meadows where we had lain entwined, a fleeting yet eternal bond etched into my soul.

Then came the shattering truth—the revelation that tore through me like a blade. My mother, the once-revered queen of Solaris, had been an evil ruler all along. Her scheming, her manipulations—they had poisoned the very kingdom that was meant to be my birthright. The people, pushed to their breaking point by her tyranny, rose in defiance, overthrowing her in a tide of anger and despair. Amid the chaos, I was thrust into the role of queen, a crown heavy with betrayal and guilt. Armand stood steadfast by my side, guiding me through the treacherous waters of royalty. Yet even with his support, the crown slipped through my grasp, grains of sand trickling between trembling fingers.

Salvatore emerged next—his darkness a reflection of my own, his blade clashing violently with mine. We fought with ferocity, but I knew he held the upper hand. Desperation overtook me, and in a moment of courage and despair, I severed the blades—their power splitting apart, cascading into the abyss, a desperate act to protect what remained of Solaris.

The memories swept me further, carrying me from the familiar streets of Solaris to a foreign realm—a place of rolling hills and sprawling forests, both beautiful and treach-erous. Earth. In this strange new world, I found Armand again, his soul intertwined with mine as if the universe had willed us together. Our love grew like tangled vines, resilient and unyielding. But just as we had built a fragile sanctuary, it was ripped from us. A fiery blaze consumed everything we had created, ignited by the treachery of Mathias—a man devoured by his darkness. He destroyed not just our home but a piece of my soul, leaving me adrift in a world that felt more alien than ever.

Each memory collided within me, forming a mosaic of

beauty, tragedy, hope, and despair. They whispered of a legacy in my veins, a lineage of immense power that had coursed through generations uncounted. I was more than Olivia James Alexander; I was the bearer of a bloodline that commanded the very fabric of time—a legacy I could no longer deny.

"Who are you?" Lazarus' roar cut through the storm of thoughts, reverberating like thunder around me. His question demanded an identity that transcended lifetimes. The weight of his gaze pinned me to the spot, forcing me to confront the fractured selves within me.

The answer slipped from my lips like an incantation, my voice steady despite the tempest raging in my mind.

"Once upon a time, I was Isabelle Farcourt in my past life. In this life, I am Olivia James Alexander. My blood is Timeborne, Timebound, darkness... and I can wield the power of a Shadow Lord."

Each syllable resonated with the echoes of my former life, weaving together the threads of my existence into a tapestry of undeniable truth.

Lazarus nodded slowly, a gesture heavy with gravity that sent ripples through my soul. "Yes, you are," he said. He leaned closer, his piercing gaze unrelenting. The corners of his mouth twitched—was it approval or merely the weight of expectation?

"But you forgot to mention one more thing..." His voice hung between us, a riddle poised at the edge of revelation. I could feel the answer welling within me, pressing against the confines of my consciousness, eager to be spoken and complete the incantation that bridged my past and present.

Summoning the remnants of my courage, I raised my chin defiantly. The storm within me quieted as clarity took hold.

With unwavering determination, I met Lazarus' expectant gaze, the final piece of my truth burning on my tongue.

In one sweeping glance, I took in the sea of faces surrounding us—the army of darkness that had once been the shadowy specters of my nightmares. They stood before me, real and tangible, their eyes glinting with readiness, waiting for the command I hadn't yet realized I held the authority to give. This was the moment to unite the fractured pieces of my existence and embrace the destiny that had pursued me throughout my lifetimes.

The power within me stirred, rising like an unstoppable tide. It filled every corner of my being, igniting an unrelenting force I could no longer deny. Drawing a deep breath, I broke the silence, my voice cutting through the charged air like a blade.

"I am the lost queen of Solaris," I declared, each word imbued with the authority of my reclaimed title. "And it's time to reclaim our realm and fight for our legacy. Together, we will restore the lost kingdom of time."

The army stood still, their breath collective and suspended as though the universe awaited what would follow. Within a heartbeat, Salvatore materialized before me, his presence suffocating. His piercing eyes burned with unbridled rage, his aura so dark and oppressive that it choked the air around him. The world around us seemed to shrink beneath the crushing weight of his power.

"Where is my father? What did you do to him?" I demanded, my voice trembling with a potent mixture of anger and desperation. My words echoed through the heavy air, each syllable a plea for desperately needed answers. But Salvatore didn't flinch. He remained still, his cold indifference cutting deeper than any blade could. It was as though my plea was nothing more than a whisper carried away by the wind.

Before I could speak again, Lazarus stepped forward, his presence a defiant counterpoint to Salvatore's suffocating darkness. His voice broke the silence like thunder, unwavering and filled with the force of a man unbowed by time.

"After all these years, we meet again, Salvatore," he said, his tone sharp, each word challenging. Though he no longer carried a blade, his resolve was sharper than ever.

Salvatore's lips curled into a cruel smirk, his dark amusement glinting in his eyes. "Oh, Lazarus," he sneered, his voice dripping with venom. "Look at you... how old and frail you've become. A shadow of the man who once dared to challenge me."

Lazarus' laughter was low and dangerous, slicing through Salvatore's mockery like a finely honed weapon. "And you," Lazarus said, his voice steady and cutting, "you shroud yourself in power and arrogance, Salvatore, but I see through the cracks in your carefully constructed facade. Beneath that illusion lies a truth you cannot hide—you are neither invincible nor untouchable. Weakness has already begun to fester within you, and no amount of posturing can conceal it."

Salvatore's smirk widened, his dark confidence filling the space like a suffocating fog. He raised the Blade of Shadows with a flourish, its energy crackling and humming with raw power. "Weakness?" he spat, his voice a commanding roar. "You speak of weakness, yet I hold the blade. I have your son, Jack—yes, the keeper of the scrolls, hidden in plain sight all this time. You will never see him again. He is mine now, as is Solaris. I will reshape this world, claim what was always meant to be mine, and rule with a darkness that will extinguish every glimmer of rebellion." His eyes narrowed, his voice dropping to a venomous growl. "You've lost, Lazarus. I am the most powerful of you all. I am the greatest Lord of Shadows. And soon, the entire realm will bow at my feet."

Lazarus' expression didn't falter. He stepped closer, his presence unwavering and his words calm but razor-edged with defiance. "Good luck, Salvatore. Continue your desperate climb to power. But know this—I have trained my son, Jack, for years, and his strength already surpasses yours. You may hold him now, but his loyalty and power are beyond your grasp. I'll see you in Solaris, Salvatore. And when I do, you will face the consequences of your arrogance."

Salvatore's mask of confidence twisted into something darker, something feral. He turned to me, his gaze as sharp as daggers, piercing through every barrier I tried to summon.

"You dare challenge me for the throne?" he snarled, his words cracking like a whip. "You think, even for a fleeting moment, that you can stand against me? Against *this* power?" He raised the Blade of Shadows higher, its energy rippling like a thunderstorm ready to strike. "My army is unstoppable. My dominion is inevitable. And you—" his voice dripped with scorn, his eyes boring into mine, "—are nothing but a fleeting spark in a storm I have already unleashed. You will fall, Olivia, just as everyone before you has fallen. And this time, there will be no rising."

My heart thundered in my chest, fear clawing at the edges of my resolve, but I refused to let it consume me. I glanced at Lazarus, his presence a storm of righteous fury, grounding me as the moment's weight pressed down on us both. He stepped forward again, his voice now a cold, dangerous growl.

"I have waited a lifetime for this," Lazarus said, his words like steel cutting through the tension. "You may wield the Blade of Shadows, but it will not save you. Your reign will be nothing but ash, Salvatore. Solaris will *never* bow to you."

Salvatore threw his head back, his laughter exploding like

a bomb of malevolence, sending a chill down my spine. It was a sound of pure darkness, a declaration of his unshaken confidence.

"Stop me?" he mocked, his tone thick with disdain. "You, Lazarus, are nothing but the echo of a long-forgotten man. And you, Olivia," he turned his fiery gaze on me, burning through the last of my defenses, "are the embodiment of futility. A fool clinging to fragile hope in a world that already kneels before me."

He leaned closer, his whisper venomous and intoxicatingly cruel. "When this battle ends, you will understand what it means to lose. Solaris will not crumble; it will thrive under my rule, reborn in darkness. Its light extinguished, its people my servants, its throne a testament to my eternal supremacy."

Before I could reply, before the storm raging in my chest could erupt into words, Salvatore's lips curled into a grin—a wicked, calculated expression that dripped with the promise of chaos.

"Let the final battle begin," he hissed, his words heavy with unshakable certainty. Then, in a swirl of shadow, he vanished, leaving mocking laughter lingering in the air like a curse.

The weight of his declaration pressed down like an avalanche, but I refused to flinch. This wasn't just his fight— it was ours. For Solaris. For freedom. For everything we held dear. And we would not fall.

The Journey Continues....
Blade of Shadows Book 4.5: Sweet Venom of Time
Amir and Elizabeth's Story
Coming Soon: Summer 2025

Blade of Shadows Prequel Novel

TIMEHUNTERS

Rise of the Shadow Lords
Coming Soon Winter 2025

The Final Saga Continues…
Blade of Shadows Book 5: Lost Legacy of Time
COMING SOON
SUMMER 2026

THANK YOU FOR READING!

Enjoy *Timehunters*? Please take a second to leave a review!

OTHER BOOKS IN THE BLADE OF SHADOWS SERIES
TIMEBORNE (BOOK 1)

DARKNESS OF TIME (BOOK 2)

TIMEBOUND (BOOK 3)

WICKED LOVERS OF TIME (BOOK 3.5)
Balthazar and Alina's Story

TIMEHUNTERS (BOOK 4)

SWEET VENOM OF TIME (BOOK 4.5)
Amir and Elizabeth's Story
Coming Soon Summer 2025

RISE OF THE SHADOW LORDS
Blade of Shadows Prequel Novel
Coming Soon Winter 2025

LOST LEGACY OF TIME (BOOK 5)
FINAL SAGA COMING SOON
SUMMER 2026

JOIN THE BLADE OF SHADOWS!
https://www.authorsarasamuels.com/

THANK YOU

Join the Club!
Blade of Shadows Book Club (Facebook Group)

TikTok
Instagram
Facebook
Goodreads
BookBub

APPRECIATION

When I began writing *Timehunters*, I was filled with nervous excitement. This is the book where the secrets and truths of the *Blade of Shadows* series are finally unveiled—the mysteries of Solaris, the depths of Lazarus and Salvatore's story. Keeping these secrets hidden since Book 1 was one of the most challenging aspects of writing this series.

As I poured my heart into *Timehunters*, I couldn't help but wonder what you, my readers, would think. But when my editor read the manuscript, she was absolutely shocked and blown away by how I had kept Solaris a secret all this time. Her reaction—she literally said, "So, when's the spin-off happening now?"—instantly eased my nerves.

Then came my beta and ARC teams. Their excitement, their shock, their sheer enthusiasm for this installment gave me the confidence I needed to know I was on the right path. Their reactions reminded me why I started this journey in the first place: to tell a story that surprises, moves, and captivates you all.

Now that you've read *Timehunters*, the journey is far

from over. The final two books in the series are on their way, as well as a *Blade of Shadows* prequel where you'll discover the origins of Lazarus and Salvatore.

Thank you, from the bottom of my heart, for sticking with me through this adventure. Your unwavering love and support mean the world to me. Prepare yourselves for what's to come—because the best (and the most shocking) is yet to come.

Chaela, thank you for everything—guiding, teaching, and always having my back when things get hard. Your wisdom, patience, and unwavering support have been a lifeline through this journey. You've helped me grow in unexpected ways, and I'm incredibly grateful for you.

Rainy, I'm beyond grateful for your friendship. Your support and dedication mean the world to me. You've made my work better and pushed me to believe in myself. Thank you for every word of encouragement and for believing in this journey with me.

Charity, I don't know what I'd do without you. From formatting to navigating the challenges of being an author, you've been my rock. Your unwavering support and encouragement mean everything. Thank you for always having my back.

Briana, you're more than an assistant—you're my best friend and confidant. Your dedication is unmatched, but your heart and friendship truly mean the most. You've stood by me, celebrated my victories, and believed in me even when I doubted myself. I couldn't do this without you!

A heartfelt thank you to Krafigs Design, whose artistic touch graced my book cover, turning it into a thing of beauty.

Finally, to my phenomenal beta readers, ARC, and the street team: your unwavering support and passion for this series have been my driving force. The energy you put into every post, reel, comment, and video has set the virtual world abuzz. My heart swells with gratitude for each of you—my most ardent and dedicated fans. Your support is truly immeasurable.

ABOUT THE AUTHOR

SARA SAMUELS is the author of the Blade of Shadow series. When Sara isn't daydreaming about her stories and time travel, she spends her day reading romance, cooking and baking, spending time with family, and enjoying life. Sara loves to connect with readers on Instagram, TikTok or by email, so feel free to email her, or message her on social media because she will reply back! Follow her on Instagram or Tiktok @storytellersarasamuels to get related updates and posts. Email her at sara@authorsarasamuels.com

Visit her website at https://www.authorsarasamuels.com/ and sign up for the mailing list to stay informed about new releases, contests and more!

Made in United States
Orlando, FL
25 March 2025

59842897R00315